Shots Fired

SHOTS FIRED

THE BLADE KINGS
BOOK 3

RUTH STILLING

Copyright © 2025 by Ruth Stilling

All rights reserved.

Cover art by Sam & Mel|Ink & Velvet Designs

ISBN 978-1-0686000-6-7 (PAPERBACK)

Interior design and formatting by Autumn Sexton

Editing by Jovana Shirley, Unforeseen Editing, www.unforeseenediting.com

Proofreading by Autumn Sexton

No part of this book may be reproduced or transmitted in any form or by any means, electronic or mechanical, including photocopying, recording, or by any information storage and retrieval system without the written permission of the author, except for the use of brief quotations in a book review.

This book is a work of fiction, including names, some places, and incidents that are either a work of the author's imagination or have been used for the purposes of fiction. Any resemblance to actual persons, living or dead, events, or locales is entirely coincidental.

TRIGGER/CONTENT WARNINGS

You should be aware that while this book is a work of fiction and is, of course, a happily ever after, *Shots Fired* does contain themes of the following: pregnancy and childbirth (without any medical complications), discussion of parental manipulation (which is off-page), representation of a toxic ex-boyfriend, sexually explicit content, and strong language.

*To those still searching for their upgrade.
Here's the standard.*

PLAYLIST

"Style" by Taylor Swift
"Lose Control" by Teddy Swims
"Obsessed" by Mariah Carey
"505" by Arctic Monkeys
"But Daddy I love him" by Taylor Swift
"Addicted to you" by Picture This
"Hey Daddy" by Usher
"Every Breath You Take" by The Police
"Treat You Better" by Shawn Mendes
"(You Drive Me) Crazy" by Britney Spears

PROLOGUE
October

ARCHER

If I was in deep before, I'm certifiably drowning now.

I shouldn't be talking to this girl; I can feel the weight of her brother's eyes as they bore into my head. My conscience is pleading with me to back away now. It knows the truth behind all my smiles, laughter, and stares—I'm obsessed with Darcy Thompson. My addiction to her grows each time I make my excuses to engage her in conversation.

The difference tonight: she doesn't have a man. Darcy's newly single with plans to move to the US in the next few months, and that's ... a recipe for disaster.

Every time I speak to an attractive woman, my mission is simple: bed her and get out before she wants more. It wouldn't matter if she made it clear it was sex with no strings; I'm hightailing it out of the hotel room or conjuring up an excuse as to why I need to leave. I've always been armed with an exit strategy, always been in control of my feelings and what we do.

But with Darcy, everything goes out the window. It's like I'm a virgin again—giddy and unable to control my heart rate or thoughts. The constant swinging between her beauty and brilliance leaves my brain zero time to compute that she's my center's baby sister with a big heart that just got broken by her shitty ex, and I'm the worst possible candidate to help fix it.

The reality: I'm in the hottest, deepest water a guy could find himself. Yet the longer I stay here, the more I believe it isn't so bad after all. I could tread water until I was scalding, and I'd still thank Cupid for the privilege of ten minutes in her company.

This cocktail bar isn't one we've visited often, and the warm, twinkling string lights overhead reflect in her huge blue eyes. She's like porcelain, a classic British rose, with pink cheeks and honey-blonde hair that stretches down her petite frame. She's smart too; this girl has brains bigger than the island where she grew up.

It's not too late to back away.

"I'm thinking I don't need a big place, especially with the cost of rent around here." Darcy runs a French-manicured finger around the rim of her empty cocktail glass, wincing at the prices of accommodations in Brooklyn.

"You could always ask your brother to help you out," I suggest, already knowing she'll hate everything about that idea.

Darcy is independent and hasn't made a secret of it.

She scoffs, pushing away her glass, and I immediately raise my arm, asking the bartender for another.

Strange approach to backing away slowly, Archer.

"I'm not owned by any man."

As she replies, I can sense the conflict in her; she wants to maintain her usually bright persona—or at least the only one she lets the world see. But tonight is different. *She* feels different.

A seed of anger takes residence in the pit of my gut, threatening to bloom into something more at the thought of her exboyfriend—the guy who made her feel less than. I know he's responsible for the slump in her shoulders.

"Why do I get the feeling that statement was loaded and not really about apartment-hunting?" I ask cautiously, dipping my head down to catch her gaze as she pulls a replenished cosmo toward her and plays with the thin black straw resting on the side of the glass.

She looks up at me then, big irises a little more constricted, stress pulling her smile lower than usual.

"Maybe because it was," she answers with a small shrug, her dainty shoulder doing things to me. "Ever wonder how the hell you let so much of your time get wasted with the wrong person?" She quickly waves a dismissive hand. "No, I guess you don't since you have never had a relationship, let alone one where you spent nearly thirty-five percent of your life with the same person."

I open my mouth to reply, but clamp it shut. She's right; I haven't ever had a girlfriend. Not even for a day. The closest I ever got to a commitment was a repeat hookup in Texas, and that was only because I forgot we'd already banged.

Darcy blows into her cheeks. "Let's change the subject, shall we? Matters of the heart don't usually make a great cocktail mixer."

Since I'm standing next to the barstool she's perched on, I can make this discreet. I shift my body closer, turning to face her before running a light finger down the outside of her hand as it rests on the bar top.

I don't miss the faint shudder as it passes through her arm or the steady kick of my heart when it beats faster. It's the first time I've ever touched her deliberately, and even though I know I'm sinking to new depths, I can't find it in me to care.

"Liam," I say softly. "That's who you're talking about, right?"

Almost like she needs a second to gather herself, Darcy quickly takes a sip of her drink, and I track her movements, blinking away when the glass reaches her mouth.

"He's not worth me giving a second thought to." Voice stern and determined, she sets the glass back down, flicking her long hair as she does. "He clearly wasn't thinking about me when he got with someone else behind my back, so why should I allow him into my head?"

This time, I take a sip of my own beer. It's practically room temperature since I forgot all about it.

"But he is in your head. Why else would you have said anything?" I don't know how she's going to handle my question; it's my addiction to this girl that forces me to ask.

Challenging her might be a mistake. The conversations we share are always lighthearted—about her studies and her dream career in editing or my hockey game she just watched.

"Forgive me for being so blunt, Archer." Darcy turns to look at me, one brow raised. "But why do you care?" She swivels on her stool, and I take a step back to give her room. "You have an entire bar full of hot women—most of them have been watching you this whole time, by the way—and here you are, talking to your teammate's baby sister about her crappy ex and refusal to pay high rent prices."

She turns back to the bar, and I make brief eye contact with her brother, Jack. He's still staring in our direction, with the same irritated expression he wears whenever I'm near his sister.

Like always, I offer him a thumbs-up and a wink before getting back to Darcy.

"Talking to you is more interesting." I throw in a confident smile to mask how fucking serious I am. "I don't know if you can tell by now, Darcy, but I like talking to you. It beats an empty conversation with some random chick about a hockey game I know she didn't watch and my own internal thoughts over how quickly I can get her naked and the deed done."

Her head whips up to mine, nothing but shock written across her face before she throws her head back with a belly laugh that never fails to spread my grin wider.

"Oh my God, you are unbelievable—you know that?" she says between fits of giggles. "I laugh, but you know what?" She draws a deep breath, pointing at me. "I think you might just have the right approach in life."

Still smiling, I shake my head in confusion.

Her pink cheeks are rosier as she takes another sip of her cocktail, and I watch her swallow it down.

"You have fun and don't take anything too seriously. Hell"—she throws an arm up, nearly knocking me out in the process—"you could have your pick of the women on this planet, and none of them could ever hurt you because you're in control."

Her pointer finger lightly presses into the center of my chest, and, fuck, I shouldn't feel that all the way into my toes.

Because I can't figure out what else to do, I continue staring at the girl in front of me, wishing away the past nine years of my adult life, along with all the news outlets that reported on it.

"Darcy ..." I begin, swallowing past the lump in my throat. I might as well start being honest with her now, even if it's to tell her she has me wrong and that the "fun" lifestyle she thinks she wants isn't all that, when my captain and one of my closest friends, Sawyer Bryce, taps me on the shoulder.

"I'm heading home, buddy."

He glances over at Collins—Darcy's friend and a pink-haired biker chick he's been relentlessly pursuing with no luck. I guess tonight is no exception.

Darcy stares down into her cocktail glass. She's only half finished with her drink, and I've got so much more I want to say.

Sawyer taps me on the shoulder again, and I know this is his version of my own warning. The one I've been ignoring.

Stay away from Darcy Thompson.

On a long breath, I pull out my wallet and set fifty dollars on the bar.

"How are you getting home?" I ask Darcy, Sawyer still hovering behind me.

She thumbs over her shoulder, and I cast a quick glance at Jack and his girlfriend, Kendra Hart. "I go home when they do. I'm keeping their spare bedroom company."

I already know where she's staying and that her brother would take her home. Still, I can't help but ask on the off chance she'll suggest taking a ride with me.

When Sawyer steps away to grab his jacket. I linger for a beat, just like the addict I am. "Liam isn't worth it, Darcy. He never was and never will be."

She smiles over her shoulder at me. "I know."

"If you need any help moving in when you get here, just hit me up, okay?" I say, a foreign lilt of desperation in my voice.

When she slides down from her stool, our height difference is obvious as she looks up at me, even in killer black heels. "I have a former NHL player for a stepdad and a current one for a brother. The biggest items I possess are my kettle and toaster, so I think I'll be good. But thank you; that's a kind offer."

I nod once, stuffing my hands into the pockets of my black jeans.

"Archer!" Sawyer flicks his hand toward me.

Jack calls Darcy's name, too, as he and Kendra shrug on their jackets.

"Will I see you again before you move here?"

She rolls her lips together. "Yeah, probably. I have a lot to figure out before I make the move here in February."

The need to bend down and plant a kiss on her forehead sends me dizzy, but even I know that would be a step too far.

Picking up her bag from the bar, she loops the strap over her wrist and then pulls her coat from the back of the stool. A part of me wonders if she's buying a few more seconds as she hesitates to move.

A part of me also concludes that's wishful thinking.

When she does finally step away, panic curdles low in my stomach. I had a chance to say something more, and I didn't take it.

"Darcy," I rush out as Jack, Kendra, and Sawyer push through the exit and into the night.

She spins on her heel, hair whipping around her.

"Just ... remember what I said. He isn't worth it."

Warmth floods her features as she tucks a lock of hair behind her ear. "See you when I'm next stateside, Archer."

CHAPTER ONE

Late August, ten months later

ARCHER

One more inch, and I swear to God, I'll cut it off.

His hand, I mean. The one that's attached to a disrespectful, dark-haired prick as it hovers just above my girl's perfectly round ass.

She isn't your girl, Archer.

Yet.

The dude's hand drops another millimeter, but Darcy doesn't react. Instead, she continues her conversation with him at the bar.

Go home and jerk off in the shower to thoughts of her. That's the safe and sensible option. It's what you've been doing since she moved here six months ago.

"Would you like a side order of wings to go with your stare session, or are you good?" Grinning, Darcy's new sister-in-law, Kendra, leans closer to me.

"Ha-fucking-ha," I drawl, trying to tear my eyes away from Darcy and the prick.

"You're still staring," Kendra sings at me under her breath.

"I fucking know I am," I sing back.

"And what are you two whispering about?" Jack pulls Kendra into his body, setting a quick kiss on top of his wife's head.

She waves a casual hand in front of her, not giving anything away and doing me a solid in the process. My obsession is getting more obvious by the second, and it's only a matter of time before I'm no longer able to pass off my infatuation as a ruse to wind up my center.

"Oh, nothing. I was just asking your goalie if he planned on drinking that beer in front of him or reading it a bedtime story."

I twist my full pint glass around on the coaster. Apparently, every time I'm out with Darcy, I can never finish a beer. "Preseason starts soon, and I'm thinking, this time, I'll cut the alcohol out early."

Kendra's hand shoots out, resting on my arm. "Okay, who are you, and what have you done with party-boy Archer?"

I deadpan and look at Jack, our team's new assistant captain. Compared to my seventh, this will be his third season with the New York Blades. I'm twenty-seven. I should be pulling up trees in the NHL like him. Instead, I'm still chasing the shutout record I set fucking years ago.

And that isn't all my best friend's surpassed me on. Recently marrying the girl he pined after for years, he now gets to call her his for the rest of time. He's living his life at a casual seventy miles per hour, chewing up the freeway at a steady pace. Whereas I'm barely off the ramp.

"How was Oxford after the wedding?" I change course, knowing they both recently got back from the UK.

Kendra sighs, tipping her head up to look at her husband. "A honeymoon from heaven. All the tea and cakes a girl could ask for."

I quirk a brow, remembering the impressive afternoon tea they put on for each guest. I nailed cream cheese and cucumber sandwiches like my life depended on it. What can I say? They were a useful distraction from staring at Kendra's maid of honor.

Which I'm back to doing right now.

Jack follows my line of vision, eyes landing on Darcy. He takes a pull of his beer and sets his glass back down on a headshake. "Don't get me wrong; having Darce here with me is awesome. We've spent way too much time living thousands of miles away. That said, I don't think I'll ever be used to watching her get hit on."

I scrub a hand across my jaw, tension building in my shoulders. "I wouldn't say she's being hit on."

She's definitely getting hit on. It's been like this every night out since Darcy moved to New York. It's like the guys in this city have some kind of unspoken agreement to hit on the hot blonde from England, just to screw with my head.

Jack scoffs. "Are you for real? That dude isn't checking out the quality of my sister's denim jeans."

I chance another quick glance toward the bar. The dude's hand has crept lower, and I look away again, inhaling a deep breath as I try—and fail—to temper my unjustified rage.

"Looks friendly to me," I grit out.

"I guess to a playboy, ass groping would be considered normal behavior." Jack laughs.

Even though I know he meant nothing by that statement—along with the truth that sits behind it—it still stings. He's not wrong; I've palmed more asses than I can count. Sure, some I went on to take home later that night, but others were purely out of harmless flirtation.

Archer Moore: Boundary overstepper extraordinaire.

"Out of curiosity, where would you categorize kissing on the getting-hit-on scale?" Kendra nods her head back at Darcy.

Don't look, don't look, don't look.

I look.

Yep, he's kissing her.

The metal legs on my chair cut through the moderately loud music, turning a few heads, as I rise to my feet, gaze still locked on Darcy while the prick works to deepen the kiss.

"I—ugh—I need the restroom," I push out, ignoring Kendra's question and snatching up my cell. "I'll be right back."

"You okay, buddy?" Jack asks, frowning at my forced smile.

"Yeah, yeah, I'm good. I think that meal we had at the restaurant earlier is doing things to me though." I circle my bowels, and Kendra scrunches up her nose.

Jack holds up a pleading hand. "Say no more. Please be my guest and relieve yourself."

If only it were that simple.

Swiveling on my heel, I head for the bathroom break I don't need. Although if I happen to come across an emergency exit, I'll be happy to make use of that.

A few seconds later, I'm pushing through the swing door and into the empty men's toilets, coming to a stop in the center of the room and unlocking my phone to scroll aimlessly through social media. Habit has me clicking on Darcy's Instagram profile, and I take a few more steps, leaning against the tiled back wall.

She hasn't posted since the last time I checked, which is unsurprising, given that was barely an hour ago. Still, I reread the caption on her last post, being careful not to like it or click on her latest story and reveal my stalker status.

The post is one she took in Hyde Park when she visited England for Jack and Kendra's wedding. Darcy's wearing a bright yellow summer dress, a puzzle book and pencil balanced across drawn-up knees as she smiles into the camera. Her hair is down and around her face, only controlled by a pair of sunglasses propped on top of her head.

I zoom in on the shot. The dress is low cut, but I'm not looking at what's on show.

I'll save that for when I finally get to explore her body with my hands.

Right now, I'm more interested in the pink that perfectly stains her high cheekbones, along with the depth of her wide eyes.

Before Darcy, I'd never seen eyes like hers. They're big and round and inviting, but more than that, they don't need the sunlight to sparkle. They only need her bright demeanor to glow.

There isn't a single thing in the world that could get this girl down—that I'm sure of. The only time I've seen that shine fade was back in October, when I asked her about Liam.

Involuntarily, my grip tightens around the phone. I'd love to do the same around his neck for the way he clearly makes her feel.

"Sorry, you plan on using that, or can I go ahead?"

Startled back to reality, I lock my phone and turn around to find the prick himself standing a couple of feet behind me, pointing at the hand dryer I'm blocking access to.

Jesus, how long has he been in here? I have zero recollection of anyone walking in, taking a leak, or using the faucet.

I step away and pocket my phone. "Yeah, sure. Sorry."

He approaches the dryer and sets it running, a smirk tracing his lips.

Fuck me, I hate this guy, and we've only exchanged fourteen words. I don't even know his name or what he does. Although I'm pretty sure I know what he'd like to do:

My girl.
Tonight.
In his bed.

The dryer cuts, and he shakes out his hands, moving across to readjust his already overstyled hair.

Try-too-hard.

He pauses and eyes me in the mirror. "I gotta ask—otherwise, I'll regret this for the rest of my life." He spins around to face me, still smirking. "Archer Moore, right? Goalie for the New York Blades?"

I scratch at the back of my head. He'd best not want an autograph—even worse, a picture. "You aren't the first one to make that assumption. But, no, I'm just a look-alike to the king." Laughing internally at my own flattery, I raise a hand above my head. "Archer Moore is at least a couple of inches taller and even better-looking."

The guy pulls his brows together, confused. "Well, you sure as shit look like him. Maybe you should check out your family history; you could be long-lost twins or something."

He turns back to the mirror and reaches into his pocket, taking out a small blue box. When he pops the lid and pulls the white strand, I realize it's floss.

Oh, this takes the motherfucking cake. He's flossing his teeth —no doubt in preparation for more kissing—while I stand here, watching him and denying my identity like some deranged make-believe twin.

I point at the box in his hands. "Do you make a habit of night-out dental care?"

On a wink, he pulls the floss from his mouth and tosses it in the trash can beside him. "Nope. However, I do like to carry floss around, just in case circumstances call for it." He holds the pack out in his palm. "Want to use some?"

I roll my lips together, jealousy coursing through me. The feeling was foreign up until I first met Darcy, and I'm no better at dealing with it today.

"I'm good," I reply, knowing I should leave this conversation where it is. "But if you're referring to the honey-haired girl you have waiting for you at the bar, I'd recommend you don't get your hopes up."

Retracting the floss, he drops it into the pocket of his pants. "Yeah? And why is that?" His previous lighter tone adopts a cutting edge.

I push off the wall and step toward him.

Leave it, Archer.

"I actually heard she's seeing someone on the Blades."

He drops his head and shakes it at the ground. "You must think I'm some kind of idiot. You are Archer Moore, aren't you?"

I don't confirm or deny, simply shove a hand into my pocket.

He continues, "Regardless of who you are, I'd check my

sources if I were you. She wouldn't be about to come back to my place if someone else were involved." He hesitates for a second. "Unless she's a cheating whore, of course."

Moving closer, I cup my spare hand around my ear, grinning with rage. "I'm sorry, I didn't quite hear that last part. I mean, it's possible I did, but you couldn't be so fucking stupid to call a girl like Darcy Thompson a whore."

His smile drops to a frown, and he backs up a few inches. "Her name is Darcy? She told me it's Jessica." He holds up a hand. "Wait, maybe you have the wrong girl."

I continue closing the distance between us. There's nothing he can say to calm my anger. He has the wrong girl all right, just not in the way he thinks.

"Aww, she's given you a fake name. If you already have her digits, you'd best check they're not fake too."

You can even check against the ones I have since I know they're for real.

His brows lift. "You're a fucking lunatic—you know that?"

I shrug. He's not wrong. "Crazy or not, I advise you to leave her alone and move on. You don't want to find yourself tangled up in a mess."

The guy looks like he's considering my warning for a split second and then resets himself, shrugging back at me. "Whatever. I'm an innocent party with no idea of her real name, let alone who she's banging on the regular. I'm only after a quick fuck with a smokeshow. And, goddamn, is she h—"

Bang.

A couple of seconds pass before I catch up to my own actions.

Spitting blood into the sink, the guy hunches over it, clutching his jaw. "Jesus fucking Christ! You *are* a lunatic. What the hell was that for?!"

I reach across to the wall and snatch a paper towel from the dispenser, handing it to him. "That was your final warning." I lean over him, eyeing his shocked face in the mirror. "Wipe her face—and mine—from your memory bank and leave without another word, or my next hit will do the job for you."

Dabbing at his chin, he slides from underneath me and heads for the restroom door, turning around momentarily. "You got some real issues."

I raise an unaffected brow. "Not really. I just hate it when a guy trash-talks a girl. Toss in the fact that this one is basically royalty, and you got yourself a problem. Or in this case, a bloody jaw."

He doesn't say another word as he pulls open the door and disappears a second later.

After a few beats of silence, the reality of my actions starts to take hold.

It's obvious who I am, and even if he has no proof of who laid the hit on him, he could take to socials and claim anything. The public loves to drag a celebrity.

Pulling out my phone and making for the restroom door, I quickly scroll through my Contacts until I find the one person who can help me right now. Or at least talk me through the self-inflicted mess I've created.

The bar music is louder as I stride past our table, ignoring Jack and Kendra as they talk to Darcy.

Good. At least she's safe and away from the prick.

The line connects, and Sawyer Bryce—my captain on and off the ice and the guy I always go to when shit gets real—says something, although I can't make it out as I head for the exit.

"It's Archer," I yell.

He says something else, but again, I miss it all as I push out into the midnight air and circle around on the sidewalk, checking that no one is in earshot.

"Archer, what the fuck is going on?" Sawyer asks.

I continue walking down the street, blowing out a breath that does nothing to steady my anxiety. "You have to promise you won't go nuclear on my ass."

"I promise," he replies, sounding less than convinced.

I consider cutting the call altogether and praying this doesn't blow up in my face. If this gets out, I'll be in the shit with the Blades and probably Jack. But worse still, Darcy will likely never speak to my crazy ass again. And I wouldn't fucking blame her.

Nausea roils through me at the thought.

"Archer!" Sawyer commands.

I jolt and swallow hard. "Oh fuck, man. I think ..." I break off, blowing out one last deep and ultimately futile breath. "I think I fucked up again. Only this time, it was over Darcy."

"Jesus Christ," he drawls. "What did you do?" Sawyer sounds more concerned than he does pissed, and honestly, that kind of makes it worse.

I shake my head to no one. "It doesn't matter. It's my mess to clean up, and I'll call you in the morning when I've got my head on straight."

"Archer?!" he grumbles.

"I'll call you in the morning," I repeat. "Enjoy your first night with your fiancée. Seriously, Collins will chew my ass up if I wreck it for you with my bullshit."

Hitting End on the call, I pocket my phone and drop my gaze to the sidewalk.

Fuck me, Archer. You're such a fucking idiot.

CHAPTER TWO

ARCHER

If the incessant knocking isn't enough to wake me, my cell's piercing alarm definitely is.

"All right, all right!" I announce, sitting up in bed and massaging my temples.

Last night's statement about cutting alcohol in the offseason was about as believable to Kendra and Jack as it was to me.

Shortly after I ended the call with Sawyer, I decided my best course of action was to drink away the mess. After that, I have little to no recollection of the events that followed.

Ripping my phone from its charger cable, I hit Stop on the alarm and breathe a sigh of relief as silence descends on my bedroom, although it's short-lived, as the knocking starts up again.

Running a hand over my face, I reluctantly slide out of bed and grab a pair of dark blue athletic shorts, my number thirty-three stamped in white over the right thigh. Whoever's paying me a visit has zero intention of leaving.

"Give me a minute," I drawl, staggering out into my hallway and heading for the front door.

"Give me a motherfucking minute," I repeat as I unbolt the door and swing it open, fully expecting my pissed captain to be waiting on the other side.

"Fucking language," a light tone replies as I wipe the sleep from my blurry eyes and focus on a set of white Converse, the left one tapping the ground impatiently. "That's no way to greet a lady," she continues, her unmistakable British accent cutting through my hangover.

Slowly, I lift my head to take her in and come face-to-face with Darcy Thompson, the last person I expected to find at my door, wearing a similar summer dress to the one she posted on her Instagram—only this one is light blue.

"I, umm ... I'm sorry?" I reply awkwardly, way too focused on why she's here in the first place. Has she ever been to my apartment? "How do you know where I live ..." I trail off, leaning against the doorjamb and attempting a casual stance.

Jesus, she looks like a fucking dream. *My* fucking dream. I look like I'm still half asleep.

I slap a palm against my cheek, checking I'm not still unconscious.

Darcy cocks her head to the side in question. Her long, thick eyelashes frame her narrowing eyes as she studies me intently, and it's then that I notice the two coffees in front of her.

She offers the tray of coffees to me. "I figured you might need caffeine."

"Umm, thanks," I reply, lifting one of the takeout cups from the holder and stepping to the side, allowing her to enter.

She doesn't move, choosing to peer down my hallway instead. "There aren't any girls lurking, are there?"

I chuckle, but it's fake. I'm still waiting for the time when her referencing my playboy reputation doesn't cut through me like steel. It's amazing how you can stop hooking up with women for the better part of a year, but the opinions others have of you still remain regardless.

"Just me," I say, taking a sip of coffee. "Want to come in?"

Darcy looks down at the remaining coffee in her holder, twisting her plump lips to the side. "Do you promise to put some actual clothes on if I do?"

I smile, scratching at my bare chest. "At the risk of sounding like an asshole"—I lean down closer to her petite frame since I'm six-four without my skates on—"you're the one who turned up at my place at the ass crack of dawn."

Her eyes sparkle with mischief before her spare hand dips into the cream Marc Jacobs bag she always carries with her. Fetching out the Amex Black Card, she waves it between us. "And at the risk of being presumptuous, I assume your fat NHL wallet won't be needing this then?" She lifts a quick shoulder as I stare at my credit card. "Fair enough. Macy's and I can keep it company."

I'm still staring at the card as I ask, "How did I lose that?"

She smiles sweetly, doing things to me below the waistline that are hard enough to hide in hockey pads, let alone flimsy shorts. "Ah, well, last night—right after you bought the entire bar another round of drinks—you handed it to me and slurred something incomprehensible. It sounded like I could keep it for anything I wanted."

I pull back and stand up straight, racking my brain for the memories. I mean, I knew I was wasted, and I vaguely remember offering random people drinks, but giving Darcy my Amex? Shit, what else did I say to her? Sure, I'm usually all kinds of crazy when she's around, but I always keep my alcohol consumption in check. Keeping my feelings hidden is hard enough, never mind with lowered inhibitions and a loose tongue to match.

"Don't worry," she sings. "I didn't use it. Not even for these coffees."

She takes a sip of her own before stepping inside, and I absentmindedly close the door behind her.

"And how do I know where you live?" She takes off down the hallway, round ass swaying in her floaty, knee-length dress. "You once told me on a night out that you moved into the most expensive apartment complex in Brooklyn, and naturally"—reaching the end of the hallway, she turns on her heel and grins at me—"Archer Moore could only live in the penthouse. It was an easy guess."

Darcy rounds the corner, leading into what I know is a messy living space, and I stalk after her, still freaking out at what the hell I might've said last night when I grind to an abrupt halt.

The dark-haired guy. The prick. Did I tell her or anyone about what had happened? And did he post anything online about it? Part of me thinks—and hopes—Darcy wouldn't be all smiles and Sawyer would be already blowing up my phone if he had.

I start walking at a slower pace until I find Darcy standing in the middle of my kitchen, coffee in hand, and her cream tote sitting on top of the island next to my credit card. Beside my card, there's an empty, unwashed cereal bowl I must've eaten when I got home last night.

She quirks a brow at me, eyes briefly dropping down my body. Despite the panic manifesting in every cell right now, a sense of satisfaction settles in my gut.

She's checking me out.

Clearing her throat, she shifts her gaze to explore my large apartment. It's nice, open plan and expensive, but I've done nothing to make it my own. It features gloss white cabinets and a butcher's block countertop in my kitchen, and a contrasting tan leather couch in my living space. The place is stark and not particularly homey.

Other than the bright girl now hopping onto a stool at my island.

"Thanks for returning my card," I say, running a hand through my disheveled bedhead.

She crosses her legs over at the knee, causing the dress to ride higher on her perfect thighs.

Oh fuck, Darcy. Don't do that.

"You're welcome." She pauses before bringing the coffee to

her mouth. "But I have to confess, it's not the only reason why I'm here."

I swallow thickly, back to freaking out over last night. "It's not?" I ask, casually walking toward the fridge.

She swivels in the stool, tracking my movements across the open-plan space. "No, it's not. I actually, umm ... I came to make sure you were okay. You seemed a little off last night." She waves a hand out in front of her, setting her coffee cup down on the island. "Like, you were your usual joking self, but you seemed kind of stressed out."

Pulling out my morning protein shake from the fridge, I twist the cap and down it in two big gulps, wiping the back of my hand across my mouth when I'm done. "What makes you say that?" I inquire.

She uncrosses and then re-crosses her legs in the opposite direction. It's more of a fidget than it is to get comfortable. "Well, last night was just weird—that's all. One minute, I had this hot guy all over me, and the next—*poof*—he was gone." She giggles. "I thought I was getting lucky and pulling off your moves."

Her face drops, and I fucking hate that it does. Sad Darcy makes me want to punch things. Equally, Darcy calling another man hot makes me want to rip them apart.

"Anyway, next thing I knew, you were storming past us on the phone and then waltzing back inside, determined to get drunk and buy everyone drinks. You were erratic and weird, so I wanted to check on you."

Her eyes soften as she looks at me, and I conclude this is way worse—I can just about temper my rage at her sadness, even my thoughts when her dress slips up her thigh. It's kind and gentle Darcy that does things to me I don't know what to do with. The beat of my heart is in unfamiliar territory; *I'm* in unfamiliar territory.

I toss my empty shake into the trash and close the fridge. At least she's clueless about what happened in the bar restroom last night, along with the motives behind slipping her my credit card. I'm tempted to slide it back along the counter and repeat my drunken statement.

"I'm good, Darce. Honestly." I don't have another response because what else am I supposed to say? Confess my obsession right here, half naked and hungover?

I've never shied away from going after what I want. Not in my career, not with anything in life, and especially not with women.

But this is one girl—my teammate's sister and coach's stepdaughter—I know I can't touch.

Wrapping a piece of blonde hair around her index finger, she nods a couple of times. "Okay. It's just that Jack said your mum and dad recently got a divorce, and I wondered if that might be troubling you. You never mentioned it before to me, so I hope I'm not overstepping here ..." She trails off, eyes softening further.

I want to tell her that she'll never overstep with me.

She eyes me carefully before continuing. "You know that my parents broke up a while back, and it sucks. Even when you're older and you know it's the right thing, it still hurts. Big time."

When Darcy was sixteen, her parents—Felicity and Elliott—divorced. From what Jack told me, it was way overdue.

Similar to Felicity and Elliott, my parents—Julia and Karl—should've split years before they actually did. My younger sister, Emma, didn't want it to happen, but I was okay with it—and that's where I differ from my sister. I'm relieved that when I next travel home to Philly, it won't be to a constant war. My parents are good people, and they deserve to find peace. Especially my mom.

I take a couple of steps toward her until I'm only a few feet away. I should probably throw on a shirt, but I'm past caring. "It wasn't anything to do with my parents, Darce."

She pins her bottom lip between her teeth. Part of me hopes she'll push me further and ask what was really up, but the second she skirts around my attraction to her, I'll be powerless to prevent my mouth from confessing how I feel—or my lips from kissing her.

As if sensing the tension, Darcy slaps a palm against the countertop and slides off the stool. She picks up her coffee—which must be barely warm at this point—and smiles sweetly at me, tossing her tote over one shoulder.

Don't leave.

I move quickly until I'm standing opposite her, and she looks up, big pools of blue inviting me to dive right in.

"What do you think of the coffee?" she asks, raising the cup a little.

I shake my head, not expecting that question. This girl is off the wall, and I love it. Darcy Thompson stokes the crazy within me.

"It's ... nice. Why?"

She giggles softly. The same sound I've imagined her making on a night out as I hold her hand and show her everything New York has to offer, free from the risk of being seen.

"Oh, nothing. It's just from Rise Up—Jack and Kendra's favorite café a few blocks away from here." She reaches up on her tiptoes, a mischievous pink flushing her cheeks.

This girl is like a doll; every part of her body and face is perfectly proportioned—something you have to see to believe it isn't manufactured.

"Although I still think the coffee I used to get from this little café back in Oxford is better. I'm not sure this is made from Arabica beans, possibly Robusta beans."

"Is that so, Miss Thompson?" I jest. "Do you consider yourself a coffee connoisseur?"

Another bubble of laughter leaves her chest, and now I'm thinking about how I could draw similar sounds from her in my bed, right after we finished our date night.

"Nope. I just enjoy proving my brother wrong."

It would be so easy. All I need to do is reach out and take her hand in mine before I ask her to spend the day with me. I could pass it off as friends enjoying time together because I know that's how she sees me.

"Do you like defying your older brother?"

The flirtation in my voice is unmistakable, but she doesn't react to it, and I fight with my frustration.

Surely, she knows I'm into her.

She falls back onto her heels, still smiling brightly. "I'm not sure I like your question, Archer. It insinuates I've, at some point, let Jack call the shots over me, and that's never been the case. Do I let him think he's in charge sometimes? Of course. But I'm always in control and nearly always right."

I can't help but grin. Jesus, she's something else. Confidence oozes from her, but not in the cocky way. Darcy's self-assured and comfortable with it.

"That's good to hear," I say, knowing I need to change up the direction of our conversation—and fast. "I'd say your brother is clueless when it comes to a lot of things."

A crimson flush deepens her cheeks further, almost like she can read my thoughts. Maybe she can since they're so loud that I feel like I'm screaming them.

Regardless, she doesn't falter under the crushing tension as I continue to build it between us.

"Enjoy the rest of your coffee, Archer." She delivers her final line and spins around, making for my hallway.

I'm after her like a dog in fucking heat. "Thanks again for returning my card," I blurt out, just as I hear the ringtone I set for Sawyer filter from my bedroom.

He's probably calling to find out what the fuck happened last night.

Darcy stops at my front door, eyes following the sound before she sets them back on mine. "I guess I'll see you around. Good luck with preseason and everything."

"Why don't you come to my house party next week?" I rush out.

She looks confused. "House party? I didn't know you were having one."

I wasn't until five seconds ago.

"Yeah, first night of preseason training, the Blades all go out to Lloyd's and then normally to a club. It's good for team building, et cetera. I figured I'd host the after event at my place this time around."

Immediately, she shakes her head, and I'm slammed with disappointment. "No can do, I'm afraid."

"Why not?" I press, keen to know why.

"Because I'm out with the girls that night. We figure we'll hit some bars and a club ourselves."

I have no right to feel jealous, but I do. Ten out of ten, there will be another guy all over her—and consequently, my fist in his face.

"Where are you going?" I ask, although it sounds more like a demand.

She looks surprised at my tone. "Probably the cocktail bars in Williamsburg."

Otherwise known as Hookup Central. I should know.

"Be careful, all right?" I tell her, unable to stop myself from sounding like an overbearing ass. "There are a lot of guys out there only after one thing."

She reaches out and pats my cheek mockingly, the front door already half open as she makes to leave. "Yes, and that's the idea. Girls like to have fun too. Catch you soon, Archer."

CHAPTER THREE

DARCY

Living in Brooklyn isn't everything I thought it would be.

When I was studying in Oxford, I worked a few placements in London, but none of that seemed surreal. Even when I spent a summer working for my now-estranged dad in Canary Wharf, it was just like any other day.

Here though, in New York, I feel like the smallest fish in the largest pond. I guess that's because I am. When Jack got traded to the Blades, he repeatedly told me life would take some adjusting if I wanted to pull off my move to the USA. In true Darcy style, I brushed off his comments and focused on the exciting parts, like working as a junior associate editor in a fancy building for a leading fashion magazine, *Glide,* and searching for a place to live. It was all about finding my own feet after a shitty end to a relationship and finally coming to terms with the inevitable breakdown of another with my dad.

I was my own version of Carrie Bradshaw, living my best *Sex and the City* life, free from my cheating ex. My eyes were finally wide open to my manipulative, controlling father, and I was ready to move on.

For the most part, that's exactly what I'm doing. I even invested in a pair of Prada heels and an overly restricting pencil skirt to carry off the look at work, and in the evenings, I hit the cocktail bars, having dragged unsuspecting colleagues along with me.

But here's the thing: New York life isn't *fully* transpiring how I initially envisaged. I'm not saying I'm unhappy or lonely exactly. I'm simply saying ... it's different from what I imagined. Unlike my brother, who had a whole team of guys to play and practice with multiple times a week, I'm seeking out opportunities to socialize. If it wasn't for Kendra, my sister-in-law; Collins Mackenzie, Sawyer's new fiancée; and Jenna Miller, Kendra's best friend and goalie for the New York Storm, I'd be lost. There are only so many times a twenty-three-year-old woman can turn up on her mum's doorstep with a Chinese takeaway for two and a bottle of Pinot.

Sienna—another junior associate editor at *Glide*—genuinely rolled her eyes when I approached her desk an hour ago and asked what her plans were for tonight. She tried to hide her expression, but I saw it as she turned her head to eye a colleague, Penelope, a few seats down.

It was fine, I concluded. Maybe they had other plans.

Or maybe I annoy the shit out of them with my high-pitched laugh and overenthusiastic approach.

"Whatever," I sigh under my breath, switching my bag of Chinese takeout from one arm to the other while I dig around for my door key in the ridiculously oversize cream tote bag I genuinely thought was a good idea when I bought it.

My A-level results might've been in UK's top percentile, but I'm about as organized as a flock of wild geese being chased by a fox, and this freaking bag only serves to remind me of that.

Tissues—*nope.*

Hand sanitizer—*not today.*

Lip balm—*ooh, the cherry-flavored one.* I wondered where that had got to. *In my bag, of course.*

Mobile phone—*not right now.*
Ah, keys.
My one-bedroom apartment in Fort Greene is cozy and has everything I need.

Mum was determined for me to move into a place owned by her and my stepdad, Jon Morgan, the coach for the New York Blades. I saw two issues with this idea. Number one: I'd never consider it as mine, even if I paid rent. Two: While I love my brother and Kendra, like hell would I live on the floor directly above them. I didn't care how many times Kendra tried to convince me of the soundproofing in that building; I was absolutely going to hear my brother having sex.

Shuddering at the thought, I step into my apartment and toss my tote on a spare chair in the cozy, but tiny, living room. Next, I kick off my Prada heels and pull the tie from my hair, letting it cascade down and around my shoulders.

"Now, where the fuck is it?" I murmur to myself, gaze roving around the room, but coming up empty.

I mean, it's possible it's in here somewhere, likely buried under a pile of laundry I gathered together with the intention of taking it to the launderette, but never quite making it.

"There you are!" I'm across the room in a flash, pulling a puzzle book from under a stack of mail.

After a grueling week, most normal people choose to binge-watch their favorite TV show with snacks or maybe even hit the gym for a workout. I guess you could classify sudoku as a workout for the brain, but I see it as the only way to unwind.

My mind never stops, not even when I'm asleep. I even talk in my sleep and occasionally sleepwalk. Mum took me to see a doctor when I was five, concerned I wasn't resting enough and it was affecting my development. Turned out, I was a certifiable genius, and while other kids my age were playing in sandpits and mud kitchens, I was solving puzzles designed for preteens.

I'm forever overanalyzing things that do not need dissecting. Prime example: why the hell did I decide to turn up at Archer

Moore's apartment out of the blue on a Sunday morning? Yes, it was to return the credit card he'd thrust into my hand the night before, but it's not like I couldn't have waited a couple of hours and given it to Jack when he stopped by later that afternoon.

And when it got awkward—standing in his kitchen, drinking tepid coffee, and trying not to stare at his bare, chiseled chest—I decided to ask him if he was okay with his parents' recent divorce.

What was I thinking?

Flicking on the kettle I had shipped from the place I shared with Liam—because he wasn't keeping my Bugatti Vera Easy Kettle in rose gold—I dump a tea bag into a mug and wait for the water to boil.

In the forty seconds it takes for the kettle to finish its cycle, I'm already a third of the way through the puzzle, powerless to prevent my attention as it wanders back to Archer.

The second I knocked on his door, I considered fleeing the scene, only to clock his smart camera and deduce that my random visit was already evidenced. So, I went all in, practically knocking his door down so I could explain the reason for my visit and that I wasn't randomly stalking his home. Despite his camera, when he pulled the door open, he looked shocked to find me standing on the other side, fighting to keep my eyes on his face and not descend to his pecs.

Fishing out the tea bag from my drink, I grab some milk from the fridge and drop a single sweetener into my brew. I bring the mug to my lips, blowing away the steam as I replay my interaction with Archer.

Had my eyes dropped to his chest, it would've been obvious, although I definitely wouldn't have felt guilty for checking him out.

The guy is stacked.

Like carved-out-of-stone, erected-in-a-museum Greek god kind of perfect. Sex oozes from every pore in his body, daring women to come closer and taste his goodness.

Only he knows it. And to me, that taints the prize.

I was genuinely shocked to find him alone when I showed up. I hadn't thought it was possible for Archer to head home by himself after a night out. There's no shame in being a playboy, but there is an inevitable reputation that goes along with it.

Despite myself and his public image, I can't deny the attraction I feel. While I've done a good job at hiding it for the large part—and especially from Archer—getting it past Jack has been harder to carry off.

Up until his and Kendra's wedding earlier this month, my brother had said nothing explicitly about it, only throwing me the occasional side-eye. That all changed when I asked why the maid of honor—aka me—wasn't paired up with the best man—aka Archer—for the day.

"Because while he might be my best friend and one of the most likable guys I've met, he's an absolute asshole to women, and I'll be damned if he tries it on with my baby sister. Keep away from him, Darce. For your sake and my friendship with him."

I take a sip of tea and smile around the rim at my response, my audiographic memory replaying the conversation.

"For the record, oh, brother"—I patted him lightly on the shoulder, smiling sweetly—*"I do not plan on going there with him. However, please note that if I were, your warning wouldn't stop me. See, I possess what's called a brain."* I tapped my temple twice. *"And I have the ability to use it."*

My brother doesn't need to worry. I've got the measure of the Blades goalie from Philly. We're alike in our outgoing personalities and confidence in social situations. He's also fun to be around, and his banter is top-tier. That's where it ends for me.

I might be in my early twenties, but that doesn't render me totally naive around guys, and that's why I'm scolding myself for turning up, unannounced, at his place.

I never do shit like that.

I'll admit, after Liam, all I want is fun. However, that doesn't involve adding to the notches on Archer's overloaded bedposts.

Something tells me I wouldn't feel good about that, and neither would he for going behind my brother's back for nothing more than a hookup.

In fact, nothing about getting with a hockey player appeals to me. Any guy I see or date will have zero affiliation with my brother or stepdad. I'm my own woman, and going there invites the kind of potential complications I absolutely do not need.

CHAPTER FOUR

ARCHER

If I buy this entire dress collection and mail it to Darcy, would that come off as obsessive?

"Earth to Moore." Coach Morgan leans forward, tipping his head over my shoulder as I lean against the leg press with my back to the rest of the room.

I hustle and lock the screen. I didn't notice him entering the gym, and we shouldn't be checking our phones during any kind of session—definitely not the first one of preseason.

Coach narrows his eyes suspiciously when I spin around to face him. "Got a girl you're shopping for?"

A couple of the boys snort out a laugh, Jack and Sawyer included as they spot each other at the bench press. I'm guessing if any one of them knew the real reason I was scouring the internet for the exact dress Darcy wore, their reaction wouldn't be as lighthearted.

I pull off my backward cap and run a hand through my sweat-soaked hair, demonstrating I've put a shift in during conditioning. I remain quiet, thinking better than to respond.

His eyes close further, but he drops the inquisition. Thank

fuck. "I've got high hopes for you this season, and I want your full attention on hockey and nowhere else." He leans closer to me, voice dropping an octave. "I know I don't get to call the shots on your personal life—and I'm not trying to either—but take it from me: These are the prime years of your career. Do not waste them on girls."

Despite Coach's best efforts to keep our conversation discreet, Sawyer's ears prick up, and as he pauses with the Olympic bar mid-rep, Jack takes it back from him and replaces it on the rack.

I turn back to Coach, anticipating my captain to head over any second.

After Darcy left my apartment, I picked up Sawyer's call and told him exactly what happened with the dark-haired guy and his likely still-bruised jaw. Following a bunch of expletives, he reamed me out for being a reckless idiot.

My crush on Darcy Thompson isn't exactly news to Sawyer—he's gathered that over the past two years. What he isn't aware of is the depth of my obsession.

I told Sawyer a version of the truth, centered around the way the guy spoke about her in a derogatory manner, only leaving out the part where I claimed she was seeing someone on the Blades. Sawyer was convinced the guy would report me and plaster it all over the internet.

Mercifully, nothing came of it. Not a single whisper made beyond the four walls of that restroom.

Maybe the prick did wipe Darcy and my face from his mind after all. Or maybe he didn't want to open a dialogue explaining why I had landed one on him in the first place.

Bringing my attention back to Coach, I offer him a reassuring smile. "I have my eyes on the playoffs and a new shutout record."

He hums something inaudible before speaking up, tucking an iPad under his arm. "The playoffs are the minimum. I think we have the potential to go all the way this season, and I need you firing on all cylinders to make that happen."

"You got it," I reply.

Seemingly satisfied, he spins on his heel and strides away right as I salute him.

Immediately, Sawyer's across the room, arms folded over his chest. I've played with my captain for a number of seasons. He lost his wife, Sophie, several years ago, and I saw him in his darkest days. I hated to see him that way, but at least he generally kept to himself. Now that he's engaged to his dream girl, Collins, he's out of his shell and content. I can't lie and say I'm not happy to see the real Sawyer back with us. I just wish the newest version of my captain weren't so fucking perceptive.

"Our coach just unwittingly caught you dress shopping for his stepdaughter, didn't he?"

I reinforce my headshake with a puzzled look, contemplating if I can pass it off as shopping for my sister's birthday. "I've got no idea what you're talking about, Cap."

He just grins, one that leaves no mistaking he's onto me. Taking a second, he checks his surroundings, likely making sure Jack is out of earshot. "Tell me the truth, Archer. Is this a case of you wanting to fuck her because you know she's off-limits, or are you actually serious about her?"

I collect my towel from the leg press and wrap it around my neck, giving myself a moment. Instinctively, my eyes track Jack as he steps onto a treadmill, talking with some of the other guys.

"Archer"—Sawyer quietly demands my attention—"you recently punched a guy because of this girl, and lately, you've been acting like she's the only thing you can think about. That, and I haven't actually seen you leave a bar with a girl, or two, since I can remember. Come to think of it, the last time I'm aware of you fucking around, it was with Kassie. You know, the one you had no idea was engaged to a former teammate."

He chuckles darkly, not finding the recollection funny. Neither do I; that was a shit show I'll never forget.

"You weren't even mentally present at my and Collins's engagement meal," he continues. "So, I'm asking you straight—as a friend, but also as your captain—what is going on with you and Darcy Thompson?"

My heart rate kicks up when Sawyer says her full name. I know there isn't a chance of either Coach or Jack hearing him, but that's not what's having this effect on me.

It's her. Always Darcy. The one girl who makes me feel emotions beyond sharing a lust-filled night in my bed.

My physiological reaction answers Sawyer's question. I don't even need to think about it. "My borderline presence is no coincidence." Using the towel, I swipe at the perspiration beading above my brow. "She's on my mind constantly."

He scrubs a hand over his jaw, unsurprised. "I know that feeling all too well, buddy. With Collins, I—"

I hold up a hand between us, cutting him off. "No offense, but this isn't anything like what you have with Collins."

That does surprise my friend, maybe even annoy him. "I'm going to need you to elaborate," he replies.

Gripping the back of my neck, I search for adequate words. "It's all-consuming, paralyzing. An overwhelming urge to protect, mixed with a fear of rejection. Like if I was to make a move, she'd laugh in my face and crush me right there and then. It's a voice telling me to back the fuck off, persistently drowned out by the deafening need to touch her and confirm that her body would mold to mine in the way I've always known it would."

"Archer, I, um ..." Sawyer trails off, and I'm relieved he does, as I continue my ramble.

"I'm pretty sure the space where I exist borders heaven and hell—I get to see her on the regular, but mainly when we're out and she's being hit on by pricks like the one from the bar. And I can't have that, man. I can't stand it for much longer."

My confession hangs in the air between us, and Sawyer never takes his eyes off mine as he draws a pull from his water bottle.

After a beat of silence, he finally speaks. "I mean, I know Jack is aware you find his sister hot, but are you being real with me right now?"

Given the reputation I've built for myself over the years, I probably shouldn't be frustrated at his doubt.

I blow out an exasperated breath. "Yes, I'm being for real. You think I want to feel this way?"

He shrugs. "Maybe. You want her, right?"

"Yes," I clip, still frustrated. Briefly, I motion toward the treadmills, specifically at Jack. "But as if being the best friend of her older brother and having her stepdad as my coach weren't complex enough, the real kicker is, none of what I've just confessed to you is reciprocated. She might find me good-looking, but that's about as far as it goes. I could see that on Sunday when she showed up at my apartment to return the credit card I'd drunkenly thrust at her right after I punched the prick."

Sawyer's eyes grow wide. "Wait. You only told me about the punching part." He thumbs over his shoulder to nothing. "You're telling me you had her in your apartment the following morning?"

I roll my shoulders back, trying to ease some of the tension in them. "Nothing happened, if that's what you're getting at. Allegedly, I said she could buy whatever she wanted, which tracks since I was contemplating an entire dress collection five minutes ago."

It's almost like Sawyer's only catching up with the program now, brows raised all the way to his hairline. "Are you telling me you want to date her?"

I pin him with a look that cannot be misconstrued. "I don't want any other man to so much as breathe in her direction. They aren't worthy and won't treat her right." I point at my chest just as Jack steps off the treadmill and starts in our direction. "She does something to me that I can't control."

Sawyer opens his mouth to reply when Jack sidles up next to

him, his golden retriever smile instantly cutting through the tension.

"We've all agreed on Lloyd's for tonight. The regular hangout seems like the obvious choice to break in the rookies with our preseason tradition." He bumps me lightly on the shoulder with his fist. "What do you say, party boy? There's bound to be a girl you can hook up with from there."

I guess it's pointless, holding anything at my place since Darcy won't be coming.

Jack's reference to girls rolls around in my gut like spoiled food I ate the night before. This is really what he thinks of me, isn't it? There isn't a chance in hell he'll ever take me seriously.

I glance quickly at Sawyer, and his empathetic expression confirms my fears.

"I'm not sure Archer's looking to hook up tonight." Sawyer speaks directly to Jack.

He snaps his fingers in response, the platinum wedding band he refuses to remove since marrying Kendra sparkling, even mocking me. "Oh, that's right. You were buying dresses for a girl." He edges closer, his humor emphatic. "Please tell me it isn't Kassie again because that was a mess the first time around."

Jack looks across at Sawyer, expecting him to laugh along with his gibe. Instead, our captain shifts awkwardly, adjusting his weight from one foot to the next.

"All right, I think we can call it. I've been impressed with everyone's work ethic and attitude today, and I want it to be the benchmark over the next few weeks and into the regular season." Coach's announcement acts like a beacon, slicing through the awkward atmosphere.

I slap my thigh and reset myself, eager to change the subject. "I'm going to head for the showers, and I'll see everyone later tonight."

Jack loiters for a second, eyes locked on Sawyer's back as our captain makes a break for it toward the locker room.

I go to spin away, but my center's hand stops me.

"You really have a girl? Like, for real?"

From absolutely nowhere, I find a casual smile, along with a lie I'll no doubt regret. "Ugh ... yeah. It's early on, but we're dating, and I just want to see how it goes. I don't want to fuck it up."

When he releases my arm, his eyes soften, kicking up my guilt. "Oh, cool. I'm sorry, man. I didn't mean to—"

"It's fine," I quickly counter, desperate to bring a second conversation to an end in as many minutes. "Like I said, it's early days, and she's not keen on taking things to the next level. She likes to keep her life private."

He nods in understanding. "I get that. Plus, you're one of the more famous NHL players, I guess."

I puff out my chest with pride. "Hell yeah, I am."

He deadpans, "Can I at least know her name?"

Shit. I really didn't think this through.

"Abbie," I blurt out. "Her name is Abbie."

He waggles his brows. "Nice name. Where did you meet her?"

For fuck's sake.

"On an away series in Dallas. We hooked up a few times in between Destroyers games, and I guess it's grown from there."

He looks practically giddy. "Oh, so a physical thing that's turned into more?"

"Yep, something like that," I reply, wiping at new perspiration forming above my brow.

He reaches out and pats me on the shoulder, a wry smile pulling at his lips, blue eyes sparkling beneath the gym lighting. "I guess I don't need to worry about you trying to fuck my sister anymore then."

I think we both know that despite his jovial tone, there's nothing lighthearted about my best friend's statement.

I scratch at my bare chest, feeling like the ultimate douche, but powerless to halt the wheels I've set into motion. "Jack Morgan being correct in his observations—I guess there's a first time for everything."

CHAPTER FIVE

DARCY

Mum always said I'd be late to my own funeral, and as I push through the doors of a random but very plush cocktail bar in Williamsburg, I once again prove her right.

"Nice of you to join us ..." Jenna looks down at her watch, one brow raised, her long, dark hair sleek and styled to perfection. "Nearly a half hour after we planned."

She passes me a room-temperature cosmopolitan she must've ordered a while back, and I take a large sip, downing nearly half of it in one go.

Jenna's bright blue eyes bug out as she looks between Kendra and Collins. My colleagues might not be all that fussed about us spending time together, but I definitely hit the jackpot with these three girls. They're my people, and I owe Jack a solid for bringing Kendra and, consequently, Jenna and Collins into my life.

Without a word, Collins takes my glass and sniffs the pink liquid that matches the color of her wavy, shoulder-length hair. "It's not a mocktail. I'd say our girl Darcy is getting wasted tonight."

I take the glass back and finish the entire thing, causing Kendra to burst out laughing.

"Stressful day?" she asks.

My shoulders slump as I replace the glass back on the bar we're all standing next to. "Could say that. My boss is a taskmaster, and I swear she leaves errors in articles just to test my proofreading abilities."

Collins nods her head in understanding, her perfectly winged eyeliner creasing around the corners when she smiles. I know she can relate to asshole bosses—her last one, before she opened her own Harley-Davidson garage, was a complete prick.

I wouldn't say Janine, my boss, is a prick or even an asshole. I just feel like she singles me out to do a lot of the heavy lifting while Penelope and Sienna get the easy ride.

"You know, it's possible she puts a lot of the work your way because she has faith in you and sees your potential in the industry. She was the one who hired you and gave you the chance, no?"

I guess it's hard to argue with Jenna's logic—Janine did interview and offer me the position at *Glide*. "Yep, you're right; she did."

I turn to the bar and lift a hand toward the barman. The next round for my girls is on me. His attention obtained, I focus back on Jenna.

"But I can't see myself staying in fashion editing. Not that there's anything wrong with it. But I do have other plans."

They all look between them.

"Like what?" Collins asks, bringing a mojito to her mouth and pausing. "With a brain like yours, I expect you to say rocket science."

I snort a laugh and ask the barman for a repeat of the last order. "No, I like maths to be more of a hobby. I have aspirations for my own business one day. Ideally, I'd love to offer independent authors services, specifically in developmental editing." I smile brightly. "You know how much I love to read, and my brain can't help but dream up stories and plotlines. I think that's my happy place, and ultimately, it's why I chose English over maths at university."

"It is the superior subject, hence why I avoided sports," Kendra agrees, a small sigh leaving her lips. "There's just something about getting lost in the pages of literature. I say go for it. Follow your dreams, Darce."

"That's how I feel about bikes. I go to another part of my brain when I'm around them, riding, fixing, even detailing," Collins adds. "I couldn't imagine doing a job I hated. I feel really lucky to have found my passion."

The drinks are placed on the bar next to us, and I begin handing them around.

"Speaking of getting lucky …" I nod my head at Jenna and then at a group of twenty-something guys, all professionals and dressed in suits. "As the only other singleton in our group, what's your opinion on the hotties at two o'clock?"

Kendra tips her head over her shoulder.

"Don't fucking look!" I swat her on the arm. "We need to play it nice and cool."

I can't be sure if the particularly handsome guy in the group spotted Kendra looking or heard my outburst, but when he glances over and smiles at me, I instinctively offer one in return.

"Oh, you are so in there." Jenna dips her head at me, flicking her eyes to Mr. Handsome.

"You think?" I ask, likely a little too enthusiastically.

"I know so." She nods. "I have a thing for boys with glasses and tattoos, so I'll take him." She subtly motions to a different guy perched at the end of the table.

Collins clears her throat, quirking a brow at Jenna. "Are you telling me you're into my fiancé?"

A couple seconds pass before we all fall about laughing.

"Ooh, looks like Mr. Handsome is making his way over here," Jenna croons, waggling her brows at me. "Someone's getting dicked down tonighhhh …"

She trails off, and I track her gaze as it leads away from the dark-haired hottie and toward the entrance.

Archer.

"W-what is he doing here?" I ask, stuttering my words.

Through the sea of people crammed into this bar, his eyes lock on mine the moment the door closes behind him.

He looks dreamy—so good that I forget about the gorgeous man now only a few feet away in favor of the mildly insane Blades goalie. He's dressed in an open-necked white shirt that reveals a platinum chain he always wears, and his dark hair is styled away from his face. And when his upper lip quirks, I'm confident his cocky smile is the reason so many women's panties melt right off.

Kendra closes her eyes, clearing her throat. She looks like she's about to say something when the mystery guy slides up alongside me, raising a welcoming hand at everyone.

"Hey, I'm Harry." He turns to me, confidence flowing from him. "Can I get you a drink ..." He waits for me to confirm my name.

"Jessica." A deep voice gets there before I can.

Wait. Jessica?

All heads—including mine—dart to Archer as he hovers behind Collins and Kendra.

"Her name is Jessica," he repeats.

"I-I'm just going to go use the, umm ... the restroom." Kendra thumbs over her shoulder.

"Yep, the need to pee is real," Jenna agrees.

"And I need to ... well, I need to get out of this dead-ass awkward environment," Collins adds, always the honest one.

Archer watches my friends leave for the restroom and then resets his focus back on Harry. Meanwhile, I'm still trying to work out why the hell he called me Jessica. I only ever use that name when I want to conceal who I really am because of my brother. But how would Archer know that?

Harry motions between us. It's obvious he's already regretting walking over here. "You know each other?"

Shoving both hands into his pockets, Archer grins at me, waiting for me to go first.

I grin back at him mockingly. "I've never met this man before in my life," I say to Harry.

Throwing his head back to the ceiling, Archer releases a single laugh that practically grinds the rest of the bar to a halt.

"Yeah, I'm going to ..." Face flushed red, Harry points toward his table. "I'm obviously stepping on toes here so I'm going to see myself out. Nice to meet you, Jessica." He throws me a weak smile and scurries off.

I take a second before looking at Archer, kind of pissed at the way he bulldozed in.

"Why are you here?" I eventually ask, still not making full eye contact with him, although I can sense his proximity and the intensity of his weighted gaze.

When I finally look at his face, I can see he wants to say something but quickly checks himself. "I was walking back home and saw you." He cocks his head toward the large window on my left. "I stopped to say hi and could see you were in need of rescuing."

I really should be fuming at him and his assumptions. "Decided against the after-party at yours then?" I gibe. "And to be clear, I didn't need rescuing. I was actually into Harry."

Ignoring my dig, he steps closer as his jaw tics, only a foot or so away from me now. His heated gaze drops down the length of my black suit dress since I came here directly from work, and he takes his time ascending my body, eyes finding mine once more.

"Have I misjudged you? Are you a bit of a playgirl, Darcy Thompson?"

I roll my lips together, not missing his flirtatious tone, but liking it all the same. Butterflies swirl in my stomach. I've spoken to Archer more times than I can count, but there's a darkness in his eyes I haven't seen before.

"Maybe I am. I thought you of all people wouldn't judge that."

He puffs out a humorless breath, pulling a hand from his pocket and scrubbing it across his mouth. "He isn't what you want, Darce."

I prop a sassy hand on my hip. "Oh, yeah? And what makes you say that? I'm single and free to go with who I please. As are you."

Archer looks uncomfortable, jaw switching from a tic to more of a grind. "I don't think it's a smart move, going home with strange guys. They can be weird. Even dangerous."

I choose to ignore that and focus on the real issue troubling me. "Why did you say my name was Jessica?"

He looks at me like I should know. "Why? Is it a significant name to you?" he asks, lips tipping up into a wry smile.

This guy's cheekiness shouldn't be so appealing to me, and neither should his intensity. Suddenly, I'm thinking less about the importance of the name I use from time to time and more about the depth of the man standing in front of me. There's more to Archer than meets the eye, and for the first time, I'm fascinated.

Reaching forward, I replace my glass on the bar, pushing down my intrigue. "Yeah, well, thanks for cockblocking me tonight."

Archer's eyes sparkle with delight. "But you don't have a cock, so technically, I didn't."

"Pussy preventer—that's what you are," I volley back.

Genuinely, I think he might wet himself. "Oh jeez," he wheezes, holding up a hand. "Darce, have mercy on me."

I wait for him to stop laughing, hand still propped on my hip. "So, let me get this straight. First, you walk into this bar, wanting to simply say hi. Then you fuck up my hookup, and *now* you're taking the pee out of me. Way to make friends, Archer."

As I finish my sentence, his cackling stops, and his head whips up to mine. "You consider me a friend?"

I shrug. How could we not be? We've always gotten along, especially since I moved to Brooklyn. "Of course I consider you a friend."

He doesn't seem satisfied with my response, shifting even closer. I can smell his spicy cologne, one that reminds me of the Dior fragrance Johnny Depp promotes. It's hot as fuck.

"You want to be my friend, Darcy?" His voice takes on a darker edge, and I wobble a little on my ridiculous designer heels.

"Absolutely," I reply, a touch shakily.

He smiles, but it doesn't reach his ears like the previous time. "Then take some advice from me. Someone four years older—"

"For now," I interject. "I'm twenty-four in a few days."

Archer doesn't look surprised at that fact. "Okay, well, three years older." He pauses, blue eyes turning as dark as the deepest part of the ocean. "Don't sell yourself short for guys who only want a one-and-done arrangement. They aren't worth it."

The fervency in his voice renders me speechless.

"I should know because ..." He pauses, swallowing once. "Because there's no way I, the biggest playboy in the NHL, would ever view you like that."

His words remind me of a conversation we had back in October in another cocktail bar. He told me Liam wasn't worth it, and I agreed with him. Back then, I interpreted it as the kind of comment anyone would say to their heartbroken friend. Though that's not how our exchange feels tonight; there's more to his voice, more meaning in his body language, than simply a friend wanting to look out for someone they care about.

And that piques my intrigue further.

My throat feels thick as I reply, "That's exactly what you do with girls though."

He shifts his weight, looking off through the window and out into the darkened street. "Not all girls, Darcy."

When he says my name, his head turns to face me, and I feel

his weighted gaze all the way to my toes. I've never felt a sensation like this before in my life. Not even with Liam.

"Some girls don't really want that kind of man. They just think they do because that feels like the safe option after their previous guy did the dirty on them."

"And you think that's what I'm doing?" I reply, my voice now as thick as my throat feels.

Rolling his shoulders back, Archer chews on his bottom lip. "I do." He tips his head at the table Harry and his friends are sitting around, now eyeing up a group of different girls. "Every woman has a motive when she goes home with someone, just like every guy does. All I'm saying is, some reasons are healthier than others. I could always pick out the women who were fucking to forget from the ones who genuinely wanted no strings attached."

I grab my cocktail glass and take a long sip, hoping the alcohol will flush away some of the truths Archer just unearthed.

"I am genuinely looking for fun," I push out. "I'm not ready for anything serious, but equally, that doesn't mean I have to wear a chastity belt."

Back to grinning, he reaches out, taking my empty glass and sliding it back onto the bar. "I never said you did have to abstain from getting with guys. I merely suggested that you're careful to be sure you pick the right one."

I wave a finger at him, convinced I've found a flaw in his argument. "Right one? As in singular?"

Archer offers a nonchalant shrug. "Perhaps that's all you need—one guy who can rock your world in all the ways your ex couldn't"—he tips his chin at Harry again—"along with most of the guys in this city."

The heat rising to my cheeks contradicts the lighthearted scoff I give him. I know he's right, but that's an ideal scenario I'll never have. That's tantamount to a knight in shining armor who cares only about the girl and nothing else. You can only find that kind of shit in the movies and not in real life. Liam is living proof of that.

"Well, when you find my Mr. One Size Fits All, then please let me know. Because I'd love to meet him."

CHAPTER SIX

DARCY

"Happy birthday, Darcy!" Janine strides up to my desk, a white envelope in one hand and a bunch of pink roses in the other. She places the card down on top of my keyboard and hands me the bouquet. "A little birdie told me you don't like chocolate all that much, so we got you these, and there's a voucher inside the card."

Sienna and Penelope are all smiles from their desks as I pull open the envelope, revealing a cute card with the number 24 stamped across the front in pink glitter. "Thank you," I say, looking between the three of them. "You didn't have to."

When I open the card, a one-hundred-dollar gift voucher for Macy's falls out.

"Since the fall weather will start to draw in soon, we figured you could use it to put toward a scarf or hat or maybe some new earmuffs for when you head out at night with your friends. New York gets cold really quickly this time of year." Penelope smiles sweetly at me.

I stand quickly and head over to hug them all, each of them

taken by surprise when I pull them into me. "It's a really sweet gift. I wasn't expecting anything, to be honest."

"Well, actually"—Sienna thumbs behind her—"when I used the restroom a second ago, I noticed there was another package being delivered for you. I think you can expect a call from reception at any moment."

I head back to my desk, checking my email and messages. "I've not heard anything."

Sienna nods confidently. "They probably haven't had the time to let you know yet, but the delivery guy definitely said your name." She chuckles. "I don't know what it is, but good luck getting it home."

My interest officially at an all-time high, I thank my colleagues and boss once more and head for reception. There's no way Mum, Jon, or Jack would mail my gift directly to work ...

"Hey," I say, leaning against the desk.

Becky, our friendly receptionist, swivels around in her chair and instantly clicks her fingers. "Ah, yes! Darcy. I just took a package for you." She raises both brows, a soft but excitable grin threatening to emerge. "I have no idea who this is from, but, girl, you're living the dream."

She reaches beneath her desk and pulls out a large white box. "It's not actually that heavy. I think the supplier overdid it on packaging."

I stand motionless. "Did the delivery guy say who it was from?"

Becky shakes her head. "No. The only name he gave was yours." She spins the box around, revealing *Saks* printed in black. "Like I said, living the dream."

On an uncertain smile, I take the relatively light box and walk it back to my desk, all the while running over who could've bought me this. As much as my girls—Collins, Jenna, and Kendra—love me, there's no way they'd go shopping at Saks. None of us have that kind of budget on our salaries. Possibly Collins, but she wouldn't be seen dead in a department store.

I return to empty desks but decide I'm not waiting around for Sienna and Penelope and quickly grab a pair of scissors, slicing the heavy-duty tape.

The box is filled with packing peanuts and white tissue paper, which I push to one side.

Oh Lord.

A medium-sized tan leather Saint Laurent tote. This style costs in excess of three thousand dollars. Easily.

Pulling it from the packaging, I root around for a card or anything to indicate who sent me this.

Nothing.

Elbows braced on the desk, I clasp my hands under my chin and stare at the beautiful handbag, convinced this has to be some kind of mix-up. If Dad had sent me anything, especially like this, he sure would've let me know it was from him.

Still clueless and kind of emotional over the most luxurious gift I've ever received, I pick up my phone and take a picture, sending it to my girls.

Me: So, this just happened. Any idea who it's from? *picture attached*

Jenna: Ah, yes, that's from me. I spent an entire two months' wages on it. Love ya, babe.

Me: Are you being for real?

Jenna: No, I am not. I actually need money to eat.

Collins: I don't even know what brand that is, let alone would I head out and buy one.

Me: Saint Laurent? Everyone knows it!

Collins: Do they manufacture motorcycles?

Me: No. I don't think so.

Collins: Exactly.

Kendra: I have died and gone to designer-bag heaven.

Me: Not from you and Jack then?

Kendra: Or Felicity and Jon. I know what they got you, and it isn't that.

Puzzled, I rack my brain for a possible sender.

Jenna: Don't shoot the messenger here, but do you think it could be from Liam? Maybe he wants you back, and this is his way of trying.

I genuinely snort at the ridiculous notion of my shitty ex even thinking about me, never mind trying to win me back with a gesture like this.

Me: I think I have more of a chance of it being from that hottie at the bar the other night.

Jenna: The one who disappeared out of sight when we got back from the restroom?

Collins: You never did tell us what Archer was doing there.

By the time they returned from their escape to the toilet, Archer had left, claiming he was heading back home alone since the guys weren't up for a house party. The rest of the night passed in a blur as I chewed over our conversation. I can still feel the way he looked at me now.

I brush off the butterflies and get back to the text chat.

Me: Like I told you, he saw us on his way home and stopped by to say hi.

Jenna: That boy is weird. Hot as hell, but weird.

> Collins: I just think he's misunderstood.
>
> Jenna: Really? I think he likes to get it on with anything that moves and thinks a lot of himself.
>
> Collins: Jenna, are you trying to tell us you want a piece of the goalie?

Something about that last message from Collins doesn't sit well with me.

> Kendra: Anyway, back to the bag. I agree with Darcy. I don't think it's from Liam.
>
> Me: Then who the hell is it from?! How can I thank an anonymous sender?
>
> Jenna: Maybe they don't want to be thanked.
>
> Collins: Are you sure there's nothing else in the box? Like an invoice or receipt or something?
>
> Me: Positive.
>
> Collins: I'm clueless then. We might have to put a pin in our investigation until the party this weekend. We can ask around then.

The birthday party Jack and Kendra are throwing for me at their place. The one I have no clue what to wear to. I guess at least my bag is sorted.

> Me: Okay, well, I'd better get back to work.
>
> Collins: Happy birthday, babe. I'll bring your gift with me on Saturday night! Ezra picked it out, so you can be sure it's cool as fuck.

I smile at Collins's text. That girl and her future stepson are inseparable, and it's truly heartwarming, especially after he lost his mum at such a young age.

> Jenna: Me too! Have a fun one. I wish we could go out tonight, but the season is kicking our asses right now. Promise we'll make it up to you.

I close out the thread, only for another message to appear. This one directly from Kendra.

> Kendra: I think I might know who that bag is from.

I sit up straighter in my chair.

> Me: You do?

> Kendra: If I'm correct, well, it's potentially all kinds of awkward. And if I'm wrong ... let's just say, it's still awkward because I'll have put my foot in my mouth. But you're my family and friend, and I feel like I should be honest.

My mind races away from me, causing my fingers to slip on the keyboard as I type out a response.

> Me: Okay, freaking out right now ...

> Kendra: I'm pretty sure it's from Archer.

> Me: A three-thousand-dollar designer bag?!

The second I hit Send, I think over her suggestion. He did give me his Amex that time. Sure, he was wasted, but he told me to go buy whatever I wanted with it.

Kendra: Girl, he earns more than Jack as center and assistant captain. Last season, he signed a record-breaking contract with the Blades. He's one of the best in the league, and he's been there for seven seasons. He can afford it, trust me.

Me: I guess it's feasible. But why?

Kendra: You are Mensa-level genius. Are you seriously asking me this question right now?

Me: I'm also scatterbrained. Intellectual intelligence does not necessarily translate into equal levels of common sense.

Kendra: True. I'll never forget the time you found your car keys in the fridge.

Me: See? Case in point.

Kendra: He wants you. Plain and simple.

Me: Wants to fuck? I mean, that's hardly surprising. He wants to fuck a lot of girls, and blondes are his type. But we both know he wouldn't go there. Not with the potential ramifications he'd face. You know what I'm referring to …

Kendra: Yes, I can't argue with you on that. I'm just saying, I think this bag is from him. I also think he's struggling to keep ahold of himself, and I wouldn't be surprised if this is an indication of his wavering willpower.

More memories of the way he looked at me in the cocktail bar resurface, but I'm still doubtful and confused over Kendra's suggestion that the bag might be from Archer. He was drunk when he gave me the credit card. Sober Archer would definitely know the limits with his teammate's baby sister.

Right?

I'm tempted to tell Kendra about my conversation with Archer, but more doubt stops me. I've likely misinterpreted all the signals from that night. He probably was being a concerned friend, and it's just me getting ahead of myself because I find the guy hot and intriguing, and that revelation has knocked what I thought I knew about him off course.

> Me: Can you stop talking in riddles, please?

Kendra: Listen, I can't say it'd be more than sex with him because I don't know, and to be honest, I can't blame Jack for being worried. Archer Moore would tear through the New York volleyball team given half a chance. I think the guy wants what he can't have, and he isn't used to that. Obviously. Just proceed with caution ...

> Me: You think he bought me a bag to convince me to sleep with him?!

Kendra: No, not exactly. He clearly likes you, and he has money to burn. Ugh, I don't know. I could be way off the mark with this. Forget I said anything. I'm not trying to paint him in a bad light; I'm just trying to be a friend and counsel you to keep your head on. I wouldn't put it past him to make a move.

> Me: I have zero idea what to do with that information. Or this bag for that matter.

Kendra: Accept the gift and maybe ask him about it this Saturday.

> Me: He's coming to the party?

Kendra: Of course he is. Why wouldn't he be?

> Me: I don't know. I figured he'd have better things to do than celebrate me randomly turning twenty-four and blowing out a few candles on a cake.

Kendra: I refer you to our above conversation.

CHAPTER SEVEN

ARCHER

Darcy's party is exactly how I expected—full of pastels, free-flowing prosecco, and enough snacks to feed a small town.

"Hey," I say to Kendra as she offers to take my jacket and hang it with the others.

Her side-eye isn't entirely welcoming. "Hey, yourself."

"Everything okay?" I ask, stretching my hands above my head. The lat pulldowns Coach set this morning have me aching like a bitch.

"Yeah, I'm good," she answers quickly, tipping her chin behind her. "The guys are back there and already hoovering up the food. I thought soccer players ate a lot, but we have nothing on hockey players."

My stomach growls at the promise of food.

"Is the birthday girl here yet?" I ask, knowing she is. I spotted Darcy the second I walked through the door.

"Don't kid a kidder." Kendra raises a brow at me.

I huff out a soft laugh and make for Sawyer and Jack standing in the living area when Kendra's palm wraps around my upper arm.

"Don't fuck around with her, Archer. She just had her heart broken and doesn't need another asshole."

Kendra isn't petite; her height suits her position as center back perfectly. Still, my tall frame towers over her. I know she's only looking out for her friend; I'd be the same with Jack or Sawyer. However, her assumption still cuts me.

"I'm not planning on fucking her about," I confirm, voice a touch sharp.

She murmurs something to herself before looking up at me, a question in her brown eyes. "Earlier today, Jack told me you're seeing a girl from Dallas. Is that true? Because a couple of weeks ago, you were drooling over Darcy."

This fucking lie gets deeper and deeper, but I can't deny it now. "Yeah, it is." I push a hand through my hair. "But like I told him, it's not serious."

My eyes find Darcy's back as she heads over to the snack table, refilling a bowl of Bugles—something she once told me she'd become addicted to since moving stateside.

Her short pink skirt bounces light from the glitter ball Jack and Kendra must've had temporarily installed, and the tight, off-shoulder black top she's wearing accentuates her perfect, shapely figure. My mouth waters at the thought of how soft she'd feel in my hands. Even though I can't see her face, she looks beautiful.

Kendra releases my arm, and I throw her a quick smile, making my way to Sawyer, who waves a hand in my direction. In his other hand, he holds out a cold beer to me, and I happily take it from him and pop the cap, trying to work out at what point would be a good time to tell everyone that Abbie is, in fact, my made-up girlfriend.

"First friendly game next week. How are we all feeling about it?" Sawyer looks between me and Jack.

Ever the confident center, Jack shrugs casually. "The Flames had a tough season and are carrying a few injuries going into this one. I'm confident we can take them now and again in the regular season."

Sawyer chuckles, beer raised to his lips. He pauses before taking a sip. "I think I've got a couple more seasons in me, and then I'll be looking to call it a day. I'm aching like a bitch from this morning, and recovery isn't getting any easier."

"You say that," I say, still tracking Darcy's every movement despite standing right in front of her brother. *Jesus, I've got some gall.* "But I'm, what, eight years younger than you and feel like I've had a head-on collision with a bus?"

"What's this about buses?" Darcy slots in between her brother and Sawyer, eyes flicking to mine for a split second.

She looks fucking breathtaking, her hair styled in waves that reach the small of her back. As she sets her eyes on me, her cheeks flush, and I can't help but recall the last time we spoke and I told her she deserved a man who could give her what she wanted.

"Nothing, Darce. Archer here was moaning about how old he feels, whereas Sawyer was pointing out how ancient he actually is and that he's considering his retirement options," Jack jokes, pulling a grumble from his captain.

She snorts softly, taking a sip of prosecco. She's wearing a white gold bracelet I don't recognize, and immediately, I'm hit with another wave of Darcy-induced jealousy.

Is that a birthday gift, and if so, who from? I wonder if she used the Saint Laurent bag I got her tonight. It was a bold—and probably incredibly stupid—idea to buy and send it to her office. But, hey, I know where she works, and I know she likes tote bags. I'd buy her a thousand more if she were mine.

"Well, I guess you have a wedding to plan and family life to prioritize now. Gotta hang those skates up at some point." Darcy nods at Sawyer and winks.

He grins, immediately finding Collins on the other side of the room, talking with Kendra and Jenna.

"I'm married, and I don't feel a day older for it," Jack pipes up. "In fact, I ..."

Darcy raises a hand. "If this is going to be one of your inappropriate sex jokes to make me cringe, just know you've already succeeded. We get it—you're in love and got the girl."

My amusement is obvious, although it soon fades when Jack looks at me. I know what's coming, and I'm powerless to prevent it.

Why the fuck did I think playing along with this crazy ruse was a good idea? And why didn't I connect the dots sooner? Of course it was going to get back to Darcy.

I open my mouth to shut him—and the entire bullshit story —down, but he gets there first.

"All I'll say is, I'm not the only one here tonight who's in love." He winks at me, and I want the ground to swallow me whole, along with Darcy so she doesn't hear what her brother is about to reveal.

"Well, duh, Sawyer, of course," Darcy replies.

"No, no. Our boy Archer here. He's been seeing Abbie from Dallas. Apparently, it isn't serious, but the other day, we caught him being a simp in the gym while buying her dresses, and the entire story came out." He takes a pull of his beer, waiting for me to verify his story.

I dare not fucking look at Sawyer. I can already feel his eyes as they bore into the side of my skull.

"Oh." Darcy's voice is weaker than earlier, dampened with uncertainty or maybe disappointment. A part of me hopes it is while the other half wants to tear my hair out for being the reason behind her flat tone. "I didn't know you were seeing someone. Congrats."

"It's not serious," I rush out, forgetting myself and glancing at a seething Sawyer.

I can fully understand why he's pissed—one minute, I'm declaring how I feel and asking him to take me seriously, and the next, he's hearing all about make-believe Abbie.

Silence falls between us. I can tell Darcy is looking for a way out, and all I want to do is haul her into my arms and carry her to one of the spare rooms, clarifying my relationship status with my tongue.

The lights go out, and our group—along with the rest of the room—is plunged into black.

"Oh God, she isn't going to sing 'Happy Birthday,' is she?" Darcy whispers.

Taking advantage of the darkness, I lean into her as Jack heads in the direction of Kendra's voice, Sawyer moving away and giving us a second.

I don't deserve that guy.

"I'm going to go out on a limb here and say she absolutely is. Happy birthday, by the way."

I don't know what the fuck possesses me to do it—desperation probably. But the second my lips connect with her forehead, I regret nothing.

She tenses against me, and I interpret it as a good sign. I affect her.

"What are you doing?" she asks quietly. "I don't think Abbie would appreci—"

"Forget about Abbie and do me a favor," I breathe against her soft skin.

I turn my head just as Kendra starts up singing and the rest of the party joins in.

Quickly, I pull away, aware that eyes will be swinging to Darcy, and we'll soon be visible in the glow from the candles.

"What favor?" she asks.

My heart hammers against my ribs. "Meet me in the spare bedroom opposite the bathroom in five minutes. I've got some things I want to say."

I spin around to face Kendra just as she makes her final approach.

"I've got so much I need to tell you," I finish, hoping Darcy can still hear and she'll give me the chance to explain what the hell just happened.

CHAPTER EIGHT

DARCY

He's got a girlfriend.

Well, there's a revelation I was not expecting when I showed up tonight.

Archer Moore, resident playboy no longer.

While my head works to process the existence of Abbie, I stand alone at the back of the living area, watching Kendra cut the cake she got me into pieces and struggling to shake an unmistakable sense of disappointment.

Did I like the prospect of Archer wanting me, with the excitement of thinking he was flirting with me the other night? Yes, I did. I was so convinced I'd never go there with him—or any hockey player for that matter—and I thought I was fine with it. But now that the possibility with Archer is dead in the water, I find myself placing way too much hope on the reasons why he wants to talk to me in private.

"Girl, you look like someone accidentally dropped your birthday cake." Jenna joins me next to the food table, reaching behind my back and stealing a piece of popcorn chicken.

I release a low groan. "Why is life so damn complex?"

She smiles at that, swallowing her mouthful. "I thought you liked puzzles. No one wants boring."

Jack passes by with a tray of prosecco, and I quickly snag a glass. Jenna grabs an orange juice since she's a committed athlete.

I, on the other hand, need bubbles.

My attention pauses on the entrance to the hallway and bedrooms. Chances are, Archer is already waiting for me since he isn't anywhere to be seen. I honestly don't know what he could want to say to me. Perhaps he picked up on my attraction to him, and he wants to make sure I'm clear that nothing can happen between us. Maybe I did go too far when I randomly showed up at his apartment, and his new girlfriend didn't appreciate it.

Shit. Maybe he did have a girl in his room, but instead of it being some random hookup, it was actually Abbie.

Feeling embarrassed, I exhale another groan, this one louder and more pronounced.

"Share with the class, Darce." Jenna sets her glass down on the table behind us, turning to me fully.

I don't even hesitate. "Did you know Archer is seeing someone?"

Her mouth pops open in surprise, answering my question. "No. No, I did not."

"He says it isn't serious, but ..." I trail off.

"Oh my God, you like him! You do, don't you?" Jenna speaks way too loudly, the music the only thing preventing the rest of the room from overhearing our conversation.

She winces and lowers her voice to a discreet level. "Is that what's got you standing over here, alone, at your own party, looking all hung up?"

A large part of me wants to deny it and make up some bullshit excuse for why I look exactly how she described earlier—like someone just dropped my cake. But that won't serve me, and I trust Jenna. Plus, she recently broke up with her serious boyfriend, Lee, so she understands the importance of leaning on girlfriends when you need them.

"I think it's possible I wanted a little more than a few laughs with him on nights out."

Jenna rolls her lips together, smirking but seeming unsurprised. "You mean you wanted to find out if he's as awesome as the rumors suggest?"

I tingle at the thought. "Maybe."

She nods in understanding. "Listen, I get that. I've read *and heard* that he can go *all* night long. Some women who have spent a night with him report he's ruined them for other men."

I take a sip of prosecco. "Well, it's not like I'm going to find out now, is it? He wants to talk with me tonight, but I'm pretty sure it's to clear the—"

Jenna holds up a hand, pulling her mobile out of her bag. The smirk she wore a few seconds ago is now a full-blown grin. "Well, well, well. Speak of the devil."

I furrow my brow as she hands me her phone.

> Archer: I know everyone wants to spend time with the birthday girl, but actually, I reserved these few minutes. Can you ask Miss Darcy Thompson to meet me in the room two doors down on the left? Oh, and this text does not exist.

I hand my friend her phone back, my excitement kicking up a notch. Even though nothing has really changed in the past thirty seconds, he sure is keen to speak with me.

Jenna tips her head toward the hallway. "Go. I'll cover for you."

I go to move past her, and she clears her throat, asking me to hold up.

"Listen, I've got zero idea what's going on with this other girl of his, but that is one complication I wouldn't want to get tangled up in. Be really fucking careful, babe."

Archer's sitting on a king-size bed, typing something on his phone when I walk into the dimly lit room.

"Hey," I say, holding the door handle with a shaky hand. I have no right to be this nervous. I turn my back on him and push the door closed, taking a second to get ahold of myself. *It's just Archer.* "Sorry, I got caught up, talking with Jenna."

A hand lands on my shoulder, twisting my body around to face the room and, consequently, him. Any calm I managed to gain in the last few seconds completely dissipates.

"I don't have a girlfriend." Archer cuts through the small talk.

He's only inches from me, and I can feel his body heat as it radiates into mine.

This boy is intense.

Swallowing thickly, I look up into bright blue eyes. He takes full advantage of our height difference, cupping my chin in his warm and slightly rough palm.

"I don't have a girlfriend," he repeats, his voice gruff and serious.

"Umm, okay," I stammer, pressing my back into the door.

He moves another inch closer, and my lungs tighten, like he's crushing me. Yet, aside from his hand on my chin, we aren't touching.

He grins, but I can't tell if it's driven by happiness or something else. It feels like there's no air in the room as I grapple to form coherent thoughts. There's that look he had in his eyes a few days ago, piercing and wanting, and it settles between my thighs as he holds me captive while I wait for him to elaborate on his relationship status.

A few pieces of dark hair fall over his forehead as he looks down at me, his platinum chain shining in the glow of the room. "That's all you've got to say about it?"

My chest grows tighter. "I don't know what to say, Archer. I'm confused. Jack just said you're seeing a girl called Abbie."

He shakes his head, still grinning. "She doesn't exist, Doll."

I hear his words and process what he's saying, but my brain can't push past what he just called me.

"Doll?" I whisper. It's more of a question than a statement.

"Doll," he repeats. "You're my doll, Darcy."

My head spins, and the floor lamp on the other side of the room—the only source of light—begins to blur under the intense weight of information.

"Say something." Archer is the first to speak, his delicious breath fanning my dry lips.

I run my tongue across my bottom lip, and he tracks the movement, imitating my action.

"Did you buy me the tote bag?"

His head falls forward on a deep chuckle, and he releases my chin, resting his on my forehead. "You're so fucking cute—you know that?"

I feel antsy and confused, and it shows in my tone. "Did you gift me the bag or not?"

His laughter trails off. "Yes. Did you bring it with you tonight?"

He did buy it for me.

More tingles shimmer down my spine. I'm not experienced when it comes to guys. In fact, I've only ever slept with Liam. So far, my quest to have fun and play the field has not been particularly lucrative. And all of a sudden, in this darkened space, with one of the most confident guys I've ever met, I feel every bit of that inexperience, along with all the butterflies he elicited in the bar.

I try not to let it show. I don't want Archer to think that being here, alone with him, isn't what I want. I can try and convince myself it's not, just like I'm sure so many other girls before me have done. I'd only be lying to myself though—the disappointment I felt when I found out about Abbie only evidences that.

"I did. Was I not supposed to?"

He lifts his head and looks at me again, darkened eyes only deepening. "I want it to be your new favorite bag, so, yeah, I'd say you did exactly right."

I'm convinced he's going to kiss me. He looks like he wants to as he presses his leg between my knees, his jeans rubbing deliciously against the sensitive skin on my thighs.

"Why did you tell people you have a girlfriend?"

He shakes his head slowly. "I didn't tell people. Your brother assumed I did when I got caught by your stepdad, scrolling through dresses on my phone. He asked me if they were for a girl I was seeing, and your brother ran with it." He breathes out slowly and studies my face, taking a piece of my hair and twizzling it around his thick finger. "I'm not into being dishonest, and I hate that I lied to Jack. But at the time, it seemed like a good opportunity and a decent cover story. I'm hoping it still is."

My heart is pounding, racing so fast that I feel sure I'll cardiac arrest at any second.

Holy shit.

"What are you covering up, Archer?" I don't know how or where I find the words as they fall from my lips.

He presses his leg higher, the rough denim skating across the thin fabric of my already-damp underwear. "My obsession with you, Darcy. And hopefully, if I get my way, the insane amount of fun we're going to have in my bed tonight."

In the space of five minutes, I've gone from being convinced Archer had a girl in bed with him when I showed up at his apartment to him inviting me into it. My instincts in the bar were right—he *was* flirting with me; he *does* want me.

Holy hell, did he show up and interrupt Harry on purpose? My head spins with possibilities as I try to stay upright against the door.

I push down the anxiety surrounding my lack of sexual experience, only for it to be replaced by a fear of my brother finding out and murdering Archer in his sleep. "Do you think this is a good idea?"

A deep rumble reverberates from his chest. "Based on what?"

I look off to the side, thinking over the best way to word this. "Because Jack will likely unalive you if he finds out, and that's before you lied to him about Abbie. Plus, and more importantly" —I focus back on Archer, my tone deadly serious—"you said it yourself the other day—I'm not the kind of girl who would happily be part of a one-and-done arrangement, and you were right. The stakes are higher with us than one of your random girls, and I'm not doing the walk of shame tomorrow once you've had your fill of me. We do this because we want each other and not because I'm the only option you have tonight. Getting with your assistant captain's baby sister is not a power flex I'm okay with."

He leans forward, our lips a whisker from touching. "Did you not hear or listen to a word I said the other night? Some girls will never be a one-and-done arrangement." He cups the back of my head in his large palm. "You are that girl to me, Darcy."

I draw in a deep breath. "I-I don't know what to say ..."

"Say you'll come home with me tonight." He runs his tongue across his bottom lip. "Don't leave me hanging because I just crossed a line, and now I can't go back. Not now that I have you in my hands, beneath my touch."

His lips draw closer to my mouth, full and wet as my eyes drop to them.

"I'm going all in here with you because I know it's only a matter of time before you go home with the wrong guy and he treats you all the ways you don't want, all the ways you just described."

I remain frozen to the spot, motionless, speechless, lost in time, as Archer hovers over me, burying his fingers in the hair at the back of my neck.

"Let me kiss you, Darcy."

"Why?" It's a fucking stupid question. Of course I know why he wants to kiss me. Still, I want to hear his version of the answer.

"Because you say you want to have fun, and I can absolutely give you that. But tell me, have you ever experienced a real man kiss you before?" His lips brush mine gently. "Or is Liam every bit the immature boy I think he is?"

Words fail me once more.

"Part your lips for me," he coaxes.

After what feels like an eternity, my body finally catches up to my brain, and I do as he asked.

The first sweep of Archer's tongue is soft and everything a first kiss should be, our tongues massaging slowly, small whimpers rising up my throat as he deepens our connection. His hand moves from the back of my head to cup my cheek, his thumb stroking me gently.

The tingles I felt in the bar are nothing compared to the fizz of electricity as it illuminates every nerve ending. It's like I'm here, but also not really, and I reach out to palm his hip, checking this is real and not another one of my crazy dreams.

A few more seconds pass, and Archer pulls back, chest heaving like he's been starved of oxygen for way too long. "And now that I've tasted you," he pants, "there's not a chance in hell I'm allowing you to say no tonight."

I know in my gut this situation has disaster written all over it, not that it's going to stop me from taking what I want.

"You could just stay at mine?" I suggest.

Archer doesn't like that idea; I can tell by the way his face falls to the crook of my neck, and he scrunches his nose, skating his lips along my pulse point.

"No. I've only ever fantasized about having you in my bed. I changed the entire frame and mattress a few weeks back because I couldn't stand the thought that any other woman had been in it. The first time I take you, it has to be this way."

"The f-first time." It's impossible to keep my voice steady, the combination of his lips and words as he whispered them against my skin proving too much.

He nips at my neck, one hand braced on my hip, holding me in place against the door, which, for all I know, Jack could be on the other side of right now.

"We're going all night, Doll." He licks up to just below my ear. "Aside from the battle I'm currently fighting, not to blow straight into my pants, I also need to be really careful with how much I tell you."

My, "Why?" is more of a seduced moan.

"Because, Darcy, after way too long, I only just got you here, and I'm not about to freak you out with more crazy-ass admissions. So, why don't you just tell me yes and ride my dick until sunrise?"

The hand still teasing my outer thigh moves inward, finding my apex.

"I'm really wet," I confess.

"I know you are—because you're nothing other than perfect. What I need is to feel your pussy between my fingers. I don't think I can wait."

"Touch me." It sounds like a plea I know I don't need to make.

"Oh, Doll. You hear that?" He shifts my now-pointless underwear to one side and runs a finger through me. "That's precisely how your pussy will sound when I push my dick inside it later," he growls and teases my hole. "I'll fuck you so good, but I swear, I'll only go at a pace you're comfortable with."

With a firm hand against his chest, I push him back an inch.

"Don't go easy on me. I meant what I said the other night. I want to have fun with guys, and I want you to show me what safe hookups look like. Your playboy days mean you have way more experience than me, and I want to finally—for once in my life—have the sex Liam could never offer."

His expression leaves me confused. I delivered my statement with all the best intentions, and I meant nothing negative by it. I somehow feel like I missed the mark though. Big time.

"What's the matter?" I ask. "Did I say something wrong?"

Like he's shaking off an unwelcome emotion, he pushes a hand through his tousled hair. "Playboy ... yeah, I know. That's what I am."

Biting down on my lip, I nod lightly. "I promise not to be all clingy and show up at your apartment, unannounced—oh, wait." I giggle. "Too late for that."

Archer moves forward, pressing against me, his fingers back to playing with my pussy, and I spread my thighs wider.

"You can show up at my apartment whenever you want. The limit for that does not exist."

I melt beneath his touch, my excitement coating his hand. "I promise I'm not that needy," I moan, my voice a juxtaposition to the words leaving my mouth.

"And I promise there's nothing you can do or say that would be too much for me, Darcy."

When I find his eyes, I sense a deeper meaning to his words. Liam always told me I was too much.

Archer's lips skate over mine. "Just come back to my place and be yourself. Don't hold back. I want every part of you."

CHAPTER NINE

ARCHER

"Come on, come on, come on," I anxiously whisper into the silence of my car, drumming my fingernails restlessly on the steering wheel.

Fucking hell, this is risky, even for me.

A few floors above, I've got my center and best friend saying good night to his baby sister, thinking she's heading home because of a headache. That's what Darcy told me she'd say right before I withdrew my hand from between her thighs and licked my fingers clean.

My engine idles in Jack and Kendra's apartment parking lot as I drop my head between my shoulders and wait outside the door Darcy will walk through at any second.

"What are you doing, Archer?" I breathe quietly to myself right before there's a light knock on my passenger window.

I dart my head around to find Darcy waiting, and I quickly unlock my car, checking to make sure I heated her seat.

She pulls the door open and immediately climbs in, dropping her Saint Laurent tote onto the floorboard between her feet.

Her eyes track to my dash and then to me.

"You realize it's not cold?" She giggles.

She's nervous—I can tell, although I'm not surprised. I know from talking with Jack and overhearing conversations on nights out between her, Kendra, and Jenna—which I likely, *definitely*, shouldn't have been eavesdropping on—that tonight, I'll be only the second guy she's been with.

Darcy isn't the only one nervous. I'm officially shitting myself. I've lost count of the number of times I've been in this position—a smokeshow sitting in my passenger seat, waiting for me to take her home. This isn't just any girl though, and tonight isn't like any other I've shared. Darcy was right when she said the stakes are higher than the average hookup.

But what she doesn't seem to realize is, for me, there isn't a chance in hell I'd fuck her and then tell her to leave. The fact that she even asked me not to do that tore me in two.

Tonight is way more than just a fuck to me. I thought I'd made my intentions clear when I pinned her up against the wall in Jack and Kendra's apartment.

Jesus. I never want to hear the word *playboy* fall from her lips again.

I grin playfully. "I use my heated seats throughout the year. No one likes a cold ass."

She rolls her eyes at me, cheeks pinkening with flirtation.

It's all the invite I need as I lean across the center section of my Mercedes and palm the back of her head, pulling her toward me.

"You've got no fucking idea how long I've been waiting for this."

On a crimson flush that descends her chest, I brush my lips over hers. Darcy's eyes flutter closed, but I keep mine open, burning the visual into my brain.

Another pass of my lips, and she opens her eyes, fixing them on the door she just walked through.

"Anyone could come through there unannounced."

"Mmhmm," I hum into her mouth. "I probably should care, but I really don't give a fuck."

She giggles again at that, doing things to my heart rate. After tonight, I've got no idea how hard I'll have to work to get her into my bed again, and I intend to savor every last noise she makes for me.

"Well, I think it's best if we get out of here."

She moves away, but I pull her back into me.

"You're right. If we stay here a second longer, doing this, I'm going to take you in my car, and that's the opposite of how I pictured us together. I want this to be perfect for you."

Her eyes sparkle with mischief. "It's just sex, Archer. Or respectful fucking, if you will."

I shake my head at her, forcing another fake grin. I hate that she thinks it's only sex to me.

I lean into her, smoothing my hand along her left knee, and her soft skin pebbles beneath my touch.

"I dare you to say that again in the morning."

"Come here." I flip my hand toward me as we ride the private elevator to my penthouse.

In her pink designer heels, she takes a step forward, and I clamp my hands on her waist, spinning her around so she's against the railing.

Baby-blue eyes peer up at me as she rests a hand on my forearm, her other holding the Saint Laurent tote bag by her side.

With my spare hand, I reach down and take the bag, hooking it over my shoulder. We're inches—no, centimeters—apart, and Darcy's sweet breath and perfume wash over me in waves.

"You're really intense—you know that?" she repeats her previous observation and swallows thickly, gaze dropping to my mouth. "When I imagined ..." She trails off, and frustration curls inside me.

"Finish your sentence, Darcy. What were you imagining?"

Her eyes widen, and I suspect that's exactly how they'll look when I slide inside her later. I can wait for that though, sensing this is a first glimpse into whatever fantasies she might've had about us.

She shakes her head, and I move my hand from her waist, snaking it up to her pulse point. It's racing, just like my heart.

"You're hiding something, Doll. Tell me what it is." I trace my fingers over her delicate skin, pushing back a few strands of hair. "What's going on in that pretty mind?"

"I guess ... I always thought you wouldn't be this attentive with women." Her eyes fall to her bag on my shoulder. "You surprise me, is all."

I know she can feel how hard I am when I press my body against her, dropping my forehead to meet hers. The elevator doors to my apartment open, though neither one of us looks away from each other.

My heart thumps faster. "That's because this isn't how it usually goes. Ordinarily, I'd already be in bed with her." I don't know how much to divulge since I've never been in this position with a girl before. I've never been this vulnerable. "I've always called the shots during hookups. I don't want to do that with you. I want to be sure that whatever I do is one hundred percent for you. I'm just lucky to be here."

Releasing a steadying breath, she rolls her lips together. "Are you sleeping with me because you're worried I'll go home with the wrong type of person? I know you've said I'm special to you, but is that because you know we'll have to see each other again after this?"

The way I want to wrap her in my arms and extract the intrusive thoughts from her head has my own mind spinning out. "It's neither, Darcy. I'm here because I want to be, because it's all I've thought about for far too long."

Her look of pure innocence as she absorbs my reassurance squeezes my chest. I've never had a woman look at me like this before, and I know exactly why—I've never allowed them to. Everything I've ever done was devoid of emotion, the complete opposite of tonight.

She reaches behind her back, and I inch away.

Holy fucking hell.

When her black top drops to the floor by her feet, she slowly lifts her eyes to look at me.

I am certifiably fucked.

Darcy stands in front of me, wearing a black lace bra, revealing that her perfectly proportioned tits make the ideal handful, and her pink miniskirt—along with the killer heels I'm seriously thinking about asking her to leave on tonight—pump my blood faster.

"Take a picture. It'll last longer," she teases.

I swipe a palm across my mouth, utterly speechless.

Liam let this woman go.

"Don't fucking tempt me," I whisper because that's all I'm capable of right now. "Seriously, don't fucking tempt me."

A bubble of laughter spills out as she lurches forward and dips her hand into my pocket, pulling my cell out and handing it to me. "Actually, take the picture. You can use it as a screensaver and show Jack."

I deadpan and fight for breath as she hooks her thumbs under the waistband of her skirt, letting it fall down to the ground. The flimsy excuse for panties I pushed aside earlier sit high on her hourglass figure, matching her bra.

"Are you being serious?" I ask, voice trembling at the sight and my need to put my hands on her.

She nods once, kicking her clothes out of the picture. "I told you, I want to have fun. You make me feel sexy, and I want to remember the feeling."

I unlock my iPhone and open the Camera app, bringing the screen up in front of me. I'm so fucking close to blowing straight into my pants. I've done some pretty outrageous stuff with women, but this, with Darcy right here, is a first for me, and it's single-handedly the sexiest experience of my life.

"Take the picture, Archer," she breathes, her chest rising and falling more quickly than before.

I snap two shots, both with her hands braced on the railing behind her, hair falling in waves around her shoulders.

It feels like there isn't any air in the elevator—or maybe it's only my lungs that are struggling to inflate.

A moment of nothing passes between us before I pocket my phone and walk a couple of paces forward, taking Darcy by the hand. I'll send the images to her later and lock them down on my phone, where no one, apart from me, will ever find them.

I look down at her, feral need burning an inferno inside me. "Tell me, at what point did you elevate yourself to the top of my priority list?"

She tips her head to the side, and I wrap my hand around the nape of her neck, waiting for her to give me the green light and take her to bed. "The moment you laid eyes on my impeccable underwear?"

On a chuckle, I drop my gaze down the length of her half-naked body, plucking at her lacy panties.

"Who bought you this set?"

She rolls her lips together, amused, maybe even entertained at my apparent jealousy.

"It wasn't Liam, if that's what you're thinking."

"Did he ever buy you underwear?"

She shakes her head. "No, never. Or a Saint Laurent tote."

My hands fall to her tight, round ass, and I palm it, ready to pick her up and walk us both to my bedroom.

"What about orgasms? Did he give you many of those?"

When I lift her up and she wraps her legs around my waist on a cute squeal, I swear I can feel the heat radiating from her pussy, seeping through my clothes.

"They were ... fleeting ..." she replies like it's no big deal.

It absolutely is a big deal. Seismic.

With my girl wrapped around me and feeling like the luckiest motherfucker alive, I step out of the elevator and begin walking through my darkened apartment, nipping and sucking at her neck.

"Yeah?" I moan against her sensitive flesh, kicking my bedroom door closed after we enter. "That's a crying fucking shame." I spin around and sit on the edge of the bed, and she straddles me. "Let me remedy that with the best night you'll ever have."

I reach behind my head and pull off my shirt in one smooth motion.

Her eyes drop to my chest, and she smooths a soft palm over my pecs, causing me to suck in a sharp breath. She isn't touching an erogenous zone, but this is Darcy.

My obsession.

"I don't know why, but I expected you to be tattooed."

I cock my head to the side, curious about her statement. "You dig the bad-boy look?"

She shakes her head, trailing a single fingertip down my abs. "No, but I am digging this perfect torso."

I let her tease and feel me for a few seconds before pushing her hair back and whispering into her ear, "Darcy Doll, I think it's time we quit fucking around and you let me do what I want with you."

I reach around and unhook her bra, bringing her nipple into my mouth and sucking it lightly.

She groans and melts beneath my touch, throwing her head

back, her long hair trailing over my legs. "Archer, that feels so good."

I move to the next nipple, sucking this one harder.

"Take these off," she commands, grabbing at the button on my pants.

I grin against her chest while she pops it open.

Both lifting up, we drag my pants and boxer briefs down together.

Darcy pauses, not moaning when I lick and nip across her chest. I look up at her as she stares down at me.

"Y-your dick is..."

I move my mouth to the underside of her jaw, desperate to leave marks but all too aware of how tricky it will be to explain how they got there.

"What's the matter?" I croon, satisfaction swelling inside me. "And before you freak out, it's absolutely going to fit. My cock is perfect for you."

She shakes her head, still looking down. "I mean, yeah, you're huge, but ..." She shuffles back a little, running a hand along the top of my right thigh, a victorious smile pulling at her lips.

Her confidence catapults another surge of need through me.

"What's got you all speechless?" I know exactly what's stolen her words. I just want to hear her say it.

She breathes out slowly when I reach between her thighs, teasing through her damp panties. "Your dick—it's pierced. A-and ... oh my God ... you have a thigh tattoo as well."

CHAPTER TEN

DARCY

He's pierced, tattooed, *and* bigger than I imagined.

Slowly—and with way more conviction than I feel—I snake my hand up to his dick. My intention is to stroke him a few times, although he's already harder than stone, the tip shining with arousal.

When I wrap a warm palm around the base of his cock, Archer's hand covers mine. My eyes flick to his. Is he trying to stop me?

"Here's the thing. It kills me to say this, but I don't think I can take one pump of your hand." He releases my grip on him, bringing my palm to his mouth and placing a soft kiss in the center. "I've lost count of the number of times I fantasized about us being in this position, and trust me when I say, they all involved you touching me like this." He chuckles, but it sounds like more of a rumble from his chest. "What's your favorite position?"

"Doggy," I reply without a beat of hesitation. "It was the only one where Liam could make me orgasm."

Archer's eyes narrow, a question in them. "For real?"

I feel my face flush hot. "Yes. Why?"

Archer rests the palm he just kissed on his shoulder. "Hold on tight."

Before I have a chance to question anything, I'm on my back and in the center of his bed. Archer hovers over me as he brackets me in between his huge forearms, pieces of dark hair falling over self-assured eyes.

"You're telling me your favorite way to fuck is without eye contact?" He braces himself on one arm, stroking a thumb underneath my right eye. For a guy with a bad-boy rep and a dominant presence on the ice, he sure can be gentle when he wants to be. "If you really want me to take you like that, then I will. I told you tonight is all about what you want. I just find doggy hard to believe. There are so many better ways I can make you feel special."

His thumb moves across my bottom lip, and my eyelids flutter at the sensation.

Bloody hell, he's so fucking hot.

"So, tell me again, what position do you want first?"

A surge of heat settles between my thighs, and my pussy tightens beneath him. As Archer rests between my legs, I'm all too aware that with a shift of his body upward, his cock will be pressing against my underwear.

My breathing is ragged, the effect he's having on me difficult to hide. "Like this," I whisper, tongue automatically swiping across my bottom lip. "I like it like this."

"Attagirl." He just smiles at me—it's one that if he wasn't already pulling my panties down and tossing them onto the bedroom floor, I'm sure it would melt them right off anyway.

He moves up, notching himself at my entrance. I'm ready, holding my breath to be stretched out and feel the three-bar Jacob's ladder on the underside of his shaft, situated near the tip of his dick.

I close my eyes, overwhelmed at the intensity of the moment.

"Open your eyes, Darcy." Archer's voice is coaxing with an unsteady lilt that lingers beneath the surface.

Surely, he isn't nervous?

Cautiously, I crack them open.

Between my legs, he palms his dick, the other hand still braced by my head, supporting all of his weight.

Archer hesitates, something flashing through his eyes. I wouldn't call it uncertainty, but it does surprise me. I never expected to see emotion in him. Kindness and care, yes. But nothing deeper.

"Are you on birth control? I realize I didn't ask you before now, and I'm sorry. I'm tested regularly, and I—" He cuts himself off. "I can wear a condom if you want me to."

Entranced by the softness in his eyes, I shake my head absentmindedly. "I'm on birth control, and fun fact: I'm actually allergic to latex. I haven't slept with anyone since Liam, and back then, we used latex-free ones. I'm guessing you don't have any of those."

I'm unsure if he's smiling at the humor in my random allergy or that I haven't been with anyone since my ex-boyfriend, but when he brushes his lips against mine, my pussy throbs.

"No, Darcy, I don't have latex-free. Do you?"

I shake my head, body tingling from his lips. "No, I don't."

"Crying shame. I guess we'll just have to feel everything," he breathes out, and I can feel the desperation laced in his voice.

I've never been this turned on or excited before. Not even when I first started sleeping with Liam.

He pushes the head of his cock inside, and small gasps fill the room, which I quickly realize emanate from us both.

Archer never takes his eyes off mine as he guides himself further, feeding me his dick slowly, deliberately, perfectly.

This is *not* the hookup I expected it to be. This boy continues to surprise me. He is nothing like I thought.

"Spread wider for me," he grits out, jaw tensing. "You're so fucking tight, and I want this pussy open."

I part my thighs, gripping the bedsheets beneath me. The way he fills me is borderline unbearable yet addictive, all at the same time.

When he's all the way inside, Archer sits back on his haunches, bottom lip pinned between his teeth as he gazes down at our connection.

"Jesus fucking Christ," he croons on a headshake. "I need you to see this, what we look like together."

He cranes his neck around, looking for something, long arms reaching for his jeans at the corner of the bed. Snatching them up, he pulls his phone from the pocket.

"I'll delete it right after."

A bubble of laughter rises up my throat.

Using the flash, he takes a photo and hands the phone to me so I can look.

"Do you always keep yourself bare?" he asks, stroking into me for the first time, his fingers smoothing over my waxed area.

The movement fires off a sensation I've only ever felt right before coming, and his phone slips from my hand, hitting the floor with a thud.

We both ignore it, too caught up in each other.

Archer takes my legs by the ankles and rolls his hips into me again.

"Y-yes," I answer his previous question, choking out the single word.

For the first time, I watch as his eyes close, and he exhales a deep breath, pumping into me in deliberate, languid strokes.

"I can hear how wet you are, and it's doing things to my ego." He opens his eyes and smirks, bringing both of my legs to his shoulders, arching his body over mine.

The change in position finds a deeper spot, pulling a pleasure-induced moan from my throat.

"Do you like being fucked like this, Darcy?"

I moan again when he quickens his strokes. "Do you like fucking me this way?" I counter his question with my own.

He puffs out a single breath, bringing a hand to where we're joined. "It's a goddamn privilege to be the guy who gets to do this with you. In my bed, with you beneath me—it's blowing my mind and pushing me to say things I shouldn't."

Two thick fingers tease the entrance to my pussy as he plays with us both.

"Can you take my fingers as well?"

My eyes grow wide when Archer starts pushing one inside.

"I ... I don't know. I ..." My voice fades out when I realize I can. He's already entering me with a second.

"That's right, Doll. Fuck my cock and fingers together. I want you all over me."

So much pressure. Building, spiraling out of control.

"So good," I moan into his bedroom.

He captures my mouth, licking into me on a grin I know will be burned into my memory for weeks, maybe months.

"That's because we're so good together." He pulls his fingers from me and breaks our kiss, sliding my release across his bottom lip. "Taste your sweetness."

On the next kiss, I run my tongue across his lip. The filth in his words and actions spark a flow of my release over his dick, and he groans.

"Are you soaking my brand-new bed, Darcy? I hope so."

I release again, a powerful orgasm right on the cusp.

"I thought you were kidding around when you said you bought a new bed."

Still moving inside me, Archer sits up. His previously sweet demeanor is replaced with determination. I can't mistake the emotion as it casts in his darkened eyes.

"I'll never lie to you—ever. I meant what I said." He brings his soaked fingers to his mouth and sucks on each one, groaning in response. "No other girl has been in this bed with me." He hesitates for a brief second, a modicum of conflict there perhaps. "And if you want the same as I do, that's exactly how it'll remain."

He pistons into me, hitting so deep that I cry out, wanting and needing more. I grab his bare ass and sink my fingertips into his flesh, feeling how toned he is.

"Come for me," Archer pushes out, swiping a hand through his disheveled hair. "Hand yourself over. I want to see how you fall apart, just for me. *Only* for me. You're never too much —ever."

Another flow of arousal coats us both as I clamp around him.

"Good girl. Can you keep it going?" Archer slows his pace, bringing a thumb to my swollen clit and working it in rhythmic circles that match the synchronicity of his thrusts. "How long can we make this orgasm last, Darcy? Over thirty seconds?"

Just as I think the peak of my high is ending, Archer plays with my clit again, pinching and rubbing it expertly. My orgasm kicks to another level.

One hand continues to claw at his ass, silently begging for more. The other comes to my breast as I knead and pinch my nipple, an overwhelming sense of confidence settling inside me.

"I never want this to stop," I plead. "Keep making me come like this."

His dick grows harder while his movements turn more erratic.

"I'm going to come. All the way inside you," he grinds out, the muscles in his jaw tensing.

The hand around his ass pulls him into me, a defiant edge to my tone as I tell him, "Do it."

Archer falls forward on a roar that fills his bedroom and my pussy, warmth spreading inside me, prolonging my orgasm further.

I expect him to collapse onto me in a satiated heap and then roll onto his side and fall asleep—that's what usually happened with Liam.

"Stay still for me, Doll. I'm not finished with you."

Apparently, rolling over and sleeping are *not* what happens on a night with the Blades goalie.

Archer moves down the bed, pushing my thighs apart with his hands, and I spread wider for him, rising onto my elbows so I can see all he's doing.

He's flat on his stomach, his breath tickling my sensitive pussy, and his eyes find mine. Mischief, need, happiness, all dancing around in them.

He licks me once, attention still on me.

I throw my head back, groaning, moaning on a slack jaw.

"Watch, Darcy. Watch me taste us both."

I refocus when his tongue spears inside me, cleaning me up so precisely.

He swallows us down and goes back to eating me out, pulling another unexpected orgasm from my body.

I overheat and thrash around, but Archer keeps his mouth firmly clamped around me. He isn't moving from his spot until he's had his fill and I'm a writhing, withering mess.

"You're so perfect," he whispers against me, taking a few last licks. "So perfect. And so fucking mine."

CHAPTER ELEVEN

ARCHER

My eyes are dry from staring so hard, and my throat is thick with emotions and feelings I've never had before, never mind while sharing my bed with a girl. My lips are sore from the number of kisses I peppered across her shoulders while she slept.

Darcy Thompson is not a light sleeper.

I smile into her hair when she releases a little snort into the room—her version of a snore.

Like I promised, we went at it for most of the night before I let her sleep—or more like she passed out—and I wrapped myself around her, covering us both under the duvet.

And that's where we've remained, the sun now rising and filtering into my bedroom, casting a glow on her long hair. She's like Rapunzel or something—and up until last night, just as mythical. Since the second I laid eyes on this girl, I've been in a tailspin. Knowing I can't touch her because she's off-limits, but falling deeper under her spell regardless.

I should probably feel guilty for going behind my friend and coach's backs, but that would mean I had a choice to walk away from Darcy, which was something I could never do, especially not after I saw the look in her eyes when Jack spilled about Abbie.

That night in the bar, when I came between her and Harry, I was making steady progress, moving out of the friend zone and easing into flirting with her. Then in came her brother with his big size nines, blowing everything up with an announcement that I had a girlfriend. I wanted to scream right there that it wasn't true, that I'd gone along with the lie to spend time with the very person I just crushed with it.

The only good thing to come out of the mess? That was the catalyst that pushed me to pin her against Jack's spare bedroom door and confess that I wanted to take her home. I knew if I didn't, then she'd eventually go searching for "fun" with the wrong guys, and there's only so many times I can get away with punching them before they lay a finger on her.

I know there's no going back now that she's lying in my bed, and I wouldn't want to. Last night was incredible, and this morning feels even better. I might be the first guy she's been with since her asshole ex, but she's the first-ever girl I've woken up next to.

Darcy makes me think about things I could never foresee myself wanting. She elicits a feeling of home I haven't experienced since before the time my parents started fighting. Whenever I'm with her, my active brain is calm. I'm not searching for the next hookup. I'm right where I want to be. There isn't another woman I want to talk to, lie beside, or draw soft moans from for hours at a time.

Last night only solidified those feelings.

Moving her hair to one side, I expose the nape of her neck, and she exhales a soft yawn into the room. With her back to me, I can't be sure if she's awake, although she's definitely stirring.

"Stay with me today, here, in my bed," I whisper against her skin, unsure if I'll get an answer.

Darcy stretches out and then rolls toward me, still in my arms. Her blue eyes are sleep-dazed and satisfied, and when she offers me her sunshine smile, I melt further for this girl.

"Did you say something? Or was I dreaming?"

Full-on fucking giddy, I pull the duvet back over our heads and form a cocoon around us. The now-bright sun penetrates my white bed linen.

"You weren't dreaming, Doll. I asked you to stay here with me, in my bed. I'll bring you food in between sex."

She suppresses a yawn, bringing a hand to her mouth and rolling onto her back. It's then I notice the white gold bracelet she was wearing at the party, but never removed last night.

"I really can't," she replies, looking genuinely disappointed. "I'm actually out for lunch."

She reaches down to her wrist, spinning the bracelet around a couple of times, and I wonder if it's nerves. I'm not ashamed to admit the pang of jealousy I felt when I first saw her wearing it last night. And now that she's talking about meeting a friend and playing with the bangle, I'm powerless to stop the words tumbling from my mouth.

"Do you have another guy, Darcy?"

Her head whips up to me, big eyes narrowing. "Okay, firstly, what do you mean by another guy? Because last I checked, I didn't even have one."

I go to reply, but she continues over me.

"Secondly, if I did, I wouldn't be lying here, in bed, with you."

I'm flooded with relief, although it's brief, as it gives way to more unease. How do I get this girl to return to my bed?

"Where did you get this?" I ask, trying not to sound like a suspicious douchebag. I'm a possessive one instead.

Darcy rolls her lips together, shifting to face me. "Oh, this?" She lifts the bracelet between us. "This is from Emmett Richards, the hot-as-fuck defenseman on your team. I woke up with him yesterday, and he gave it to me as a birthday gift."

"Don't fuck with me, Darcy."

She's on her back in seconds, and I'm hovering over her, a caveman growl I've been fighting to suppress escaping my chest. I'm tempted to slide inside her right now and demonstrate how I'm the only man she needs.

Small hands rest on my shoulders as the bracelet slips down her arm.

"Did your dad get it for you?" I ask softly. I know from Jack that she doesn't have a relationship with him anymore. That doesn't stop me from hoping the guy didn't miss his daughter's birthday.

"No." She shakes her head, a subtle sadness dulling her eyes. "I haven't spoken to him in months. The bracelet is from my mom. She bought it for my twenty-first birthday, and I wear it on special occasions."

Although I wouldn't describe us as estranged, I'm not especially close to my dad. Darcy might be right to keep Elliott out of her life—just like Jack cut him out completely too—but that doesn't mean there isn't residual hurt.

"Do you miss him?" I ask cautiously.

She peers up at me like she hasn't been asked that in a while.

"That's a complicated question, Archer."

I settle down between her parted thighs. I know she can feel my hard cock as it presses into her. Casually, I run my fingers down her stomach, holding myself up with an elbow braced next to her shoulder. We're both completely naked, but that isn't the most intimate part of this moment. I want to explore every part of Darcy, well beyond the conversations we've previously shared.

"We've got the time."

She clears her throat and shifts beneath me. "My dad is one of those people who always has an agenda with everything he does. When I was younger, I couldn't see the games he played or the way he would emotionally attack Mum, not until I got older. Then, when Jack joined the Blades and met Kendra, Dad tried to come back into his life after he learned what my brother was earning and how much his girlfriend's family was worth. Kendra told me all about it when I moved to Brooklyn, but I'd already hated his guts anyway." She pokes her tongue into her cheek. "And I don't hate anyone. Ever."

My blood boils on behalf of Jack and Darcy, two of the kindest people I've ever met. If they despise this guy, I can only hope we never cross paths.

"Did he hurt you?"

Shaking her head again, she presses her lips into a thin line. "No, never physically. Dad doesn't need to get physical to cause hurt. He likes to weigh and measure people, and when he has a drink, the venom really starts spouting. He once told me I'd walked away from a good relationship with Liam because of my ego."

"But he cheated on you," I immediately fire back, my rage simmering.

"He did, although Dad never saw it that way. He said Liam was going to have a great career in finance." She laughs darkly. "Funny, because that's what my dad does—he's a stockbroker in London."

I remember Jack telling me his dad worked in Canary Wharf. A place where some of my own investments are run. He'd better not manage any of my offshore accounts.

"After Liam and I split, Jack admitted he could see more and more of Dad in Liam's behaviors. Mum spent a lot of time detangling herself from Dad's grasp, and Jack was afraid I'd go down the same route. I once failed a test at university—"

I release a mock gasp, and she swats me on the chest, giggling.

"Yes, Archer. Believe it or not, I did. Anyway, do you know what Liam's reaction was?"

I shake my head, already convinced I'm not going to like it.

"He told me not to worry because a woman's place is really in the home and with the kids, not out earning money because he could take care of that. It was a carbon copy of what Dad used to say to Mum."

I can't imagine Darcy ever accepting something like that from a guy. They do say love is blind.

When she looks up at me for a reaction, I know my jaw is clenched, molars grinding hard.

"There were plenty of red flags I chose to ignore because I'd invested so much time into the wrong person, but I didn't want to feel like all of it was wasted, so I kept plowing ahead with him. I guess that's why now I'm not keen to get into anything heavy. The next person I date, I want to be sure they won't screw me over."

My tongue burns with the need to tell her that I'd never let her down. Then I consider the evidence of my past and what she has to go on.

"A woman's place is wherever she wants to be." They're the only words I can find in a sea of confessions I desperately want to profess. "No one owns you or gets to tell you what to do with your life, Darcy. When a real man says, *You're mine*, it's because he can't stand the thought of living a day without you in his life. Not because you're a possession he can show off to his friends. You're a treasure, not an accessory."

In the silence of my bedroom, she scans my face slowly.

"What?" I ask, unable to hide my smile.

Her hand cups my face, and I can't help but let my eyes flutter closed at the touch. "You're smart, smarter than you let on, Archer. Smarter than me in so many ways."

I set a kiss against her forehead. "We're so alike, Darcy."

When she swallows thickly, my mind travels back to the conversation we had right after I basically told Harry to fuck off. This is risky, and I know it, but I have to shoot my shot.

"Let me be what you need, Doll."

Pushing her head back into the pillow, she examines me. "What do you mean? Because I don't want to get into a relationship right now. I—"

"No," I cut her off, knowing she isn't ready for that. "I'm saying I can be your Mr. One Size Fits All." I swallow down the fear of rejection. "I'm saying I can give you the fun you're looking for and we can be exclusive. I get you, I know what you need, and I promise I'll treat you right."

When she shakes her head again, my heart sinks into my gut.

"We can't do that, Archer. One night we can get away with, but sleeping together on a regular basis? I'm not so sure. I'll say now that I have zero intention of telling Jack or Jon about what I get up to behind closed doors, but that doesn't mean we won't be caught at some point. The fun we have with each other won't be worth the pain you'll experience when my brother and stepdad go crazy. It's the betrayal they'll hate, Archer. I might know you're not an arsehole to women, but Jack's especially convinced you're the wrong type of guy for me. He's protective after Liam."

She might be telling me no, but it isn't because she doesn't want to spend time with me, and that knowledge spurs me to keep going.

"Let me worry about Jack and Coach. If you want me to talk with them, I will, but I think if we're careful enough, we can keep this just between us." I move my hand—which is currently splayed across her stomach—to her face, pushing strands of stray hair out of her eyes. "Focus on yourself for a second. I'm asking you if you want to have an exclusive thing with me. Yeah, we'll have to be careful, and that kind of sucks since I can't take you out when I want and spoil the shit out of you."

Darcy quirks a brow at me. "That's what boyfriends do."

I know I need to rein myself in here. "Listen, all I'm saying is, I want more of you, like this, in my bed beneath me, rolling around in the sheets and talking about our lives. I can be all of those things you want because I *want* to be them for you. You can trust me."

I cut myself short before I say way too much and she bolts from my apartment.

A few more agonizing seconds pass before Darcy speaks again. "Like an exclusive fuck-buddy arrangement?"

Jesus Christ, I *hate* that description. Darcy is anything but a fuck buddy to me.

"If that's what you want to call it, then that's what we can be."

I watch as she considers my offer, and I feel the way my heart hammers against my rib cage, wondering if she can sense how seismic this moment really is for me.

Another beat of nothing, and she finally makes a decision. "Okay, if you're comfortable with the high stakes involved, then we can give it a try. I trust you and really like spending time with you, and last night was ... it was amazing."

I know I'm grinning like a fucking lunatic right now.

"BUT!" She holds up a finger between us, scolding me like a teacher, which is nothing but fucking adorable. "We have to be really careful how we play this, *and* that includes you not turning up on my nights out with Kendra, Jenna, and Collins and giving random guys the death stare. You have to trust me."

It's not you I don't trust, Darcy Doll. It's the men who think the way I have for most of my adult life.

"Okay," I say, agreeing to all the terms. They're only temporary anyway until I make her my girlfriend.

"Okay," Darcy repeats quietly, her shoulders relaxing into the pillow.

I'm aware she has a lunch to get to, and she'll need to head home to get ready. Still, that doesn't stop me from notching myself at her entrance.

"Are you sore from last night?" I ask, feeling how wet she is when I run a soft finger through her pussy. "I know my piercings make it amazing for us both, but they can take some getting used to."

Drawing her lip between her teeth, she reaches down to fist my cock. "I'm sore in the best way."

Slowly, we both feed my dick inside her, a low groan echoing in my chest. Darcy is the first girl I've slept with and not used a condom and it's incredible, although I know so much of that is down to the girl I'm with.

"You feel so good," she breathes out when I push deeper inside, stretching her delicious pussy out slowly.

I set another kiss against her forehead. "Yeah, well, get used to it. Because now you can have me whenever you want."

CHAPTER TWELVE

DARCY

Sitting alone at the restaurant table that Jenna booked for a last-minute girls' lunch, I'm halfway through completing an online sudoku challenge when Mum's text pops up.

> Mum: I need your honesty on something really serious.

> Me: Oh, yeah? What's the issue?

I've always had a good relationship with my mum, and it's grown stronger since I moved to New York.

Shortly after my parents divorced and my dad's temporary work contract in Seattle ended, meaning he would be returning to the UK, I was keen—no, gasping—to get back to Oxford and see Liam after way too long apart. Back then, our relationship felt different and exciting, until it didn't anymore. The compromise was living across the other side of the Atlantic from my brother and mum.

Like I blurted out to Archer last night, it wasn't until I was older when I started to piece together the narcissistic side to my dad, especially when he didn't have Mum in his life anymore and his controlling ways focused more on me as a result. That's when I took a step away and started considering the benefits of moving back to the US to be with the blood family I respected. Liam cheating and behaving like a first-rate arsehole sealed the deal, and I guess the rest is history.

> Mum: Do you think the dusky pink or the sage green? *pictures attached*

I chuckle when I open two images of Mum wearing dresses in a fitting room. They're both similarly styled, with thin straps and a cowl neck, in a satin material that clings to her stunning figure and falls to the floor.

Mum and I are alike in so many ways, but we do have our differences—she has deep emerald eyes and wavy chocolate hair.

I study the pictures for a few seconds, rotating my phone to see all angles. She's not wrong; dress shopping is a serious matter.

> Me: You know my preference is pink, but Jon has always been right—green truly is your color.

> Mum: Okay, thanks, honey. I've been agonizing over them for what feels like forever. Dress shopping without Jon here to give his opinion is a bloody nightmare.

I shake my head to thoughts of my stepdad. He might be one of the biggest names in ice hockey, but sports isn't his only talent. That man has an incredible eye for fashion.

> Me: Where is Jon?

> Mum: At the rink for practice. The Blades have a preseason game tomorrow, and he wants to iron out a few plays with the team.

I'm immediately thinking about Archer in his goalie kit. *Jesus.*

> **Me:** What do you need the dress for?

> **Mum:** Didn't Jack tell you? Last week, the Blades general manager confirmed he's leaving after ten years with the team due to poor health. His replacement—who is yet to be announced—is attending a dinner the week after next. He's going to meet the team, and it's doubling up as a farewell to the existing GM. Not great timing ahead of the start of the regular season, but it can't be helped. Players and coaching staff, along with close family and friends, are all invited.

> **Me:** No, I hadn't heard.

"Look at you, sitting over here, all alone."

I place my phone face down on the table and look up to find Jenna hovering over me.

Picking up the wine I ordered when I arrived, I take a sip. "I was early for once."

Jenna takes the seat next to me, looping her bag over the back of the chair. She looks like a woman on a mission, and I'm confident that mission is me.

"Since we have a few minutes before the others arrive, care to tell me why a certain Blades goalie wanted your undivided attention last night?" She tags a wink onto her question.

I quirk a brow at her, considering how many details to divulge. Fuck it. It's not like Jenna—or any of my girls—is untrustworthy. Plus, if I start sneaking off with Archer, the first people to notice are going to be my best friends.

"All right, bitches." Collins plops down on a seat opposite us, followed by Kendra.

Jenna's still looking at me, and Collins and Kendra share a

glance. The entire table is now in silence, apart from the gentle Italian music playing in the background.

"Oookay, what did we just walk in on?" Kendra finally speaks up.

I drop my head between my shoulders. "Jenna was asking me about the party last night."

"Annnd …" Kendra pushes. "What happened? You're over your headache, right?"

I flush pink because I'm a terrible liar, and I knew she could see through me when I left the party early.

They do say honesty is the best policy.

Inhaling a deep breath, I look around at my friends as they gaze back with equal intensity. "I didn't go home sick. I left earlier because I wanted to spend the night with Archer. He'd invited me back to his place and … yeah …"

"H-O-L-Y HELL." Kendra's jaw hangs open.

Collins tips her head toward her friend, whispering low, "You're drooling."

Kendra scoffs once, eyes bugging out. "Y-you slept w-with …"

"Yep," I reply, sitting up straighter in my chair. I fold my hands on the table in front of me. "I did, and it was fucking amazing."

Jenna leans forward, elbows braced on the table. "Ladies, you didn't see the text I received from him, asking to talk to Darcy alone, but I think we have a boy obsessed on our hands."

"Pah!" I swivel to my friend, the short outburst garnering a few turned heads. On a wince, I lower my voice and hold up a hand. Anything Archer said last night was in the heat of the moment, and, boy, was it hot. "That's completely ridiculous. We're just friends with benefits, and we've agreed to have fun together. Last night was the first time, and I can't lie—we both find each other attractive. Call it scratching an itch."

Jenna, Kendra, and Collins all raise their eyebrows, staying silent.

"Okay, are we ready to order?" A server approaches our table with a bright smile and notepad in hand.

I fluster and open the menu in front of me, finding the first item on the list. "Yes, I'll get the chicken Parmigiana, please, and a side salad."

The rest of the table goes about ordering while I zone out of the conversation.

Sure, Archer wants a fuck-buddy arrangement, but that doesn't mean anything. He's a friend, giving me what I want and benefiting from it himself in the process. To me, that sounds like the perfect scenario for a playboy.

"Earth to Darcy." Collins waves a hand in front of me. "We aren't done with this conversation."

I rest my chin in my palm. "It isn't as big of a deal as you're making it out to be. It's just sex. He's hot, he thinks I'm hot, and you all know I wanted some fun after Liam. This is the perfect solution. Plus, we agreed to be exclusive, and I guess that's ideal because I'm not sure how safe sleeping around really is."

Kendra clears her throat. "Well, I, for one, have multiple questions." Collins and Jenna hum in agreement before my sister-in-law continues, "Number one: what happened to Abbie?"

"Didn't work out," I reply on a casual shrug.

Kendra narrows her eyes, doubtful. "Question number two: who suggested a fuck-buddy arrangement?"

"He did."

They all look between each other again, more brows raised.

"Question three," Kendra presses on with her inquisition, "at what point are you both planning on breaking the news to Jack? Because I sure as hell am not. He's already convinced Archer wants to fuck you around, and this just confirms it." She crosses her arms, sitting back in her chair.

Drinks are set down in front of us, and I finish the last few sips of my wine before speaking. "I don't plan on telling my brother. Ever. Archer offered to come forward and straighten things out, but I really don't get why we should. It's just some fun that will eventually fizzle out. Why do I need my brother's permission to do what I want with who I want? He also doesn't need to know everything that's going on in my life. I'm telling you all as my trusted girlfriends and because all three of you clearly worked out something was going on. I'm not even sure I'll tell Mum since she has no clue, and again, this whole thing isn't a big deal."

They all nod in understanding.

"I get that, Darcy." Jenna smirks at me, mischief in her tone. "But my question to you is this: was he as good as the rumors suggest?"

Every single one of them edges closer, waiting on the tea, as memories race back and settle between my thighs.

"I'd say *good* is the understatement of the year."

Collins picks up her water, the glass halfway to her mouth. "Details, Thompson. We need details."

I shake my head at her. "You're engaged to be married. And you"—I motion to Kendra—"already are."

"Looks like I'm the only one finding out the deets then." Jenna looks particularly smug. "My best guess is, it all started when he asked you to meet him in Jack and Kendra's spare bedroom. That's what his text said after all."

Collins throws a hand up. "What the fuck is it with that spare bedroom?!"

"Tell me about it," Kendra replies between laughs. "First Sawyer and Collins hooking up with handcuffs in there, and now ... wait." She looks at me, jaw agape. "Did you actually bang while Jack was in the other room?!"

My entire body flushes—I swear it does.

"Oh my God! You did, didn't you?!" Jenna squeaks out, way too excited.

Waving a hand in front of me, I shush them quickly. "No, I did not," I whisper-hiss. "We might've gotten a little close, but even Archer isn't crazy enough to think we could get away with that. You just know Jack would have been heading to the bathroom right as I screamed his goalie's name."

"He made you scream, did he?" Collins croons. "That's the best—when you come so hard that you can do nothing except wail." She looks off into the distance, sighing.

"Annnd now I feel like a lonely old woman. I need me a good fuck-buddy arrangement," Jenna puffs out. "Preferably with a hockey player since you three are only confirming what the romance books report—that these boys know what they're doing."

"Archer's pierced." The words leave my mouth before I can stop them.

"Come again?" Jenna says.

"I'd say she likely did—multiple times," Collins adds.

"Well, my flabbers are officially gasted." Kendra picks up her Diet Coke, eyes wide. She takes a sip, glass suspended midair. "Now, you agreeing to a fuck-buddy arrangement makes complete sense."

Collins's phone vibrates on the table in front of her, and she picks it up. "It's Ezra. I need to take this."

She rises to her feet and makes for the restaurant door; all the while, I track her movements with a smile. For so long, that girl was convinced she didn't need a man—or a family—in her life. Now, she's a wife-to-be and an absolute rock to her future stepson.

"And I'm going to head to the restroom before the food arrives." Jenna picks up her phone and waves it at me and Kendra. "Maybe even join a dating app and bag me a hot hookup." She pushes back her chair, wrapping a soft arm around my shoulders. "For what it's worth, I'm really happy for you. Have some fun, girl. You deserve it after fuckface Liam."

Alone at the table, I turn back to Kendra as she swirls the ice cubes around in her drink, deep in thought.

"I won't say anything to Jack because girl code and I get where you're coming from about privacy." Her brown eyes find mine, a hint of concern behind them. "Just don't go falling for him, yeah? You seem to have your head on straight, and I know, underneath the bravado, Archer is a good guy. But I'm a friend to you." She places her glass down on the table, reaching across to take my hand in a move I wasn't really expecting. "And also, now, you're family. I don't want to see you get hurt, and I *will* cut Archer's balls off if he fucks you around."

I'm hit with an emotion I didn't anticipate, and I wrap my hand around hers, squeezing it softly. "I love you so much, Kendra, and I understand your worries. If the shoe were on the other foot, I'd for sure be having the same conversation with you." I release a long breath. "I'm twenty-four years old, and I spent almost a decade in a long-term relationship with a guy I thought was forever. Turned out, he was the bad kind of fuckboy who couldn't keep it in his pants."

I push a hand through my hair, and my phone vibrates next to me. I ignore it, maintaining my focus on Kendra.

"What I'm saying is, you never really know the real person until they show you their true colors. My gut tells me Archer is genuine, and to be honest, the hookup surpassed my expectations. I felt confident around him. He made me feel great, and I want more of that feeling. Liam broke me more than I realized —or maybe more than I've admitted to." My voice shakes a little, more emotions surfacing.

Kendra's eyes soften with an easy smile. "Then that's all I need to know. I assume the Abbie story will be spun out a little longer."

I shift in my chair, hating the lie Archer told, but kind of understanding why he went along with Jack's assumption that he had a girl.

"Neither of us wants to lie." I smirk at her, a thrill running through me. "But the sex-in-secret thing is kind of hot."

She bursts out laughing, nodding along. "Yes. Yes, it is." Her amusement fades to a cheeky grin of her own. "I can't believe he's pierced. Wait, no. Actually, I can absolutely believe that Archer Moore is pierced."

"And his thigh is tattooed with his jersey number."

Kendra's eyes grow wider, if that's even possible. "Why is a thigh tattoo so hot?"

I shrug, tingles racing down my spine. "Who knows? But I can't wait to get my hands on it again."

"Oh, I bet you can't. When will that be?"

My attention falls briefly to the mobile phone sitting face down on the table, and I flip it over.

> Thigh Boy: I have you pinned as a size four. I hope I'm correct …

I look over at Kendra. She's busy on her phone, no doubt texting Jack.

> Me: Do I dare ask what you're doing now?

> Thigh Boy: It's not what I'm doing—aside from you. More what I'm buying.

> Me: You can't keep using my birthday as an excuse for whatever gift you're buying me this time.

> Thigh Boy: I don't need an excuse to do what I want. When can I see you next?

> Me: It's been less than a day since I left your bed. And thank you for whatever you're buying me.

> Thigh Boy: Tonight?

Pure excitement sparks beneath my skin. I'd love to see him again tonight, but this is where I have to heed my own warning. Sex with Archer is every now and again and not a daily occurrence. Too much time together risks complications that I do not want or need.

> Me: No can do, I'm afraid. I've got work to catch up on.

Thigh Boy: Are you playing hard to get, Doll?

> Me: No. I'm playing out exactly what we agreed. I'm coming to the GM dinner, and I'll see you then …

Thigh Boy: Nope, sorry. That's the week after next and way too long away. I need to see you sooner than that.

I close out our message thread and open my Camera app. Quickly snapping a picture and sending it to him.

> Me: Now you've seen me.

Thigh Boy: Stunning.

Thigh Boy: I'm coming over to your place tomorrow night.

> Me: You're intensely horny.

Thigh Boy: For you? Yes.

> Me: I need to go; I'm out with the girls.

Thigh Boy: That was my next question since you didn't tell me earlier—who you are having lunch with. Dates with your girls are the only ones I'll accept. Aside from dates with me.

> Me: Scratch that. You're just intense. Period.

Thigh Boy: I'll be at your place just after seven. We have practice, and then I'll head over straight afterward.

Jenna takes a seat next to me, and I move my phone out of

sight before throwing her a wink and grinning like a giddy teenager.

> Me: I didn't say yes to anything.

Thigh Boy: You didn't need to. The smile I know you're wearing right now is answer enough for me.

Thigh Boy: Speak soon. Stay pretty, A, x.

CHAPTER THIRTEEN

ARCHER

"Man, you were on fire tonight." Jack claps me on the back as we step off the ice and head for the locker room.

I pull off my helmet, tucking it under my arm. "My low angle game could use some work. Overall, not bad."

Jack stops, setting his stick on the rack just inside the tunnel. "Something on your mind? You've been quiet all practice."

Oh nothing, just thinking that I'll be balls deep inside your baby sister in around an hour.

"Nope. I'm good," I reply, pushing a hand through my hair. "Locked in on the regular season and determined to beat my shutout record."

My center cocks his head to one side, studying me.

Jesus, am I that transparent?

I tear my gaze away from him and look down the tunnel, concluding the less eye contact we have, the better since I'm a terrible fucking liar.

"How are things going with Abbie?"

My molars meet as I focus back on my friend. "She's good. Busy with work."

He nods lightly. "What does she do?"

Crap, crap, crap.

"She's, eh, a teacher. Kindergarten."

"Oh, nice. Will she be coming to the GM dinner? It'd be great to meet her."

Actually, no. Because the girl I'm really involved with is your sister.

I wince, partly at the dead-ass awkward situation I'm in right now and partly to help sell yet another fucking lie. "She's not big into events or loads of people. I'll probably introduce her if we get more serious."

Jack pulls off his gloves, jutting his chin down the tunnel. "You got a picture of her?"

And now all I can think about are the two photos I have of Darcy posing in my private elevator, dressed in only underwear. Along with the other photo I took when I first slid inside her and the one she sent me at lunch yesterday.

I'm getting hard.

In front of her brother.

I'm a bad friend.

"No," I blurt out. "No pictures."

Jack's brows pull together. I can't say the confused look he's giving me is surprising. I sound like a total fucking weirdo.

"All right, well … I know Kendra is keen to meet Abbie, so don't keep her locked away forever."

I just smile because, honestly, what the fuck else am I supposed to do?

"Sure," I reply, trying my best to engage in the conversation. "I guess the other girls will want to meet her too, especially Darcy." I literally have no idea why the fuck I said that. As if the hole I've dug for myself isn't big enough already.

Jack puffs his cheeks out, scratching at the back of his neck. "You know my sister …"

I do.

"She's the ultimate social butterfly." He drops his hand from his neck, slapping it against a padded thigh. "Well, I don't suppose she's feeling very sociable right now though."

Immediately, I'm back in the conversation, pulse kicking up, along with my adrenaline.

"Oh, really? Why's that?"

I haven't spoken to Darcy since we texted yesterday. In truth, I want to speak with her every goddamn second.

On a sigh, he shakes his head. "Mum called me last night, asking if I would stop by her apartment with a prescription for Darcy."

"Why?" I ask quickly.

He props a hand on his hip. "She has a history of lower respiratory tract infections that the doctors are familiar with, and it looks like another one has hit her. You know what she's like—fiercely independent, like Kendra—but she needs an antibiotic, and Mum is tied up with work. I dropped them with Darcy first thing this morning, and she looked ... yeah, I'm worried about her."

I'm halfway to the locker room when Jack catches up to me.

"Are you sure everything's good with you?" He wraps a palm around my arm, twisting me around to face him. "My gut is rarely off, and right now, it's screaming that something isn't right with you."

How in the hell I force a smile, I'll never know. "I'm honestly fine, Jack. I'm tired, and I didn't get much sleep last night. I just want to head home."

What the fuck is this piece of shit?

I could kick this in, using only my big toe.

Knocking a couple of more times on Darcy's poor excuse for a front door, I wait for her to answer, bracing a hand on the dark wooden frame above my head.

"Excuse me, are you the boy I spoke to a second ago?" An older lady peers around her door, watching me closely.

"Yeah," I say, going to knock again.

I only know the building Darcy lives in because she told me once on a night out, just after she paid a deposit on the rental agreement. Finding her actual apartment would've been a lot harder had it not been for her neighbor—aka the lady who buzzed me up on the intercom and told me Darcy lived next door.

And now she's standing in front of me, holding what I assume is a key to Darcy's place.

"Are you her boyfriend?" she asks, sliding the key into the lock.

I'm both grateful and fucking petrified over the current situation. In around three minutes, I've seen how easy it would be to break into my girl's apartment. My best guess is, she isn't answering her door or phone because she's passed out in bed, and that hurts my heart.

"Yes," I reply, spinning more lies as I go.

"Her mom just left, you know. Family have been coming and going all day."

As I step inside Darcy's apartment, I'm tempted to ask the old lady how she knows all this, but my gran was exactly the same before she died last year—she knew everything going down on the street where she lived.

"Thank you for your help ..." I break off, unsure of her name.

Smiling sweetly, she pockets Darcy's key. "Elsie. And you are?"

I suppose I shouldn't be surprised she doesn't watch hockey. "Archer." I offer my hand out to her.

"Archer?" a weak voice calls from behind me. "What are you doing—"

I spin around to find Darcy coughing up a lung.

"Best you go and take care of your girlfriend." Elsie winks before disappearing out of sight, her front door closing with a click.

I close Darcy's door and head straight down her hallway, stalking the few yards toward the girl doubled over and dressed in a fluffy pink robe.

Still coughing, she holds a hand up in front of her.

All I want to do is pull her into my arms and ask what she needs. That's not how this girl works though.

"You c-called m ..." She heaves in a deep breath.

I'm unable to stop myself as I wrap my arms around her small frame, smoothing a hand down the back of her head. "Take a second, Doll." I close my eyes. She smells insanely good, even when she's sick. "Don't get worked up. You've got an infection."

A few more beats, and the coughing fit subsides. She looks up at me, blue eyes still big and gorgeous, even with a dull sheen to them.

Fuck me. She's not doing well.

"Do you need to see a doctor?"

She shakes her head slowly. "I've already been, and I have the antibiotics I need."

Darcy breathes out against my chest, nuzzling into me. I know she's vulnerable and searching for comfort, and right now, she's finding that with me. My lungs inflate for the both of us.

"Some people get throat infections or repetitive migraines; I get chest infections. A few days and a course of medication, and I'll be fine."

My hand comes under her chin, tipping her face up to look at me. "You aren't fine. I'm worried about you."

I can tell she wants to roll her eyes.

"I'm a big girl, Archer." Darcy turns to look down her hallway. "And I'm not your girlfriend either. Elsie speaks to my mum when she visits and could drop us both in the shit."

"It's fine. If asked, Elsie would describe me as a tall, dark-haired guy, and that's hardly narrowing it down. Aside from my incredible looks, there's not much else that sets me apart."

She deadpans and takes a deep breath, trying to force oxygen into her lungs.

The temptation to brush my mouth over hers is too strong, and I do exactly that.

"Your lips are dry. When did you last take on fluids?"

She rubs them together, swiping her tongue over them. "Why are you changing the subject?"

I wrap my arms under her ass and carry her into a room just off her small living space. I presume it's her bedroom since there aren't many other options.

"Archer," she continues, "you aren't my boyfriend, and you just told Elsie you are." Her voice is more prominent, demanding an explanation as I lay her down on the king bed and pull a pale pink duvet over her body.

"I know I'm not your boyfriend, but you weren't answering the door or my calls, and I panicked. Elsie asked who I was, and I figured she'd already met your brother." I wink.

Darcy sits up in bed when I pick up an unopened bottle of water and unscrew the lid, handing it to her.

"You play with fire, Thigh Boy."

a low chuckle. "Thigh Boy? Where the fuck did that come from?"

Her eyes drop to my gray sweats. "I think the clue's in the name, don't you?"

Another coughing fit overtakes her weakened body, and, fuck, I feel so goddamn helpless.

"Get some rest."

Nodding, she takes a sip of water and sets the bottle on her nightstand, sinking down into the bed. All I want is to be lying next to her, making sure she's okay.

"You should go," she whispers, already falling asleep. "When I'm sick, Mum usually visits a couple of times a day. Jack said he might stop by, too, and there's no way I can hide your six-foot-four ass in my tiny closet."

"I'll stop by again tomorrow after morning skate."

She shakes her head, face down into the pillow. "No. It's too risky. You will one hundred percent be caught, and I can't be doing with a pissed-off brother, alongside an infection from hell."

"I don't want to leave you."

"Tough," she coughs into her pillow.

I lean down, bracing a palm beside her head. With my other hand, I tuck the hair covering her ear behind it. "You're such a brat—you know that?" Kissing the shell, I watch the way her skin reacts beneath my touch. "And while I might not be your boyfriend, you are mine for however long we're sleeping together." I kiss her again. "I'm going to need regular updates from you throughout the day. Seeing you like this is killing me because I care about you, Darcy."

She groans in response, turning her head to look at me. All I can see is an eye and the corner of her smile.

"Okay, you got yourself a deal."

"How many days do I need to keep away?" I ask, convinced I won't last more than a few hours.

"I'll call you when I'm better and the coast is clear."

"I don't want to leave you," I repeat.

Darcy lifts an arm behind her, motioning to the door. "I'm fine. I promise."

It must be another few minutes before I finally turn to leave. Darcy's breathing is more even, along with a soft snore.

Walking out of her bedroom, I close the door behind me and look around her kitchen and living space. It's not exactly tidy, although I can tell someone has taken the trash out and wiped down the kitchen surfaces. Probably her mom when she was last here.

A pile of paperwork sits on the corner of her breakfast bar, and I make my way over to it, taking a seat at one of the stools.

This is technically classed as snooping, but, hey, I'm telling lies and claiming relationships with anyone I want these days. What's another immoral act?

On top sits a master-level sudoku book. Most of it is completed, and there are little doodles—hearts, flowers, and smiling faces—dotted around the pages.

I know Darcy is smart and has a high IQ—I didn't need her to tell me to figure that one out. This though? This screams of someone with next-level intelligence. Like, who the fuck does this stuff for fun? She's even made up her own problems in the corners, challenging herself further.

Searching underneath the puzzle book, I find a letter from Premium Rentals, titled: *Welcome to your new home.* Blowing out a sarcastic breath since this place is about as secure as my confidence when it comes to other guys chasing my girl, I scan the contents and land on a name and number. This must be her landlord.

Don't do it, Archer. Put the letter down and walk away.

Pulling my cell out of my pocket, I pause on punching in the number, one last attempt to stop myself.

It doesn't work, and a few seconds later, I've got the phone to my ear, listening to cheesy hold music as I drop down from the stool and pace Darcy's living area.

"Hello, Ian Rands speaking."

I pause my pacing. "Hi. Are you the guy who owns apartment fourteen in Deuce House?"

There's a beat of silence before Ian replies. "I am. And you are?"

Pinching the bridge of my nose, I blow out a long breath. "I'm Darcy Thompson's boyfriend, and I need to speak with you about the security in this place."

CHAPTER FOURTEEN

DARCY

"Okay, your temperature is on the way down. I think the antibiotics are finally doing their thing." Mum runs a hand across my forehead before cupping my cheek in her soft palm. "I just called your boss and said you're going to need a few more days off."

I release a pained groan. "I wasn't going to tell her that; I was going to send an email this afternoon and suggest I work from home for the rest of the week."

Mum's soft gaze turns more serious. "This infection has knocked you off your feet, Darcy. You've been cooped up in this room for four days now, and only today are you starting to show signs of a recovery. I've never seen sickness like it. I want you warm and rested. Mother's orders."

I grumble below my breath when she stands from the bed and tucks in my duvet.

Mum ignores my protests. "Chicken or tomato soup?"

"Chicken, please, but you know I can make my own soup. I'm twenty-four," I reply, already restless to get on with life again.

She's right; today is the first day where I'm starting to feel myself, the vomiting and diarrhea finally subsiding. I'm used to antibiotics, but these ones were new and didn't sit well in my stomach. Still, they did the job—my chest isn't as tight, and the coughing is beginning to ease.

"I'm quite aware of your age and ability to heat a pan of soup. What I'm saying is, I can do it for you. Jon and I are heading to Seattle the day after tomorrow, and I want to make sure you're all set and okay. It's a mother's prerogative." Mum makes for the door, spinning around to face me. "You'll understand if you have children of your own one day."

I screw up my face. "Don't hold your breath on that one. I think Jack and Kendra might be your best shot at becoming a grandma."

Mum opens her mouth, probably to protest at the use of grandma, when a drilling sound stuns us both.

"Is that ..." Mum doesn't finish her sentence, thumbing in the direction of my front door. "Is that coming from outside?"

I shrug and pull the duvet back, sliding out of bed and grabbing my robe. "No idea, but I guess there's only one way to find out."

The drilling starts up again just as Mum reaches the front door and opens it, and I stay back a few paces.

Dressed in full overalls, with safety goggles on and an electric drill in hand, my landlord, Ian, stands in the doorway.

"Can I help you?" Mum asks, sounding genuinely confused.

Ian looks equally flummoxed as he takes our shocked faces in. He points to my doorframe. "I'm here to fit the smart doorbell." He bends down, pulling a package out of his toolbox. "Also this dead bolt on the inside of your door."

I have zero idea what he's talking about, but get the feeling I shouldn't argue. The guy is doing me a favor. "Oh, okay, thanks."

He nods his head once and gets back to drilling just as Elsie pokes her head around the frame and smiles at me. She might be the nosiest neighbor I've ever had, but at least she knows when to keep her mouth shut. She's never breathed a word to anyone about Archer's visit.

Mum makes her way back down the hallway, running a light hand across my shoulders as she passes. "He seems like a very attentive guy. You can never have too much security, living in the city."

My gaze lingers on Ian for a beat as he continues to work, still perplexed as to why he's here. I *never* forget a conversation. "No, I guess not."

With Mum heating soup, I head back into my bedroom and close the door, sliding back into my warm bed when my phone buzzes on the side table.

> Thigh Boy: How are you feeling?

I smile down at the hundredth message he's sent since I banned him from coming over while I was sick. I told Archer not to come around for several reasons, the first being risk—I wasn't lying when I said family could show up at any point. Plus, I looked and smelled like absolute crap. There is no way I'm letting him see me like this. However, all that aside, I didn't want him here, spending too much time with me. He might be able to separate his feelings, treating me like a friend in need one second and fucking my brains out the next. I can't. There's a sweet side to this boy, and slowly, I'm starting to understand why—aside from him being insanely handsome—women fall at his feet.

I wonder how many hearts he's broken.

> Me: Actually better. My temperature is coming down. Plus, this morning, I had this random package from my favorite dress store. All in a size four. Do you happen to know anything about this?

> Thigh Boy: You have no idea how happy that makes me. And, no, no idea about the dresses. Who do I need to beat up?

> Me: Well, thank you. I knew they were from you. That said, you can drop the sweet-boy act and just ask when you can come over and bang me.

> Thigh Boy: Wow, Doll. That cuts deep.

> Thigh Boy: So, when can I come over?

A spontaneous bubble of laughter spills from my rattly chest. He's so fucking cheeky.

> Me: Not right now. I have Mum here, heating soup like I'm ten years old, and my landlord is upgrading the security on my apartment.

> Me: I can't even remember agreeing for him to come over today. Clearly, the sickness-induced hallucinations were bad this time around.

It must be five minutes before another text comes through from Archer, just as Mum hands me a tray of food and a glass of water.

"Who the hell is Thigh Boy? Or shouldn't I ask?"

I pick up my spoon and take a first mouthful of soup. It's only premade and from a packet, but it's a universal fact that anything made by your mum always tastes better.

Swallowing my mouthful, I smirk around the spoon. "Just a friend."

Mum picks up the phone and hands it to me, eyes a little wide at the message on display, and I cringe, wondering what the hell he wrote.

"A friend to you, perhaps. I'm not sure that feeling is mutual, honey."

I open up the message thread just as Mum leaves the room, closing the door behind her.

Thigh Boy: It's funny you mention hallucinations because I can't stop thinking about you or the way you looked beneath me. So fucking beautiful.

Me: You wouldn't be saying that right now. More like the bride of Frankenstein.

Thigh Boy: Show me.

Me: No.

Thigh Boy: *picture attached*

My tray of food almost cascades to the floor when I open the message from Archer. He's standing in front of a mirror—in what I presume to be a changing room—completely naked from head to toe, pointing at his thigh tattoo with one hand while flexing and holding his phone in the other. I can see everything —and I mean, *all* of it.

Thigh Boy: Make sure you keep that image on lockdown in your phone.

Thigh Boy: Now you've seen me. Let me see you.

Me: Where the hell are you?

Thigh Boy: In the gym changing room.

Me: And where is everyone else—aka my brother and stepdad?

Thigh Boy: Both at a safe distance. Jack is in the shower stall behind me.

Me: You're crazy—you know that?

Thigh Boy: Maybe I am. Still waiting on your picture …

I open my Camera app and flinch. Unwashed hair over several days, combined with a general look of malaise, is not attractive. On a sigh and with a face like a slapped arse, I snap the photo and send it to him.

> Thigh Boy: Yeahhhh ... I'm gonna need to see you.

> Me: I promise I don't feel as bad as I look.

> Thigh Boy: That's not what I was thinking. Let me come over, even if only to watch a movie with you and heat you some more soup. I'll be on my best behavior.

> Thigh Boy: If I told you I missed you, would you freak out?

> Me: Well, you just did, and, no, I'm not freaking out. I kind of miss you too.

> Thigh Boy: Of course you do. Anyone would miss this face. How about tomorrow? I can sneak off after our warm-up game against Philly.

By tomorrow night, there's a chance I'll be feeling way more human. That, and I'll have at least had a shower.

> Me: Yeah, that works.

> Thigh Boy: I'll bring all your favorite snacks.

> Me: You don't know my favorite snacks.

> Thigh Boy: Oh, Doll. I thought you were finally working me out when you said I was crazy. Now I'm thinking we have a long way to go.

> Thigh Boy: See you tomorrow night. Stay pretty, A, x.

CHAPTER FIFTEEN

ARCHER

I'm on for my first shutout of the season when the Philly center—and my former captain—picks up a loose puck, reaching it just before Sawyer.

Shit. Their rookie winger is one of the fastest in the league as he comes barreling toward me, catching up to his captain and leaving me in a two-to-one situation and our slender one-goal lead at risk.

It's only the preseason, but as I've learned over the years, good habits start early, and with only an away series in Boston left to play before the regular season starts, I need this final play to go my way.

Typically, their center likes to deke—faking to pass off to his wingman before taking the move on himself. I'm not falling for that shit though. I've played with and against him enough seasons to know where he's going with this. Top right with a snapshot.

And that assumption is my first mistake. My second is ignoring the rookie and first-round draft pick when their captain fires a pass to him at the final second, immediately followed by a onetime slapshot, heading for the bottom left.

I keep the puck out, dropping into the splits, the very edge of my pad making contact with the puck, but not in the way I wanted it. It spills out with zero control or direction, only to find their captain's stick and, consequently, the top right, just as I originally anticipated.

The lamp lights, and I flop onto the ice, frustrated. The only saving grace is the empty arena since tonight is a simple friendly away from the media rather than an exhibition game.

I look across at Coach as he scrubs a hand over his jaw before holding it out to shake with the Philly coach. The game ending one to one.

"I should've been on the puck. That goal's on me, man." Sawyer glides across, pulling up just in front of me as I climb back to my feet.

I shake my head. "Nah. They exposed my weakness. Coach has been talking to me about rebound control, and my low angle game has been off for a while."

"That reach was wild! Unlucky on the rebound." Jack slides up to me, chewing on the corner of his mouth guard.

"Yeah, Archer isn't seeing it that way," Sawyer replies for me, skating off to head for the locker room.

I should do the same, but right now, the only thing holding up my mood is the thought of finally seeing Darcy tonight.

I pull off my helmet, smiling at Jack. "I'm getting in my head over the shutout record I set in my rookie season. I should be way ahead of that by now."

Jack looks confused. "You are way ahead of it." He thumbs behind him toward the emptying ice, and it's then that I notice Coach as he makes his way over. "When I arrived at training camp at the start of my first preseason, all I could think was how fucking relieved I was, playing for you and not against you."

I clamp a gloved hand on his shoulder, squeezing gently. In the brief seconds we make eye contact, the urge to tell him exactly what's happening with Darcy overwhelms me. The words *I've got feelings for your sister* are right there—teasing, taunting, telling me owning up and being honest is the right thing to do.

"All right, Morgan, nice play out there."

On Coach's approach, Jack spins around, a moment of pride passing between him and his stepdad before he skates off toward the tunnel, leaving me feeling anything but proud over my performance on the ice and lack of balls off it.

"Before you say anything, I know." I speak first, eager to get to the point. "I fucked up and should've anticipated the pass. I also need to work on my rebound distribution."

Coach runs a hand through his dark hair, zero signs of frustration. "Yeah, it wasn't the best, but the initial reach was excellent." He releases a long breath as I turn and grab my water bottle from the goal. "I want to try a new approach with your training and was going to speak with you about it after conditioning tomorrow. However, now seems like the best time."

Taking a pull from my bottle, I snap the lid shut and eye him for signs of being dropped to the farm team. "Should I be worried?"

Coach shakes his head with a dismissive laugh, and I heave a sigh of relief.

"Jensen Jones."

"What about him?"

He scrubs a hand over his jaw. "He's a good friend of mine and former Scorpions teammate. Recently retired from the game."

"Go on," I reply, already knowing all this.

"His rebound game is generally acknowledged to be one of the best ever seen, and I'm calling in a favor with him. He's agreed to temporarily join the coaching staff and work specifically with you. I think if we can get this element of your game nailed down, then you'll be unstoppable." He chuckles. "Maybe not the best analogy for a goalie, but you catch my drift."

I nod once, taking another sip of water. This isn't the worst news. I could learn a lot from probably the best NHL goalie in recent history.

"I told you I want to go deep into the playoffs this season, ideally lift the Cup. To do that, I need you locked in and focused on hockey and hockey alone."

Not on your stepdaughter then ...

"I told you I wanted this season to be my best yet, and I meant it."

I begin skating off the ice, and Coach follows.

"Good. Since we have a short rest period coming up, I'm actually due to go see Jensen in Seattle tomorrow after our conditioning session. We're going to discuss contracts and terms then. I'll let him know you're okay with the plan."

"Oh my God, you weren't kidding when you said you'd bring the snacks with you."

With two brown bags loaded with everything I could think of, I follow Darcy down the hallway in her apartment, setting them down on the counter in her kitchen.

She spins around to face me, and I immediately close the few feet between us. When she opened the door a second ago, I wanted to pull her into me, but didn't get the chance.

She's wearing a purple dress I bought her with tights and a cute cardigan over the top. "You look amazing in my dress."

With a cocky smirk, I breathe her in like a drug I've been reluctantly detoxing from. "How are you feeling?"

She looks at her nonexistent watch. "Since you asked me a couple of hours ago? Still a lot better than when you were last here."

There's an easy silence between us as we stand in the center of her living and kitchen space, the light fading fast outside. Only a floor lamp and her under-cabinet spotlights are on, bringing a soft glow to her apartment that shines on her rosy cheeks.

I don't feel the need to say anything as I appreciate her warm body against mine, dropping my face into the crook of her neck.

"Can I ask you something?" Darcy's voice cuts through the silence.

I hum into her soft hair, nodding once.

"How many girls have you slept with?"

I pull my head back up and study her closely. "Why do you ask?"

She twists her hands around in front of her, and I take them in mine—confident I'm, once again, crossing fuck-buddy boundaries. That said, so is she with her question. She knows I'm tested for STIs by the team.

"Why do you ask that, Darcy?" I softly repeat.

She looks down, and I release a hand, bringing a finger under her chin. I need to see her right now. I get a sense that ensnaring this girl in my world involves her understanding the real me, which isn't what the rest of the world sees. I know it isn't because I've never treated a woman in the way I do Darcy.

Her soft breath dances across my lips.

"I guess I've never had a fuck-buddy arrangement before, so I don't know what they usually look like. I will say, I never expected it to look like this though."

Finger still looped under her chin, I can't prevent my rogue grin. "How does it look, Darcy?"

"Different." She chuckles softly. "Do you know all of your former hookups' favorite snacks?"

She cocks her head toward the brown bags I set down earlier, a packet of Bugles just visible at the top.

"How honest do you want me to be with you?" I ask.

Darcy shakes her head like that shouldn't even be a question. Trouble is, if she knew the depth of my feelings and what I want, the full truth might not be so appealing.

This is just fun for her, Archer.

"I want you to be really honest with me. Always."

I tuck a piece of hair behind her left ear while my stomach knots with a barrage of emotions—mainly anxiety—as I search for the best way to put this. "You want to know how many women I've slept with?" I brush my thumb across the hand I'm still holding, and I see the goose bumps as they rise on her bare arms. "I don't think I can give you a number because I don't know myself. My past is littered with bad decisions and one-night stands, some of which I've buried at the back of my memory."

Her eyes search my face. Fuck, what is going on in that head?

"I mean, this—you and me—we're a risky hookup, aren't we? Will you bury us ..." She pauses for a second. "Me. Do you plan on burying me at the back of your memory when you're done with whatever this is?"

Up until this moment, I've done a good job of hiding the way her assumptions about me cut deep. Assumptions I can't blame her—or anyone else—for having. It's a reputation I've built up since my college years, and now it's biting me in the ass.

I can't hide my frustration or hurt any longer, and as a result, I feel the mask disguising the true depth of my emotions slip a fraction.

"I have no plans to be done with you, Doll. And what we're doing, I'll never forget it."

She nods once, never taking her eyes off mine. "What did

you mean when you said you buried some of your one-night stands at the back of your memory?"

This is a conversation I wasn't expecting to have today, and my anxiety kicks up a notch. "Some of the women I got with weren't single."

Her eyes flare wide, and I quickly rectify her spiraling thoughts about me.

"I didn't know that they weren't, and if I had, I would've never gone there. Ever." I punctuate the last word to get my point across.

"Kassie, the last woman I was with before you, was engaged to a guy I used to play with. When I found that out, I could've buried the knowledge and let him go ahead and marry her. That didn't sit right with me though, so I told him what happened."

Darcy grimaces. "How did he react?"

I can still feel the sting as his fist collided with my jaw. "Not that great. After that, I made a vow to quit playing around and grow the fuck up. Choosing to be with multiple women or men is nothing to be ashamed of, even if the reckless way I was going about it was questionable. I was literally hooking up with strangers I knew nothing about, other than they were hot and I was horny."

The words burn my mouth like acid as I voice them, unease creeping up my neck in a crimson rash I know is visible. I want to tag on that I also stopped sleeping around because I couldn't stop thinking of her. It's not the right time though, and I force down another admission, my throat burning as I do it.

With everything she knows, I wouldn't blame Darcy if she ended our arrangement right now, although I keep holding on to her body, waiting and hoping she won't back away.

"So, you haven't slept around for a while?" she asks, no judgment or malice in her voice, only a simple question.

I shake my head, the truth spilling from me in easy waves. "Not for a while, no."

Her surprise is obvious, or maybe it's relief that causes her shoulders to relax. I can't be sure.

"You have nothing to feel guilty about or ashamed of, Archer. You're a good person, and you did the right thing in telling that guy about his unfaithful fiancée. I'm not sure how many times Liam went behind my back. I can only hope I found out after the first time."

This time, it's my shoulders that drop with relief as I place a chaste kiss on the bridge of her nose, working my way down to her mouth.

Just like that morning we shared in my bed, nothing about this moment feels like a fuck-buddy arrangement, and I let that reality sit between us without words. I don't know how much she shares of what I'm feeling. All I can do is keep showing up for this girl.

When I go in for another kiss, she pulls back a little, something more on her mind. "So, this, what we have"—she motions between us—"I get to call time on it?"

Releasing her hand, I wrap my palms under her ass and lift her up. She loops her legs around my waist, interlacing her fingers at the nape of my neck.

"I've told you from the beginning that you're in control of us. Nothing has changed that."

Beneath the dress I bought her, I feel the heat between her thighs.

Goddamn, I want her so badly.

"Do you want to watch a movie?" I ask, thinking she's probably not up to much with being so sick this week.

"No," she whispers, pupils dilating. "I don't want to watch a movie *or* eat snacks."

My heart rate kicks up, pumping blood to my dick. "Well, given you're in control, tell me what you want."

She looks over her shoulder, gazing through the open bedroom door and then back at me. Her skin's flushed red, chest moving more rapidly. "I want you to take me to bed."

CHAPTER SIXTEEN

DARCY

The way this boy undresses me—like it's his birthday and I'm the only gift he's ever wished for. It's all-consuming. I sense he's trying to hold back from tearing the clothes from my body, determined to savor each part of the process.

I feel the same way. I would be lying if I said I didn't. Archer is a work of art—every curve to his abs exquisite and refined over years of gym work and conditioning.

And now that I'm seeing the man beneath the bravado and beautiful body, I can't help but get sucked into him further. He might've slept with more women than he can remember, and he might want to bury the memories of those he can recall, but I'm confident the man before me is not the version the rest of the world has seen. The trouble is that realization both excites and terrifies me. Even though he isn't asking for it, I know I'm not ready to put my heart on the line and go for more. With anyone.

He's kneeling between my feet as I sit on the edge of my bed, palms flat to the mattress and supporting my weight. Just like when he ate me out and tasted us both, I want to watch the careful way he peels down my tights. He tosses them across my bedroom, along with my cardigan, and then brings his hands to the hem of my dress. I sit up straighter and lift my arms, allowing him to pull it off in one motion.

Now I'm only wearing a lacy pink bralette and matching thong, but Archer remains kneeling, running his hands up my thighs on a deep exhale.

"What are you thinking about?" I ask quietly.

He shakes his head, though it isn't negative, more in awe. It's possible he doesn't realize he's looking at me in this way, or maybe I'm being sucked in even deeper. But getting naked with the Blades goalie is one of my favorite things.

"Reconsidering my religious beliefs," he whispers against my navel between kisses.

"What do you mean?" I half laugh.

He works his way up my body, kissing past my sternum before finding the underside of my jaw. "Because I think I just found a reason to pray." He reaches my mouth, sweeping his tongue against mine. "You know you're incredible, Darcy. And if you don't, then you should start believing it, right the fuck now."

I hold my breath, tingles dancing along my skin, all in response to his mouth.

He leans into me, and I collapse onto the bed, scooting back so he can climb on while we continue to kiss.

"Are you sure you're up to this? You've been really sick." He asks the question, although I can see the same desperation in his eyes that I feel deep in my core.

We've been vulnerable with each other, and I trust him to go gentle—not just with my mind, but with my body also. Even though I'm exhausted, I'm needy to relive the orgasms he gave me in his bed.

"Just go easy with me." I'm already panting, my shallow breathing has nothing to do with the infection I'm recovering from.

He smiles into my mouth, tongue running along my bottom lip. "Lie back on the pillows, Doll. Let me look after you."

A second later, I'm exactly where he wants me, watching as he pops the button on his jeans and pulls them down his thighs. Naturally, my eyes fall to the tattoo, and I pull in a breath when his boxers go as well. Somehow, his dick looks even bigger than it did last time.

Next, he removes his shirt until he's fully naked in front of me. Archer pulls down my damp thong, and I reach behind my back, unclipping my bralette and tossing it onto the floor.

He lazily pumps himself, lying down beside me. "Roll onto your side for me."

"But then we won't have eye contact," I reply, remembering what he said the first night we hooked up.

Archer kisses my shoulder. "This is very different. Tonight is about going slow and being gentle. I promise I'll make you feel special like this."

My stomach flips in the best way, and I do as he asked, facing away from him as he pulls me into his body. His hard cock presses into my ass, the cold metal piercings a delicious contrast to my burning skin.

"I'm obsessed with your hair." He pulls it away from my neck, wrapping it around his fist. Next, his lips caress just below my ear. "I'm obsessed with your skin."

He kisses me, and I moan quietly.

Archer slides his arm underneath us both, placing his warm palm over my heart. "But mostly, I'm obsessed with this right here. Don't let anyone break it again, Darcy. It's too kind and trusting and all the things a real man would never take for granted."

For a brief second, he pulls his hips back before entering me slowly.

He releases a low moan I feel against my back.

"Is that good?" he whispers against my already-pebbled skin. "Your heartbeat tells me it is."

I answer his question by hooking my leg over his, spreading me wider.

Archer releases my hair, his hand sliding to my hip, pinning me against his body. He's so deep.

"Taking you raw is my new favorite thing," he whispers between the kisses he sets along my collarbone. "You're the first girl I've ever done this with."

I turn my head to look at him. His blue eyes are already searching mine out as he slowly grinds into me, and while I appreciate every inch of his dick, my heartbeat kicks up in response to his candidness. Another piece he's shared with me slots into my latest puzzle as the real Archer picture continues to take shape.

"I feel privileged. And me too, I guess that means we've both shared a first with each other."

Archer continues fucking me, joint gasps bleeding into our words. "I've only ever wanted it like this with you, Darcy. I know I couldn't tell you how many women I'd been with, but you should know I've never had sex in this position. I've never held anyone like I hold you."

My sudden and unexpected release coats his dick, a whimper falling from me.

He leans over me and seals his mouth over mine, tipping my chin up with his finger so he can drive the kiss deeper.

"Are you drowning my dick, Darcy?"

I whimper again, like the needy girl I am. "Coming all over it."

Another moan emanates from his chest, climbing up his throat, and we both swallow it down.

"Do you like the thought of that, huh? Being my girl."

Archer's dick swells, turning impossibly hard before I feel his warm cum spill inside me. He tries to keep his movements smooth but fails as he pistons into my pussy, sending me over the edge for a second time.

I can feel him pulsating along with our release as it slides down the inside of my thighs. It's without a doubt the hottest sex I've ever had.

My eyes flutter shut, exhaustion pulling me under.

"Before you go to sleep, I need to know your answer."

My eyes snap open. Initially, I didn't take his question seriously, convinced he was fooling around when he alluded to me being his girl. But now, as he asks me a second time, my heart spikes for an entirely different reason than honesty over his past or the orgasm he just gave me.

I pull my hips away, far enough so he's no longer inside, and flip over to face him. "Y-you're serious?"

Archer shifts toward me on the bed, one hand reaching to my waist, and I pull back a little more. My hazy brain trying to figure him out.

He goes to speak and then stops, uncertainty written in his expression. A second later, he relaxes into an easy smile. "No, Doll." Between his fingers, he plays with a piece of my hair, studying my face carefully. "I got carried away and didn't think about what I was saying. Sex with you makes me all possessive and shit."

I narrow my eyes at him, trying to come off as playful but still reeling inside. "Don't go getting too possessive, Thigh Boy. Orgasms and yummy snacks are what I'm after. Not strings and needy men." I cup his chin in my palm, just like he frequently does with me. "The last guy who claimed me subsequently put his dick in another woman."

The moment the words are out, I regret them. Archer is nothing like Liam, and I just insinuated he was or could at least have the capabilities to hurt me.

There's a long beat of nothing as I search for the right thing to say when Archer clears his throat.

"No, yeah. I get that."

He sits up in bed and grabs my TV remote from the nightstand, flicking it to the first channel he can find. "Okay, let's get the snacks and watch a movie."

I follow him and sit up, still feeling some kind of way over our conversation. I gently place a palm on his forearm. "Archer."

He sets the remote down, yet still won't look at me.

"Archer," I repeat.

After a moment, he turns to face me, brows pulled together and jaw tense. "It's all good, Darcy. I'm known for saying stupid shit, and clearly, this was another one of those instances."

He's infuriated with himself, and so am I. There are so many dangers with what we're doing.

"It's just ... you sounded serious, and then you said that you needed to know my answer before I went to sleep."

He blows out a harsh laugh, pulling my body against his. "What? No. I told you I say stuff and don't think it through. I've never had a relationship in my adult life." He tries to grin, but I see through the pain I've caused. "Once a playboy, always a playboy, right?"

Something doesn't feel right. His facial expression doesn't match his tone or the words tumbling from him.

I want to drop the subject and eat Bugles with a movie, but I can't push past the gnawing guilt or doubt that he isn't being completely honest with me. Still, in what world would Archer Moore ever want a girlfriend? Just because he's stopped sleeping around doesn't mean it's because he wants someone. His experience with Kassie would be enough to put anyone off the lifestyle.

Releasing a slow breath, I know I'm the only one who can address the elephant in the room. He put all the power in my hands. "Do we need to end this? I don't want everything between us to get complicated."

Archer picks up the remote, muting the TV. "Is that what you want?"

I bite the inside of my cheek, totally conflicted and confused. "I don't want to end it. Like I said, I'm having fun, and I can't deny that spending time with you is one of my favorite things." I catch a blooming smile as it pulls at his lips. "I'm just not ready for anything more—with anyone." I kick my feet under the duvet. "I'm not sure that I ever will be."

Archer nods a couple of times, placing a lingering kiss against my forehead. "I get it, and that's something you *can* be sure of with me, Doll. Fun."

CHAPTER SEVENTEEN

ARCHER

> Me: I'm bored. Let's sneak out when no one's watching.

I hit Send on my message to Darcy and look on from my position in the corner of the room for her to read it.

She's standing at the bar, dressed in a silky pale pink gown that crisscrosses down her back, stopping just above the curve of her ass. Looking phenomenal.

The entire Blades team is here tonight with their families and partners, celebrating the appointment of our new GM and the long tenure of our retiring one. I should be socializing or even flirting with the blonde server who keeps bringing me drinks even though I haven't finished my current soda.

Instead, I'm laser-focused on my girl as she laughs and jokes with Kendra and Collins, sipping on her favorite cocktail—a cosmo.

Her purse—containing her cell—rests on the corner of the bar, and she hasn't looked at it once all night. I know we're trying to keep a low profile, but I've barely spoken to her all week since she reaffirmed what we are—fuck buddies.

With a hand to her chest, she leans back, laughing at something one of the girls just said, when Jack joins the group, wrapping an arm around her shoulders. He's as proud of his sister as he is protective—anyone with eyes can see that.

I see that.

"Dude, you have got to stop staring. It's making *me* feel violated, never mind the girl." Sawyer takes a seat at the empty round table I'm sitting at, setting his half-finished pint on the white tablecloth. He mirrors my position, resting his leg across the opposite knee.

Groaning, I sit back in my chair. I've confessed to wanting Darcy, but I'm not about to tell my captain about the latest mess I'm in with her. If he discovers I'm boning Jack's sister for "fun," as Darcy describes it, then he'll throttle me with the bow tie I'm wearing.

"I really think you need to let it go." Sawyer twists the pint glass around in front of him, dropping his foot to the floor when he leans forward, elbows braced on the table.

I continue watching Darcy have a good time as she accepts another cocktail from one of our forwards, and a smack of unjustified jealousy hits me straight on.

"I've been giving this entire thing you have for her some thought, and you need to let it go." He repeats his advice, but it washes over me for a second time. "Archer," Sawyer demands my attention, frustration in his voice.

"I'm not letting anything go," I reply. "That isn't an option for me."

From beside me, Sawyer grumbles something inaudible against the ambient music. I choose to ignore whatever he said, watching as our rookie forward, Blake Harrison, lingers with the group. He just bought her a drink, and I don't like it.

Not one fucking bit.

"You're going to tear the team apart. With the story about

Abbie and your secret obsession with his sister, Jack won't forgive you for the deception."

My molars grind. Stress and tension taking ahold of me. "It doesn't matter what you say; you aren't going to change the way I feel."

Sawyer sits back in his chair, running a palm across his mouth. "I don't know what to say to you. You're playing with fire. Has Darcy even hinted that she feels the same way?"

I huff out a despondent laugh.

"I'll take that as a no then," Sawyer replies.

"Have you and Collins set a date yet?" I pick up my soda and take a large pull, my mouth dry and throat thick.

"Way to change the subject." Sawyer chuckles, although I can sense his relief since we're heading nowhere fast on the current topic. "Collins wants a small wedding at the city clerk's office with a meal for friends at a restaurant we like at Brighton Beach. We're thinking in the offseason, so maybe July and then go all in on a big honeymoon to Japan—she's always wanted to head back after she visited when she was younger."

As I twist around to face my captain, I can't help but smile.

"What's the grin for?"

I shake my head. "Nothing, just thinking how fucking stoked I am for you. You deserve the world, Cap."

Sawyer inhales deeply, rolling his lips together as he studies me. "You know, I thought I had you all figured out when you joined the Blades from Philly. But you just keep proving me wrong, don't you? When Ezra had the motorcycle accident, you were there with words of wisdom. You've always had my back, and I've always had yours."

Now feels like a better time to revisit the previous conversation. "I'm serious about Darcy. I don't know how many ways I can say it, but I am, and I'm not going to let her go. There's something there between us."

I'm desperate to tell him I've fallen harder since I had her in my bed.

Sawyer hums like he understands, but doesn't necessarily agree while I glance over my shoulder to find Darcy.

Christ, she's beautiful. Every time I look at her, she realigns my brain chemistry. Her contagious laugh brightens everything in her vicinity. My parents might've separated after years of marriage, but I'm confident I could never let Darcy get away. I could make her the happiest girl on this planet.

"You chased Collins when she kept blowing you off." I say the words and bite down on my cheek—hard.

Sawyer rises from his seat and clamps a hand on my shoulder. "That's true, and I remember talking to you about it. You told me to go after the girl and tell her how I felt." He squeezes his palm, and I know it's to comfort me ahead of whatever he's about to say. "The thing is, you were also correct when you said your situation with Darcy wasn't the same as mine with was with Collins. I wasn't trying to bone my best friend's sister, and neither was I trying to push something I knew was a lost cause. I don't want to see you get hurt, Archer. I want to see you happy and settled and with a woman who makes you feel worthy. Darcy isn't at that time in life. She wants to have fun and explore the new city she just moved to. Be a friend to her, man. Be a friend to yourself and let it go."

He picks up his pint, and the words *I'm sleeping with her* are right on the tip of my tongue. They won't materialize though because perhaps he's right; maybe I am fooling myself, and the only reason Darcy climbs into my bed is purely out of fun and nothing more.

Maybe my playboy days aren't just actively playing against me, but fully laughing in my face. Revealing to Darcy that I haven't slept around in a while might have done nothing to change her opinion of me, even if she'll never judge me for my past.

Still, I want her next to me again tonight. My addiction to this girl won't allow anything else. And if I have to lean into my playboy reputation, then that's what I'll do to keep her coming back to me. I guess you could say that at this point, I'm caught between the ultimate rock and a hard place.

"I'm worried about you, Archer." Sawyer's voice permeates my thoughts.

I wave a nonchalant hand in front of me, eyes still on Darcy. "I'm good. You don't need to be concerned."

Before walking away, he hesitates for the briefest of seconds, and I pray he doesn't say anything more. In the past, I might've turned to him for women-related advice, but he knows this circumstance is different, and he's aware I'm reluctant to pull him into it too.

"You won't change my mind," I breathe out. "No one will."

He disappears, and I squeeze my eyes shut, whispering to myself, *What the fuck are you doing, Archer?* only for it to be absorbed by the music and open dance floor in front of me.

When I open my eyes a few seconds later, it's like she can sense my pain. From across the room, Darcy glances at me briefly. Jack's arm is still around her shoulders as she throws me a quick smile.

In your purse! I mouth to her, pointing toward the end of the bar.

She looks confused, and I feel frustrated.

Grabbing my cell, I wave it at her subtly, being sure not to capture anyone else's attention in the process.

Check this, I mouth again.

For good measure, I type out another text.

Me: You look fucking incredible.

Making her excuses, Darcy shimmies out from beneath her brother's arm and grabs her purse, fetching out her cell phone.

I can feel my adrenaline spike, watching her read my messages and type out a response.

> Doll: Let me guess ... in your mind, you're already peeling this dress off me.

> Me: I've got your dress, bra, and panties in a heap by my feet.

Doll: Well, that's an interesting revelation …

Doll: Since I'm not wearing any underwear.

The rumble as it vibrates in my chest only leaves me more grateful for the music in this place.

> Me: I need to be inside you. Now.

Doll: No can do, I'm afraid …

She sends the message and leans across the bar, lifting her cocktail at me with a smile.
Brat.

> Me: Are you trying to play me?

Doll: Tell me, is it working?

Jesus, if only she knew.

> Me: I'm hard as fuck, if that's what you mean.

Doll: That's exactly what I was getting at.

I can feel the throb of my pulse as it beats in my ears.

> Me: I need to fuck you. Right. Now.

Doll: You're a dirty boy, Archer Moore.

> Me: Tell me you aren't desperate for it.

I watch the way her fingers hover over the keyboard.
Come on, Darcy Doll. Keep coming back to me.

Doll: I cannot tell you that. Because I am.

> Me: Tell me you're desperate for my cock.

She pauses and looks up at the group, Jack standing a few feet away.

> Doll: If I were wearing them, my panties would be soaked.

> Me: In around thirty seconds, I'm going to walk out of this room and into the lobby. I want you to follow me a few seconds afterward. Bring your bag and things.

> Doll: Why would I need my stuff?

> Me: Because once we leave, we aren't coming back.

CHAPTER EIGHTEEN

DARCY

I've figured out that I'm a sucker for secret sex, and I'm absolutely fine with that.

Replacing my phone, I zip up my clutch bag and loop the small strap around my wrist. I can feel the anticipation and excitement fizzing through me, and it only kicks up when I rejoin my friends and brother just as Archer leaves the room, throwing me a daring wink on his exit.

"What do you think, Darce?" Jack turns to me, assuming I've heard everything he's been saying these past few minutes.

"Hmm?"

Jack rolls his eyes mockingly, pulling me into his side. "We're talking about heading to a few bars at the end of the function. The team leaves for Boston the day after tomorrow, and we'll be gone for five days while we wrap up preseason."

I look around at Jenna, Kendra, and Collins.

"I was actually going to have an early night." I take a deep breath. "That chest infection took me right out, and I'm exhausted."

It's the truth; I am way more tired than I normally am after an infection. It's hardly surprising with the insane hours I've been working to catch up on the time off I took.

The corner of Jenna's lips tips up, and I feel my cheeks heat. She's worked out my real reason for wanting to leave.

"Girl, I've had one respiratory infection in my life, and it took me out for, like, a month straight. I say get yourself home."

"Do you need a lift home?" Jack asks, releasing me from his side.

I shake my head and plant a kiss on each of my friend's cheeks, blowing another kiss across the room to Mum and Jon, who are both deep in conversation with the new GM.

I turn back to Jack, "No, I'm good. I'll be just fine."

Without looking back, I'm heading for the exit, nerves and excitement now swirling in my gut. It's been over a week since I spent time with Archer, and despite me wanting to play it cool, I can't deny I've missed him.

But as I step into the plush lobby, other than the concierge and a couple of people I don't recognize, there's no sign of Archer.

I move to one side and reach into my bag for my phone.

"I'm right here, Doll."

Tingles settle in my toes as I look up at Archer.

He takes a step toward me, and my back finds the wall. His eyes are molten, a cocky smirk playing on his lips. *This* is the Archer I expected to find when I first agreed to sleep with him.

He towers over me, breath fanning my face.

"Where do you want to go?" I say under my breath, so incredibly turned on.

Like he's enjoying holding me here—locked in his penetrative gaze—Archer doesn't immediately answer, one hand finding my waist and sending a searing heat through the thin fabric of my dress.

"You told me you wanted to have fun, right?" When he finally breaks the silence, his voice is gravelly.

"That's precisely what I want."

"All right then." His other hand intertwines with mine as he turns and leads me toward a door just off the hallway.

Checking that the few people in our vicinity aren't watching, Archer opens the door and guides me into a dark room, closing us inside and flicking the lock behind us. Only a crack of light from the bright lobby creeps underneath the door.

In a flash, my back is against the door, his huge hand flat above my head. I've got nowhere to go in this small room, not that I'd want to escape his clutches.

Archer's ragged breathing slows as he gazes down at me. The urgency we had when we entered the room has all but disappeared as he brings his other hand up to cup my cheek.

"I know I already told you tonight, but I think it warrants me saying again that you look fucking incredible."

My eyes drop to his perfectly finished bow tie, and I reach up and pull it apart until it hangs open around his neck. "And you're giving me James Bond vibes."

Archer studies my face, as he does so often when I see him, only his observations seem more deliberate tonight, and I hold my breath in response. Just like in Jack and Kendra's spare bedroom, it feels like I'm fighting for oxygen.

"Tell me something, Darcy." Keeping his hand against my cheek, he rubs his thumb along my bottom lip, and instinctively, my tongue darts out to track the movement. "Do you plan on making me wait a week between each time I see you?"

Voices sound from the other side of the door, although at this point, it's just noise; nothing can penetrate the atmosphere building inside this tiny room.

"Or maybe I should put it another way ... did you deliberately make me wait a week to see you because I'd freaked you out with what I said the last time we were together?"

"I-I'm not freaked out." My voice is about as strong as the wobbly knees that are trying to keep me standing.

His spicy cologne envelops me, along with the determined look in his eyes. He wants answers.

"So, you aren't avoiding me?"

I shake my head once. "No. I've been busy catching up at work."

He seems satisfied with my answer, although I can tell there's something else playing on his mind.

"Just go ahead and say whatever else is eating at you, Archer."

Our lips are barely apart when he leans down to my height, moving his hand from my cheek to my hip.

"Why is it that Blake Harrison can buy you drinks in front of your stepdad and brother, yet I can't even be near you without Jack giving me the death stare?"

I fight back a smirk. *He's jealous.*

"Don't play with me, Doll. You know I'm right in my observations. While our rookie forward gets cozy with my girl, I'm left on the sidelines, hating that everything I do with you has to be in secret. If I'd bought you that drink, you'd have had to claim that it was from someone else."

I'm tempted to appease him with a kiss. "Maybe it's because there's a clear difference between you and Blake."

Archer pulls back slightly, a crease forming between his brows as he frowns down at me.

I reach onto my tiptoes and smooth out the line. I hate it when he isn't smiling.

He catches my hand as I bring it back to my side, kissing the center of my palm in a move that's so sweet that it melts me as much as the first time he did it. "Blake isn't your brother's best friend?"

Cocking my head to one side, I nod once. "Well, that, I guess. Although that isn't the real reason."

Archer presses his body into mine. "You're killing me here."

My mouth suddenly turns dry, and I lick my lips. I know this is a risky admission on my part, but Archer has only ever been open with me. Last time we were together, I know I hurt him when I compared him to Liam. This time, I want him to know how much he and the time we spend together mean to me.

I force down the temptation to back out and push out the words. "Because I don't look at Blake the way I look at you, and neither does he make me feel special."

Air leaves his lungs in a whoosh that fills the space around us. Although his eyes tell me everything I need to know as they soften in the glow of the room. "Making you feel special is all I've ever wanted to do."

Without another word, Archer lifts my long dress around my waist and drops down in front of me, then lifts one of my legs onto his shoulder.

A swift bubble of laughter leaves my throat. "You see what I mean? You're even on your knees for me now."

I expect him to laugh along with me. He doesn't. Instead, he swipes a single finger through my pussy before taking it into his mouth and sucking it.

"Doll, if your man doesn't get on his knees for you daily, then trust me when I say you don't want him."

I can form no words when he swipes his hand through me again, burying his face between my thighs.

"You weren't lying, no underwear," he whispers against my sensitive pussy.

I push my head back into the wooden door. My clutch slides off my wrist and hits the floor as my entire body goes limp.

"I was thinking about buying you lingerie to go with your tote and cute dresses. I'm now thinking I prefer you like this—bare and ready for me whenever I want."

The charge in the room morphs in an instant as Archer switches from sensitive and caring to full-on possessive.

So many sides to this man.

I groan when his tongue passes through me again, followed by his fingers as they pinch my sensitive clit.

Archer spreads me apart, licking and sucking so well, ruining me for any other man.

He pauses and looks up at me, lips shining with my arousal.

"Is that what you want, Darcy? For me to take you whenever we can, wherever we are?"

An agreeable noise rises up my throat, and he drops my leg, rising to his full height as he brackets me in with his arms.

"Since you want to be a dirty girl for me, go ahead and suck my cock."

I quirk a brow at him. It comes off as challenging, but really, I'm nervous. I rarely went down on Liam. I rarely did anything with Liam.

My hands fall to the button on his trousers. "What if you can't handle my mouth and you blow straightaway?" I pull down the zipper, popping the button and pushing his pants and boxers below his ass. "I want you to fuck me too."

His breathing is back to ragged. His lips are millimeters from mine, and his voice is hoarse as he says, "Is that what happened with pathetic little Liam? Was it a choice between a blow job or sex?" He brushes his mouth over mine. "That's not how it works with me. Especially not when it comes to you. I could shoot down your throat a thousand times and still be hard enough to make you scream."

I swallow thickly, dropping to my knees in front of him.

When I pass my tongue over the head, he pulls on my hair, and I look back up at him, wondering if I did it wrong.

His eyes are softer and laced with awe. "This is a fucking dream for me, Darcy. You, like this, ready to swallow my cock."

I keep my gaze on his when I take him into my mouth, pushing his huge cock to the back of my throat. I force back a gag and pop off.

"I guess I could say the same thing—if a girl doesn't drop to her knees in front of you, then she must be freaking crazy."

Archer's jaw hangs open as he pushes his cock back into my mouth. I accept it gladly. "Goddammit," he bites out, his hand caressing my cheek. "It's like your mouth was made for me."

My tongue finds the piercings on his shaft, and Archer sucks in a sharp breath when I tease them, pride inflating my chest.

"I'm ready to blow, Darcy." He tilts my face up to look at him.

Right as Archer grits out his words, the door handle moves beside me followed by familiar voices that flip my stomach.

"Is this the cloakroom? I can't remember."

"Shit. That's Jack," Archer hisses.

I bring him out of my mouth and smile, excitement coursing through me. "But the door's locked, right?"

"Fuck it," Archer breathes, right before he reaches down, looping his hands under my ass. "I need inside you. Now."

I'm suspended and pressed against the door, legs wrapped around Archer's waist, just as Jack tries the handle again.

"Holy fucking shit." Archer drops his face into my neck, muffling his low voice and entering me slowly. "You're so fucking tight. So fucking perfect."

"I think it's locked. Either that or the handle's busted." Jack's voice filters from the other side.

Archer sucks on my collarbone right as he strokes into me again. "Don't make a sound, Darcy. I need you to keep really quiet while I make you come. Can you do that for me?"

The tiniest whimper leaves my throat, and after that, all I can hear is the way my pussy takes him. Over and over again.

"That's really good. You're being so good for me," he whispers again, growing harder and harder.

I can tell this is turning him on, driving him to the edge. It's no different for me—I've never been this wet. Ever.

My pussy clamps around him, and I feel his smile against the shell of my ear.

"You're so fucking naughty—you know that? There's nothing British or ladylike about you when you let me spread you open and plow into this cunt."

His hips pump into me, grinding deeper each time.

I turn my head to look at him. "Does forbidden fucking get you off?" I murmur against his lips.

Archer runs his tongue along my bottom lip, and I draw it between my teeth, tasting him.

"I know I shouldn't be touching you like this. When I put my hands on you, I know I'm crossing a line. But the thing is ..." He rolls into me again as I overhear Jack, Kendra, and Jenna trying to find a key so they can get their jackets and leave. Archer swallows thickly. "I'm prepared to take the risk because I can't stay away from you. We're just the same, Darcy. Other idiots might say that your laugh is too loud or you talk too much. I say I can't get enough of it. Of you."

My orgasm hits me. Hard. Like a cannon between my thighs, ricocheting throughout my body. Archer covers my mouth with his, swallowing down my cries as he kisses me through it.

I pull back, whispering so quietly that I can barely hear myself, "Come inside me, Archer. Do it." I know I'm letting my emotions take over, but fuck it; this boy is all I want in this moment. In so many moments.

Archer hated being apart for the past week—well, that makes two of us.

He supports my body weight with one arm, holding the door handle when someone on the other side tries it again.

When I feel his warm flow spill inside me, we're both rendered speechless, mouths locked on each other as we fall from our silent highs.

He drops his forehead against mine, grinning like an idiot, while I press my lips together, fighting back laughter I know will give us away.

"Shhh!" He brings his pointer finger to his lips, laughing under his breath too.

"How do we get out of here, unseen?" I ask, slightly panicked, eyes darting around the darkened space.

Archer kisses the underside of my jaw, shoulders still vibrating with humor. "We wait it out. This is a storage closet." He points toward a faint outline of a mop and bucket. "Not the cloakroom. As soon as they figure that out, we'll be in the clear."

I narrow my eyes at him. He's still hard and inside me. "You had this all worked out, didn't you?"

He shakes his head. "No. It's just blind luck I picked this room. My brain doesn't function well whenever I'm around you."

He grins wide and rolls his hips again, and I gasp.

"Are we going again?"

He nods once, taking my mouth in another searing kiss. "We are. And then again when I get you back to my bed."

CHAPTER NINETEEN

ARCHER

"This has been the longest five-day series ever." Jack rolls onto his back, fingers interlaced across his chest as he stares up at the hotel ceiling.

Ordinarily, I share a hotel room with Sawyer, but the new GM has come in and immediately shaken things up, including the comfortable routines we got ourselves into. I can't say he's made himself popular with the team or Coach Morgan, especially since our preseason friendlies have largely been wins.

We've rolled Boston over twice, and I've played well, securing two shutouts. Jensen Jones is due to start with the coaching staff when we head back to New York tomorrow, and I'm hopeful that with his added input, I can make this my best NHL season yet.

Jack's right though; despite the successful preseason away series, this has been the longest time ever. Only made longer by having to hide my phone and text Darcy in secret.

And I feel shitty for it. Secret sex in the closet is exciting, fun, and so fucking hot. But replying to messages when her brother takes a shower is not what I want for our friendship.

It irks me because I look around and see all the other guys on our team video-calling and messaging their wives and partners while I'm stealing a quick text from my girl like it's a drug hit, feeling ashamed when I do it. Hell, I'm pretty sure I caught the back end of Jack and Kendra's phone sex when I walked into the hotel room the other day, having finished a gym session earlier than expected.

"I don't know how you do it." Jack sits up on his bed, pulling out his phone and typing something—no doubt to his wife.

I study him with envy. "Do what?"

Finishing up, he sets his cell phone on the bed. "With Abbie. It's hard enough, being married and trying to fit around soccer and hockey schedules, let alone what you have to do. I mean, when was the last time you saw her?"

It's hard to look at him. *Fuck me*, I hate lying.

I roll onto my back, crossing my ankles over and trying to look relaxed. In reality, I'm anything but. "With her work schedule and everything, it's hard to see her. But we try and make it work."

"I dunno, man." Jack shakes his head. "That's a whole lot of long distance." He reaches over to our shared nightstand, picking up his water glass and taking a couple of sips. "Still, I guess you have July and August to spend time together."

My brows crease with confusion, and he must notice.

"That's when kindergarten teachers get their summer break, no?"

Remembering that is, in fact, the make-believe job I gave my entirely fictional girlfriend, I clear my throat and nod in agreement. "Yeah, yeah. We'll have to make the most of that time. Just sucks, having to wait out the year."

"At least away games in Dallas will work."

I don't reply, choosing to close my eyes instead.

"I guess I'm shocked, is all. I never expected you to be a one-woman guy."

Keeping my eyes closed, I will away this painful conversation. That said, every twinge of discomfort is my own making.

I sit up and grab my phone, which is face down on the nightstand. Anything to busy my hands and mind since the tension rolling off me must be noticeable. "Things change, Jack. I'm not getting any younger, and hookups don't carry the same appeal anymore."

"I get that," Jack replies before falling silent.

Please be it, please be it, please be it.

He opens his mouth, and my heart sinks.

"Do you think Abbie's the one then?" His face lights up, probably on my behalf. "I knew with Kendra, and I get the feeling it's the same for you with Abbie."

Puffing out a doubtful breath since the woman doesn't even exist, I can't help the laugh that follows. "Why would you think that?"

He shrugs a shoulder. "You've been different these past few weeks. Quieter, maybe even subdued. You've been heading home earlier on nights out, and I assumed it was so you could call your girl."

Nope. So I could bone your sister.

When I finally pluck up the courage to look at my friend, he's waiting for me to speak. The guy is happy for me, and here I am, keeping multiple secrets, which I know, in the end, will tear our friendship apart. Possibly even the team.

Since that night at the dinner, Sawyer hasn't spoken about Darcy with me again. He said his piece, and he was likely right. However things end with Darcy, whether I make her my girl or not—*who am I kidding? Of course I'm making her mine*—Jack is going to be pissed. And the longer I let the lies and deceit go on, the deeper the damage will get.

I can hear the words I want to say as they echo in my brain. *I've got feelings for your sister, and you need to know we're sleeping together.* They're right there, dancing in the space between our hotel beds, screaming at me in the silence that's descended on our conversation.

It's obvious Jack can tell something isn't right. The guy isn't an idiot.

Still, the early nights, the elusive behavior, and not hooking up with other women—all my actions are explainable with Abbie. Darcy doesn't want Jack to know all her private business. The problem is, she doesn't want him to know because she sees us as fun and nothing more.

My hand curls around my phone, growing frustration threatening to crush it.

"I-is everything okay, buddy?"

Jack's question breaks the spiraling thoughts, and I sit back, pushing my head into the plush headboard.

"I'm good. It's just been a series."

Grabbing his phone, Jack stands and rests a hand on my shoulder. "Tell me about it. I'm going to head out for a walk; I can't seem to shake the lactic acid buildup from last night." He squeezes his palm and smiles at me. "Also, it'll give you some time to call Abbie. I guess she'll be finished with school about now."

All I can do is smile back because telling Jack and breaking Darcy's confidence is not an option. She'd never forgive me, and I'd likely lose her forever.

When he throws on a jacket and steps out of the hotel room, I unlock my phone and bring up the text chat with Darcy. We haven't spoken today, and I know that's because she's at work.

I fucking miss her and hate even more that I don't know when we'll next meet up.

Sitting up on the bed, I curl my biceps and take a picture, sending it to her.

Doll: Was this supposed to impress me?

I burst out laughing.

> Me: Brat. Yes, it absolutely was.

Doll: The visual only winds me up. I like to feel it.

> Me: Funny you should say that since that's why I was texting. When can I see you again?

Doll: You're insatiable—you know that?

> Me: Yes. Tomorrow night? We land back from Boston at lunchtime.

Doll: No can do.

> Me: Girls' night?

Doll: Chess club.

Fuck me. This girl and her brains.

> Me: I have a confession.

Doll: Go on.

> Me: When you were sick, I snooped a little bit and found your sudoku book.

Doll: Oh, well, that would explain why it wasn't where I'd left it.

Doll: Did you try to solve one?

> Me: Bahaha! Baby, I got an F in math. I couldn't solve it, even with the answers you had written down.

Doll: Sudoku isn't centered around maths; it involves the application of logic and deduction. I can teach you sometime if you'd like.

> Me: Is that your kind of foreplay?

> Doll: Problem-solving is my favorite thing.

I huff a laugh out into the empty hotel room. I wonder if she'll be any good at fixing my broken heart when she shatters it into a million pieces.

> Me: Sure, if you've got the patience of a saint, then go ahead and teach me how it works.

> Doll: Okay, this is such fun! We can start at the beginner level and progress from there.

I don't need to ask her to send me a picture to know how big her excitable grin is right now.

> Me: How about I pick you up from chess club? Unless you think I'll cramp your style?

> Doll: And do what afterward?

> Me: I thought you were supposed to be smart …

> Doll: Fair point. Chess club is at Franklin Park and finishes at eight. Just stay in your car or something, and I'll meet you outside.

My fingers hover over the keyboard. I guess this can only go one of two ways …

> Me: What if I took you out for dinner?

> Doll: Are you kidding? You'll be recognized, and our cover will be blown.

> Me: I have that issue figured out.

> Me: Let me take you out. Spoil you a little.

It's five minutes, two anxious bathroom breaks, and one attempt to delete the message later when Darcy finally replies.

> Doll: You've got yourself a deal, Thigh Boy.

Don't dance in the hotel room, Archer.

> Me: Perfect. Stay pretty, A, x.

CHAPTER TWENTY

DARCY

The exhaustion I was feeling a little over a week ago has not improved at all, and neither have the headaches that started a few days back.

When I said yes to dinner with Archer, I really hoped I'd be feeling much better than I currently am.

I've dragged myself into work all week, and when Sienna unexpectedly asked me out for a cocktail two nights ago, I passed it up, not even wanting Chinese since the thought of food left me feeling wretched.

I'm sitting at the breakfast bar in my kitchen, thinking over what to do about tonight with Archer, when my phone starts vibrating next to me.

"Hey, Mum," I say when I answer, head dropped between my shoulders.

"Okay, you don't sound good. What's the matter?"

I switch the call to loudspeaker and lean forward, resting a cheek on my granite worktop. "I'm really not sure. All I know is, I feel like shit."

Mum blows a soft breath down the phone before speaking to

someone I assume to be Jon. "How long have you been feeling this way?"

"I guess since the infection."

"But you finished your course of antibiotics, right?"

"The whole ten days."

"Hmmm," she muses. "You should be feeling better by now. Maybe there's something low grade going on. Why don't you call the doctor?"

I groan; I hate going to the doctor. For starters, I have an irrational fear of needles, and you can bet they'll want to take blood. "I really don't want to."

"Yes, well, sometimes, we have to do things we don't want. Take me right now, for instance. I have Jon talking to me about the correct amount of time to heat pasta—from spaghetti to fusilli to lasagna. I don't particularly want to engage in said conversation, but I'm nodding along agreeably."

I snort a laugh when I hear Jon grumble something in the background. He's likely updating the menu at Luigi's, the Italian restaurant he jointly owns with his best friend and former Scorpions teammate, Zach Evans.

"Go to the doctor, Darcy."

"I have work." I try one more time to wriggle out of making an appointment.

"Call him and schedule something in. Tell the receptionist you've been feeling unwell for a while. Dr. Hughes will want to see you quickly. He's never let you, me, Jon, or your brother down when we need him."

"Okay," I relent. "I'll call him when I get to work. Or rather drag myself to work."

"Now, Darcy," Mum scolds me like I'm still ten years old. "And let me know what he says, please."

I pick up the phone and say my goodbyes, immediately scrolling to the contact I need, already feeling like this entire process is a complete waste of everyone's time.

"Miss Thompson, it's so great to see you. How are you doing?"

Ever the nice guy, Dr. Hughes—our family doctor—welcomes me with a warm smile.

I slump down on the blue sofa next to his desk, arguably feeling worse than when I spoke with Mum earlier.

"This is probably nothing," I say on a long sigh, "but I'm just not feeling myself."

A crease forms between his brows. "The receptionist passed on a few details, but can you be more specific?"

My gaze drops to the tiled white floor. I'm not even wearing my heels today, opting for black pumps since I don't have the energy to battle even the prettiest Pradas. "I just feel ... off. I'm exhausted all the time, I hate my favorite foods, I've got an incessant headache that won't go away. Plus, I've had some sharp shooting pains here ..." I circle the lower part of my abdomen. "I've felt like this since I recovered from the infection."

With a frown, Dr. Hughes spins toward his computer, checking a few details in my medical notes. "You aren't taking any other medication, and you haven't started taking any supplements I'm unaware of, correct?"

I shrug a single shoulder. "Nothing. Other than my oral contraceptive pill."

He nods a couple of times. "Yes, that matches my records."

He pauses for a second, eyes flicking back to me cautiously. "I'd like to run a few tests, if that's okay."

I know I look like a petulant teenager. "You're going to take blood, aren't you?"

He smiles knowingly, already aware of my phobia. "I'm not going to draw blood, but I do want to take a urine sample to check for infections." He spins on his chair, wheeling across to a cabinet.

Opening a drawer, he fetches out two sample pots, along with clear bags. "When you were unwell, did you vomit?"

I nod slowly, wondering where the hell he's going with this. "Yes, multiple times. I couldn't stop coughing, which made me retch. I think the antibiotics messed with my stomach, too, because let's just say, some days were not pretty in the bathroom ... if you know what I mean. It's never been like that with antibiotics before, but I guess bodies can react differently."

He wheels back across to his desk and marks up the containers with a pen. "Yes, you're right. And if you haven't had that particular antibiotic before, especially since you recently moved to the US, then that does track. To be clear though, Darcy, are we talking sickness and diarrhea?"

"Yes. Not pretty." I snort out a nervous laugh.

He presses his lips together in a thin line. "Can I ask, have you been sexually active in the past few weeks?"

I swallow thickly at the sudden change in conversation. I guess I have doctor-patient confidentiality. "I mean, sort of."

He pauses on writing. "Can you be more specific?"

I wince with no idea why. "I've recently started sleeping with someone. It's exclusive, and he's checked regularly since he's a hockey ..." I trail off. Dr. Hughes doesn't need the finer details.

"Well, that's good to know, but being totally honest with you, it's not only STIs I'm concerned about. Although we are testing for those too."

The headache I was nursing now pounds inside my skull. "Y-you think I might be pregnant, don't you?"

Dr. Hughes swipes a palm across his mouth, eyeing me carefully. "Were you taking your pill at the same time each day?"

"No—yes—I mean, I don't really know. I know they're gone from the packet. I just can't be sure I took them at the same time each day since I was in and out of sleep."

He pulls off his glasses and sets them on his desk. "And you were also experiencing vomiting and diarrhea too."

I don't need the doctor to finish as I drop my face into my palms. "I'm such an idiot," I mumble, cold realization hitting me like a tidal wave. "I barely had sex with my ex-boyfriend, and when we did, it was always with condoms. The pill was just a backup because I'm so scatterbrained." I throw out my hands, the bright surgery lighting stinging my eyes. "I've been so far up my ass and so carried away with life—what with moving across the Atlantic, my new job, everything," I ramble on, knowing none of this changes anything, only making me madder at myself for being so goddamn unreliable.

Not to mention the way I've been wrapped up in my fling with Archer.

Oh Jesus, Archer. He's the father.

"You can be a real fucking ditz sometimes, Darcy," I scold myself quietly, covering my face with my hands again.

"I think the best thing to do is get the test done and everything set out, and then we can go from there." Dr. Hughes confirms.

For saying I just found out I'm likely pregnant with Archer Moore's baby, I'm surprisingly calm. Only three times in the past two minutes have I nearly emptied my stomach onto the pristine floor beneath me.

Dr. Hughes rises from his chair, offering me a comforting smile. It does nothing to quell the rising panic I feel though.

"Why don't you complete both tests for me?"

Head spinning out, I stand from the sofa and take the sample tubes from him, hands shaking.

I turn on my heel and go to leave the room.

"Darcy?"

I stop at the soft way he says my name, emotions threatening to overwhelm me.

He smiles again, obviously worried that I'm going to lose my shit at any second. "Whatever the results, you always have options. And whatever you decide, you will have all the support you need. So, please try not to worry too much."

Five minutes later and with two full pee pots in hand, I push back into Dr. Hughes's office. With my heart beating out of my chest, I feel no calmer. And as I hand the samples over, I shake my head at myself and take a seat back on the dreaded sofa.

Walking both samples across to a side table, Dr. Hughes opens one container and begins the test, then the other and does the same. "Okay, let's see what we have."

I fidget with my hands, twisting them around in my lap, when my attention snags on the Saint Laurent tote by my feet. A small smile pulls at my lips, right as a tear hits my cheek.

This was all supposed to be for fun.

"Okay." Dr. Hughes retakes his seat and swivels toward me, hands clasped in his lap, wearing a smile I don't need a degree to interpret to know what's coming. "The first test confirms there aren't any infections."

He pauses, and for a second, I think he's going to reach out and take my hand.

I wish he would.

"The second test," he continues, "did come back as positive, and you are pregnant, Darcy."

A second tear runs a track down the opposite cheek and to the edge of my chin before falling onto my white blouse. I don't bother to wipe at my eyes. I'm too exhausted, too shocked to move. I can feel the throb of my pulse as it beats a fast rhythm in my ears, and I can see Dr. Hughes's mouth moving, but I can't hear any words.

"Are you okay?" This time, he does reach out and places a firm hand on my shoulder. "You look a little wobbly."

"I-I didn't hear anything you just said." I half laugh, although none of this is funny.

He smiles his usually warm smile. "That's okay. You have a lot to take in, and I know this has come as a shock to you."

I half laugh again.

Dr. Hughes stands and walks across to the water cooler, pouring a cup before handing it to me.

I take a couple of sips, the freezing ice water helping to steady my senses.

"Just over a week ago, I had three cocktails. I'm pretty sure I was pregnant then too."

"Try not to worry about that. Many women don't realize they are pregnant and have alcohol. I was going to ask if you could give me a firm date of conception."

I shake my head and put the cup down on the floor by my feet. "It could be one of multiple times. I mean, most likely, it was right after I got better." I think back to the intimate way Archer spooned me. "But I can't be a hundred percent sure."

"Well, we can never be one hundred percent because the pill isn't infallible, especially when not always taken at the same time each day."

"Right," I say, flushing. "Of course."

"With that in mind, we would calculate your gestation period based on the first day of your last period." He picks up a pen, hovering it over his notepad. "Can you tell me when that was?"

"September 8 ... I think," I reply.

Dr. Hughes makes a quick calculation. "Okay, well, given today is October 6, that puts you at four weeks, plus four days."

My eyes practically bug out of my head. "That works out at, like, mid-June, right?"

He nods. "It's a rough guide, but right now, your estimated due date is June 15. I'll be referring you to your OB-GYN now, and at eight weeks, you will be invited for your first scan, which will help pin down a more accurate timeline."

All I can do is stare out of the window situated behind my doctor. None of this feels real.

"Are you okay?" he asks me for a second time.

I brace both elbows on my knees, massaging my temples slowly. The pounding headache I was nursing is now kicking into a full-blown migraine. "I don't know what to think."

He sets his pen down and mirrors my position, ducking his head slightly to capture my wandering attention. "I'm going to conclude a pregnancy is not something you personally had in mind at this stage in your life."

I blow out a harsh breath, picking up my water and taking a sip. "No, it most definitely was not."

"Okay." He nods. "Before you took the tests, I told you there are always options available. I think one of the first questions you need to ask is, do you want to keep the pregnancy? Because whichever route you choose, we will be able to support you. This is your body and your decision, Darcy."

"I had my whole entire life set out in front of me." Another tear trickles down my cheek, and this time, I swipe it away angrily.

I'm angry at myself for being so careless. That said, the efficacy of my pill was not at the front of my mind when I was throwing up and racing to the bathroom. And I'm angry on Archer's behalf because I know this isn't what he would want either. He asked me if we should use condoms, but I declined.

"I need to think it over." I gulp down the rest of my water, and the doctor takes my empty cup from me, throwing it into the bin next to him. "I need to talk to the dad."

He rolls his lips together. "And just to clarify, there can only be one father?"

"Yes," I whisper. "We were hooking up in secret since he's my brother's teammate and best friend."

I don't miss the raised brow before Dr. Hughes quickly resets his professional demeanor.

"I'm going to send your details across to the OB-GYN and

some pregnancy information directly to your email. Were you on your way to work?"

"Yes," I repeat.

"Well, my best advice is to take the day off and use this time to think over everything we've discussed. Reach out to your family or a friend you can confide in. The symptoms you are experiencing are perfectly normal for this stage in pregnancy, but if you start to experience any symptoms listed on the information I send to you, then I'd ask you to contact your OB-GYN or head to your nearest emergency room."

I nod once, now completely speechless.

"Are you going to be okay, getting home?" he asks softly.

"I got an Uber here. I can get one home."

"All right." He picks up my bag, and I take it from him, simultaneously wanting to clutch the damn thing to my chest and toss it out the nearest window.

"Think everything over for me, Darcy," Dr. Hughes says just as I reach his office door.

I tip my head over my shoulder, looking back at him. The Darcy that walked into this room earlier feels so far removed from the one leaving right now.

Everything has changed. *Forever.*

"I will," I reply, voice thick with emotion. "Thank you for your help."

CHAPTER TWENTY-ONE

ARCHER

Tonight is one thousand percent a date.

I'm wearing my favorite gray button-down shirt and black dress pants, and I made sure to apply what I know is her favorite cologne—the spicy one Darcy inhales whenever she's near me.

And I want her close to me all the fucking time. Twenty-four/seven.

When people start filtering out from the address for the chess club Darcy gave me last night, excitement thrums through me as I wait to catch a glimpse of the girl I haven't seen in nearly a week.

Away series used to be one of my favorite times, but not anymore. Now I'm in the same camp as most of my teammates —wishing time away so I can get back to my girl in Brooklyn. I can't get enough of her smile, bright clothes, and addictive personality. She bleeds into me like osmosis, and I soak every last drop of her up, hungry and desperate and never feeling fully satisfied.

Life before Darcy Thompson is a blur to me. I've got the images in my phone to prove I was alive back then, that my lungs were working and my heart was beating. Only I wasn't really living; I was existing, waiting for Darcy to walk into my life and give me purpose aside from securing shutouts on the ice. That isn't the kind of feeling you can let go of. Even if I wanted to forget about her, I'm not sure it would be possible. I feel grounded when I'm around her, locked in on whatever she's saying, eager to know what she's thinking and will say next.

Perhaps my initial fascination was sparked because she didn't fall at my feet like other women had, and I saw it as a challenge. But whatever it was that drew me in, there's no going back now.

On the flight home, I found myself researching sudoku so I could sit on the couch and play alongside her in the evenings. That's how far removed I feel from my previous life, and I'm not mad about it at all. Not one bit.

Every time she swoons at my thigh tattoo, I get a hit that feeds my addiction to her. Not because she runs her soft palm over it each time we're naked together, more because it reminds me that despite the ink serving as evidence of the passion I hold for hockey, nothing is as profound as the feelings I have for her. Darcy Thompson is the deepest tattoo I've ever gotten; she just can't see it yet.

The ringtone I set for my mom spears through my daydream, and I hit Accept on the car steering wheel, automatically connecting the call to Bluetooth. It's been a couple of weeks since I last spoke to her, which is the typical amount of time we go. However, with my parents' divorce recently being finalized, I've been trying to check in a bit more often since she's taken the split worse than Dad.

"Hey," I say in my softest voice, eyes still pinned on the doors I expect Darcy to walk through at any second.

"Hi, sweetheart."

I can tell she's been upset. Mom and Dad freely admit that going their separate ways was the right thing, but I think the reality of what that looks like is finally hitting Mom, especially since Dad has already moved on with someone else.

My heart drops an inch in my chest. She's a good mom and a kind person, and she deserves to live a happy life.

"I'm sorry I haven't driven over more often to see you. Preseason has been crazy, and the regular season starts tomorrow, but—"

"It's fine, Archer. Honestly. You're living your life, and I get it." Mom blows a soft breath down the phone. "I should come and watch one of your afternoon games, and maybe we can go out for dinner afterward."

I smile at that. I love spending time with Mom. "Yeah, why not? One of our first games is against the Scorpions." I chuckle right as Darcy emerges, and my entire body trips out.

Fuck. How can someone make tight blue jeans, an oversize pink sweater, and a casual braid look so stunning?

"Would you be able to do that for me?"

"Hmm?" I reply to Mom, reentering the conversation.

She huffs out a soft laugh. "Are you even listening to me?"

"Yeah," I say right as a dude who has to be at least ten years older than Darcy steps up behind her. He must be another member of the chess club.

Rage builds when he sets a hand on her shoulder, and she spins around to face him.

"Want to talk about whatever's going on?" Mom asks.

How is it that from two hours down the road and with no hint whatsoever, my mom just knows when something's up?

I tear my eyes away from Darcy and stare out of the windshield. "It's nothing."

"Who is she?"

A single burst of laughter leaves me. "Should I even bother to ask how you guessed it had to do with a girl?"

Mom releases a long sigh. "Archer, sweetheart, I carried you for nine months and birthed you and your sister into this world. I know what my lovesick son sounds like, even if he's never had a girlfriend before." I hear her shift, probably her getting more comfortable. "Now, spill."

On another laugh that eases the tightness in my chest, I shake my head. "Yeah, it's a girl. Although I can't talk about it right now, because I'm picking her up."

"I see. Are you dating?" Her voice takes on a breezy tone, sounding like she's excited on my behalf.

I don't want to be the one to let her down and tell her the truth that all we are is fuck buddies. I might be good at fooling myself into believing this is a date, but I'm not about to lie to my mom. I've spread enough bullshit lately.

As Darcy continues talking with the random guy, who I want to punch square in the face for even looking at her, I focus back on my call with Mom.

"Not exactly." I wince, pushing my head back into the rest. "It's more like I want to get serious, but I'm pretty sure she doesn't share the same feelings." I close my eyes, rolling my tongue across the roof of my mouth. "So, I'm doing what any down-bad guy would do, and I'm chasing her like a fucking idiot."

She chuckles softly. I'm happy my misery can bring her some relief. "And you don't think you've broken a few hearts along the way? The other day, I opened a magazine while I was waiting for my pedicure to set, and there, across two pages, was a picture of my son on a night out with two beautiful girls, one hanging off each arm. The title of the article read, 'Shots Fired: The NHL's Leading Goal Scorer Off the Ice.' "

Despite myself, I can't suppress a smile as it tugs at my lips. "What did the article say?"

"I don't know," she quickly answers. "I immediately closed the magazine and moved to *Horse & Hound*. Do you know I can barely surf the web or open any kind of article without seeing a supermodel wrapped around you?"

"Was this supposed to make me feel better?" I drop my head between my shoulders.

Mom clears her throat. "Sorry, sweetheart. The article was at least eighteen months old, if that helps."

My gaze finds Darcy as she finishes up talking and scans the street for my car.

I flash my lights to capture her attention.

"Yeah, well, any images or posts you find are all recycled from a while back. I haven't played around in a long time. Everything that's been printed recently is purely speculation. I only need to look in a girl's direction on a night out, and the media automatically concludes I'm banging her."

Mom releases a low groan.

"Sorry," I reply. "Probably too much information?"

"Just a touch," she confirms. "Am I to assume you've quit messing around because of this girl?"

I hum my confirmation.

Mom's breezy tone immediately makes a reappearance. "I like this mystery girl already. You know all I've ever wanted for my only boy is for him to fall in love and settle down. You can't play around forever, Archer."

In the past, I'd have rolled my eyes in response, but now I'm nodding along in agreement. She's right; it is what I want.

"I gotta go, Mom. Just keep this all close to the vest, okay? It's complicated, and I'll explain why another time," I rush out when Darcy starts crossing the road, walking toward my car.

"Okay, sweetheart."

"I'll get you tickets to a game, and we can do dinner afterward."

"Yes, that's what I was asking when you zoned out on me earlier. Anyway, let me leave you to your girl. Love you. Bye."

Mom disconnects the call just as I unlock my door and Darcy climbs in.

If I wasn't sitting down, I'd be bouncing on the balls of my feet over the chance to take my girl out and spoil her.

"Hey, Doll," I greet her, leaning over the center section and planting a soft kiss against her collarbone, her oversize sweater granting my lips the access they need.

Her skin reacts, pebbling with excitement. Except Darcy's

face doesn't hold the same enthusiasm. Her usually bright and sparkling blue eyes shine, but with a gloss I never want to see again.

Worried as hell, I cup the right side of her face in my palm. She doesn't look away, although I can tell she wants to.

"Talk to me, Darcy," I say, coaxing her to explain what the fuck has got her feeling this way. I nod my head toward where she was talking to the guy a few minutes earlier. "Was it him? Did he say something to hurt you?"

A single tear falls from her left eye, and, fuck, I'm going to murder the son of a bitch.

I'm opening my driver's door before she can say anything, ready to hunt the fucker down and bury him.

Chess-playing prick.

"Wait, no." Her warm palm wraps around my shirtsleeve, sending a shot of comfort through my veins.

I turn back to my girl, reaching out to wipe a second tear with my thumb. "I need you to talk to me, because I'm around ten seconds away from committing a felony."

Her head shakes, followed by her shoulders, and I slide my chair back. Next, I wrap an arm around her waist, asking her to straddle me.

"Come here and tell me what's going on. No one can see us through my tinted windows."

On a final sniffle, she clears her throat, trying to get herself in check.

As she climbs into my lap, my fingers find the end of her braid, playing with her soft hair.

"I've told you before, but I'll tell you a million more times: you don't need to hide your feelings from me, Darcy. It's an honor to witness every part of you, even if I hate seeing you this way."

A wry smile pulls at the corner of her mouth, and it alleviates the pain tearing through me on her behalf, just for a moment. I've seen Darcy deflated before, but never like this. She's always been the girl lighting up a room, pulling grins and laughter from everyone else.

She exhales softly. "I don't even know where to begin." She rubs at her temple. "I'm sorry. I have the worst headache."

"Are you sick again? Baby, this can't be normal."

She shakes her head again. "No, no. Well, not exactly."

Instantly, my hands frame her face, and I can't hide the panic as it rises, acidity burning my throat. "Darcy, what the fuck?!"

Her watery eyes soften in response as she senses my distress, and she covers my hands with hers.

My shoulders drop, and I rest my forehead against her sternum. The rhythmic beat of her heart calms my erratic pulse. Even though my real feelings are on display, I'm powerless to hide them as worry races through me, along with the foreign feeling of rejection.

She's going to tell me that she can't hook up anymore.

Darcy shudders out a breath. "Archer ... I ..."

I lift my gaze to look up at her as she hovers over me. This girl is effortless, yet the hold she has on me is vise strong.

"If you aren't sick, then are you trying to tell me you want to stop?" I whisper. "Do you want this to be over?" I never thought words could taste so rancid.

She drops her hands, twisting them in her lap. I keep mine on either side of her face. Waiting, hoping, praying.

"Archer." She tries to speak again, and suddenly, I'm not so sure this is about me and her or our arrangement.

The knot forming in my stomach contorts further.

"I'm ..." The tears start to flow more freely down her cheeks. "I need you to know I haven't told a soul about this, and I wasn't planning to tell you tonight. But since I can't seem to control my emotions"—she puffs out a disbelieving breath—"or my hormones ..." She chews on the inside of her cheek, brows creased together as she examines my face for a beat.

"I'm pregnant, Archer."

The silence surrounding us is deafening.

Darcy's last two words play on repeat in my brain. *"I'm pregnant."*

I drop my eyes to her flat stomach. "Y-you're ..."

She nods, taking my hand in one of hers. Pulling it into her lap, she interlaces our fingers. "I'm just over four weeks pregnant."

I do the math. I know zero about gestational periods, but that timeline stacks up ... to be mine.

Darcy cocks her head to one side, studying me. "Why are you smiling?"

I roll my lips together. "I didn't even realize I was," I say, reaching up and brushing my mouth over her tear-soaked lips. "But I guess my subconscious tracks because, wow. Incredible. Tell me you're having *my* baby. Say the words and make my fucking life."

CHAPTER TWENTY-TWO

DARCY

Wait.

Did I just hear that right?

I shake my head, convinced the hallucinations are back. Or maybe I'm just going mad because with the day I've had, anything is possible.

"I'm sorry. You're going to have to say what you just said again because I think I heard you—"

"Tell me you're having my baby." Archer smooths his smiling lips across mine. "I can say it again if you need."

I pull back, still straddling his lap. The ambient lighting in his Mercedes glows on his face, high cheekbones drenched in light blue.

God, he's so beautiful.

"We've been exclusive, haven't we?" he continues, an ounce of worry creeping into his features when I don't speak straightaway.

"We have. It can only be yours. I haven't slept with anyone else since Liam, and that was a long time ago." I immediately reply, never more certain of anything in my life.

I'm ready to launch into a long explanation about how the

timeline stacks up for the baby to be his when a large palm wraps around the back of my head, bringing our mouths closer.

He pauses for a second, the faint noise of traffic passing between us while he studies my face. I'm not sure what for, but it's intense, and I feel the weight of his emotion as it settles inside me.

Perhaps he can sense my worry. After all, this isn't what either of us planned or even wanted.

Is it?

"I want you to know something, Darcy."

My eyes blur. I can tell by whatever he's about to say that this isn't easy for him, but he's the kind of person—a kind of man I never thought him to be—who would do and sacrifice anything for the people he cares about the most.

"I want you to know," he repeats, voice heavy and thick, "that this is the best fucking news of my life. Nothing compares to this moment." He takes one of my palms and rests it in the center of his chest. Through his shirt, I can feel the fast and heavy beat of his heart. "Not when I got drafted, not when I made my NHL debut. The only moment in my life when my heart has raced this fast was when I first laid eyes on you and then when I finally got the chance to carry you to my bed."

"But ..." I look around the car. It feels like I'm having an out-of-body experience. None of this can be real. At some point, I'm going to wake up, *in my bed*, and realize this was all one crazy dream.

"But what, Darcy?" Archer coaxes, only care in his voice and steady eye contact as he starts twisting my braid around his finger. "Tell me what's going on."

"But you don't want any of this. With me, with anyone." My own heart races as the little composure I had remaining unravels before him. "You've never had a girlfriend before, and I just told you I'm having your baby. Do you know how huge that is?"

Maybe he's just as delusional as me.

"I heard everything you said." Archer's voice is as even as the ice he plays on. "And I'm not scared."

The second those words leave his mouth, I see a flicker of unease, and he shifts his weight beneath me.

"Do you want this, with me?" he asks.

I drop my face into his chest, my entire body deflating against him. "I can't even think straight anymore. I came to chess club tonight because I got back from the doctor's office and I didn't know what to do or where to put myself. I needed to distract my mind. The only place I could think to go was here. In the end, I just stared at the chessboard and ended up withdrawing from the tournament. I wanted to call you and cancel tonight because I didn't even know how I was going to look at you."

A shudder racks through me. "This was all supposed to be fun. I wanted to have a good time with you, and I know that's all you wanted with me too." I inhale a deep breath, laughing at the mess we're in. My emotions are all over the place. "And here I was, telling you not to use a condom because I was on birth control even though I apparently couldn't take it correctly or account for when I was sick and—"

"None of this has ever been just fun to me, Darcy."

I stop dead when he cuts through my ramble.

Archer interlaces our fingers, bringing our joined hands from his heart to his mouth, where he kisses the center of my palm.

"This—me telling you what I'm about to say—was inevitable. I guess the timeline has just been brought forward because you're carrying my baby."

He smiles proudly, and I drop my gaze from his, feeling the opposite of pride and more anger at my own stupidity when it comes to contraception.

"Show me your eyes, Doll."

I hesitate, and he props a finger under my chin, asking me to look at him without words.

I do as he asks.

"Good girl. Now, I need to know how much more you can deal with today."

I laugh at the thought of me having anything left in my emotional reserves. Despite how drained my body and mind are, curiosity wins out. I need to know what Archer has been hiding. I felt something was off when I more than likely fell pregnant that time he visited my apartment and I asked him to take me to bed.

"I can handle whatever you have to say," I reply.

He raises a single brow, bottom lip pinned between his teeth. He looks really unsure, more uncertain than when I told him he was going to be a dad.

"Do you want more than just a fuck-buddy arrangement?" I whisper.

I could be well off the mark, but I don't think I am, and I hate to see him torn up like this.

He shakes his head, and just like the time at my party when Jack announced that Archer had a girlfriend, my stomach drops. Disappointment flooding my insides.

"No, Darcy. I don't want more than a fuck-buddy arrangement with you."

I swallow so hard that I can practically hear it.

"I want it *all* with you."

My mouth runs dry, my words completely stolen.

The hand not laced through mine finds my lower abdomen, his warm palm offering some light relief to the bloating and discomfort I've been experiencing.

"I want it all," he reiterates. "Our baby, this life, with you. The truth is, I wanted it before I got you pregnant, and now that you are? I'm going to take everything you can give me with both hands and never let it go."

His blue eyes shine brighter beneath the car lighting as he looks at me with awe. "Some might say I've been an idiot to continue sleeping with you when you've made it repeatedly clear what we are. The thing is though, I haven't had a choice. I've been trying to stay away for longer than I can remember, and all the while, I've been falling deeper for you."

A single puff of laughter leaves his chest as his hand dips underneath my top, palming my bare stomach. His thumb rubs slow circles that fire off delicious tingles.

"I think, deep down, you know I'm all in with you. Each time we're together, the mask that I fixed in place when I first met you slips further. You're right when you say I haven't ever had a girlfriend, but that doesn't mean I can't develop feelings for a girl who literally won't leave my head. It's been this way for a long time, Darcy. Only now, I feel compelled to tell you my truth. You need to know where my head is at, and, goddammit ..." He squeezes his eyes shut, dark lashes resting against his cheeks before he opens them again. "I need to know where you are with me because either I'm going fucking crazy or you feel something for me too."

He leans into me, lips ghosting my ear. "I'd tear down entire cities and whole-ass countries to keep you and our baby safe. So, just know, if you're thinking about running away, I'm going to chase you. Anywhere, everywhere. Forever."

"I literally don't even know what to say." My entire body trembles. "Maybe I wasn't ready to hear all that."

Stress pulls at his face as he releases my hand, wrapping an arm around my waist. "I knew it would be a lot for you, but like I said, voicing it was inevitable."

As my tears reemerge, Archer wipes them from my cheek.

"I genuinely thought I'd be sitting in that passenger seat"—I motion toward the empty chair next to us—"trying to figure out how I'd cope as a single mum. I thought you were going to lose your mind and tell me you couldn't do this. Instead, you've not only told me you're in this, but it's the best news of your life and ... and ..." I sniffle again. My whole body weighed down with intense exhaustion. "That you have feelings for me?"

Archer cocks his head to the side, the crease between his

brow much deeper than before. "Do you remember when I told you over text that you have a lot to learn about me?"

I shrug a shoulder and nod at the same time. "Yeah, I do."

"Well, consider this lesson number one in Archer Moore. If you'd like, we can even name the class." He taps his chin in thought, eyes growing wide.

I automatically chuckle.

"Lesson One: How to Figure Out When the Former NHL Fuckboy Is Actually into Only One Girl." He reaches up, planting a kiss on my forehead. "I'm down bad, Darcy. And I'm not going anywhere. Especially not now."

CHAPTER TWENTY-THREE

ARCHER

We didn't make it to the restaurant.

Instead, we switched up the seafood for Taco Bell. Cheesy bean and rice burritos were all my girl could think about, repeating her need for them as I drove us to the nearest drive-through.

After she inhaled three—the first in less than four bites—she asked me to take her home. But that was where the compromises stopped for me. I might've missed out on my unofficial date with her, but I wasn't about to let her sleep anywhere else but in my bed.

And that's where she passed out, straight after I carried her in my arms from the elevator to my bedroom, helping her exhausted body get undressed. I didn't miss it when she said she hadn't planned on telling me about the pregnancy right away, but, fuck me, am I relieved she did. By the time I pulled the duvet over her body and grabbed her toothbrush—yes, I'd made sure she would have everything she needed when she stayed over at my place—Darcy was fully asleep, her soft snorts filling my bedroom.

It's amazing how the presence of one person—no, two people—can turn an otherwise empty and cold penthouse into the home you never knew you were searching for.

When I wrapped myself around her warm body, resting my splayed palm against her lower belly, I felt her melt into me, a gentle sigh leaving her lips.

We haven't had much chance to talk, and it's fucking killing me to know what's going through her head right now as I drive the short journey to the practice rink for morning skate. All I have to keep her from leaving is the hope that she'll sleep through until I get home, along with a note I left on the nightstand, confirming I'll be back as soon as I can.

Did I consider skipping skate in favor of staying curled around her warm, pregnant body, waiting until she woke up so I could repeat the same assurances I had given her last night in my car? Best fucking believe I did.

When Darcy had told me she expected to be figuring out life as a single mom the moment she broke the news to me, the only comfort I could find in her words was the realization that she was planning to keep the pregnancy. Ultimately, this is her body and decision, but I want our child in the same way that I'm desperate to have this girl in my life. Permanently. Irrevocably. There isn't a flicker of doubt in my mind that her birth control not working for whatever reason was the greatest failure in the history of forever. Because now ... now I get my shot to prove how goddamn serious I am about her.

As I pull into the rink parking lot, I turn the volume down on Aerosmith's "Don't Want to Miss a Thing" and flash my ID at the security guard.

But the second I round the corner and see Jack's black truck parked next to Sawyer's, I'm hit with the heavy thud of reality. It's not lost on me that the fuck-buddy arrangement I had with Darcy has morphed from risky to a full-blown atomic bomb, waiting to blow one half of my life to pieces in the wake of the other half finally gaining some traction.

Jack Morgan is going to fucking murder me.

At one time, when we were joking around about my crush on his baby sister—well, pretending we were joking—he told me if I touched her, he'd put my balls in a vise. And I knew he meant every fucking word.

I put my Mercedes into park and check my cell for messages from Darcy—none.

When he finds out I've not only been fucking his sister, but now have her knocked up and that she has a newfound addiction to Taco Bell, I'm pretty certain my balls and their fate will be the least of my worries. Because let's not forget that the girl lying in my bed, carrying my baby, is also, for all intents and purposes, my coach's stepdaughter.

You. Could. Not. Write. This. Shit.

Unless you're Archer Moore and you have a habit of getting yourself into binds with women you can't resist.

A knock on my car roof interrupts thoughts of which method Jack and Coach will use to castrate me, and I peer out of my driver's window to find my captain waiting. With one hand in the pocket of his gray sweats, he motions for me to get moving since I'm already pushing time, and if there's one thing that pisses Coach off, it's delinquency.

Although right now, I might hazard a guess at something else that could really fuck up his day.

I lower my window, offering an easy smile. "Fucking roads, man."

He lifts a brow. "At six a.m.? Did you detour via London?"

Opening my driver's door, I step out as Sawyer backs away, and I head for the trunk, pulling out my gear. "You're getting cocky these days—you know that?" I tell him, closing the lid and locking my car.

He smirks but doesn't respond, knowing I'm not far from the truth.

Turning toward the building, we both head for the entrance, the automatic doors opening as we step into the reception area.

Sawyer grabs two towels from the dispenser and throws one to me. I catch it against my chest right as one of the physiotherapists pushes through the swing doors.

Fuck.

Amelia—if I remember her name correctly—throws me a sweet smile, tucking a piece of blonde hair behind her ear as she heads for the water cooler.

"You hooked up with her, didn't you?" Sawyer whispers beneath his breath, tipping his head toward Amelia as she stands with her back to us.

I swipe a hand through my hair, but really, all I want to do is pull it out at the roots. It was years ago, and we weren't breaking any rules since Amelia worked for the leisure facility attached to the training rink and not for the team itself. We got into it on her massage table, and I regret fucking around, even if it was before Darcy.

He chuckles; not judging or berating me, but my frustration grows all the same.

"I'll take your silence as my answer," Sawyer says as we walk through the doors toward the locker room.

I pull up in the empty hallway, and my friend grinds to a halt alongside me.

There's so much I could say, and in so many ways, I want to tell him.

"What is it?" he asks, speaking before I can find the right words.

I know I can trust him with anything, even something as big as Darcy's pregnancy. But I know it's not what my girl would want. Hell, I don't even know *what* she wants at this point. This is why I shouldn't be here but back home instead, in our bed, giving her everything and anything she needs.

Pulling my cell out of my pocket, I check again for messages. Still none. Hopefully, she's sleeping and not freaking the fuck out over last night.

A hand lands on my shoulder, and I look up at my captain.

"That night, at the meal for the GMs, you left with Darcy, didn't you?"

My eyes dart around the still-empty hallway. "I don't think this is the best time."

He puffs out a despondent breath, and I meet his green eyes. My cocky friend has disappeared. Now only my captain stares back at me.

"No." I lie on Darcy's behalf.

He releases another despondent breath. "Am I going to need to pry this from you as your captain and the guy who has a responsibility to look out for team dynamics, or are you going to wise up and offer me the truth?"

I look off to the side as my fist tightens around the strap of my bag. "I left with her."

As much as I don't want to see it, I center my attention back on his face, checking for a reaction.

He just nods, dropping his head to the floor as he scuffs it lightly with his sneaker. "Jesus, Archer. I hope you know what you're doing."

I have no fucking idea.

"I do," I reply confidently. "And it was the best night of my life." Other than admitting I left with Darcy, it's the first truth I've told him during this conversation. It feels good.

Sawyer's eyes soften, and he opens his mouth to say something right as the locker room door swings inward.

Coach Morgan stands in the threshold, Blades cap pulled low and a folder tucked under his arm. He looks between us both, confused. "Sorry, did I just interrupt a women's weekly meeting, or are we actually planning on doing some work around here?"

A couple of snorts sound from behind him.

I thumb toward my captain, my mask of the expected Archer Moore slipping back into place with ease. "Cap forgot his cup and asked me if he could borrow one. Turns out, they're all way too big."

Coach and Sawyer simply roll their eyes, and just like that, it's as if the previous five minutes never happened.

"Okay, well, now that you've both finished literally dicking around ..." Coach begins as we step into the room, and I make straight for the usual bench, dumping my gear down. "I'm glad I have your attention since I've got a new member of the team to introduce."

I turn on my heel. Fuck. With everything swimming around my head, I totally forgot today was the day.

"We're honored to have him working with us on a temporary coaching contract. He's a good friend of mine, and with his skills and knowledge, I'm confident we can expect great things this season."

Rising from the bench next to Jack, Jensen Jones comes to stand beside Coach Morgan.

The room falls silent as he tucks his hands into the pockets of his gray sweats and scans the room, acknowledging each player before finally landing on me.

"Thanks for having me," he says, clearing his throat. "Jon—Coach Morgan," he corrects himself, "has told me nothing but good stuff about each and every one of you. The plan is for me to work with the team over the next couple of months, but perhaps longer. I'll be here in a mentor capacity, although mainly working with Moore." He looks at me again and then my training bag. He's probably wondering why I'm not already padded up.

Because I'm having a mild breakdown over my personal life.

"I'm looking forward to working closely with you and helping achieve your goals this season—"

"Which is lifting the Cup," Coach finishes Jensen's sentence for him. "Okay"—he points at the clock above the exit leading to the rink—"I want everyone ready and out on the ice in the next five minutes."

As Coach leaves the room, Jensen looks like he wants to say

something directly to me, but then pauses, swiping a hand across his mouth. I catch a flash of his platinum wedding band.

I vaguely remember reading an article about his wife and the circumstances in which they got together. Allegedly, she got pregnant unexpectedly with twins, and then he made some kind of grand gesture in a TV interview about them getting married someday.

He walks over to me, a warm smile on his face. "Nice to finally meet you beyond a handshake and a few awkward stares from the crease," he says with humor in his voice.

I hold out my hand, and he takes it, offering me the eye contact he never did at games. He was the ultimate professional during his career, but that's where the pleasantries ended.

"Looking forward to working with you. As you're aware, Jon has employed me in a coaching capacity, but we can shape that in any way that will work best for you. I'm here to give you pointers on the ice, off the ice, as part of game prep or postgame analysis. Whatever you want. As much as we are a part of the team, goalies are a different breed, and this job can be lonely as fuck sometimes. It's a whole different perspective from the blue line, and at times, it feels like we'll never be understood."

I swipe a hand across my mouth, eyes flicking to Jack as he passes by, wearing a grin.

"Yeah," I say, already liking this guy way more than I thought I would. "Ain't that the whole damn truth?"

CHAPTER TWENTY-FOUR

DARCY

Sunlight pours into the bedroom, and I immediately know it isn't my own, drenching me in a warm October sun.

I snap an eye open, the other side of my face still buried in Archer's soft white pillows. I always sleep well in his bed, and last night was no exception, despite feeling like utter crap. Aside from dropping the Hiroshima bomb on him and stuffing my face with Taco Bell, all I can recall is Archer carrying me to his bed, where I promptly passed out.

And, *my God*, could I stay here all day. This mattress is a cloud. I mean, I've never actually felt or slept on a cloud, and if I did, I'd obviously fall to my death since they aren't really—

A loud beeping sounds from behind me, and I forcibly roll over, reaching for the bedside table.

Shit.

Holy fucking shit. I have work in thirty minutes.

I snatch my phone up from the charging pad, muting the alarm as I sit up in bed, eyes scanning my upper half.

Wait.

I push back the duvet to reveal lacy white bottoms that match a silky top. *Where did this sleepwear come from?*

Swinging my legs out of the bed, the heated floor quells my panic as it warms the soles of my feet. I know I'm going to be late for work.

I look around Archer's luxury bedroom. He must be reeling over what I told him. To be honest, I wouldn't have been shocked if he'd packed his bags and left the country, fleeing the crazy parental reality we're both faced with.

But when my eyes land on a note scrawled in his handwriting, memories of the way he reacted to my news cling to my skin as softly as the silky sleepwear I know he bought me.

All he did was reveal something of his own—the depths of his feelings.

Jesus. After yesterday, *I* should be the one boarding a flight out of the country. Except I didn't run or balk or feel any semblance of fear. All I felt was a repeat of the warmth and comfort that'd grown to be familiar in his presence.

I fall asleep so easily in his bed because he makes me feel safe. I don't hold back or feel like I'm overbearing or too much when I'm around him because he makes me feel seen. Why would I want to run away from that?

I stand from the bed and stretch my arms above my head, the Brooklyn Bridge just in the distance through Archer's floor-to-ceiling windows. The headache from last night is still present, but the throbbing has at least subsided, and I pad towards his en suite.

I'm a few feet across his bedroom when Archer steps into view, leaning against the doorframe. Keeping his eyes on me, he dips a hand into the pocket of his black sweatpants, tossing his mobile phone and keys onto a plush chair just inside the door.

"I'm going to conclude you didn't see my note and not that you read it, but still chose to get up and ignore it."

He reaches behind him, pulling his Blades hoodie overhead,

and I catch a flash of toned abs as his T-shirt rides up with the action.

I can't help it. Regardless of my current condition, my mouth waters. Truthfully, I think I could be placed into a medically induced coma, and this man could still elicit the same response from my body.

He flashes me a quick smile, pushing off the frame and heading towards me. I know my thoughts are transparent. I've always worn my heart on my sleeve, and oftentimes, it's gotten me into trouble, especially with my ex-boyfriend.

He wraps a large palm around my hip, pressing my body into his. *More trouble ahead.*

"How do the pj's feel?"

Heat from his touch penetrates the soft, thin material.

"Let me guess … another one of your purchases?"

He leans forward, pushing a piece of matted hair away from my ear. "Want to know something else I bought you?"

I can feel the goose bumps as they flare across my body. "I have a feeling you're going to tell me anyway," I jest, totally wanting to know.

His other hand finds my hip as he kisses just below my ear. I know this exchange is way more intimate than a fuck-buddy arrangement. Our dynamic has shifted, and Archer is driving us, with me as a willing passenger.

"You might've been sick with an infection, but you weren't suffering from hallucinations. The security system your landlord fitted"—Archer pulls back, shaking his head with a proud expression—"you didn't ask for it. I did." His attention rests on my stomach. "Back then, I was protecting the girl of my dreams, and now I'm protecting my family."

"You're so intense," I reply, my throat thick, voice hoarse.

He just smiles, one that creases the corners of his eyes. "I know." A hand dips under the hem of my top, coming to rest against my flat stomach. "I could ask if my intensity is okay with you, although I won't waste my breath or yours with an answer." He pins me in place with his stare. "This is how it is for me, Darcy. You, me, and our baby. It's really that simple." He chews on the corner of his bottom lip. "Oh, and trying to stay alive when we eventually break it to your brother."

The calm bubble I was in bursts, unease trickling through my veins. Of course I knew my family would find out I was pregnant —it's inevitable. But in the overwhelm that was yesterday, I didn't get to the part where I considered Jack finding out or his reaction.

"I don't want to tell him. Not yet anyway."

Archer cocks his head to the side, a mix of relief and worry etched across his face.

"It's common knowledge that pregnancies are at their highest risk during the first twelve weeks, and I'm not going to spill my business to everyone apart from those I want to know." I shrug, a growing sense of conviction in my decision. "Maybe not even until I start to show. It's our choice who we tell, and it's my body to divulge news about."

Archer nods lightly, drawing gentle circles against my stomach with the pad of his thumb. I'm not completely sure the action is conscious.

"I know I laid all my cards on the table for you last night, and when I drove here from practice, it was my intention to ask you if you had made a decision about keeping the baby. I think I've already figured out what you want, but you always have options, Darcy. I just want y—"

"I'm keeping the baby," I confirm without a single falter. "I know I have options, but I genuinely can't see a situation where terminating the pregnancy is the right route for me. I don't even need to think about it, but I do want to keep my business private."

Relief doesn't just fill Archer's face; it takes ahold of his entire body as every muscle visibly relaxes. He doesn't need to say anything for me to know how much my decision means to him.

"Holding on to secrets or being liberal with the truth isn't my strong suit, Doll. But you're my priority. You and this baby. That said, when we eventually tell my mom, she'll likely lose her shit. In the good way," he clarifies.

I snuggle into his cotton shirt, Archer's freshly showered cologne delectable. "Is she nice?"

He hums softly. "Yeah, family is everything to her." A light chuckle rumbles in his chest. "And I'm beginning to understand why she feels that way."

Instinctively, my arms wrap around his waist, and he loops his around mine, resting his chin on top of my head.

"Starting a family, was it something you wanted someday?" I quietly ask. "It was for me, even though I couldn't picture a time when it would happen."

As he inhales a deep breath, I cuddle further into Archer's chest.

"Honestly? Not for the majority of my adult life. I guess I didn't see settling down with a family, however that looked, as a barometer for my success. It's always been about hockey and records and ..." He pauses for a second. "Maybe I feel ashamed to admit it but ... how desirable I was to women." He releases a puff of air into the room. "Yep, out loud that sounded about as shallow as it had in my head."

Pulling away from his chest, I peer up at him as he watches me carefully, searching for my reaction.

I don't have one to give him, other than my respect for how honest he's being with me. If Jack and Jon deduce that this man is a deceitful arsehole, then they're wrong. All I see is someone trying to do the best they can to go after what they want under difficult circumstances. And the more I think about Archer's predicament, the more I can relate to it.

"In that case, I find you even more amazing."

His arms tighten around my waist. "How so?"

I've concluded I'm going to be really late for work. Not that I can find it within me to care.

"For not freaking out and for giving me exactly what I needed last night—and I'm not just referring to Taco Bell. If having a baby was never a part of your plans, then you did a really good job of staying calm."

His hands move from my waist to my ass as he picks me up with ease, and I loop my legs around him.

"I didn't say a baby was never a part of my plans, Darcy. I said it hadn't been for the majority of my adult life. Things change; people change."

I can't help but play with the hairs at the nape of his neck as he stands, holding me in the center of his bedroom.

"If you had asked me two years ago if I was happy with my life and the way I was living it, I would have told you yes. On the face of it, I wanted for nothing. Money, the lifestyle, my dream career ... the attention from women."

As he stares up at me with his blue eyes, so sincere, all I can think about is how it would feel to bend down and kiss him.

"It was a safe way of living, but it wasn't as fulfilling as I thought. I just didn't work that out until I set eyes on the one woman I wanted. No amount of money, fame, or shutouts could win her over or even make her take me seriously. I hung on every word I could get on nights out and searched for opportunities to hint at how I was feeling, just to see if you felt the same way too, but I didn't dare let it show because of my friendship with your brother, along with the shitty relationship you were in. That's right, Darcy. I could see you weren't happy with Liam."

My fingers are still in his hair. "You could?"

He nods slowly. "If you had been happy, then you would have worn the same smile for him as you do for me. And that's what kept me going, kept me hoping that I was still in with a shot. You say I'm amazing for the way I reacted when you told me about our baby—I'm not; I'm waiting and praying that this isn't a dream, that holding you in my arms like this is as real as the feelings I possess. The obsession over you that's growing within me every day."

My whole gut wants to blurt out that I'm on my way to being right there with him. If I admitted it, I don't think I'd regret the words or ever want to take them back. Fear of history repeating itself and caution are the only emotions that hold me back. Everything I thought I knew about my life has changed, and I don't know how to wade into deeper, unknown waters. I don't know if I can.

My fingers tease his hair again as I pinch my lips together. "You're right; my relationship with Liam was shitty, and now I'm pregnant with your child. I'm a little fucked up to be thinking straight, let alone jumping into something else that could blow up in my face, whether it's with my baby daddy or not."

Archer lifts me higher in his arms, pulling my top up until my bare skin pebbles against the morning air. His lips ghost over my stomach as he whispers, "Do you think you can help your mommy fall for daddy?"

I laugh toward the ceiling, but it's only to disguise the flutters as they shimmer throughout my body. I've *never* been wanted like this, never been pursued so relentlessly. Every woman should experience this at least once in their lifetime.

"Don't listen to him, Baby." I rub my stomach gently. "Daddy's getting carried away."

He smirks, determined to have the final word as he kisses my palm and places it over my stomach. "Looks like we've got our work cut out for us. Don't worry though, Pipsqueak. I've got this."

CHAPTER TWENTY-FIVE

ARCHER

Two wins, two shutouts, and two of my best-ever performances to kick off the regular season.

Leaving the ice to cheers from our home crowd, I'm wearing a victory smile as I replace my stick in the rack and pull off my gloves.

"You were a goddamn wall out there." Jack catches up to me, offering out his fist, which I bump. "Seriously, so impressive."

Right at that exact moment, Jensen walks past, tipping the bill of his cap at me as he heads for the debriefing room.

He wasn't down on the bench with Coach for the game against Colorado, instead opting to watch from behind my net. I could feel his eyes on me the entire time, and rather than freeze under the weight of his observations, I thrived.

I've never had an issue with being the center of someone's attention, and this past week, working one-on-one with Jensen Jones has lit a fire under my ass. I want this season to be a turning point for me, and I'm prepared to do whatever it takes to achieve my dreams.

Yet the drive I feel isn't solely down to the new coaching staff

—I know that. Now I have another reason to excel and be the best player and person I can be.

And that reason is around the size of a sesame seed, nestled warm and safe inside the girl I can't stop thinking about.

"Since you started seeing Abbie, you've been fucking weird."

The sound of Jack's voice breaks my daydream.

"Weird, as in more focused on hockey?" I cock a brow at him.

He shakes his head, one hand on the locker room door. "Nah. Weird, as in aloof and not interested in going out." He props a hand against his hip, still not pushing through the door. "You're coming out tonight though, yeah? This is a win we need to celebrate; Colorado is a favorite to make the play-offs, and we just rolled them over like they were a beer league team."

"Of course I'm coming out," I reply. "Two back-to-back wins and zero goals against us. What's not to like?"

Plus, Darcy's going to be at Lloyd's, and like hell am I leaving my pregnant girl to be ogled by some fucking loser.

"Darcy's going to be out."

"Oh, is she?" I respond, attempting to sound surprised, but not entirely sure the execution is there.

He seems to buy it though, eventually pushing into a locker room full of pumped hockey players. He pauses and turns on his heel, wearing an expression I can't decipher.

Please, for fuck's sake, don't tell me she's sick again.

I've barely seen her this week since she's been working all fucking hours at *Glide*.

"Thinking about it, my sister has been acting weird lately as well."

A cold shiver chases down my spine as I will myself to look at him.

Does he know?

He shakes his head, looking pissed, but not at me, and I breathe an internal sigh of relief. Fuck knows why—my fate is sealed regardless. All I'm doing at this point is kicking the can down the road.

"So, a couple of nights ago, Kendra told me Liam messaged Darcy, asking for her back."

He blows out a disbelieving breath, and I'm ready to put my fist through the nearest fucking wall.

I smile. "Really? Maybe he finally realized what a dick he's been to her."

He grinds his molars, almost like he's chewing the guy up. "He's got some fucking nerve. Apparently, he's ended it with the girl he cheated on Darcy with, and he wants a second chance. He wants to travel to New York to see her."

He can't. I'll murder him and be a first-time Dad while in custody.

I run a light palm across my mouth, ignoring all the guys around us as they head for the shower stalls. What if she decides to take him back? But also, why hasn't she told me when I've called her every morning, afternoon, and evening?

"What did she tell him?" I ask.

"Obviously, no. My sister knows a fucking idiot when she sees one."

But does she?

I smile again, and this time, it's genuine as relief washes away any niggling doubts that Dickface Liam could come back on the scene and I'd be rendered an inmate before turning twenty-eight.

"Does he still plan to come to New York?"

He just shrugs and heads for his bench on the opposite side of the room to mine. I follow him, not caring how fucking desperate it looks. I need to know her ex's intentions.

"Not sure. All I know is, he told her that leaving her alone 'is not going to happen.' " He mocks Liam, repeating his words.

"Well, he should've thought about that before putting his dick in another girl and fucking up the best thing that had ever happened to him," I snap, and Jack looks up at me from his seat on the bench.

He starts unlacing his skates.

"You're beginning to sound like a relationship guy. Abbie really does have you wrapped around her little finger, huh?" He winks, smirking.

Another icy sensation creeps through me as I opt to ignore his comment and head for my own bench, ripping my jersey overhead before starting on my pads.

I need to see her.

I need to know she's okay.

The instant we step into Lloyd's, my eyes are roving the space for honey-colored hair and a bright smile I can't get enough of.

I ignore my teammates as I walk alongside them and through the ropes cordoning off the private area, and my eyes finally land on the main reason I came out tonight. She's sitting at her usual place at the bar, wearing a peach bodycon dress that rides high on her smooth thighs, her long hair resting in classic waves against her back, hovering just above her ass.

My mouth runs dry as she picks up her water glass and takes a sip, giggling over something with Jenna as she waves her arm around expressively. I love how she talks with her entire body.

"I'm getting the drinks in. Beer, I assume?" Sawyer steps in front of me, snapping his fingers to garner my attention.

"Nah, I'm good," I reply, eyes never leaving Darcy.

Inconspicuously, he turns to identify what's got me so distracted, although he doesn't need to. He should know by now.

"Jesus fucking Christ, tell me you aren't going back there with her."

I focus on my captain for a second. The words *she's carrying my baby* battle to break free. "It's probably best if you keep out of this, Cap. I'm your friend, but you've also got the team to think about. I guess you could say you're facing a conflict of interest."

He turns to look at Darcy again and then back at me. "True, but I'm your friend first. I'll be sharing a beer with you long after our hockey careers are through. You're going to tear yourself to pieces over this girl." He scratches at his chest, pained on my behalf. "Trust the first girl you fall for to be the one you can't have."

My eyes snap to his face. Not because he freely admitted I'm falling for Darcy since there's nothing to deny there. I'm just sick of hearing the same rhetoric from him. I can have her; we can have each other. It's going to happen.

The glare I give him leaves no doubt over my thoughts, and Sawyer holds up a hand in surrender.

"Liam wants her back," I bite out over the music.

He just nods casually. "Of course he does. If she's got the NHL's biggest playboy all twisted up and chasing her every which way, you can best believe some loser like Liam will eventually realize his loss."

Darcy swivels on her chair, probably on her way to the restroom, when she stops dead in her tracks at the sight of me staring.

"Annnd that's my cue to leave and pretend like I haven't seen any of this." Sawyer says, making his way over to the booth, where a few of the players, along with Collins and Kendra, are seated.

Like I'm her latest catch, she reels me in, and I head toward her. But unlike a fish awaiting its grizzly fate, I'm not thrashing or fighting against her bait. I'm desperate to be caught up in her.

I don't want her to cut the rope and release me back into the ocean. I want to be right here. No matter how much it hurts or how long I have to wait.

I flash Jenna a quick smile, not wanting to be rude, but she takes the hint anyway and turns to order another drink. I don't know how much she knows about me and Darcy, and to be honest, I don't especially care. Jenna has never struck me as a girl who plays by the rules. She's got a wild streak to her—I can tell. And that's why I messaged her that night at Darcy's party. I get the feeling I can trust her; in fact, I'm pretty sure she appreciates a boy who couldn't care less about etiquette in his pursuit of what he wants.

Trying not to make the action too obvious, I lean down to Darcy's height on the stool, my breath shifting a few strands of hair, and I watch the way her throat hitches.

"You know, I swear to God, your hair is thicker, and your rosy cheeks are glowing even brighter tonight. Or is it the fact that, once again, I've hardly seen you all week?" I smile into her big blue eyes as she stares up at me. "And this fucking dress." Surreptitiously, I graze a finger down her thigh. "It's really unfair to make me go any time at all between seeing you. You can really kill a guy with that kind of mean behavior."

She rolls her lips together in amusement.

Yeah, she knows she's got me hooked.

Reaching back to the bar, she picks up her water glass and takes a sip. "For your information, thicker hair and a natural glow are all signs that a girl might be ... you know."

I step a little closer.

Jesus, talking like this in public—with Jack, Coach, and the team only a couple of tables away—is dangerous.

Regardless, the risk isn't enough to stop me.

"Are you pregnant, Darcy Doll?" I whisper so only she can hear.

She wets her lips at the depth of my voice. It feels like we're already in bed, wrapped around each other while I make her come all over me.

"I am. Although I still don't think I believe it."

I can see and sense the uncertainty as it manifests in her brain. Fear of the unknown. Who can blame her? She's just had her whole world flipped on its axis. It's understandable that, one minute, she feels steady and okay, and the next, she feels like life is anything but. My job right now is to help stop her head from spinning and give her the love and stability she and our baby need.

"You don't need to worry, Darcy. I promise everything is going to be okay."

Her hand cups my elbow, being careful to make sure it's the one closest to the bar so no one can see.

"This is really complicated for me, Archer. My head is telling me so many things; my emotions and hormones are everywhere. Then Liam decides to get in touch, and it's like I'm reminded of the reasons why I walked away from him. I guess you could say he's triggered me." She drops her eyes to the floor. "Add to that, it feels like I've got no control over my own life when I came here to get exactly that. I moved to escape the toxic people from my past and be closer to those I love and care about."

I edge even closer, desperate to wrap her in my arms. "You're doing so well though, Darcy. You're killing it at work, taking everything in your stride. Do you know how much respect I have for you? I could never move to a new country and fit in so seamlessly, so quickly. I've never met a person like you before. It's like you have this aura that encapsulates people. Liam and your dad either couldn't see that or didn't want to because they felt threatened, and that's on them and their insecurities. I see it though, and I want more of it. I want to watch you soar in your career and live out all of your dreams. You make me want to better myself on and off the ice, and now that you're carrying my baby ... those feelings have only intensified."

When Darcy's smile reemerges, warmth floods my insides. I helped to put that back there, on her lips, where it belongs.

"Thank you, Archer." Her voice is soft, but I'd hear it over the loudest music. "I can't explain how much that means to me."

If I cupped my hand around the back of her neck and pulled her smiling mouth to mine, I wonder how many seconds it would take Jack's fist to connect with the side of my face ...

Like I can sense eyes on us, my attention snags on the team booth, and I look straight at Jack. He's staring right at us, a beer to his mouth and Kendra's hand on his arm.

Offering a salute to my center, I hope that will be enough to placate him.

"What did Liam say to you exactly?" I try hard to keep my voice gentle for Darcy's sake when all I want to do is rip her ex's head off.

Darcy chews on her bottom lip. "It doesn't matter because I have no intention of engaging him in a conversation. We're done, and that's all there is to say."

"Jack says he wants you back." This time, I'm working even harder to keep my voice calm, to keep my jealousy and rage simmering below boiling point.

Darcy doesn't say anything as she takes another sip of water, clearing her throat.

Fuck. All I want is to throw her over my shoulder and take her away somewhere, anywhere, where it's just the two of us and no one else. Fuck hockey, fuck *Glide* and chess club and anyone else who wants to get in our way.

"Liam says a lot of things, most of it being bullshit. God, Jesus. Why is life so complicated?" She pushes out a frustrated breath.

"If anyone can figure it out, I know you can."

I wink at her, and she does a double take before a rogue grin pulls at her top lip.

Darcy sets her glass down and straightens on her stool. "Is that so, Thigh Boy?" Her voice takes on a bratty tone, and I fucking love it when she's like this. Challenging me. "Please do enlighten my masterful problem-solving brain. How can this be uncomplicated?" She subtly circles her lower stomach, and my chest swells.

"We can work as a team. Your brain is built to break codes and mysteries. Mine is designed to care for you and our child."

Her face softens in the wake of my words, shoulders relaxing. I know she wants to say more.

When Darcy slides off the stool and heads for the restroom, I can tell that she needs a minute. I'll always give her the space she needs.

"Don't suppose you have any teammates who want to be obsessed with me and break a few rules along the way, do you?"

Jenna's half laughing, half serious. That much is obvious as she pulls my attention back to the bar, and I rest a foot on Darcy's stool, playing with the strap on her wrist bag. I'm surprised she left it behind since all girls like to powder their nose and shit when they take an hour in the restroom.

Especially British princesses.

"Why? Are you hoping to snag a hockey boyfriend too?"

Jenna scoffs. "Yes, no, maybe. What with Kendra, Collins, and now Darcy dating a Blades boy, I'm the odd one out. As per fucking usual." She breathes the last part quietly, and I'm not about to correct her on my relationship status.

Jenna's a real enigma. Outwardly, she's your usual girl and pro athlete. But this conversation only proves my initial impression of her correct. She wants a boy from the bad side of town and one who will push all her buttons and excite her. I'm certain of it. I've seen enough girls to know what they want.

"Emmett Richards is single," I suggest.

She takes a sip of her cocktail, shaking her head. "No offense to him, but he doesn't float my boat." She shrugs a shoulder, turning to face the rest of the room. "No one here does. I guess I'm looking for a unicorn."

She doesn't wait for my response as she pushes off the bar,

heading for the restroom herself. I guarantee Darcy will be another thirty minutes now.

And that gives my brain just enough time to center back on Liam. It's not lost on me that Darcy didn't tell me what he had said when he contacted her, and a part of me wonders if her omission was deliberate.

He doesn't deserve to lay eyes on her again, let alone have her back in his life. Rage sprouts from anxiety, fire singeing my veins.

She's carrying *my* baby, and *now* he comes waltzing back into her life like they can just start over. Sure, he doesn't know she's pregnant—or at least I think he doesn't—but who the fuck is this guy?

I stare down at her bag.

Don't do it, Archer.

The small voice of reason loses, and I snatch up her bag, unzipping it and pulling out her phone as I head for the door, praying no one on the team is witnessing my exit.

The chilled fall air clings to my thin dress shirt as I stand outside Lloyd's, staring at Darcy's locked phone. A picture of her, Kendra, Collins, and Jenna on a night out fills the screen.

Fuck. I want that picture to be of me, bouncing our baby on my knee.

My first attempt to unlock her phone fails. The code isn't her date of birth then.

I try a second—Jack and Kendra's wedding date.

No luck.

Chewing on the inside of my cheek, I contemplate the impossible. She wouldn't go with the first night we hooked up, would she? I try it since that's my passcode.

The screen unlocks, and I swallow down a lump of emotion, navigating to her messages.

Shit, I know this is an invasion of privacy, but my protective instincts tell me Darcy is only letting me see the tip of the Liam iceberg.

Liam: Why are you dodging all of my calls?

Darcy: Because we've got nothing more to say. I don't want to talk to you, and it's my right to have peace.

Liam: Speak for yourself. I have plenty to say.

Darcy: Like what? I'm at work, and I need to concentrate on an article that's due to be published first thing in the morning.

Liam: Like I want you back. Like I think we made a mistake, splitting up. You shouldn't be in New York. You should be here with me, planning our lives together.

Darcy: Are you for real? The last I heard, you were in love with Libby. Get a grip, Liam. Does she know you're texting me?

Liam: Libby and I are over. So, no, she doesn't.

Liam: Are you seeing anyone right now?

Darcy: You lost the right to ask me that a while back.

Liam: What's his name?

Darcy: This is ridiculous. Leave me alone.

Liam: Not going to happen. What's his name?

Darcy: My life has got nothing to do with you anymore.

> Liam: It will if I board a plane to New York and see you. You shouldn't be there, Darce. And why have you suddenly decided to work for a lowly fashion magazine? I thought you had aspirations that were higher than that. You always screamed about your dreams enough, LOL.
>
> Darcy: The only aspirations I have right now are ones that involve ending this conversation.
>
> Liam: And there's the problem, right there.
>
> Darcy: ...
>
> Liam: You've always thought you were above me, always had the witty retorts to try and shut me down. Is it any wonder I cheated when you're so fucking full of yourself? So fucking self-assured all the time.
>
> Liam: Good luck to whoever your guy is. He's going to fucking need it.

The fact that it's Darcy's phone I'm holding is the only reason it isn't crushed into a thousand pieces.

Motherfucker.

I stand, staring down the lit street, cars passing and people walking by as I think over—or more try and talk myself out of—calling this prick.

Fuck it. He won't know my voice. He's likely never watched a hockey game in his life. Probably into some weird shit.

At the international dial tone, I can't fight back the smug smile. Good. He's still thousands of miles from her—exactly where he needs to be.

"Hello? Darcy?" a sleepy male voice croaks down the line.

Instantly, my adrenaline is pumping. The rage I felt before has nothing on now.

"Is everything okay?" he asks when I don't reply.

As I hear him shift in bed, since it must be three a.m. in the UK right now, I wonder if he's actually alone or still shacked up with the girl he claims he's ended things with.

"Baby, are you still there?"

"Don't call her baby," I growl.

There's silence for a beat before Liam speaks again. "Um, okay. Who the fuck is this?"

I snarl, and even though he can't see me, it still feels good. "Who I am really doesn't matter, but what I have to say to you absolutely does. So, clean out your arrogant British ears and listen very fucking carefully."

"Excuse me?" he replies, sounding offended.

I chuckle, loving every second of this as I lean against the streetlight next to me, switching Darcy's phone to my other ear.

"At what point in your miserable fucking life did you conclude that you had the right to say the kind of shit you did to Darcy over text?"

He huffs out a laugh, a condescending tone dripping from his voice. "Ah, so you must be her new fella."

"Damn right I'm her new *fella*," I mock in a broad London accent. "I'm also your new worst nightmare."

All he does is laugh, and I picture my fist as it extends across the Atlantic Ocean, landing straight between his eyes.

"Listen, whatever your name is. I appreciate the call and everything, but I don't respond well to threats, and neither does my solicitor."

I double over, my stomach muscles genuinely hurting as I explode with laughter.

"Solicitor?! No one is breaking the law. I'm referring to breaking bones—specifically the ones in your face—should you even consider messaging my girl again. She was done with you the first time, and she's definitely done with you now."

"Dude, you're a sandwich short of a picnic." He snorts, but I can hear the slight tremor as it enters his voice. "Does Jack know his sister is dating a fucking lunatic?"

My knuckles form an even tighter fist around Darcy's phone as I check over my shoulder to make sure the coast is still clear and no one is eavesdropping.

"What anyone else knows is inconsequential," I tell him. "The only person who matters is Darcy and her happiness. You don't make my girl happy, which means you need to be eliminated from the equation. So, why don't you go ahead and see this as your warning? Stay away from her; don't even contact her. Whatever you both had, you fucked it up, and now I get to enjoy the consequence of your actions. You picked the wrong girl, but for me, there's only ever been one. Don't get on a plane. In fact, don't bother to keep her name saved in your Contacts because you won't be needing it."

I might as well be standing right next to him as I bite out my words with increasing menace.

"And if you even think about telling Darcy or anyone else I called, the next time we interact, it won't be over the phone. You were right with what you said to Darcy—she is way above you. You're like a blip on her radar, but don't think I won't come for you if you even *think* about overstepping her boundaries again."

"Dude, you're fucking insane."

I cock my head, smiling. He's not wrong.

"Are we clear?" I press.

He says nothing, but I'm not worried. This dude is a fucking wimp. He doesn't love Darcy enough to take a beating from me. He cares only about himself.

"Crystal," he eventually says.

"Good. Have a nice life."

I hang up and quickly delete the call from her log, heading back into Lloyd's before she returns from the restroom, adrenaline rolling through my system as I scan the bar for signs of my girl.

The second I round the corner for the private area, I come face-to-face with Sawyer.

Hands in his pockets, he lifts a brow, staring down at the

phone in my hand. "Jesus fucking Christ. Do not tell me you just did what I think you did."

Sliding her phone back into her bag, I zip it shut and scratch at my chin, a sense of pride I probably shouldn't feel falling over me. "I've got zero idea what you're talking about."

He looks unconvinced. "So, if I search Darcy's phone log, I won't find a recent call made to Liam?"

"Nope." It's the partial truth, one up from the full-blown lies I've been spouting.

"I'm going to take Darcy home." Jenna approaches us from nowhere, thumbing over her shoulder toward the restrooms.

She looks worried, and instantly, my adrenaline is pumping for a whole different reason.

"What the hell is wrong?" I ask her, already heading for my girl.

Jenna catches my arm. She's got a strong grip, good enough to hold me back. I guess soccer and hockey goalies have more in common than simply being unhinged.

"No, you can't go in there. Other women are using the toilets."

"Then what the fuck is wrong?!" I snap, eyes flicking to Sawyer and then back at Jenna.

She looks taken aback at my reaction. I'll apologize later.

"I don't know exactly," Jenna explains. "One second, we were talking, and the next, she got ahold of my arm, trying to keep herself upright. She got dizzy and asked to go home."

I'm pulling out my phone, immediately bringing up Google to search her symptoms, but then stop when I remember I'm not alone.

Sawyer speaks first, his hand coming to rest on my shoulder. "Jenna, head back into the restroom and make sure she's okay. Let us know how she is."

Jenna nods once, eyes dropping to Darcy's bag in my hand. I can see she's wondering why I have it, but doesn't question it. I pass it to her, and she takes it, scurrying back to the restroom.

Now alone and with the sound of panic ringing in my ears, I set eyes on my captain. He doesn't say anything, but the cogs are turning in his head. He's a dad himself, and I wonder if Sophie experienced similar symptoms. I fucking hope so since her pregnancy turned out to be fine.

"We need to talk," he says calmly. "But not now and definitely not here."

"There's nothing to discuss," I reply. Knowing Darcy wants to keep the pregnancy private for as long as possible.

He looks off to the side and down the hallway leading to the restrooms before scratching at the back of his neck. "I've known you for a long fucking time, Archer, and I can tell the difference between your truthful and bullshitting faces, and right now, you're wearing the latter."

"I've got everything handled."

He shakes his head. "See, there's that bullshitting face again."

"What's going on with Darcy?" Jack joins us, breaking the staredown between me and my captain.

He looks between us. "Jenna just messaged Kendra to say she's taking her home."

I pocket my phone, and Sawyer looks at Jack, jutting his chin at the restrooms.

"We were just speculating on that ourselves." He looks back at me, more concern than anger in his gaze. "Although whatever it is, I haven't had a drink tonight, so I can give her a ride home."

CHAPTER TWENTY-SIX

DARCY

Pregnancy is not fun. Sure, it's a blessing in so many ways, but right now, as I lie here, trying to sleep past the banging in my temples and sporadic plummets in blood pressure—which are apparently normal as my body adapts to growing a baby—I'm thinking I've had better mornings.

Squeezing my eyes shut, I will myself to grab a few more hours of sleep. It's not even light outside, and I don't have work, making today the perfect opportunity to recharge my batteries.

Only the harder I try to rest, the more elusive sleep becomes. The only time I pass out and sleep well is in a certain boy's bed—that fact isn't lost on me. And neither are his words from last night.

"Your brain is built to break codes and mysteries. Mine is designed to care for you and our child."

Warmth floods my belly, and I dip a hand underneath my silk top—another set Archer bought me—palming my stomach.

"It's all going to be okay, Pipsqueak," I whisper into my darkened room, smiling at the nickname Archer gave to them. "He's going to stand by us."

It's the first time I've spoken to my baby, and despite feeling like utter crap, I guess it's the first time I've really felt a connection to my new reality—I'm pregnant, and in a little over thirty-four weeks, I'll be a mum.

I crack my eyes open, peering around my bedroom. In the faint lighting coming in from the street, I see my disorganized dresser, makeup bottles and products strewn across the top in a haphazard fashion. My shoes and coats are scattered around the room, some jackets hanging from my closet door, others piled on top of a single chair in the corner.

I need to get my shit together. Literally. I also need to work out what the hell I'm going to do about my living arrangements. A one-bedroom apartment isn't going to cut it.

Overwhelmed at all the challenges I have to face, I roll onto my back and exhale a long breath into the room. "It's going to be okay, Darcy. All of it."

"Do you frequently make a habit of talking to yourself?"

A voice rips my soul clean from my body, and I almost tumble out of bed.

"Whoa! What the fuck?!" I panic, reaching out to my side table and flicking on a lamp.

"Relax, Babe. It's just me, Jenna." She chuckles, sitting up in bed, wearing one of my silky hair caps and an eye mask.

She pulls the mask off and looks at me, grinning. "Seriously, before you started rambling on, I was sound asleep. These masks are a game changer."

I giggle and point to the cap she's wearing. "You think the masks are good? Wait until you style your hair later." I offer a chef's kiss. "No crunchy ends or dry hair. Only smooth, salon-worthy locks."

She snorts a laugh. "Shame my new look will be wasted in a messy bun at practice later today."

I stretch, lifting my arms above my head. "Yeah, that sucks." I pause and look across at my friend as she takes a sip of water. "You stayed overnight."

She nods once, replacing her glass on the side table. "I did. After Sawyer dropped us back, I wasn't comfortable leaving you." Jenna turns to look at me, only intrigue and kindness in her eyes. "I'm not quite sure how best to put this, but can I ask you something?"

Holding her gaze, I have a pretty good idea what's coming. Especially if she heard me talking to my stomach. "Sure."

Bringing her bottom lip between her teeth, she chews on it softly. "Darcy ... are you ..."

"Yes," I quickly answer, "I am."

Even in the dim lighting, the sun only just starting to rise in the Brooklyn sky, I see the way her eyes grow wide, brows raised into her hairline.

"Oh my God," she declares, gaze dropping to my stomach. "Is it Archer's?"

I nod my head, an unexpected sheen covering my eyes. It's a strange sense of relief to tell someone, especially Jenna, who I know I can trust. Even if I hadn't planned to tell anyone soon, apart from Mum, I've never been more grateful to be caught talking to myself.

Her hand reaches across the duvet, one little finger wrapping around mine. "How many weeks are you?"

"Just shy of six, although I'll have a better idea at the eight-week scan."

"Wow," she breathes out softly. "No wonder you aren't showing yet. My mom didn't start showing with my brother Holt until she was, like, fourteen weeks—or so she tells me."

A stretch of silence passes between us before I speak again.

"Only you and Archer know. I plan to tell Mum and maybe the rest of the girls since you all know about our fuck-buddy arrangement. But that's how it's staying until at least twelve weeks."

She picks up her water, taking another drink but holding on to the glass this time, almost like she's caressing it. "I won't ask how Archer took the news since I already know he's in love with you."

I balk at her directness and certainty. "He's got feelings for me, yes. I'm not sure it's lo—"

"He's in love with you," she immediately repeats. "The way he looks at you melts my bones to jelly."

And mine.

Jenna says it like she's craving the same thing, and on instinct, I move my hand over the top of hers. When things broke down with her ex, Lee, I know she took it harder than she let on. Jenna wants a love story of her own, and here I am, with a man at my feet and his baby in my womb. Yet all I wanted in the beginning was fun.

"He'll look after you and the baby. We'll all be there with you." She looks at me. "If you decide to keep it."

"I am keeping it. I considered the alternative for a while, but when Archer stepped up to support me, I knew I could do it. My mind has been reeling since I found out, but I'm not as scared anymore."

Like it's suddenly registering, she pops her jaw open. "*Oh fuck.* Jack."

I nod once. "Yeah. Jack. And Jon."

Jenna winces, slipping under the duvet like she's hiding from the thought of their reaction. "That isn't going to be pretty." Like a yo-yo, she sits bolt upright this time. "Holy shit! Jack … he thinks Archer is dating a girl named Abbie." She points at me and then my stomach. "But you're really Abbie, and now you're … you're …"

"Yep," I quip. "Although it looks a bit bad, Archer didn't deliberately lie to Jack about Abbie. He made an assumption that Archer was dating, and he's sort of let my brother run with it. Only now I'm pregnant, and our secret hookup arrangement is going to get out, which was never the plan."

She snorts, kicking her feet out in front of her. "Seriously though, Babe, you might be a single mom after all when Jack finds out."

I shrug. "What's done is done. Archer and I will tell him when the time is right, and he'll have to deal with it."

She drops her head between her shoulders, sighing. I don't like the way it sounds or perhaps what's going to leave her mouth next.

"I know sports aren't your thing, but it's a little more complicated than that. These guys thrive on trust and respect, especially in team sports like soccer, football, and hockey." She rolls her lips together, discomfort all over her face. "Then factor in a new GM for the Blades and the fact that your stepdad is the coach. Shit. This could rip the dynamics apart."

My blood runs cold. I get where she's coming from, but I never considered the seriousness of our situation. "What are you trying to say, Jenna?" I ask, needing her to be direct with me.

Her brows crease together. "I'm saying this is the kind of stuff a lot of teams don't come back from. Not unless ..." She trails off, and panic swirls in my gut.

"Jenna," I plead, "finish what you were going to say."

She clears her throat. "If the boys can't work it out or if the new GM is an asshole, I'm just saying I've seen shit like this force a player to leave."

"Like, be traded?" My voice shakes.

With regret laced in her features, she nods. "Yes. And given your brother is the assistant captain and pretty much the MVP these days, I'd say Archer would be the one forced out. Sure, goalies are hard to come by, but the AHL team in Connecticut has a good alternative, and normally, they're on two-way contracts so someone can step into the NHL whenever needed."

I go to speak right as my phone lights up with an alert from my smart doorbell.

The one Archer had fitted.

I turn and pick it up, unlocking the screen.

"Who is it?" she asks.

Against the odds and with everything Jenna just told me, an involuntary smile pulls at my lips when I turn the phone to show her the camera. "Speak of the devil."

CHAPTER TWENTY-SEVEN

ARCHER

In a pink pajama set I bought her—because of course I fucking did—Darcy brews two mugs of Yorkshire tea. One for me and another for her. I don't have the heart to tell her I can't stand tea.

Would it be a deal-breaker?

Jenna left around ten minutes ago, and since the moment Darcy answered the door to me, my girl has been really fucking quiet. Disconcertingly quiet.

Slowly, she stirs a tea bag around one mug and then moves to the other, releasing a small sigh.

When Sawyer took his eyes from my phone and Darcy and Jenna back home, I spent the next half hour Googling her symptoms, and—thank fuck—lightheadedness is a normal part of pregnancy, thanks to lower blood pressure.

That didn't stop the burning desire to wrap her in my arms at Lloyd's and be the one to take her home, with me, to my apartment—a place I know we'll call ours soon.

I approach her from behind, not stopping until my chest

brushes her barely covered back. Even though I'm wearing a hoodie, her skin still reacts to my presence.

Reaching around, I fold my hand over hers, taking the teaspoon from her and setting it in a cute-as-fuck spoon dish I know she brought with her from England because we don't have that kind of shit here.

"Spin around for me, Doll."

Another small sigh leaves her lips. I can smell her shampoo, and I appreciate the perfect curve of her exposed neck since she's wearing her long hair in a messy bun.

"Please?"

Picking up a small milk jug, she adds a few drops to each mug and sets it down softly. "When all this gets out ... about you, me, and the pregnancy, is there a chance you will be traded?"

Her question comes out of nowhere and hits me right in the gut.

This time, I don't ask her to turn around and face me. I plant both hands on her small waist and do it myself. Her lower back is pressed into the countertop, and worried blue eyes peer up at me through thick, dark lashes.

I cup one side of her face with my hand, my large palm dwarfing her delicate features.

We haven't kissed in days, but like that's going to stop me. I duck down and brush my lips over hers.

She smiles against my mouth, and fuck if I don't do the same back.

With her pinned to my body, I'm convinced she isn't going anywhere, so my other hand leaves her waist, slipping between our bodies. I palm her stomach, rubbing small circles around her navel with my thumb.

The question she asked still hangs between us, but kissing Darcy is my priority. I know it makes her feel good, and if it offers her some semblance of comfort, then I'll gladly give it to her every damn day.

The truth is, I can't be sure what will happen when I ultimately break the news to Jack and Coach. I know the new GM doesn't take any prisoners, and if it fucks with team dynamics, then best-case scenario is, I'll be benched. So much of my fate rests on how Jack will react.

I think about if the shoe were on the other foot and this were my baby sister, Emma, and my best friend ... yeah, I'd be pissed at the betrayal. But if he treated her right, I'd have it out with him for being a secretive douche and then try to push past it.

"Why do you ask?" I breathe into her mouth as she wets her lips, clearly not done with the kiss.

Neither am I.

She exhales, and I swallow down the taste of her. I want to consume every inch of Darcy Thompson.

"Just something Jenna said. She knows, by the way. It's a long story, but she'll keep it quiet until the time is right for us to announce we're having a baby."

I close my eyes. Despite the tension rolling off her in waves, the last part of her sentence feels like a melody.

"We're having a baby." I repeat her words in a tender whisper, wanting to hear them again.

In her usual way, she cocks her head to the side, smiling sweetly. "You're one of a kind, aren't you, Archer Moore?"

Instantly, my hands are around her thighs, and she's sitting on the counter next to our cooling mugs of tea.

I hope they turn cold and undrinkable.

I step between her legs, one palm braced beside her, the other wrapped around the nape of her slender neck. "I'm not that complex, Darcy."

She still looks worried over whatever Jenna said, but we'll get to that soon. I want to hear what she has to say about me first.

"You're deeper than you—or anyone else—gives you credit for," she responds.

I play with the soft strands of her hair, and goose bumps

bloom along her bare arms. "Perhaps you see it that way because you're under my skin."

She leans forward and kisses me, and my heart grows another inch with hope that I'm under her skin too.

"What did Jenna say?" I ask, returning the kiss. "Was it about me getting traded?"

She nods, face twisting, body tensing.

I clear my throat, searching for the best way to deal with this. "I'll never lie to you, Darcy. I know I've been flexible with the truth from time to time, but with you, I'll always be honest. I think a lot of my fate hinges on Jack. If he finds out and decides to kick my ass in the locker room and let his emotions overpower his professionalism and it destroys everything Coach has built between us as a team, then, yeah, the new GM will be concerned. The thing is, his potential reaction aside, your brother is the future captain of the team; he's where the money's at, and he's the one all the fans are talking about right now. I'll be twenty-eight in a couple of months, and while I'm a fucking good goalie, if it's a choice between him or me, I'm not so sure I'll win that kind of face-off."

A sheen coats her eyes.

Fuck.

I hustle, thinking of something that will calm her. "I'm hopeful it won't come to that though. I don't think it will either."

She wets her lips and rolls them together. "You don't?"

I shake my head as an urge to take a risk and go somewhere that might help ease her worries rolls through me.

"Let's get out of here." I intertwine our fingers. "Throw on clothes and come with me somewhere."

"Brooklyn really is beautiful in the autumn." Darcy's eyes scan the multicolored trees as they line the empty pathway we've been walking for the past five minutes.

It's a beautiful, bright day, and we're fortunate that hardly anyone is around.

I pull the bill down lower on my cap and shove my hand back into my pocket, resisting the urge to reach out and wrap my arm around her shoulders.

"I haven't been to Fort Greene Park before, which is a crime for saying I live here, and I love open spaces. This place reminds me of the good parts of the UK."

"Do you miss England?" I ask as she breaks off the path and picks up a conker, which lies beneath a large horse chestnut tree.

She turns it around in her fingers, and I watch her study its grooves and smooth surfaces. Her analytical brain examining it carefully.

"Sometimes. It's mostly memories of my childhood that I miss and not really my time at university. I loved studying. The company? Not so much."

Walking over to the tree, I pick up a similar-sized conker, wondering what all her fascination is over. But before I can ask her more about university, she quickly changes course.

"Did you ever have conker fights in school? I used to kick Jack's ass every time we played."

"You're speaking another language right now," I tell her. "I seriously have no idea what you're talking about."

Her eyes light up like this is the best news ever as she continues walking, holding the conker up to show me.

"Okay, so basically, you have to drill a hole in the top, being careful not to split the skin because that weakens the conker. Then you pass a string through it and tie a big knot at the bottom. The idea is to destroy your opponent's conker as they hold it out in front of them."

She turns and walks backward, demonstrating what to do. I just smile because she's in her element.

She huffs out a breath and finishes up explaining the rules to me. "Back before my dad became at total arsehole, we used to have family championships each October. I looked forward to it every year, and I usually lifted the conker trophy. That was, until one year, when I caught Jack preserving his chosen conker from the chestnut tree at the bottom of our garden in a jar of vinegar. Cheater," she bites out.

I make the assumption that vinegar intervention is frowned upon and skip to what I really want to know.

"Does my girl have a competitive streak?" I ask, pocketing the conker in my jeans. Fully intending to keep it somewhere safe when I get back home.

Her brow quirks in a menacing way. "Will it get dark tonight? Of course. But only when it's necessary."

"Like with family conker championships?" I muse.

"Precisely." She nods once, turning on her heel before coming to a grinding halt. "Oh fuck. I didn't expect that to be so huge."

Hold in the inappropriate comments, Archer.

I walk up next to her as she pockets her conker too.

"That's the Prison Ship Martyrs Monument."

Darcy continues walking until she reaches the couple of large steps leading up to it and turns to take a seat. I do the same and sit next to her.

This feels like the date I never got at the restaurant. But

despite being an impromptu idea that came to me in her kitchen, it feels even better than sitting in a restaurant I booked out so we could have some privacy.

Beneath her black winter jacket and beanie, Darcy rubs her hands together and breathes out, a small puff of air clouding the space. I can tell she's getting cold.

"I should've used the voucher my colleagues at work got me for my birthday to buy more winter clothes," she says on a shiver. "It really says something when I'm too overwhelmed to go shopping."

I scan the area around us; there are only a few people walking in the distance, and they're not close enough to recognize us.

"Come here," I say, picking up both her hands and pressing them together between my large palms.

She releases a small whimper as warmth seeps into her freezing fingers. "You aren't even a bit cold."

I shake my head. "Hockey players run hot since we spend most of our lives on the ice. Call it adapting to our habitat."

She giggles at that, staring up at me with her baby blues. "How did you know that coming here was just what I needed?"

I kick my feet out in front of me, constantly searching the area for people who could see us and blow our cover. "I've been here more times than I can count. To most of the parks around where I live, to be honest."

Darcy cocks her head to the side, studying me again. "Like for runs and stuff?"

"Sometimes, but mainly to center myself when things get difficult. I do my best thinking in the outdoors, whether it's before a game or afterward."

She nods her head slowly. "Oxford University is a beautiful place. I found myself walking the grounds around my campus a lot. Took the edge off the loneliness."

My relaxed jaw tics when I think about Liam.

"Loneliness? I can't imagine you being without friends."

She shrugs, and I interlace our fingers on both hands, holding them down between us. "The first year was good. I went out partying a lot. After that, everything changed, and I decided to take on elective courses in my second and third years."

I know she did since she's told me before.

"That's when it all went wrong with Liam," she continues, moving into territory I'm not aware of. "I tried explaining that I took them on because I was finding my course easy and I wanted to bolt on additional subjects to help pursue my dream career in editing, but he didn't get it. With increasing responsibility, I had less time to party. Friends became more distant, especially since I shared so many with Liam. By the time my undergraduate degree was done, I was so ready to leave but stuck it out to finish my master's degree because I knew that would help secure a job, like the one I have with *Glide*."

My heart breaks for her.

He really is a fucking piece of shit.

"In hindsight, maybe I should've gotten into sports and been drafted into the NHL, like you were. That sounds like a much better option."

I know she doesn't really believe that, although I can't deny I've had a fucking good life.

It's just better now.

"Your experience in college isn't a reflection on you as a person, Darcy. Only the people who were around you. But now all that's changed because you're in the right place, surrounded by people who care about and love you."

She just looks at me with eyes sparkling in the bright fall sunshine when a couple approaches the steps below us and takes a seat, turning their backs to face the same way as us.

I don't think they recognize me, but I don't want to chance it.

Keeping hold of her hands, I stand and guide her toward the monument.

"Where are we going?" she asks in a giddy tone.

I turn back to her, the usual cocky grin plastered across my face.

When we reach the back of the monument, I waste no time as I press her into the side. Darcy props a foot up against it as I lean over her frame, tipping her chin up with my finger.

In her flat black boots, she's tiny beneath me.

"Do you feel better now?" I ask her, my voice breathy.

I see the way her chest rises and falls, but this time, it isn't because she's turned on. This time, it's different. And I like the way the shift between us feels.

"Are we talking about my low blood pressure, headaches, hormones, or panic over you getting traded?"

"All of it."

I cup the back of her head, and she spins my cap around so it's facing backward.

Reaching onto her tiptoes, she brings her lips up to mine, and I can smell her sweet scent.

"My headache is gone, and my hormones are in check. The panic has also eased, thanks to you bringing me here ..." She trails off.

I lower my lips until their barely touching hers. "And your low blood pressure?"

Her tongue pokes out, smoothing across her lip. "Actually, I'm now having the opposite problem. And that *is* your fault."

My heart hammers in my chest. "How so, Darcy Doll?"

Finally, she presses her mouth to mine, still smiling. "Because it's sky-fucking-high."

CHAPTER TWENTY-EIGHT

DARCY

There are two elements to a hockey game I particularly love.

Number one: the warm-ups. If you haven't watched the way the players stretch and flex, then I'm afraid you haven't lived.

Number two: when the goalies cut up the fresh ice prior to a game. Especially when number thirty-three for the Blades does it.

And as I sit here, in the family box, ahead of today's game against the Scorpions, it's entirely possible I'm drooling.

With a smirk, Kendra whispers from her seat next to mine, "A while back, I asked Archer if he'd like a side of chicken wings to go with his stare session. Now I'm thinking you're as bad as him."

I roll my eyes and act like I wasn't doing what she's accusing me of. "The Blades are playing their rivals. It's intense, and I'm locked in on the action."

"Mmhmm," she hums, less than convinced. "I assume your little fuck-buddy arrangement is still alive and well?"

I flare my eyes at her, darting them around us. "A little discretion please, babe."

Kendra takes another sip of her soda and offers some popcorn out to me. I take a couple of pieces because I'm starving and skipped lunch like the idiot that I am.

"We're still on for Rise Up next week, right? Collins and Jenna can make it too. It's been a whole three days without cake, and I'm craving." Kendra throws her head back, groaning. "That bakery is going to be the death of me and my soccer career. Jack can literally eat through England and not gain a single pound. I only have to *look* at the cake stand and I'm tipping the scales."

Snorting a laugh, I take a few more pieces of popcorn. "Yeah, I'm free and ready to eat all the scones. Jack's right; no one around here does them like Rise Up. The coffee is mediocre, but the cakes are …" I give a chef's kiss.

A shot of anxiety passes through me. Rise Up will be a great opportunity to break the pregnancy news to Collins and Kendra. They're the best friends I've ever had, and I know they'll be there for me. Still, I'm nervous all the same. I just hope Kendra understands the reasons why I'm waiting to tell Jack. There's zero point in rocking the boat for Archer or the team until the pregnancy is in the clear.

At the end of the warm-ups, the players skate off the ice, just as a door behind us swings open, and a woman I've never seen before rushes into the room, dressed in a Blades jacket and hat.

She pulls off the hat and shakes out her silky, dark hair. I'd pin her as in her early fifties. She's incredibly glamorous with piercing blue eyes and perfectly applied makeup.

"Damn traffic!" she mutters to herself, stuffing the hat into her shoulder bag before casting her eyes around the room, orienting herself.

Her attention lands on me, and she smiles. I can tell she has no idea who I am, and despite the fact that I don't know her either, she feels familiar.

My gaze drops to her jacket once more, where I see Archer's number stamped across the chest.

"Oh my God," I say low, eyes flicking to Kendra as I motion to the lady.

"Have you never met Julia before?"

My whole body turns toward my friend. "I'm sorry, and you have?"

She just shrugs, taking a sip of soda. "Archer's mom occasionally drives over for games. I guess you've never crossed paths since you were in the UK. She's nice."

I pull out my phone and type a quick text as Julia makes her way over to a seat a few feet away from us and casually begins talking with my mum.

> Me: So, in the past three nights we've spent together, you didn't think to tell me about your mum coming to today's game?

I realize the text sounds a bit shitty the second I hit Send.

> Me: I'm not angry. Just shocked.

> Thigh Boy: That's the equivalent of "I'm not angry, just disappointed." Actually, it might be worse. She wasn't sure if she could make it, so I didn't say anything. In hindsight, I probably should've. Sorry, Doll.

> Thigh Boy: Do you still plan to meet your mom tonight and tell her about the baby?

> Me: Yeah. Why?

> Thigh Boy: I'm going to tell mine too. If that's okay with you?

> Me: You don't need my permission to tell your own mum. Are you nervous?

> Thigh Boy: Nope. Like I said, Mom's a family woman. Plus, I don't really care what anyone thinks. Only about you.

My heart rate kicks up, just like it did against the monument.

> Me: Sweet talker.

Thigh Boy: Is it working?

> Me: No.

Thigh Boy: That's bullshit, and you know it.

> Me: How are you even texting me back? My original message was for when you finished the game.

Thigh Boy: I'm hiding in the bathroom. Saw my phone light up with your name.

> Me: Go and play hockey. Another shutout, please.

Thigh Boy: If I make it, will you stay in my bed tonight?

> Me: I'll think about it.

Thigh Boy: I'll DoorDash Taco Bell for you.

> Me: Deal.

Thigh Boy: One day, you'll love me as much as cheesy bean burritos.

> Me: You're incorrigible.

Thigh Boy: Yep. Stay pretty, A, x.

Thirty minutes later—with the Blades already a goal ahead, thanks to a slapshot from my brother—I make my excuses and head for the bathroom.

When I reach the toilets, the door swings away from me just as I go to push through, and I narrowly miss falling straight on my face. I stumble into the room, laughing the entire time—half from embarrassment and the other because I must look ridiculous.

A hand wraps around my arm, saving me from catapulting across the room.

The woman—and I assume the person keeping me upright—laughs along with me. "This is the kind of thing that could only happen to me. At least I'm not alone."

When I finally get ahold of myself, I spin around and come face-to-face with Archer's mum.

She hitches her handbag further up her shoulder, warmth radiating from her. "You're Felicity's daughter, aren't you?"

"Darcy," I confirm, feeling a little nervous, knowing I'm meeting my baby's future grandma, and in a few hours, she'll know all about it.

She clicks her fingers. "That's right! Felicity mentioned your name. I've met her a couple of times at games, but never you. I'm Julia, Archer Moore's mom." The smile still hasn't left her face. "I presume from your very strong British accent that you live in the UK."

Julia steps all the way back into the restroom, releasing the door, and it shuts behind her.

"Oh, sorry!" She shakes her head, motioning to the toilet stalls. "I bet you're busting to pee, and here I am, going on." She rolls her eyes at herself.

"I'm good," I reply. "Actually just taking a breather away from the arena noise."

She nods her head, chuckling again. "I think we might be kindred spirits—both a little clumsy and loud noise not being our thing."

Julia's eyes fall down the length of my body. I'm wearing a dress, tights, and knee-high boots since I'm heading out with Mum straight after this.

"I don't normally get this dressed up for games," I clarify, feeling my cheeks heat a touch.

She shakes her head, but it isn't judgmental. "I was actually thinking how beautiful you are." Her voice is full of awe, and my face flushes redder.

She hesitates for a brief moment, eyes narrowing slightly. I can't work out what she's thinking, but the wheels are definitely turning in her brain.

"Thank you," I reply. "I recently made the permanent move to New York. I was living in Oxford up until early this year."

She nods softly, fiddling with the leather strap on her shoulder. "This might be a really random question, but have you met my son, Archer?"

I'm a shit liar, and I'm even worse at acting chill. Heat creeps across my entire face, burning the tips of my ears. "I have. He's one of my brother's closest friends. I speak to him on nights out sometimes."

Biting on her bottom lip, Julia studies me in the way her son does. They're so alike with the same eyes and dark hair, but also in their mannerisms.

I can sense she wants to say something but is holding back, and I wonder if Archer has spoken about me. Maybe he hasn't mentioned my name but told her there's a girl he likes.

"He's a good man," she finally says. "Since the minute he left the womb, he's always known what he wants and gone after it. I think that's what makes him one of the best goalies to ever grace the NHL—his determination to follow his dreams."

In isolation, her comment is kind of abstract, but there can be no doubting now that she isn't talking about hockey. She's talking about me; her eyes confirm it.

Julia reminds me of my mum with her maternal instinct; it's never pointed her in the wrong direction. I hope I have the same gift when it comes to our child.

"Anyway ..."

As if snapping back to reality, she clicks her tongue and takes hold of the door handle behind her, spinning to face me once more. Her warm smile is still there, and although our encounter was spontaneous and brief, there's nothing weird or uncomfortable about it.

"Enjoy the game, Darcy," she continues. "I really hope to see you around again at some point."

And as quickly as I fell into the restroom, she exits, the door closing behind her with a click.

> Me: I know you're on the ice now, but I just met your mum. She's like the double of you in every way possible. But in spite of that, I like her. A lot.

CHAPTER TWENTY-NINE

DARCY

"Well, fuck me." Kate Jones, wife of Jensen Jones and an all-around badass woman and lawyer, stares down into her glass of Pinot Grigio.

When I asked my mum to meet for lunch, I wasn't anticipating Kate to come too. In hindsight, it's probably not a bad thing. Kate and JJ—the nickname she has for her husband—fell pregnant with their twins unexpectedly a few years back, and I guess I could use her advice. Although, at this point, all she's said is three words.

We'd been in the restaurant for all of five minutes before I blurted out the news. The second Mum started talking about grandchildren and her desperation for them, I dropped the bomb, which has left her open-mouthed and with a green olive in hand, suspended midair.

I reach across and take it from her, popping it into my mouth before grabbing a napkin and disposing of it.

Bleurgh. Another food fallen victim to this pregnancy. I used to love olives.

I take a sip of water to rinse my mouth, and both Kate and I look at Mum.

"Say something," I breathe, trying to remain calm.

Still silent, Mum rises from her chair and rounds the table. I can already feel the tears as they prick in the corners of my eyes as I stand and she wraps her slender arms around my shoulders, and everything nearby fades to a blur.

Ten, maybe twenty seconds pass with me held in her embrace. I can smell her familiar perfume and coconut shampoo, and I realize this was exactly what I needed. Not her words, but her touch.

Pushing back her chair, Kate comes to stand beside us, and Mum opens her arms out for her to join the hug. We must be attracting attention in the restaurant, but I couldn't care less.

After a few more beats, Kate breaks from the hug and steps back a pace. "Okay, so practical-talk time. Is Liam back on the scene?"

I part laugh, part sniffle. "Umm, no," I reply and take my seat, Kate and Mum doing the same. "I mean, he's been in contact, and he wants to talk, but if you're asking if the baby's his ... it isn't."

Mum hands me a tissue, and I dab at my eyes. She takes a sip of wine and places the glass down carefully on the pristine white tablecloth.

"Who is the father, honey?" Her voice is soft and encouraging, and I wipe at my eyes again.

Kate sits back in her seat, arms folded across her chest. Then she flicks her hair over a shoulder. "Well, if Emmett Richards is the dad, then you're good. With the injury he sustained on the ice earlier, I'd say he'll be out for the season. He sure took one for the team to secure a Blades win."

I shake my head. His knee injury looked serious, and I hope he's okay. "It's not Emmett's. I've barely spoken more than a few words to him."

Kate leans forward, arms braced on the table in front of her.

"Girl, I could barely *look* at my husband, and he still put twins in me. That means nothing."

Mum turns to Kate as she begins crunching on a breadstick.

"What?" Kate asks. "It's the truth." She points the breadstick at me. "He still pisses me off now, from time to time. It does make for great sex though."

"Yes, yes. We get it." Mum waves a hand in front of her before focusing back on me. "If it isn't Liam"—she rolls her eyes toward her friend, who's still chomping on the breadstick—"and it isn't Emmett, then who is he?"

"Fuck!" Kate announces. "Did you bang Archer Moore? Everyone else has, so ..."

I don't need to answer because I'm sure my face says it all.

Mum tips her head to the side, analyzing my response. "Holy moly, it is, isn't it?"

Is it me, or has it suddenly gotten really hot in here?

"Yes." My voice is a whisper. "I've been sleeping with him for a while, and ... well, not taking my birth control properly. Then I got sick, and I think it failed to work altogether."

Mum holds up a hand. "Wait. How long have you known?"

I shrug. "A little over two weeks."

"Two weeks?!" Mum exclaims, and heads turn towards us. She clears her throat and reaches for my hand, taking it in hers. "Why didn't you say something sooner? You told me all was fine after your latest doctor's appointment."

It would be so easy to chalk my silence up to shock and trying to come to terms with the news. Maybe even living in denial. But none of those reasons would be the truth, and I know it.

Twisting my lips, I look between Mum and Kate. A server approaches our table, but she must sense now isn't a good time to take our order, and she immediately spins on her heel.

"Archer's not the guy everyone seems to think he is. He really cares about me. The day I found out I was pregnant, I was due to meet him after chess club. I wasn't planning to tell him right away, but then I got in his car, all upset and overwhelmed, and he looked at me like his whole world was about to crumble beneath him. He thought I was going to end our hookup arrangement, and I could tell he was worried about me. He pulled me into his lap and looked at me in a way no one had ever done. He makes Liam look like a poor excuse for a man, and the words tumbled right out of me."

My eyes flick from the menu lying on the table in front of me and up to Kate.

"He's changed a lot. Sure, he's fucked women around in the past, but he blew all my theories about him out of the water the second he told me he wanted our baby more than anything. I think he wants to be with me. No, I *know* he does."

I then look Mum straight in the eyes. "That's why I haven't told you before now. Not because I haven't wanted to, but I think, deep down, I've enjoyed sharing these past two weeks living in a secret and peaceful baby bubble with Archer. In the beginning, the whole hookup arrangement was about having fun because we found each other attractive. I think that fun might be turning into something more. It was, even before I fell pregnant."

I stop talking, wetness balancing on the rims of my eyes, and I notice the same in Mum's too.

"Wow, Darcy," Kate breathes out, shaking her head slowly. "I don't know if this is the right time to say this, but ... I'm really happy for you. For both of you."

So much of me wants to leap from my seat and hug Kate again. I knew she'd get it. Instead, I stay planted in my chair, staring at Mum as more tears emerge, casting wet streaks down her flawless makeup.

"How many weeks are you?" she asks, voice thick with emotion.

"Seven." My hand is still in hers, and I squeeze it tightly. "I have my first scan at eight weeks."

She nods once, picking up a napkin and using it to swipe at her cheeks. "Do you want me to come with you?"

If I'd fallen pregnant with Liam's child, I know my answer would've been an unequivocal yes. But I'm not carrying Liam's baby, and I'm so damn relieved he isn't the father, even if, at one time, he was the only future I could imagine.

"I want you to be involved in my pregnancy journey, and I'm going to need you and all your experience and love. I know this isn't going to be easy."

"But you want Archer to be there with you?" she asks, no bitterness or upset in her tone, only understanding.

"Yes. And I don't think he'll want to be anywhere other than at my bedside."

"He's in love with you."

My gaze moves to Kate as she speaks, twisting her wineglass around with the stem between her fingers.

"Head over heels, in fact." She looks up and smiles at me. It's possible she's the most beautiful woman I've ever laid eyes on. "I speak only the truth, Darcy. I'm also only repeating what my husband has told me. He's said on multiple occasions that Archer's in love. He can tell by the way Archer's game has stepped up a gear. After all, the same happened to him when we started dating." She eyes me carefully. "With that in mind, just do me a favor, okay?"

Emotions are high around the table. Even Kate's stoic eyes wear a gloss.

"What's that?" I ask.

Kate swallows. I can't tell if there's regret or she's simply reminiscing. "Don't waste the next seven months of pregnancy convincing yourself that you want to co-parent with a man who would do anything and everything for you and his unborn family. Embrace it, girl. Embrace him and all that he is—because trust me when I say there are women out there who would kill to be in our position. Being a mother—from conception to the day we leave this earth—shouldn't be something we do alone. The person who should step up to the plate is your man or partner. I know Liam—the fucker—ripped your heart out, but don't let that stop you from loving Archer with everything you have. Life's too short, and pregnancy is too special."

If I wasn't sitting in a packed restaurant, I'd let the sobs break free. In thirty seconds, Kate has nailed exactly how I'm feeling, hitting right at the heart of my fears.

"You know what I think?"

"What's that, Mum?" I croak out.

Her tears are flowing freely now. "I think I'm the luckiest woman alive." She wraps her spare arm around Kate's shoulders. "I have the best friends and the strongest, smartest, and most beautiful daughter I could've ever wished for. I also think you should heed every single word Kate said because she's one thousand percent correct, and I couldn't have said it better myself."

We sit with our words and my reality, one that feels more exciting with every passing second. I'm not naive enough to believe that my short- and long-term future won't be full of difficult moments. However, I am wise enough to believe and trust in the people around me.

I have to trust them. I have to trust Archer.

"I'm assuming Jack doesn't know?"

I shake my head at Mum, a kernel of unease reappearing. "No, he doesn't." Emotion is replaced by insistence when I speak again. "And that's the way I want to keep it. I think we all know that regardless of Archer's intentions with me and the baby, this is going to go down like a lead fucking balloon. Jack thinks his goalie has a girlfriend over in Dallas when, in fact, he's been hooking up with his sister behind his back, and now we have a baby on the way. It could tear the team apart, and I'm not going to share anything about my pregnancy until at least twelve weeks. The only people who do and will know are you both, my girlfriends, and Archer."

"Jon shouldn't know either. It would be unfair and awkward as fuck if he did. Having to coach and keep it a secret from Jack

—I know he'd hate that," Mum says, and relief floods through me. "Plus, you are my daughter, and you come above everything for me. Always. So, if you want to wait on telling people, then we wait."

I twist my hands around in front of me. "Do you think Jack will go crazy?"

Mum shrugs. She isn't dismissing my worry, but she clearly doesn't see it the same way. "Probably. But that's something the boys have got to work through. You are your own woman, making a decision for yourself, your pregnancy, and for your man. If Jack wants to get into it with his friend, then that's on them. As are the consequences that the new GM will rein down on anyone who steps out of line."

I wince. "He rules with an iron fist?"

Mum raises her brows. "Between the three of us, Jon isn't so sure about him. He's making some changes that aren't going down well with the non-playing staff, and his ideas for the direction he wants the team to go in aren't exactly conducive with Jon's. I don't think the GM has loyalties to anyone on the team, regardless of how long they've been working with or playing for the Blades. So, if Jack and Archer want to get into it over their egos, then let's just say, it might not sit well, and they could find their asses on the bench, on the farm team, or worse still, on the trade list before the March deadline."

In a roundabout way, Mum's only confirmed what Jenna said to me, and my stomach rolls. The thought of Archer being shipped off to another team, maybe even the other side of the country, brings a whole new level of fear.

And comprehension—Kate's right. I don't just need Archer; I want him too.

My mobile pings on the table next to me. It's face down as my eyes fall to it.

"One hundred dollars says that's your obsessive baby daddy."

I roll my eyes at Kate. Giddy excitement courses through

every artery as I pick up my phone and open our message thread.

> Thigh Boy: That's so weird because Mom likes you too, along with the fact that you're having my baby.
>
> Thigh Boy: Anyway, enough about parents. When can I come get you and take you back to bed? I have Taco Bell on speed dial and an entire night free to be at my girl's beck and call.

CHAPTER THIRTY

ARCHER

"This is craziness. I thought we were pushing our luck at Fort Greene Park, but the movies?!"

Darcy takes a step back and looks at me beneath the thick scarf and new yellow beanie I bought her. I can only see her cheeks, nose, and eyes as she peers up at me.

I thumb over my shoulder toward the theater entrance. "Your favorite movie is showing as a rerun, and I knew you'd want to see it. This is the only night they had tickets left."

Her eyes flare wide, and I can't help but laugh as I pull my cap lower.

It's true; I am a fucking idiot for doing this. Crazy comes naturally around this girl.

"Do you even like this kind of film?" she asks with a raised brow as she takes a tentative step forward.

Up until last night, when she told me about her obsession with history surrounding the Enigma code—more specifically the codebreakers in England who had helped to break it—I hadn't heard of the actors, never mind the movie. That was nothing I couldn't quickly fix with an internet search.

"Truthfully ..." I wince and drop my head when a few people walk past us. "I'm more of a sci-fi guy."

"I like that genre too," she says, peering around me to see how busy it is inside. "If we're going to do this, then we need to go now; it's quiet in there."

I reach out and take her hand in mine, and she gasps, pulling it away.

"Archer! If we pretend like tonight isn't a date, then we can at least pass this off as two friends heading to watch a film." Her eyes go even wider. "I mean, this is a date, right?"

My lips are on hers before I can even stop myself. "It's a date, Darcy. They've all been dates to me."

"We're going to get caught," she sings against my mouth.

"Not if we're careful," I reply. "Plus, they have Bugles."

I feel her moan into my mouth.

"I really want Bugles. I think Pip does too."

Being anything other than careful, I bring my palm to her stomach. There are so many layers between us, but it doesn't prevent the fizz of electricity I feel whenever I touch her.

"Come on. Let's get inside so I can geek out with my girl and then take her back to my bed straight afterward."

Five minutes later, we're sitting right at the back of the theater with all the snacks I could carry. As predicted, the place is packed, and Darcy is still freaking out about being seen.

"I think my beanie would make a better disguise," she suggests, pulling it off her head and offering it out to me.

Setting the Bugles, popcorn, and candy on the floor, I smooth a palm over her braid, pieces of static hair sticking up at all angles. "You look like I did when you first stopped by my apartment that day. Hair everywhere."

I take her beanie, jacket, and scarf and drop them onto the empty seat beside us. We're on a row of five in the very top corner, and luckily, no one booked the seats right next to us. I can't say I'm surprised since we can barely see the screen from way back here.

"I'm sorry the seats are shit, Doll. It was all they had left."

She reaches down and picks up the packet of Bugles, pulling it open and offering it to me. "Meh." She dismisses the issue entirely. "I pretty much know this movie scene by scene and line by line. It's just nice that someone wants to actually watch it with me."

I choose not to ask if Liam ever did because I already know the answer.

"When I was ten, I had an obsession with trains. If I wasn't railfanning, then I was playing hockey." I think back to the catalog of photos I put together over a two-year period. All of which my mom keeps in her place now. Darcy is the first person I've talked to about my former passion, something that I'd long forgotten about until now. Nostalgia shoots through me as hazy childhood memories reemerge.

"Railfanning, as in trainspotting?" Darcy asks, already on her third Bugle.

"Yeah. Some, my dad took me to spot; others, I researched and followed online. Then I turned into a preteen and found girls." I smirk at her, and she deadpans.

I lean forward and snatch the piece she's holding between her fingers with my mouth, and she balks at me in surprise.

"I could teach you some lessons in Darcy Thompson, if you'd like?"

I continue to crunch on it, a smirk still playing on my lips as the lights go down and the movie starts to play.

"Go on," I whisper. "It's probably nothing I don't already know about you anyway."

She side-eyes me as an image of Bletchley Park—the place where most of the codebreaking took place in England—comes into view.

"Never steal my favorite foods, especially not while I'm pregnant."

I reach into the bag and take another out before she can scrunch it shut.

"Gotta be quicker than that, Doll." I hold it between my lips and wait for her to reach up and take it from my mouth.

Her eyes rove the theater as she braces one hand on the seat and reaches up to snatch it. I take full advantage, pulling her into my lap.

"Archer ..." she whispers just before she takes the Bugle from my mouth and begins crunching down.

The woman sitting directly in front of us shifts in her seat, but doesn't look behind her as she continues to watch the movie.

I push back Darcy's braid and brush my lips along the shell of her ear. "I'm going to need you to calm down. Or you're going to get us busted."

Her cheeks flush pink, and her skin pebbles along her bare arms. She's only wearing a black T-shirt and purple skirt with tights and boots, and all I can think about is how easy it would be to slide—

"Do you have any intention of watching this film with me?" Darcy asks, cutting off my daydream.

With my hand on her knee, I slowly trail it up and under her short, pleated skirt, dipping my fingers beneath the hem. "It's like you can suggest other things we could be doing?"

"Shhh!" the woman in front scolds, still not looking our way.

I roll my lips together and try not to laugh. Darcy buries her head into the crook of my neck.

"You know what we can do in silence?" I whisper so quietly that I can barely hear my own voice as she loops both arms around my neck, the shine of her eyes reflecting off the screen.

"What?"

When I run my tongue along her lower lip, she parts for me. Just like my memories of railfanning, this kiss takes me back to when I was a young boy and started to kiss girls for the first time.

Butterflies dance in my stomach, and a small whimper rises up my throat when I massage my tongue against Darcy's. But unlike when I was a teenager, nothing about this moment feels naive.

I'm in love with this girl. The feeling is unmistakable, even if I've never said the words to anyone before or felt the way I do about Darcy. The realization washes over me in a flood of relief, mixed with a silent prayer that she will catch up to me. This is beyond wanting her as my girlfriend or being obsessed enough to stalk her around town or call her shitty ex. It's beyond wanting to raise a baby with her because I know she'll be the best mom in the world.

She is what I want for the rest of my life—silly dates at the theater where we don't actually watch the movie but make out instead. Walks around the park so she can clear her head of stress and tell me all of her eccentric British traditions.

This is why I couldn't get enough of her when she visited from the UK. Why—from the moment I set eyes on her two years ago—the only place I could picture being was right by her side.

I break the kiss and study her swollen red lips as I pull away, finding her eyes when they lock on to mine.

"What's the matter?" she asks in the softest voice.

I swallow hard, my mouth as dry as the popcorn by my feet. "I need you to promise me that you won't freak out in the middle of this packed theater."

Her fingertips tickle the back of my neck. "I promise I won't."

"Good, because I can't hold it in anymore." The woman in front of us stirs again, and I bring my mouth back to hers. "I'm in love with you, Darcy. I'm going to need you to be my girlfriend now."

When a smile tips up her lips, I know that despite being in a packed theater as I whispered the words, this, right here, was exactly the right time to go all in.

"Okay."

My arms tighten around her waist as I check that this isn't a dream.

"Oh Jesus ..." I blow out a slow breath. "For real?"

She chuckles softly and brings her mouth down over mine. "For real. I *want* to try with you."

Bringing her palm to my lips, I set a kiss in the center before resting it over her stomach. "You hear that, Pipsqueak? Let's fucking go."

CHAPTER THIRTY-ONE

DARCY

We all have that one pair of jeans that just fit. They make your ass look good and don't dig into your stomach when you sit down.

Well, these jeans *were my pair*. And as I pour myself into them, fighting with the zip and button while I lie flat on the bed, I slowly come to terms with that cold, hard truth.

My Levi's 501s are about to become a thing of the past.

"Are you wrestling or getting dressed?"

From flat on my back, I roll my eyes toward the ceiling. "Both," I grunt out, securing the button on a deep inhale.

Archer stands over me, arms folded across his chest. In a black T-shirt and dark blue jeans that hug his sculpted thighs, he looks anything but bloated. Unlike me.

He smirks. "I would offer to help, but my expertise centers more around taking your clothes off."

I circle my stomach. "I reckon you've done enough already, wouldn't you say?"

With two hands underneath my ass, he scoops me off the bed

and carries me through to the kitchen, where he sets me on the island, coming to stand between my legs.

He runs his hands along the tops of my thighs. "This was the first place you sat when you came over to my apartment that time. You brought coffee and asked me if I had a girl in my bed."

"That seems like a long time ago." I reminisce. "So much has changed since then. I feel like I've grown ten years older."

He cups the sides of my face in his huge hands. I've never craved the security or safety of a man before in my life, and I was convinced I wouldn't ever. Now I'm thinking I simply had the wrong type of guy.

Archer kisses the underside of my chin, working his way down my neck. "I'm so fucking happy we could get the eight-week scan on my day off."

The way I want him to take me back to bed so we can do unholy things ...

"And if we don't head out now, then we're going to miss it," I reply.

He pauses on kissing me and glances at the clock above the oven. "We have at least another ten minutes."

"Your maths is appalling—you know that?" I'm aiming to sound bratty. Instead, I come off as turned on because I absolutely am.

He smooths his tongue across my pulse point, fingertips dancing toward my apex. "I like to think of it as optimistic calculations. I drive a Mercedes AMG GT Coupe. I promise we'll make it on time."

I quirk a brow at him. "You know I'm a good girl, and you're a bad influence, don't you?"

He moves to my earlobe, biting it gently between his teeth. "Yeah, but you're officially mine now, so there's no point in fighting it. Just let me have my way with you."

I part my thighs wider for him. "When you say you want to have your way with me, be specific."

He groans and pulls me forward until I can feel his hard cock pressing into my jean-covered pussy. "Lots of sex and plenty more babies."

I pull back, ready to tell him one is more than enough, when his mobile starts buzzing at the other end of the island.

Reaching across, Archer picks it up and then looks at me. "It's my mom."

I wave an excitable hand around. I haven't spoken to Julia since Archer broke the pregnancy news. "Answer it. Answer it."

He groans like a petulant teenager. "I wanted to have sex."

I raise a brow. "Archer Moore, answer the phone to your mother."

"Hey, Mom," he says in a bright tone, his spare hand reaching for the top button of my jeans.

I bat him away and strain to listen in.

"Hang on. Darcy's here and wants to say hi. Let me put us on speaker."

"Oh! Of course, it's your scan this afternoon. Why don't you put me on video call so I can see you both?"

Archer narrows his eyes at me when I nod profusely. "Hang on a second. Let me get dressed."

"Archer! You did not just answer the phone while having—"

"No, he did not. He's playing with you," I cut across Julia.

Talking to her about sex is *not* how I envisaged our first proper conversation.

Flicking the camera around to face us, Archer stands just in front of me as I peer over his shoulder from my seat at the island. He holds the phone out in front of him, and Julia's bright smile fills the screen.

"We can only be a few minutes, as we need to leave for the clinic."

Julia just continues smiling at us both before she bends down and picks something up off the floor.

"Oh my God!" I gasp, hands covering my mouth when a ball of fawn-colored fluff with pointy ears and an attitude for days sits on Julia's lap. "Is that a Chihuahua?"

"Sure is," she confirms. "This is Stella. She's my baby. Say hello to your brother and his girl." Julia lifts her left paw, waving it at us.

I'll be honest, the dog does not look impressed.

"Archer is her favorite," she continues. "I've been telling Stella that she can't go getting all jealous when the baby arrives. Can you, my love?" She finishes the last part of her sentence in a sickly-sweet voice.

I love her even more.

Something off-screen catches Stella's attention, and she releases a muted bark, ears pricked like a meerkat as she launches from Julia's lap.

Julia chuckles and brushes the hair from her trousers. "I just have to say, Darcy, I knew you were my son's love interest when I saw you in the arena restroom that day. You're exactly his type."

Archer rolls his eyes, but despite his apparent disapproval, I can see the love he has for his mum; it rolls off him in waves.

"Maybe one day, he can convince you to give him a shot and start dating?" she asks, hopeful eyes flicking between me and Archer.

"Well, actually ..." My boyfriend's face morphs into the biggest damn smile I have ever seen. He wraps an arm around my shoulders and pulls me into his side, planting a kiss in my hair. "We already figured that part out. She's officially mine, Mom. All fucking mine."

I can't help but blush at his actions as Julia scolds her twenty-something son for dropping the F-bomb.

"I'm so happy for you both." Her eyes soften at her son. "I know you've been chasing Darcy, and now you have the girl. Now all you have to do is—"

"I know; I know," he quickly confirms, pressing a kiss against my forehead. "I'm not going to fuck anything up. I love her too much."

If I don't melt into a puddle right here, I'm pretty sure Julia will.

"Just ..." Archer trails off, clearing his throat. "Just make sure you don't say anything to anyone, okay? I'll tell Emma and Dad after the twelve-week point, but the pregnancy and us is ... it's kind of complicated right now."

I can tell that Archer's statement serves as more of a reminder than it does a request to his mum, and she nods her head quickly. "I got it."

"Only you, Darcy's mom and her friend, and Darcy's girlfriends know about the pregnancy."

I smile at that, recalling the look on Kendra's face yesterday in Rise Up when I said I'd be skipping caffeine for the next seven months. Naturally, our group chat hasn't stopped with ideas and suggestions for the nursery styling and links to cute baby clothes from Jenna and Kendra. Collins, on the other hand, wants to know when she can apply for the baby's motorcycle license.

Fat fucking chance.

Just like Mum, Kendra agreed it was wise to wait to tell Jon. Unfortunately, she also agreed that Jack would lay Archer out the second he found out.

"Okay, before I go—because I know you need to head out—I have to ask. Are you going to find out the gender? After eight weeks, you have the option to via a blood test."

I swallow hard. I knew this from the research I'd been doing and conversations with Mum. So much of me wants to find out since I hate surprises and love shopping—which is only made easier when you know what you're having—but ... needles.

Archer looks at me, rubbing my thigh in slow circles. He doesn't know about my needle phobia, and that, combined with the way I always seem to be sick, I'm sure he'll think I'm a wimp.

"I'm going to leave that decision to my girl."

He leans down so only I can hear. "About a year ago, Jack mentioned your fear of needles. We were talking about my thigh tattoo at the time. I want you to know that if for any reason you're scared or holding out on any tests you want, like for the gender of our baby, then I'm here to hold your hand. Nothing bad is going to happen to you when you're with me."

Every nerve I possess sparks as crackles dance across my skin, and I look at Julia when Archer kisses below my ear.

I can see the pride she has for her son, it's palpable, even via a brief video call.

"I'm going to let you two get to your appointment," she says.

"Okay, Mom." Archer wraps his arm around my waist. "I'll send you some pictures from the scan."

She grins like that's exactly what she was about to ask him. "Good. And then I want you both here for Thanksgiving ..." She pauses. "Actually, what about Christmas?"

Archer gazes down at me, phone still outstretched in his other hand. "I'll be spending Christmas wherever my girl is." He looks at his mum then. "And I want you with us for sure."

Julia's face lights up. "I would absolutely adore that."

Archer tears his gaze away from me, focusing back on Julia. "Our last Christmas before we're a threesome."

CHAPTER THIRTY-TWO

ARCHER

It's amazing how you can stare at the same thing over and over, yet you see something new each time you look at it. At the eight-week scan, the sonographer confirmed Darcy's final due date as June 16, which was pretty much in line with what we expected, and the second our baby's heartbeat filled the quiet room, I was ready to fall apart. A week later, I can still hear the soft thump of my child's heart.

We made that.

I was right when I said scan day would be the best day of my life. After we finished up, I took Darcy back to my apartment, undressed her, and made love to my girlfriend all night. We got zero sleep, and I regret nothing. To be honest, sleep has been in short supply for both of us since we got together. Why rest when you can fuck in every room you own? I like to look at it as preparation for the disturbed nights we'll have when the baby finally arrives.

"Is there, like, a secret passageway in this bathroom I'm not aware of?"

Still staring at the scan photo I keep inside my wallet, I quickly fold it shut and pocket it in my sweats.

Jack lets the bathroom door close behind him.

I push off the far wall and randomly wash my hands. I don't need to since I already rinsed them, but it's a great way to busy myself and an excuse not to look at him.

He sidles up next to me, arms crossed over his chest and his training bag slung over one shoulder. We just had practice, and some of the guys want to head to the driving range to hit a few balls this afternoon—a new hobby they've taken up.

Ordinarily, I'd go, and as Jack stands next to me, his lips pressed together while I finish up drying my hands for a second time, I know he wants me to tag along.

"If it had a secret passageway, then I wouldn't be standing here, would I?" I volley back, smirking as I do.

Anyone who knows Jack Morgan knows that he's the excitable, fun-loving guy on the team. I once told him in his first NHL season that he had all the ingredients to make a captain, and I still stand by that statement today. Only, as he drops his head between his shoulders and slowly shakes it, I see none of the usual brightness he shares in common with his sister. And that reality makes me feel a blend of guilt, as I wonder if he knows about Darcy, along with fear, for the exact same reason.

Clicking his tongue, he scuffs the floor with his sneaker. "I'm worried about you, bro."

I look up from the faucet and into his eyes, realizing he doesn't know anything about Darcy and me, but not feeling any easier. "Why are you worried?" I ask in a light tone.

Jack exhales deeply. "You aren't the same person." He lifts his head to look at me. "Back when we first met, you were different. You'd go out for one thing."

"I do still go out," I reply.

He lifts a brow, arms still set across his chest. "So, I'll assume you're coming to the driving range with us then?"

I push a hand through my hair, unease coating my insides.

Darcy's back at my place, waiting for the clinician to arrive and take her blood. She decided to go through with the prenatal blood test to determine the gender of our baby, and I need to leave in around five minutes to make sure I make it back in time. She's shitting herself over the process, and I need—no, I *want*— to be there with her. It isn't just my duty as the dad, but supporting my girlfriend brings me a sense of belonging I've never had before.

I find myself in another awkward-as-fuck situation, scrambling for excuses I can offer my friend without actually lying.

"I can't make it. I'm sorry." It's all I can think to say.

Jack moves toward me until we're only a few feet apart. "Is it Abbie?"

"Is Abbie what?"

Clearing his throat, he looks just as uncomfortable as I feel. "Is she, like, not letting you hang out with us? I mean, I know you've got a reputation, but she can't think you'd play around with someone else behind her back?"

There are a thousand different lies I can give him, but my brain won't allow me to spill any more. My mouth wars with my mind.

"We actually broke up," I say after a few beats, too exhausted to continue the ruse. Like I said before, I'm not a good liar, and if I have to hear that make-believe girl's name one more time, I swear I'll lose my mind.

There's only one girl's name I like to hear.

He looks genuinely shocked, but I can't say he's gutted for me.

Reaching out, he clamps a hand on my shoulder. "Do you want to talk about it or ..."

I shake my head; the last place I want to be right now is in this bathroom. "Nah. I ended it because the long-distance thing wasn't going to work, and she wanted more from me, which I couldn't give."

He nods in understanding. "I get it. I struggle being away

from Kendra for an away series, never mind months on end. Fuck that shit."

His trademark cocky smile blooms, and I can't say I'm mad about it. Just like with his sister, Jack looking down is not the kind of world I want to be a part of.

"So, I guess that means you're single as a Pringle and ready to mingle?"

I roll my eyes at him, feeling my cell vibrate in the pocket of my pants. It's probably Darcy freaking out again.

"Technically, yes," I reply. "But the breakup is all kinds of fresh, you know? And that's why I can't make it to the range. I'm going to head home and get some rest. I've not been sleeping well."

"Yeah." His hand drops from my shoulder, and he circles around his eyes. "You do look kind of tired, to be honest."

Yeah, fucking your sister every way to Sunday will do that to a guy.

Jack steps aside, allowing me to leave.

Right before I reach the bathroom door, I swivel on my heel as he pulls out his phone and starts typing.

"I respect you—you know that, right?" I wasn't expecting to say the words, but I know why I said them.

At some point, I know he'll doubt how much I value our friendship, and while I have the easygoing Jack standing in front of me, I want him to absorb my truth.

I think the world of this guy.

He looks confused but smiles anyway. "Yeah, I know, man. I've always got your back."

My hand wraps around the door handle, and I pause again, closing my eyes slowly as I try to convince myself of a reality where he won't want to take me out when he finally finds out about Darcy. "See you tomorrow at skate."

The elevator doors open to my apartment just as the smart doorbell sounds.

I made it home just in time.

Dressed in black Lycra leggings and a cropped white T-shirt with a braid hanging over her left shoulder, Darcy appears in the entryway, separating the hallway to the kitchen and living space.

She looks pale as fuck, gray almost, and I can tell she's trembling, even from the other side of the vast open-plan space.

I drop my training bag at my feet, not bothering to move it to the side, and head straight for her.

My lips find the top of her head as I wrap her in my arms, and she melts into my chest.

The doorbell sounds again, and she releases a sigh into my hoodie. "We need to get the door or else the phlebotomist will think we're not here."

Generally, a gender blood test is conducted with an at-home kit, and as it's a finger prick test, it doesn't require a professional. But given Darcy's fear of needles, I paid for someone at the clinic to visit and carry it out. I figured she'd feel more confident that way.

I grip her shoulders and pull back so I can look at my girlfriend. "You don't have to do this. We can wait until eighteen weeks, when they can confirm by ultrasound."

She shakes her head. "No, I want us to know. This is a good opportunity for me to start getting used to the fact that I'm going to be poked and prodded for the next seven months. I want to prove to myself I can do it."

I think I just defied gravity and fell a little bit harder for this girl.

I take her hand in mine, and we walk across to the door. I pull it open to find a smiling middle-aged woman with curly brown hair and warm, rosy cheeks.

She holds her ID card attached to a lanyard around her neck. "You must be Archer and Darcy. My name is Amanda, and I'm here to help with your early gender test."

I swear to God I hear Darcy gulp from beside me, and I squeeze her hand in mine.

"Hey there," Darcy replies, squeezing my hand back.

Her palm feels clammy, and I watch the way her chest rises and falls more quickly. Fuck, she doesn't have to do this.

But if there's one thing I'm learning about this girl, it's that she's got the strength to match her beauty. This is more than about finding out the baby's gender. This is an internal war with herself and one she's determined to win. I wonder if something happened in her past that triggered her phobia of needles or if it's simply inherent for her.

Truthfully, the reason doesn't matter. I just want to protect and care for her in any way I can. For the rest of my life.

Amanda steps inside, shrugging off her jacket, and I break from Darcy, taking it from her and setting it on the coat stand.

Heading across to the couch, Darcy sits tentatively, and I retake her hand, stroking my thumb across the top.

"You must think I'm such a wimp." She snorts, looking at Amanda as she pulls some paperwork from her bag and begins filling it out.

Amanda just smiles. "Actually, you'd be surprised how many people suffer with trypanophobia. I do more home visits than you can imagine, but I promise this is a noninvasive procedure, and you will only feel a tiny scratch."

Darcy swallows hard and fast as she watches Amanda

complete the paperwork. I can tell she's a few seconds from puking as anxiety overwhelms her.

I lean into my girlfriend, speaking softly. "When I was ten, I wasn't just into railfanning. I also liked to skateboard in places I shouldn't, including down my mom and dad's steep street."

She looks up at me, wincing when I pull off my long-sleeved shirt and show her the faint scar that runs from under my armpit all the way to the crook of my elbow.

"I figured you'd gotten that from hockey."

I shake my head. "Nope. Let's just say, I only stopped when I hit some barbed wire. I needed a small blood transfusion. I've never been so scared as I was that day."

Darcy eyes my scar, reaching up to run a finger down the faint line. "Your mum must've been terrified."

"Yep." I nod. Faintly remembering the look on her face. "My sister passed out at the sight of my injury, and my dad went fucking nuts. I didn't get back on my skateboard for a long time."

Her eyes flick across to Amanda as she finishes up the paperwork, and I catch her chin between my thumb and forefinger, demanding her attention.

"I know the level of anxiety you're feeling right now is extreme, and I wish with my whole fucking heart that I could take that away from you. Every damn day, you amaze me with something new, and I sit in constant awe of you. Facing your fears like this is incredible. You are incredible."

Now that I have her eyes on me alone, I remove my hand from Darcy's chin to cup her cheek. "Just like my mom promised me that day—that nothing bad was going to happen because she was there with me—I can promise you that too. You have nothing to fear today or any other day because I'm here, with you, fighting for you. When you love someone as much as I do you, it isn't possible for bad shit to happen—because I simply won't let it. I'll annihilate anything or anyone that tries to hurt you."

Darcy's breathing slows a fraction, and her pupils dilate. "I'm so fucking scared, Archer."

My lips find the corner of her dry mouth. "Of course you are. But I believe in you, and I know you wouldn't be here, sitting on this couch and pushing your comfort levels, if this wasn't what you wanted."

She looks down at her hands as she twists them in her lap, and I take one of them back between both of mine.

When I focus back on Amanda, her eyes flick between us, and I have to hand it to myself—I'm pretty sure I just made the phlebotomist swoon.

Add it to my list of talents.

"How is it you can have everyone wrapped around your finger so easily?" Darcy asks. Her voice is lighter, and I might even detect a little humor in there.

I take advantage of the moment and hold out our joined hands to Amanda. In a split second, she completes the test. Darcy jolts but quickly smiles against my mouth when I press it against hers.

It's possible Amanda wasn't expecting to get a show to go with her two o'clock appointment, but I couldn't care less. I've got my girl right where I want her. Her ragged breathing has calmed and she's fucking putty in my arms.

"I beg to differ, Doll. It's impossible for everyone to be at my mercy when I'm too busy on my own knees for you."

"You just have all the lines, don't you?" she croons.

I tip my head toward the kitchen. "Okay, well, if that one didn't work on you, then maybe this one will."

She narrows her eyes at me suspiciously, and just like that, it's almost as if the blood test never happened.

"Give it your best shot."

Briefly, I look at Amanda, who's busy bagging the sample.

I reach down and spread my palm across her stomach. It's probably my imagination, though I swear it feels rounder. "What if I told you I have all the ingredients to make cheesy bean burritos, Archer Moore–style?"

Her face lights up. "If you can pull them off like Taco Bell, then I'll wrap around anything you want."

Darcy's eyes flare, darting to look at Amanda, and the phlebotomist waves a hand in front of her, smirking.

Through my tears of laughter and wheezing, I'm pretty sure I hear my girlfriend curse under her breath, explaining it wasn't supposed to come out like that.

My shoulders are still vibrating when I kiss her. "Mistake or not, I'm all in on this challenge. Taco Bell doesn't stand a chance."

She quirks a brow, cheeks still stained with embarrassment. "You can cook? How did I not know this?"

I set one last kiss across her mouth, nodding. "Let's call this lesson number two in the class of Archer Moore."

CHAPTER THIRTY-THREE

DARCY

A week later, and I can still taste those damn burritos. They were that good. Let's just say, my stomach wasn't the only satisfied part of me that night.

Sitting at my desk at work, I squeeze my thighs together at the memories of the way Archer wrapped me around him in every way possible, trying to focus on the fall edit I need to have back to Janine in the next hour. Good job my first pass was excellent. All it needs is a light proofread.

I'm well over halfway through my final pass when I feel my bag buzz against my leg.

Being the queen of procrastination and apparently too damn obsessed with my boyfriend to hold off another half hour before I check it, I reach down and grab it.

> Kendra: I've made an error in judgment, and I need one of you to bail me out ...
>
> Collins: This has got my name written all over it.

> Jenna: Whatever you did, I'm pretty sure I can take your "error" and raise you several stupidity notches.
>
> Collins: One at a time, please. Kendra, you go first.
>
> Kendra: I kind of just dropped way too much of my salary on baby clothes, and now I have nowhere to hide the bags.

I snort out loud in the middle of the office.

> Me: Girl, I'm ten weeks, and we're still waiting on gender confirmation.
>
> Kendra: I know, I know, but I couldn't help it. The rompers were too cute, and then I saw these tiny little sandals, and it snowballed. Everything is gender-neutral.
>
> Kendra: And have you checked your email? Because I NEED to know what you're having.

I navigate to my email and refresh the inbox. Nothing. My heart sinks a little more. If news doesn't arrive today, I'm fairly certain Archer will drive to the lab and run the test himself.

> Me: Nothing yet, but we were told it could take a week or so. I need you all to remain calm because my boyfriend is about to burst a blood vessel. He's the most impatient person on this planet.
>
> Kendra: I still can't believe you're pregnant.
>
> Collins: Your bank balance can though.
>
> Kendra: True that.

Jenna: You can stash the clothes here. I promise I won't go through them and squeal at their tininess …

Kendra: Lifesaver. I'll be over later.

Collins: Next order of business: Jenna. How have you fucked up on this fine morning?

Jenna: If you take the word "how" and rearrange the letters to form a common pronoun, your question will be more accurate.

Collins: I mean, I'd rather not …

Me: Easy problem. So, who did you fuck?

Me: WAIT. WHO DID YOU FUCK, JENNA?

Jenna: I was horny, okay?

Kendra: WHO?

Jenna: One of the Storm's team physios. We've had a thing for a while, and … yeah. I'm still in his bed, and he's taking a shower.

Kendra: OMG, you fucked Phil, didn't you?

Jenna: Yes.

Kendra: Girl, if word gets out, you're both in so much trouble.

Jenna: I think that's what made it so good—the forbidden nature of it all.

Collins: Is he kinky?

Jenna: Unfortunately not. Decent-sized cock though.

Me: I have no words.

Jenna: Oh, don't pretend like you're a good girl.

> Me: True. The first time I had sex with Archer, we took photos.

> Kendra: That's my biggest fear—a sex video or a photo of me and Jack leaking onto the internet. I'd fly to the moon and never come back.

> Me: I already deleted it—because same. It was still hot though.

> Collins: Are you going to go there again, Jenna?

> Jenna: Probably. Who knows? He isn't boyfriend material, but I'm resigned to the single life. So, I might as well have fun.

> Me: That's what I was saying a few months ago. Oh, how the tables have turned.

> Jenna: You mean by having the hottest guy in the NHL at your feet with his baby inside your womb, all while he worships the ground you walk on? I'll take the surprise pregnancy to have that.

> Me: When you put it like that …

> Collins: Practical question, but what are you doing about your job?

I stare ahead into Janine's office as she talks with Penelope over something, dread festering in the pit of my stomach.

> Me: Actually, that's a really good question and one I don't currently have an answer to. I was talking to Mum about my plans after maternity leave, and we hit upon a snag, which her lawyer brain is trying to work through. My contract with Glide—and work visa—ends in just over eleven months, at the end of October, since they extended my initial twelve-month contract. So, unless Janine offers me a permanent position beyond that point, then I'm out of work, and the baby will only be four and a half months old. That's if she doesn't terminate my contract when I have to leave and give birth in June since that was never the agreement. When I moved here, I figured I'd be able to find another job once I had some experience behind me, and I was prepared to take that risk. But who's going to take me on now? I refuse to go back to work after only a few months with our baby. The whole entire situation is shit.

Kendra: Wait, so having a baby in the US with an American man doesn't mean you can automatically stay?

A wave of nausea passes over me.

> Me: Nope.

Kendra: What does Archer say?

> Me: I haven't told him. I found out, like, two days ago, and I'm still trying to work through it. Mum is getting some advice.

Collins: You need to tell Archer.

I close my eyes, trying to temper my rapid heart rate.

> Me: I know.

> Collins: I'm so sorry this is happening, Babe. Am I the only one without drama in my life?
>
> Kendra: It appears that way.
>
> Me: I feel like a girls' night is overdue. Drama requires cocktails. Or in my case, mocktails.
>
> Me: I JUST WANT A COSMO!
>
> Jenna: Agreed. And if this whole thing with Phil blows up in my face, I'll be sure to have your quota of alcohol, trust me.
>
> Kendra: I will return with dates, venues, and times. Girls' night is on!

Dropping my head between my shoulders, I inhale a deep breath and blow it out for eight seconds.

It's all going to work out, Darcy. You've got your mum working everything out.

Collins is right, and I know it. I need to tell Archer because I know he hasn't considered any of this. We've spent the past five weeks trying to get our heads around becoming parents, and now this.

I'm halfway through the same page I've read multiple times when my phone buzzes again.

> Jack: Is it me, or does it feel like I see you less now that you're in New York than when you were in Oxford?
>
> Me: It's definitely a you thing. I've been coming to games. I'm just busy with work—so many deadlines.
>
> Jack: Yeah, well, I miss my baby sister, even if you are annoying. My wife sees you more than I do.

> Me: It's funny you should say that because we're arranging cocktail night. Girls only though, I'm afraid.

> Jack: Are you seeing Liam again, and that's what's got you busy?

My brother's question acts as a further reminder of how crazy my life has become. Since I heard from Liam when he asked me to give him another chance and he wanted to visit me in New York, he hasn't contacted me again, and I haven't even thought about it. It's just as well, given the way he spoke to me. A part of me hopes he got the message that I didn't want to talk. More likely, he's already moved on to another girl and forgotten all about me a second time.

Whatever.

> Me: No. He's fallen off the radar, and I can't say I'm mad about it.

> Jack: So, what's going on, Darcy? I'm worried you regret moving here.

> Me: I regret nothing, and you don't need to worry. There's nothing back in the UK for me, other than an asshole Dad and a dickhead ex.

My stomach drops again. The *last* place I want to be is stuck in the UK.

> Jack: When I get back from the next away series, we're going out.

> Me: As like a brother-and-sister bonding session?

> Jack: Exactly that.

> Me: Only if you're paying.

Jack: When have you not made me pay?

I snicker, sending the next text.

> Me: True. I want to go somewhere big and fancy and really expensive.

Jack: Well, given you're the only other person I know who loves raw fish, I figured we could go to that new sushi restaurant across town. It's lavish and expensive enough for your tastes.

Every single hair on my body feels like it's standing on end. Jack's right; I do love sushi. But I can't eat it.

Get out of this one, brainiac.

> Me: Already been there, and it wasn't that great.

Jack: It opened three weeks ago. Who with?

Fuck.

> Me: Some girls from work. Let's just go to an Italian or something.

Jack: Boring.

> Me: But at least the food will be nice.

Jack: And you will have Pinot Grigio on demand. I'll book us a table.

Double fuck.

CHAPTER THIRTY-FOUR

ARCHER

I'm horny as hell.

What the fuck is it about pregnancy that turns my already-high sex drive into feral need every time my girl is around? Like magnets, every inch of my skin flares in response to her proximity, and the feeling won't let up until I'm touching her in some kind of way.

When I'm on the ice, I'm thinking about getting home so I can see her. If she's staying at her place that night, I'm scrambling for reasons why I need her in my apartment.

This away series in Dallas is going to be the death of me—five days away from Darcy and more sneaking around as I hide text exchanges and phone calls from her brother and the rest of the team.

The one saving grace? The boys know Abbie is out of the picture, so no one expects some random chick to turn up at a bar one night, claiming to be my girlfriend. The downside? They're all going to expect me to leave the bars with one, maybe even two girls on my arm.

Because that's what Archer Moore does.

Even though I haven't actually done it since last October, when I finally realized if she wasn't Darcy, I couldn't go through with it.

I get all the reasons why Darcy wants to wait on telling her brother and stepdad. My parents didn't announce their pregnancies until Mom started showing. It's a standard decision to make. I can't lie and claim it isn't killing me though. The thought of holding in our secret another couple of weeks and the prospect of breaking the news equally terrify me.

Not that I'd tell Darcy or anyone else that. She's got enough spinning in her head. Whatever comes my way—whether it's her brother's and stepdad's fists or congratulations—I'll deal with it. I'll tell them I'm in love with her. I'll own the Abbie ruse, and I'll take what they throw at me on the chin.

For her.

For us.

For our baby.

The other thing that's killing me? Waiting on the gender test results. It's been over a week, and I have plans, goddammit. I know Darcy loves to shop, and I intend to drop some serious cash on her, the baby, and getting us all set as soon as we hear what we're having.

It's possible she'll want to wait until she's twelve weeks, but this is where I'm drawing the line. It's happening the second I get back from Dallas.

As I spoon my naked girlfriend, my palm finds her belly, and I gently run circles over her perfect skin. "You going to tell us what you are today, Pip? Daddy doesn't want to be in Texas when the news drops."

Darcy shifts in response to my whisper, and I move some hair to one side, exposing her neck.

When my lips find the sensitive skin underneath her ear, she stretches out like a kitten. I feel a little bad for waking her, but our time in bed is limited since she's got to head to work, and I'll be boarding a plane before she finishes.

I probably shouldn't be so hung up on how many hours I get with her since I plan to spend the rest of my life by her side, but still, every second feels like a goddamn blessing.

My phone buzzes on the side table, and I reach across and grab it, opening up a message from Jack.

> Jack: *shirtless picture of him working out in his home gym*
>
> Jack: I'm sending this since Archer doesn't bless us with his naked chest any longer.

I smirk. The kid's got some fucking gall.

> Me: I remember you and Sawyer telling me to keep it to my OnlyFans page.
>
> Sawyer: We did, and it thankfully worked. Put it away, Jack. I just ate breakfast.
>
> Me: You're up early.
>
> Sawyer: Ezra has a motocross meet, and Collins is taking him. They had to leave early.
>
> Jack: Why don't you send early morning workout pictures to us anymore?
>
> Jack: Wait. Don't answer that because I already know what's coming—you're too busy in bed with my sister or some shit like that. Change the record.
>
> Sawyer: Did everyone get the amended practice schedule from Coach? He emailed it late last night.

Jesus, way to divert, Sawyer.

Another text comes through. This time, it's directly from my captain.

> Sawyer: You are in bed with her right now, aren't you?

Darcy turns over to face me, smiling sleepily as she sets a kiss on my bare shoulder.

> Me: Yes.

> Sawyer: Jesus fucking Christ. I don't want to know anymore. When you get found out, I'm denying I ever knew anything about this—got that?

Protecting Sawyer from getting caught up in the fallout is a priority to me. At one point in Lloyd's, I figured he'd guessed, but he never said anything, even if he had suspicions.

> Me: I got it, Cap. I also got the amended practice schedule.

> Sawyer: I know you did. I was deflecting.

> Me: And I love you for that.

> Sawyer: Jack's messaging the group chat ...

> Me: I know. I can see them coming through.

> Sawyer: This is all going to blow up in your face, Archer. And I'm not sure I can help you pick up the pieces on this one.

"Who are you texting?" Darcy sings at me, her palm wrapping around my already-hard dick.

"Sawyer," I reply, leaning in to set a kiss on her forehead.

> Me: So, you want me to end it with Darcy? Because that would be the very definition of fucking her around which is, in fact, what Jack thought I would do. I'm not going anywhere, and he's going to have to deal with it when the time comes.

> Sawyer: Wait. Are you guys dating now???

> Me: Yeah.

> Sawyer: Is it serious???

> Me: Yeah. Very.

> Sawyer: You need to tell him.

> Me: I will.

> Sawyer: Now.

> Me: It's … complicated. Just let me handle it, and you have my word I'll keep you out of it.

> Sawyer: All right. I'm not happy, but all right.

> Me: I gotta go. She just woke up, and we're about to spend five days apart.

> Me: If you catch my drift.

> Sawyer: I've got NO IDEA what you're talking about.

I toss my phone off to the side and hover over her.

"I think you're starting to show a little, Doll." My hand smooths over her stomach. "You're doing such a good job at growing our baby."

She whimpers a little, and I grin down at her.

"Wait. Does my girl like being praised?"

Darcy flutters her long eyelashes at me. "I mean ... I guess there are worse things in life than being told I'm a good girl."

Yeah, that'll fucking do it.

Throwing back the covers, I lift her into my arms and walk us to the shower.

"I was all warm and snuggly," she whines as I hold her in one arm and crank the walk-in rainfall shower.

The water heats up fast, and since we're both already naked, I move us straight through the stream, pinning Darcy against the far wall with both hands under her ass.

"You literally carry me around like I weigh nothing."

Running my tongue along her bottom lip, I can feel my cock as it presses into her stomach. "Hence your nickname—you've got doll-like features and weigh about as much. So fucking beautiful."

My cock is lined up perfectly, and I push inside my girlfriend.

"I want you to know something," I tell her, eyes falling to her tiny, round belly.

She cocks her head to the side, lips parted on a gasp. "What?"

My grin is so wide; it aches in my cheeks when I stroke inside her for the first time. "I'm really fucking happy you're allergic to latex."

She bursts out laughing, playing with pieces of hair at the back of my neck as I fuck her slowly. "Well, we can get latex-free ones afterward."

"Never going to happen." I shake my head. "This right here" —I pull out and push back inside, spreading her perfect cunt— "is the only way we're going to fuck. From now until the day I die, Darcy. You're never going anywhere, and neither am I. This is it for us both."

Something flashes in her eyes when I spread her legs wider. I can't tell what's going on in her head, and I hate that.

"We're having a girl," she whispers.

My hips pause, and my throat grows tight. Water from the

shower trickles down my forehead, where it gathers in my lashes, although I know the wetness coating my eyes isn't from that.

"A baby girl?" I choke out.

She cups my face in her small palm, stroking the scruff I haven't shaved yet. "I got the email while you were texting Sawyer. I was going to tell you right when you marched us into the shower."

My tears spill over, running down my cheeks.

Fuck. I'm a mess.

"A baby girl?" I repeat since I'm incapable of forming other coherent sentences.

"Yes, Baby. I'm going to be insufferable, shopping for her."

My hips piston into her again, and she sucks in a breath. I can feel her getting wetter as her pussy grips me tighter.

"Yeah, I got plans for that, Doll. Both of my girls are being treated like queens."

She goes to open her mouth, but I silence her with a thrust that steals both of our breaths. I drop my face into the crook of her neck, fighting for air.

"I don't want to hear anything other than *yes* fall from those pretty lips. Both when you agree to me dropping a ton of money on you *and* when you come all over my cock in a few seconds."

A few more strokes, and she's practically wailing. My fingertips sink further into her ass, and I lick into her mouth, a possessive growl rising up my throat.

"You going to come for me, huh?"

She can't form words, and I don't push her to. The way her pussy squeezes as I feed it my cock is evidence enough.

"I'm going to put so many fucking babies inside you, Doll. I can't stop giving you my cum."

"Is that what you want?" Her voice is raspy. "I bet it turns you on, doesn't it? The thought of you inside me, taking over my body."

Pressure draws my balls tighter. I'm ready to go off like a fucking rocket.

"Come in my pussy, Archer," she orders. "I want to be your dirty, bad girl."

I am deceased.

"Are you going to come with me?" I rush out the words. "Because I'm about ten seconds—"

She pushes her head back into the tiles. "Oh-my-God, yes!" Her body shakes and quivers in my hands as I feel her release all over my cock.

"Fuck it."

I pull out and drop to my knees, her body suspended in my arms.

Thank the sweet Lord for leg presses.

My mouth is clamped around her pussy as I savor her release. I lick from one hole to the next as she continues shaking, clawing, and pulling at strands of my wet hair.

"I'm sorry if I'm hurting you; it's just s-so good."

I pop off her with Darcy coating my lips as they tip into a wicked grin. She's like damn royalty, staring down at me like I'm her servant.

At this point, I basically am.

"Hurt me, Doll. Make it really fucking sting. I've got five days without you, and I'll take any reminder of the way it felt as I drank you down."

When I take her back into my mouth, her nails dig into my shoulders. Her clit feels swollen against my tongue, and I tease it between my teeth.

"Oh fuck, oh fuck," she cries out. "I'm coming. Again."

Yes, she fucking is.

Her nails scrape down my skin. It's fucking exhilarating to know I'll wear the marks from my dream girl.

As Darcy's second high subsides, I lick her clean, the shower still flowing behind us.

"That was amazing," she croons when I lower her body and come to stand in front of her.

She reaches out to take my cock, but I interlace our fingers, resting my forehead against hers. I've only got the time to fuck her in my bed, and that's exactly what I'll do after we've showered.

"I don't want to leave you for five days."

She rests her spare palm against my chest. "It'll fly by."

I shake my head. "I can't do five minutes without you, let alone five days. All the guys call and text their families, but I can't with you, and it sucks fucking ass."

Her blue eyes find mine. "Do you want to tell him now?"

Yes. No. Maybe.

"You want to wait, and that's what we're going to do."

She nods once. "I do want to wait. I only told Mum and my girlfriends because I need them beside me. But if you—"

"I can hold out," I tell her, brushing my lips across her mouth. "Now or in a couple of weeks isn't going to make any difference. Not when we have the rest of our lives."

She looks heavy. Heavier than when we've previously talked about telling her brother. I know she's worried about how the team will react, but something has shifted in her, and it's freaking me the fuck out.

"What's going on, Darcy?"

She swallows hard, and for a second, I think she's going to say something.

"Nothing. I'm just a hormonal mess that's going to miss her man."

I decide to let it go. Maybe it is nothing. Maybe she's struggling with me going away just as much as I am.

If she is, then she definitely loves me.

"Are you going to see the girls while I'm away?"

"Yes. We're heading out for cocktails—or in my case, mocktails."

A seed of jealousy blooms in the pit of my stomach, but it's possession that overtakes it. "Out, as in around town?"

She nods, smirking just like she did that first time she came to my apartment.

"Don't play with me. One man even so much as looks at you, and I'll be on the first fucking flight."

"Oh, Archer." She brushes her lips across mine. "Maybe it's time for a little lesson of my own?"

Now I'm the one smirking. "What's that?"

Reaching up, she wraps a hand around the nape of my neck, bringing our foreheads back together. "You should be able to recognize a girl when she's falling for a boy."

CHAPTER THIRTY-FIVE

ARCHER

No one can tell I'm grinning like a fool behind this helmet. But I totally am.

She's fucking *falling* for me.

I've worn this smile for four days straight, and it shows no sign of fading. Neither does my performance on the ice this season.

We're three goals up against the Dallas Destroyers—a team that's nearly always kicked our asses, especially in away games—but not tonight.

Just like Darcy's heart, this shutout is going to be mine.

In a rare turnover, the Dallas captain collects the puck at center ice and wastes no time as he comes racing toward me. It's possible he'll lay off to his forward and the only other player in a position to support him.

It's also possible he'll use him as a decoy.

Memories of the preseason game come crashing back, but so does the advice Jensen has given me since we started working together. He identified that I was committing a fraction too early, and this was because of my anxiety around rebounds. Every goalie wants to gain possession, but flying pucks four inches from the ice aren't that easy to bury, and sometimes, you just have to call the opposition's bluff.

It was a genius call, and one that's given me more control over the puck. Jensen concluded there was nothing wrong with my ability to rebound to the corners; it was all in my head. Years of psyching myself out. I had made it big in the NHL because of my unmatched puck possession, but everyone knew my weakness revolved around distribution. And now I'm standing my ground at the crease a split second longer, and I'm psyching out forwards instead.

On this occasion, I don't need to call on my newfound confidence as Sawyer checks their center before he has a chance to shoot and the buzzer sounds.

Another W.

Sawyer skates across to me as I head toward the benches. The arena noise is muted while home fans leave, feeling underwhelmed by the result.

I grin bigger.

He pulls off his glove and taps the top of my helmet once. "Now, that was a motherfucking performance, buddy." He shakes his head in awe. "I can't put my finger on what it was out there, but you just felt more …"

"In control?" a voice calls from behind Sawyer, and he spins to look at Jensen when he approaches us.

Hands in the pockets of his black dress pants, he smiles at us both. "Seriously, I think my work here is done." He points to the crease. "Bryce got a hit on him because their center hesitated. My best guess is, you've thrown a lot of teams' pregame prep for a loop with your performances early season, and the oppositions just don't know how to handle it."

I pull off my helmet—smiling, of course. "I feel different out there. I mean, I've always felt composed and like the crease is my home, but something's definitely changed."

Jensen pats my shoulder a couple of times. "I get what you

mean, and I can see it in your eyes." He narrows his at me, but not in a suspicious way; it's more studious than that. "You look happy too. Happier than at the beginning of the season. I also know exactly how that feels. I don't think I played my best hockey until I met my wife." He chuckles, hearts in his eyes. "Or at least until she stopped hating me and started looking in my direction."

I cast a quick glance at Sawyer as he removes his helmet. I can tell he's wondering what I've said to Jensen, but the truth is I've kept it strictly professional during practices.

Jensen shrugs, shoving both hands back into his pockets. "It was just a hunch I had. I heard you were dating."

"Who's dating?" Jack slides up behind Jensen and Sawyer, hanging both arms around their shoulders.

Rolling his eyes playfully, Sawyer shrugs him off, the action quickly followed by Jensen.

"I swear to God, you've got the hearing of an owl or something."

Jack chews on the corner of his mouthguard. "I do when it comes to matters of the heart. Who's getting hitched?"

Dropping his head between his shoulders, Jensen shakes it. "Fuck me, you are just like him. I need to get back to Seattle, stat."

Almost offended, Jack's irreverent smile falls. "Like who?"

"Who do you think? Your stepdad."

"You are a bit like me, Jack." Coach Morgan joins from behind, the usual iPad tucked under his arm. "Take it as the compliment it is."

He turns to me, his business mask slipping back into place. "I know this isn't the best time, and you guys no doubt want to head out and celebrate the win, but some team news has just been confirmed ..." He pauses, looking like it's anything but good, and I'm guessing it has something to do with our new GM. "It's going to break to the press in the morning, and I want you all informed first."

Sawyer raises an unimpressed brow. "Is this about what I think it is?"

Coach Morgan clears his throat, shifting anxiously. For the first time in four days, my smile falters.

There's no way this is about me and Darcy. My face is still intact, for one thing, and my assistant captain is smiling.

"Let's get dressed, satisfy the postgame interviews, and meet in the team briefing room. And, Bryce?"

Sawyer pauses on skating away, waiting for Coach to finish.

"Let the rest of the team know. I've got a call with the GM I need to make."

"Take a seat, gentlemen." Coach stands at the foot of the briefing table as we all pile in, dressed in postgame suits.

The palpable tension in the locker room in anticipation over whatever team news is about to be delivered is not alleviated by Coach's tone. If anything, he sounds more pissed than he was on the ice.

"Is everything all right?" Emmett Richards asks as he balances one of his crutches against the table.

After a bad hit that twisted his knee, he was confirmed as being out for the season, and despite our excellent results, there's no doubt we need another defenseman. Everyone's best guess has been Noah Statham from Connecticut since he's been killing the AHL this season.

Now, as I look at Coach's creased brow and pursed lips, I'm not so sure that's the case. He likes Statham, and I heard that was who he wanted as Emmett's replacement. If he'd gotten his way, I'm confident I wouldn't be looking at a scowl right now.

"All right, as you all know ..." Coach begins. "Richards has sustained a season-ending injury, which has thrown the defense into turmoil. After all, he's a fucking wall."

Everyone begins laughing at the compliment because it's true, but Coach doesn't react, waiting for heads to refocus.

Amusement dies down quickly.

"The GM and I have been in deep discussions over a replacement and where we want to pull resources." He takes a breath and, fuck, here goes. "There were a couple of options available to us, both internally from the AHL and externally from elsewhere in the league."

Apart from Coach's, every single pair of eyes darts around the room, casting glances left and right to see who knows what. I think, at this point, we all definitely know it's not Statham.

I can tell Coach is fighting with everything he has to maintain a professional demeanor. He doesn't like this acquisition. And neither will we.

"Aside from the rookies, I know a lot of you have played with him. Let's just say, his style is memorable. In addition to his last name."

More heads turn to one another. My permanent smile is well and truly wiped.

"The GM feels we need to replace and intensify our presence in the back lines." Jon closes his eyes momentarily. Screw keeping a professional demeanor. This is personally hurting him. "The trade with Detroit is about to be finalized, and I'm ... well, I'm *pleased* to announce that Tommy Schneider will be joining the Blades. Effective immediately."

"Tommy Schneider?" Jack's voice cuts through the stunned silence. "As in the dickhead who doesn't actually play hockey?"

Jon side-eyes his stepson, but Jack's already lost his shit, and

I find myself wincing as I witness a prequel to what I can no doubt expect from him when he finds out about Darcy. Only I get the feeling this reaction I'm seeing is just the tip of the iceberg.

"As in Alex Schneider's estranged son?!" Jack continues. "As in the son of the guy who almost killed former Scorpions legend, Zach Evans, on the ice?"

Coach drops his head to the floor, hands stuffed inside his pockets. "Yes, Jack. As in Tommy Schneider."

"Yeah, well, he can't come. Terminate the damn trade!" Jack growls. "We just got this team playing like an actual unit, and now you want to throw an atomic bomb that is the biggest fighter the NHL has ever seen right into the center of our season."

Coach's head whips up, eyes narrowing at his assistant captain. He points his finger in the center of his chest. "I expressed my opinion on a number of occasions, but ultimately, the decision sits with the GM. And he's decided Schneider is what we need."

He points to Sawyer, and I know what's coming. Our captain hasn't hidden his intentions to retire, likely at the end of this season. "We know Bryce's plans, and we have to move now to strengthen the team."

He motions to me, and I shrink back in my seat. I want nothing to do with this since I'll be public enemy number one soon enough. "And we have to protect Moore's shutout stats. We're almost two months deep into the season, and he's smashing it."

Jack folds his arms across his chest, kicking his feet out under the table.

Coach looks at Sawyer next. "Maybe a few words from the captain?"

I know for a fact that Sawyer couldn't stand Alex Schneider. Sawyer was with the Blades when Alex was kicked off the team —or more accurately, his contract wasn't renewed.

The truth is, Tommy Schneider spent the first couple of years of his career wreaking havoc in the AHL before he was pulled into the Detroit side. No one really knows how much he's capable of since he spends the majority of his time in the penalty box.

Before Sawyer opens his mouth, I already know he's seething inside. He likely had a better idea than the rest of us that this was coming, but clearly, he never truly thought it would happen. This move from the GM is like two fingers to our fans and a step back in time to when the Blades were struggling at the foot of the league.

Clearing his throat, he scratches at his stubble. "I can understand concerns around the trade."

Jack huffs out a sarcastic breath.

"Hey!" I call across to him with a raised brow. "Cap is speaking. I know this is personal for you—it is for all of us—but let's keep it professional."

Pushing a hand through his hair, Jack nods in response. "Yeah, I'm just pissed, is all. Sorry, Cap."

"No worries," Sawyer replies. "So, yeah, I know this decision has come way out of left field, and it's going to leave a sour taste in a lot of people's mouths. That said, there's nothing we can do about it. The deal is done, and Schneider is joining us. All we can do is make him feel welcome and keep our focus off team politics and on the ice."

When he delivers that final sentence, his gaze tracks to me. Perhaps he sees this trade as small time compared to the bomb I'll drop.

He's right.

After Darcy turns twelve weeks, I was thinking the sooner, the better to tell Jack and Coach, but now, with this news and the state of mind both are in, I'm concluding we need to let the dust settle before we tell them.

Jack already looks livid, and I can't say I blame him. He knows that next season, he'll replace Sawyer as the C, and that his beef with Kendra's ex, Tyler Bennett, in his rookie season will have been a side show compared to the chaos Schneider will bring.

People label me as the NHL's biggest playboy. Well, that's nothing compared to the bad boy rep our new defenseman carries.

CHAPTER THIRTY-SIX

DARCY

Morning sickness has taken me out these past few days.

Not that Archer needs to know. He needed to concentrate on the away series against Dallas and keep up the run of form he's had since he started the regular season. His knowing about my sporadic puking wasn't going to change anything, other than having him on the first flight out of Texas.

He needed to be there with the team. When he says Jack is the more valuable player, he's doing himself an injustice. And now, with the contentious trade of Tommy Schneider, his teammates need him more than ever. He's the backbone and steady ship that steers them, even if he doesn't recognize it in himself. He shows up for his people, and they love him.

I'm falling in love with him.

Truthfully, I think I've known it for a while. I've certainly felt it in my heart. From the moment I found out he was "seeing" someone else, I tumbled into his world and abandoned my inhibitions. Yes, I was determined not to become another notch on his bedpost, but honestly, I don't think there was ever a risk of that happening. Archer Moore is the kind of boyfriend you dream about taking home to your parents while simultaneously counting down the hours until you can leave the family dinner table and get him alone again.

He's perfection personified.

He's the father of my child.

And he's mine.

He's also half an hour fucking late.

Wide awake at past midnight, I roll onto my back and stare up at the white ceiling. It's been nearly a week since I last stayed at my apartment, promising Archer I'd stay at his place instead. Apparently, a dead bolt, smart camera, and an incredibly nosy neighbor weren't enough to convince him I would be safe.

"So possessive," I whisper into the dark, smiling the whole time.

Reaching across to the side table, I tap the lamp base and flood the room with a warm glow. When I sit up and the duvet pools around my waist, I see the faint outline of a bump. To the onlooker, I've probably had a big meal, but to me, it's obvious.

I swipe my sudoku book and pencil from the table since my brain needs some kind of distraction and begin filling out the first problem when I hear the faint sound of elevator doors opening.

Every nerve tingles while I listen for footsteps following the familiar noise of his keys being set down on the console table.

I fight back a giddy smile and focus on my puzzle when the bedroom door cracks open, and Archer carefully steps inside.

His eyes drop to my puzzle book, balanced in my lap. "Does your brain ever get tired?"

He's already halfway to my bedside when I begin chewing on the tip of my pencil, appreciating the way his black tailored trousers and open collared white shirt hug every part of his perfect body.

Pretty much every year, he's voted by a magazine as the hottest guy in the NHL. Come to think of it, I'm fairly sure I voted once too.

He takes a seat on the edge of the bed next to me, cupping one side of my face in his hand while he slowly undoes his shirt with the other.

The first kiss he sets on my lips is soft and sweet, allowing me to taste what I've missed for nearly a week. He pulls back, eyes sparkling with mischief.

"I'm fucking crazy about you, Darcy."

If I couldn't feel the mattress beneath me, I'd feel sure I was levitating.

"My mind only rests when you're around," I breathe, trying to fill my lungs with the oxygen they crave.

His shirt now half undone, I notice he's wearing the platinum chain I love so much. "Where did you get that?" I ask, smoothing my fingers over it.

Archer takes the chain between his thumb and forefinger, eyes dropping to it. "I bought it myself. The day I got my signing bonus from the Philadelphia Bolts, I went and got it. It serves as a reminder of how far I've come and what I worked hard to achieve."

I never anticipated such a simple question to evoke the emotions forming in my throat as I take in a man who surprises me every day.

"You're sentimental?" I ask.

He dips a hand into the pocket of his pants and pulls out the conker he picked up in Fort Greene Park. "I guess you could say that, yeah."

I take it from his hand and turn it around in front of me, tears filling my vision. I know I'm all kinds of hormonal, but this is one of the sweetest gestures ever. "You kept the conker and took it away with you."

"Anything to help me get through the days without you, Darcy Doll."

Leaning forward, he presses a searing kiss against my lips, and I part for him, tongues tangling in perfect harmony. Nothing with Archer is forced—from our kisses to our conversations and more.

When we break for a second time, he picks up my puzzle book, turning it the right way up so he can study it.

Next, he picks up my pencil and begins scanning each square on the sudoku board.

After a few beats, he inserts a four into the central square on the third row down and hands the book back to me.

I check it over to make sure it doesn't clash with any other row or column. "You learned how to play?"

He flushes the cutest color, placing the pencil down on the side table. "Some of the team flights can be long and boring. It's kind of fun when you get used to it. Good for the brain."

He taps his temple twice, and I swear I fall further.

"That said, I still hope our baby girl gets her mom's brains." He chuckles as I slide the puzzle book next to the pencil.

He lowers the duvet from around my waist and lifts my sleep top to just below my breasts.

"You're definitely starting to show now." His warm lips rest against my bump, the vibration of his voice firing more sparks beneath the surface of my skin. "The way your body will change as it grows my baby will be a sight to behold."

Another kiss, and I'm melting.

"I've been chewing over potential names, and I think I might have one." He lifts his gaze to mine as he rests his chin on my growing belly.

"I'm not calling her Archer," I muse, running a hand through his soft brown hair.

"Damn." He clicks his tongue. "Good thing that wasn't the name I had in mind."

"What did you have in mind?"

He exhales a long, smooth breath, and I feel my shoulders relax in response to his calm.

"Emily."

Okay, that wasn't the kind of name I expected him to say. I was anticipating something more modern.

But I love it so much.

"Why Emily?" I ask, already choking up.

Archer climbs up my body, hands pressed into the mattress on either side of my ass as he looks into my eyes.

So much emotion, so much depth to this man.

"Back before I first met you at the Scorpions game, I was winding Jack up about his sister. Little did I know that when I met her, I'd be enraptured within minutes and fully in love with her a couple of years later." He sets a kiss against my forehead. "When we were talking in the group chat, I called you Emily since that was the first British name I could think of, and fuck did I think it was beautiful."

We're so close that I can feel his breath as it caresses my face, the beat of my heart growing faster.

"You know what I think?"

"What's that?" he replies, his voice intense.

"I hope Emily gets her daddy's brains because that will make her the kindest, smartest, and most thoughtful person I've ever met."

I see the shine in Archer's eyes as he lifts my top overhead, and I raise my arms for him.

It's late, and I have work in the morning, but screw it. I want him. All of him.

Archer kisses his way up my body, starting at my stomach and continuing past my breasts. I reach for his pants, but he stops me with a hand.

"No. This is about you tonight. Chasing your high is the ultimate prize for me. Plus ..." He kisses my left breast, and my nipple tightens at the sensation. "We have all the time in the world to explore each other."

When he moves to my right breast, I know what he's going to say; I can feel it in my gut as it squeezes.

"We're never going to be anywhere but with each other."

His soft words cut me like a thousand knives, and I recoil. Not at him, of course, but at the reality I'm faced with. Mum is still looking into options for me to stay in the US, but every process takes so long. I know, some point soon, I'm going to have to talk to Janine about my job and if there's any chance she will keep me on as a permanent member of staff, even throughout my maternity leave.

I might feel the pain, but Archer looks like I took a blade and shoved it right through his heart.

"What's going on, Darcy?"

He slides off the bed and removes his shirt and pants in front of me. Not saying a word, I watch on, mesmerized by his beauty and forced into silence at the spinning thoughts in my head.

I truly hoped that we'd have a solution to my visa dilemma by the time I had to tell Archer. But I don't, and suddenly, the sight of his warm eyes and concerned voice, coupled with the general overwhelm of pregnancy, slam into me.

Angrily, I swipe at my eyes. Crying about it isn't going to change my situation.

"Come here."

Dressed in only his boxers and me in my tiny pink sleep shorts, Archer reaches out and takes my hand in his.

I climb out of bed, loose hair that's fallen out of my braid tickling my cheeks.

With my hand in his, Archer turns and walks us to a chair in the corner of his bedroom. He takes a seat, spreading his thighs and pulling me down onto his lap.

I sit across his body, and he interlaces our fingers together.

There're a few seconds of silence, noise of late-night traffic faint but audible from the streets below us.

"What's going on?" Archer asks again, pushing my braid to one side and kissing my left shoulder. "I thought that maybe something wasn't right before I left for Dallas, and now I'm convinced of it."

"Umm ... I'm not quite sure of how to put this?" I can hear the stress in my own voice.

"You should know by now that you can say anything to me. Nothing is off-limits between us." In contrast to mine, my boyfriend's tone is cool and collected. He's likely shitting himself, but he doesn't let it show.

"Over the past few days, Mum and I have been looking into my visa options," I begin, taking a deep breath before continuing. "You already know I was here on an employer-sponsored visa and planned to get a permanent job out here after my contract with *Glide* ended."

He closes his eyes, face twisted with frustration and a painful realization. "And now you're pregnant, so getting another job won't be easy."

I nod once. "Just because I'm having a baby with an American doesn't automatically allow me to stay here in the US. In fact ..." I swallow down a pain I've never experienced in my life, one that makes me want to wail. Tears reemerge because I'm incapable of controlling them. "When my job at *Glide* ends, I'll have to return to the UK soon afterward, and our baby ..."

"Would likely remain here as a US citizen," Archer finishes for me, putting all the pieces together.

Instead of nodding, I gulp this time, a puking bout threatening to strike again.

Archer shakes his head slowly. "I can't live without you, Darcy. I *won't* live without you by my side." He lifts his head back up, a burning determination taking over his eyes. "I've fought this hard to get you, and I'm not about to give you up, not for Jack, Coach, Liam, or the fucking Atlantic Ocean. They can all go fuck themselves because I've found my future and she's five feet three with honey-blonde hair and the biggest blue eyes I've ever seen."

We don't say anything more to each other as he carries me in his arms to the bed he bought especially for us and lays me down on the soft duvet.

My sleep shorts are over my knees and lying in a heap on the floor in seconds, and Archer drops to his knees, pulling my bottom half off the bed. Next, he rests my legs over his shoulders.

No more words pass between us, only the sound of his mouth and tongue as they play with my pussy, eating me with a slow intensity I know only he's capable of delivering. And when he enters me with a single thick finger, curling it upward as he licks and sucks my clit, I move my right leg onto the bed, sliding my foot along the edge of the mattress so I can open wider for him.

"Good fucking girl," he groans against me. "Spreading yourself without me even asking."

I lean up on my elbows so we can make the eye contact I know he demands when we're having sex.

He strokes my front wall again, and my jaw hangs open. I'm so wet; I can hear it.

Clearly not satisfied with my pleasure levels, Archer pushes a second finger inside my pussy, and this time, when he crooks them, I feel an involuntary release into his mouth.

"I'm thirsty for more. Give me more of your sweetness," he demands, running a slow lick through me.

My knees shake. No, my entire body trembles from the way his mouth and fingers work me into such a frenzy. I know why he's doing this. He wants me to forget the stresses we're faced with since there's nothing we can do about them right now. Instead, he wants me to bask in the comfort of his love.

Just as I come, my elbows give out, and he works his fingers faster, not letting up when I repeatedly cry out his name.

When I'm fully satiated and limp, he climbs to his feet and pushes down his gray boxers, taking his leaking dick into one hand. "Fuck, Darcy. You turn me on so much. I'm always so goddamn hard for you." He rolls his head back to the ceiling, pleasuring himself in front of me on deep breaths he pulls into his lungs.

"Let me suck you," I whisper. "I want to make you come now."

As he grips his shaft tightly, his heated gaze holds me captive. "I already did—in my pants, around thirty seconds ago."

He steps between my still-parted thighs, and I spread as wide as I can for him.

Archer presses the tip of his cock inside me. His next words are a little shaky as he says them. "Just in case the universe isn't receiving the memo clearly enough, I said what I said: I've found my future, and she isn't going anywhere."

CHAPTER THIRTY-SEVEN

ARCHER

It's been seven days since Darcy broke the news I hadn't seen coming.

Maybe I should've thought through the practicalities of her staying in the USA and being unable to work after she had our baby, although it's probably fair to say I've been too caught up in falling in love and winning the heart of the girl lying next to me.

And now that I have her? I'm not giving her up. Perhaps to Darcy and her mom, this is a problem not easily solved, but to me, the answer is clear as fucking day.

All I needed to do was check out some facts and make a couple of arrangements.

We've got forty-eight hours—the time I have before I need to be back at the rink for next practice, as Jon gave us two days' rest before Tommy Schneider starts training with the team, and Darcy is due in work.

"Wake up for me, Doll," I murmur against the soft skin of her neck.

She turns in my arms to face me, yawning the whole way.

I can't help but smile as she cracks an eye open, her yawn morphing to a groan. "What time is it?"

"Really early," I reply. "It's still dark outside."

She groans again, and I kiss the underside of her chin.

"Then what are we doing awake? I need to conserve my energy for the mall you're determined to take me to today." She giggles, fully acknowledging that shopping is one of her favorite things.

Wrapping my leg over hers and my arm around her waist, I pull Darcy into me.

Here goes fucking nothing.

"Yeah, well, here's the thing. I still plan to take you somewhere. It's just a little bit farther than the mall."

Sleepy Darcy immediately springs to life. "What do you mean?"

I lean further into her until my mouth brushes the shell of her ear. "Get on a plane and come away with me," I whisper. "Just the two of us, for forty-eight hours, in Miami."

She looks at me like I've lost my mind.

And this is news to her?

"Archer. W-what are you talking about?"

I push a few strands of hair away from her face, biting the inside of my cheek to steady my nerves. "There's a way to keep you here, in New York."

I know she'll have considered this option, but I also know Darcy would never be the one to approach it.

"What are you suggesting?"

I can't keep my mouth off this girl, and my cock stirs to life. "Remember when I told you confessing my feelings was brought forward when I found out you were pregnant with my baby?"

She rolls her lips together, nodding her head.

"Well, this dilemma we're facing with your visa just sped up what I already want, but haven't asked you yet." My stomach swirls with anticipation and excitement as I pull air into my lungs. "Be my wife, Darcy. Marry me and wear my ring on your left hand. You already own my heart, so go ahead and take my last name too."

For a couple of beats, she studies me carefully. "But there's still a waiting period for marriage green cards to be accepted."

I smile because, fuck, she *has* thought about being my wife.

"Please don't be mad at me ..." I pause and dare a glance at her. She already looks pissed, but I continue anyway, "I spoke to Janine and told her everything."

She gasps, throwing a hand over her mouth.

I pull it away, kissing her palm. "She told me she fell pregnant unexpectedly with her daughter, and it left her in a financial bind when she was younger, so she can relate to curveballs in life. She will talk to you about the logistics of maternity leave when you head into work on Monday, but the bottom line is, she isn't terminating your contract early. There's enough time for the green card to be granted."

She puffs out a breath, and I spread my palm across her growing stomach.

"So, what do you say? Pip and I are waiting for an answer."

Her eyes are glassy, and my breathing is ragged while I wait for her to speak.

"Yes, I'll marry you, Archer." Her face blooms into the smile I know and love, one that she saves especially for me.

I grip her tightly against my body as I roll us over so she's looking up at me. There are so many words I could say in this moment. Lines about spending the rest of our lives together and growing old, watching our favorite movies in the back of packed theaters.

None of those could do justice to the euphoria as it washes over me.

I'm turning my dream girl into my wife.

My fiancée holds up a finger. "I have to ask, though, why Miami?"

I knew she'd be curious about that. "Because I want to take you away where it's only the two of us. I'd take you to Paris if we had the time between our jobs."

Her body melts into me and I consider the option of getting married in this bed and never moving.

If only.

"I love you—so fucking much." I kiss the tip of her nose. "And when we get home, I think we should tell your brother. Shit is going down in the team right now, and I didn't want to add to it, but I think it's time we said something." I hesitate. "If that's okay with you?"

She cups my face in her warm palm, and my eyelids flutter close. *This* is what true love feels like.

"I agree; it's time. Have you told your mom or family that you planned to propose to me?"

"I'll tell my mom when we tell your family. Plus, my sister is coming to visit soon to watch our game against the Philly Bolts, so you can meet her then, and I'll drop the baby and marriage bomb." I chuckle. "Emma loves a good surprise. And Dad ..." I blow out a breath. "I guess I'll tell him when we next speak."

"Is your sister as nice as your mum?" Darcy asks.

The way this woman is so keen to embrace my entire family. This alone is reason enough to love her for the rest of my life.

"She is, but we aren't as close as you are to Jack. It's just the way our family is."

Darcy shifts slightly. "I'm not sure how close I am to Jack anymore, to be honest. I feel like we've drifted, and life has changed for both of us. He wanted to meet up for lunch, but that didn't happen, and I didn't push it either. It felt awkward to be around him with everything going on."

I tip her chin up to look at me. "We can call and tell him right now if you want. Lay it all out for him." My lip quirks up. "I'll take the beating like a man and marry you with two black eyes if that's what it takes."

I can see that she's considering my suggestion, but finally shakes her head. "No. It would be the worst timing; it needs to be face-to-face and ..." Softness overtakes her eyes as she pauses. "I think I want just two more days like this."

"Like what, Darcy Doll?"

"Like this," she repeats. "You and me, living in our peaceful bubble. No outside noise, just us."

My lips brush over hers. I'm in so far that I feel sure my love for Darcy rests at the bottom of the deepest ocean. "It's always been just you and me, Darcy. Even before you knew it. We've been falling in love for a long time, in secret. Preparing for our first child together, in secret. And tomorrow afternoon, in Miami, I'll make you my wife, in secret. The truth is, we don't need a witness or for anyone to validate the way I love you. I'll take whatever's coming from your brother and Coach on the chin because despite what they might think, I know I'm the only man for you. I'm going to light up your already-bright world every damn day, for the rest of my life."

I'm back to kissing her jaw when she shifts slightly. "I want to tell my mum now, but I'm going to wait until we get back. I've asked her to keep enough secrets from Jon when they usually tell each other everything, and it feels unfair to burden her with something else. Same with the girls—I'll tell them when we get back. Anyway, Kendra is in Spain at the moment, watching her brother's football game. Sorry, soccer game," she corrects, shaking her head at the constant debate we witness between Jack and Kendra over what the sport is actually called.

Holding her in my arms, I spend the next few minutes making out with my girl. Languid kisses that pull me deeper into her world.

"I know this might not be the wedding you wanted," I say, resting my forehead against hers when we finally break for air.

"Hey, look at me, Archer."

With our eyeballs practically touching, I do as she asks.

I'll do anything she asks.

"What exactly defines the perfect wedding? Because I, for one, think it has nothing to do with the day and everything to do with the person you're marrying."

I can't help but smirk. "I'm not sure your stepdad would agree. I've heard he's all about the grandeur."

Darcy rolls her eyes, sinking further into my body. "I think he's almost as crazy as you are."

Tipping her chin up, she looks at me, and we share another kiss that I'm desperate to turn into more, but we're already running short on time.

"We need to head to the airport," I murmur against her mouth. "I booked a private jet, and it leaves in two hours."

Throwing the duvet back, she bolts right up in bed. "Oh Jesus. I haven't got anything packed, Archer. Not even my toothbrush! And what am I going to wear?"

I wrap a hand around her arm, pulling her back down to the bed. "I've got it all handled. Your bags are packed and set to one side in my closet."

"B-but ... I don't have many clothes here and ..."

I silence her rambling with a finger to her lips.

"I bought you an entire new wardrobe." Her eyes flare when I smooth my thumb across her bottom lip. "Jimmy Choo, Prada, Gucci. All of it. I have your engagement ring already, but I have a plan for that too."

"Are you for real?"

Rolling onto my back, I pull her on top of me before cocooning us under the bedsheets. "It's funny you should say that. Because I've been thinking that exact same thing about you." I pull my bottom lip between my teeth, plastering on a pained expression. "I do need you to know something before we do this though, about me."

With one brow raised, sass rolls off her. "Is this another Archer Moore lesson?"

I chuckle. "Yeah, I guess you could think of it in that way." I take her hand in mine. "I know this is going to be difficult for you to take, but I genuinely believe we can work through it."

"Archer," she drawls, "what the fuck are you about to tell me?"

I blow out a long breath. "I-I can't stand tea, any kind of tea. It makes me gag."

CHAPTER THIRTY-EIGHT

DARCY

Collins: I know you're all aware of how much I hate birthdays—or just celebrations in general, to be honest. However, this year, Sawyer is determined to throw me a party. He says since it's my last one as a Mackenzie, I should make the most of it. He also wanted to do invites, etc., but I drew the line. He's already getting carried away with wedding plans. So, consider this text as your invite.

Kendra: Where is this party?

Collins: Sawyer's hiring out a fancy place or something. The entire team and their partners are invited.

Jenna: You sound so thrilled, Collins.

Collins: I won't lie, when he first made the suggestion, I shut it straight down. But I'm warming to it a little, I guess.

Jenna: Well, I'm free around your birthday, and if partners are invited, I might bring a plus-one.

Kendra: Phil?

Jenna: Hell no! I stopped sleeping with him because he wanted more with me, and I'm not seeing it. He's not my type in that way.

Me: She wants a hockey player.

Jenna: Show me a girl who says she doesn't, and I'll show you a liar.

Kendra: I cannot argue with that logic.

Jenna: I'm holding out for Tommy Schneider. He's hot and a bad boy. Exactly my type.

Me: He's also a complete douche and hated by pretty much every Blades player. His dad is an even bigger dick for what he did to Scorpions defenseman, Zach Evans, back when Jon played for them.

Kendra: Yeah, Jack has been in a bad mood since he found out about the trade. He isn't looking forward to Tommy's first practice session with them on Monday.

Jenna: So, sleeping with him and bringing him to Collins's party is out of the question?

Collins: I mean, he'll already be at the party since we're inviting the team and can't exactly leave him out, but you've heard of the movie Sleeping with the Enemy, right? Another classic from my queen, Julia Roberts.

Jenna: Sigh. Strike him off my list then. Why do the bad boys always have to be dicks? Like, can't they act the part, but underneath, they're all gooey and romantic?

Collins: What about a biker? They might fit your needs.

Jenna: At this point, I'll take any viable option.

> Collins: Okay, so I'm going with six places between the three of you.
>
> Kendra: Who is Darcy bringing?
>
> Collins: I guess I assumed everything with Archer would be out in the open by January ...

I stand in the middle of our hotel suite on Miami Beach, staring down at my phone and the Vivienne Westwood ivory satin minidress Archer picked out especially for today.

It's perfect. The second he unzipped the bag and showed it to me, I cried—big tears. If I'd chosen my own dress, I'd have gone for something completely different. Likely a long fishtail with a lace bodice.

This one is a peplum style that's cinched at the waist, the skirt puffing out and stopping mid-thigh. Thick straps lead down to a V-shaped neckline, accentuating my petite figure.

And just when I thought it couldn't get any better than the dress fitting me perfectly, Archer showed me the pearl earrings he had bought to match.

I kept my hair in the long braid I know he loves and my makeup natural.

Everything about today feels natural. Like it was meant to happen. And as much as I want to scream to my friends about where I am and what I'm doing, I also don't. After today, we'll need to burst our own bubble and let the world in.

> Me: Yes, it will. I can't hide this baby bump forever, and it's time to tell everyone. We plan to soon.
>
> Kendra: Oh, thank the Lord. I, for one, am terrible at secrets, but I did it for you.
>
> Collins: I enjoy a good secret.

> Jenna: I'd enjoy anything other than the spin bike I'm on right now.
>
> Collins: Exercise is gross. Ezra tried to get me to go on a run the other day. It was a hard pass from me. So, instead, we went for a ride.

The suite door cracks open, and Archer steps into the room. Dressed in dark blue suit trousers, tan loafers, and a white open-necked shirt, he looks delicious, especially with his chain on show.

When he styled his hair this morning, he kept it simple, dark pieces falling over his eyes. He also kept the scruff on his jaw since he knows I like to feel that against my fingertips.

Along with other places.

I close out the text thread and place my mobile face down on a side table. No phones today.

Just us.

Archer still hasn't said anything as he walks toward me, carrying a small white bag in his left hand, eyes locked on mine the whole time. When he left to go run an errand, I took the opportunity to get dressed.

The second he reaches me, he loops his big arms around my waist, locking my body against his.

He smells incredible. All woodsy and spicy and manly.

I tip my chin up to look at my fiancé. The difference in our heights is especially noticeable since I'm not wearing any shoes.

"You've rendered me speechless, Doll," he purrs into my ear. "When I picked out this dress ..." He smooths a palm over my ass, squeezing it a little, and I feel my underwear grow damp. "I knew it was the one, I knew you'd look perfect in it." He pulls back from me, gaze descending my body. "But you look like a fucking angel. An angel carrying my baby."

He walks a few feet to a wardrobe, setting the white bag he was carrying inside before he pulls out a white shoebox. As he removes the lid on his way back over to me, a pair of white

Gucci pumps comes into view. They're flat and simple but with the cutest yellow bows stitched to the toe.

"I hope you don't mind that they haven't got a heel. They just screamed my girl when I saw them and then had the yellow bows added."

I move my gaze from the pretty pumps to his face. "You had the bows stitched on?"

He shrugs, cheeks pinkening slightly, and it's the cutest thing I've ever seen. It's rare Archer flushes, but I guess it isn't everyday you get hitched.

Especially not in secret.

"Yellow reminds me of you. One of my favorite dresses you wear is yellow, and it's the color of sunshine."

He bends down, taking the shoes from the box and placing them to the side.

Carefully, I slide each foot into a pump while he holds them for me.

A bubble of giddy laughter climbs up my throat. "You're like Prince Charming or something."

Standing back up, Archer cups the nape of my neck in his hand. "You've always reminded me of Rapunzel, with your hair and cute features."

I cock my head to the side, thinking it over. "I can get on board with being a Disney princess."

On a slow exhale, Archer dips a hand into his pocket. "I bought you something else yellow too."

My breath catches in my throat. As a girl, I always dreamed of the moment a boy asked me to marry him. I pictured him down on one knee with a beautiful landscape behind us, my hair blowing in the breeze while he wore a suit and bow tie. I imagined a crowd of our friends and family surrounding us and a party into the small hours of the morning.

It's amazing how societal norms can be the complete opposite of what we truly want—and need—in our lives. With Liam, I thought that's what I wanted too. But as Archer pops the lid on a small velvet box and a princess-cut yellow diamond on a thin white gold band stares back at me, I realize this is what fate planned all along.

Archer was right when he said we were always meant to be.

Just like the old horse chestnut tree in Fort Greene Park, a love like this grows from the deepest roots. And even though it can take a long while to surface, its strength is unwavering.

Like everything else Archer buys me, the fit is perfect when he slides it onto my left hand, interlacing our fingers together.

"Do you like it?" he asks, his voice thick, his eyes glossy.

"What do you think?" My throat is as tight as his sounds.

We both stand in the silence of our suite, taking in the moment.

He pulls me in for a searing kiss, his mouth moving over mine. I grow wetter, thinking about how he'll touch me tonight. As his wife.

"I think it's time for you to become Mrs. Darcy Moore. Are you ready?"

This time, it's me who kisses him. Beautiful butterflies shimmering throughout my body. "Yes," I murmur against his lips. "I'm ready."

Other than the moonlight casting across the still ocean and the faint lights from our hotel, we're drenched in complete darkness with no one else around.

I've lost track of time. It could be midnight, or the sun might be about to rise as I lie back on the sun lounger, legs spread, with my feet buried in soft sand while my husband devours me.

He licks his way up the insides of my thighs, capturing every drop of release as it trickles down my legs.

It's been like this since he woke me up, told me to wear his jersey, and led me by the hand to the hotel's private beach.

We couldn't get married here, for fear of Archer being recognized and pictures appearing on the internet. From the airport to the hotel, we took a private taxi, and Archer wore a low baseball cap, shielding his face. So, instead, we said our short vows in a small private room and exchanged rings.

I cried the whole time before Archer carried me back to our room.

But now that everyone's asleep, we finally have a moment to enjoy the beach together. And, oh my God, am I enjoying it.

Archer's lips shine with my arousal as he stands from the lounger and pushes down his shorts. He steps out of them and comes to sit in front of me, straddling the lounger as he does.

His cock is hard, and pre-cum leaks from it as I reach forward and wrap my palm around the base.

"Fuck me like this," he breathes out, voice raspy when I drag my grip to the top. "I want my wife to fuck me, just like this."

Releasing his cock, I rise from the lounger and sit back down, straddling his hips.

With darkened eyes, he looks into mine, tucking a piece of stray hair behind my ear.

I lift up and sink down onto his cock. Our jaws hang open from the way he stretches my pussy, coupled with the delicious sensation of me taking him.

I rock over him for the first time, and he moans into the night, his pleasure blending with the ocean waves as they break against the shore.

"Loving you as my girl was a privilege; loving you as my wife is the highest honor I'll ever be granted." He pushes his hips into me, and I take him and his piercings deeper. "Tell me you want more babies with me."

When I push a hand through his hair, my rings sparkle in the moonlight. "I want so many babies with you. But I also want it all—the career, the lifestyle, and the family."

Archer runs a hand across his name, which is stamped on the back of the white jersey he gave me. Even through the thin material, my skin tingles from his touch, and I tighten around his shaft.

"I'll tell you a million times over until you truly believe it one day: nothing about you or what you want from this life is too much. I promise that, with me, you can have it all."

As Archer grows harder inside me, I come all over him. I'm impaled on his dick, moving over his body in rough, ragged motions as I fight back my cries.

He reaches beneath the hem of the jersey and finds my swollen clit, pinching it between his fingers. "It's okay to scream, Doll. In fact, now that you're officially mine, it's mandatory. Every time you take my cock, I want to hear you chant my name, right in between the delicious sounds this pretty wife's pussy makes."

"Your mouth—it's filthy," I moan as he gathers our joint arousal onto his fingers and takes them into his mouth.

He offers his fingers to me next, and I open, sucking them clean.

Archer's cocky grin appears, his top lip quirked. "What were you saying about dirty mouths? Because I'd say this NHL playboy has infiltrated his innocent British girl."

Lifting up, I drop back down, and he grits his teeth, trying not to blow.

"You're right about that. Now, come in me."

I feel like a world away from the girl who first slept with Archer, the one who thought she preferred zero eye contact and could only orgasm in one position. "I can't wait to have your baby."

He releases my clit and pulls the jersey over my head, throwing it on the lounger next to us. My breasts feel sensitive against the cool night air, and it only kicks up the intensity. Next, he loops his hands under my thighs and lifts me up until only the tip of his dick is inside.

He holds me there, staring down at the small bump, which I swear gets visibly bigger each day. Or maybe that's just my excitement to meet Emily.

I'm suspended, my feet off the ground as, slowly, he fills me again. Archer does all the work in taking my full weight, although he handles me like I'm lighter than a feather, his biceps flexing as he guides my body over his. He fucks me slow, staring up at me with awe in his eyes, need etched into his features and perspiration above his brow.

I spread my legs wider and grip his shoulders, leaving the marks I know he loves.

"I'm going to blow," he grits out. "Your pussy is strangling the willpower out of me."

My words sound more like a pleasure-filled moan when I press my forehead into his and reach down between us, cupping and playing with his balls. "Don't hold back, Thigh Boy. Be a good boy now and fill your wife up."

CHAPTER THIRTY-NINE

ARCHER

I'm a married man.

A sentence I never thought would apply to me and, oftentimes, never thought I wanted it to. That was, until Darcy Thompson waltzed into my world and flipped it upside down, and now I can't stop staring at the platinum band on my hand or thinking about how good she sounds with my last name.

Darcy Moore.

To my wife, I know we've been a whirlwind, but to me, it's been over two years of waiting for her to see me for who I am.

A complete fucking simp for her.

Reciting my vows was the single greatest honor I've ever had. Even if it was in a small room with only an officiant to bear witness, it was perfect.

When the double doors had opened and Darcy stood in the entryway, a single yellow rose clutched between both hands, I couldn't have been prouder. She looked incredible and every bit as stunning as I'd imagined in that dress.

Her reaction when I had revealed it was pure shock as she

shook her head in denial, repeating that she'd never have gone for a dress like the one I'd picked out.

Perhaps she thought it was blind luck on my behalf.

It wasn't.

Back before she had moved to New York and whenever I knew she was in town, I would find myself rushing to get through my postgame routine, excited to catch a glimpse of her at Lloyd's. Even if she only gave me a few minutes, I'd take them with both hands and then head home to only fantasize over what it would be like if she'd come back with me.

I stared into many mirrors, convincing myself I hadn't been batshit crazy over what I did when I walked past a boutique in town one day and saw that Vivienne Westwood dress in the front window. A sane man would've kept walking, thinking how beautiful his crush would look in it. But I wasn't that man, and Darcy wasn't just a crush. She's an obsession that's only grown stronger since that day a year ago, when I pushed through the shop door and dropped four thousand dollars on it right there and then.

And the yellow bows stitched into her pumps?

I stand, waiting for our bags to be returned, and flush again at the memory of me trying to use a sewing kit last week. Originally, I had planned to have a pair made especially for our day, but time was short, and I had an uncompromising vision of how she'd look when I married her.

"Is everything okay?" Darcy steps toward me.

Since the airport is dead and there's no one around, I let my inhibitions drop a fraction, and I lean across, setting a kiss on the top of her head before our bags are returned to us.

"I'm good, just thinking over everything."

She reaches up onto her tiptoes and pulls down the bill of my cap, smiling the whole time. "Thinking's good, but try not to overthink. I find it never ends well. Not unless you have a spare sudoku book."

I pick up her hand and kiss her palm. "Does downloading the app count?"

Darcy rolls her eyes, but I see the way she swoons in response.

"I was thinking of asking Jack and Kendra over to our place for a meal after practice tomorrow night. We could tell him then."

She nods right before her eyes flare. "Wait. *Our* place?"

I interlace both our hands, holding them down between us. "You're aware that we're married, right? I don't recall needing to drug you to say yes."

Her eyes narrow to slits. "It's a fair point, well made. But I will miss my little apartment, even if it's cold and unsafe."

"Keep it if you want. We can cover the monthly rent," I say as we head toward the doors leading to the airport exit, me pulling both cases behind.

Her nose scrunches up at the idea. "No. Affordable housing is hard to come by in this city as it is. I couldn't justify keeping my apartment for purely storage and nostalgic reasons."

"Storage?" I question. "We live in a huge penthouse apartment. You don't need storage space."

"Have you *seen* my shoe collection?" she volleys back.

I stop walking, and Darcy pulls up alongside me. "And that collection is only going to grow bigger. Anything and everything you want, it's yours."

"Where did the driver say he'd wait for us?" Darcy reaches onto her tiptoes as I pull my bill even lower and scan the room for a board with my—our—last name on it.

"I don't think he's—" Darcy starts talking, but cuts off abruptly, her face paling.

"What's the matter?" I ask, trying to follow her line of sight.

"Jack." Her voice is weak, barely a whisper. "H-he's here and staring straight at us."

At first, I think she's joking. She *has* to be. Why would Jack be here?

"Archer!"

It's his voice I hear first before he steps through the double glass doors directly in front of us.

Beneath the bill of his cap, his face is beet red. Even from here, I can see how the muscles in his jaw clench and strain. Enraged eyes travel from me to his sister and then back to me.

Heart racing, I take Darcy's hand and start walking toward a different set of exit doors at the back of the building, trying to get away from prying eyes. There are only a few staff members and other passengers around, but I don't want to give them a show. That's the last thing we all need.

As we keep walking, Darcy and I don't speak, even though the silence between us screams a thousand words.

This is not how it was supposed to go down. He wasn't supposed to see us here. This is worst-case scenario number one, playing out right in front of us.

A huge part of me wants to head straight for a taxi since our driver obviously isn't here. But I know in the long run, that would only make everything worse.

Closing my eyes, I force back my doubts over how badly this could all play out and turn on my heel to face my new brother-in-law.

Standing around ten feet away from me and with both hands shoved into the pockets of his jeans, Jack reminds me of a bull that's just been shown the red flag. His chest is heaving, eyes glazed, although even darker than they were before.

He looks like everything I imagined he would when we eventually broke the news, only worse.

"Jack, listen. Let's not do this here, okay?" My mouth is dry as I deliver a sentence I hope will remind him of how precarious this environment is. I hold up a hand. "We were going to head straight back home from here, so why don't you come with us? We can talk there."

"Why *the fuck* are you both here? Together?"

I've only ever witnessed my friend like this once before. It was right after he found out about some texts Kendra's ex had sent to her in an attempt to break them up. Let's just say, it didn't end well for that dude, for his face especially. That day, I saw a different side to the golden retriever personality. He might be all smiles and jokes ninety-nine percent of the time, but on the rare occasions he feels betrayed—just like he does right now—a much darker character emerges.

I predicted the Tommy Schneider news would only be a prequel to the main event, and I was correct.

"Jack," Darcy whispers, taking a step forward, "Archer's right. Let's not do this here, okay?"

In response to her plea, his eyes soften as they flick to Darcy. "Why are you both here?" he repeats, eyes growing harder again. "I drove here to surprise Kendra since her flight from Madrid is due in at any second. I planned to take her out for a meal, but now I'm thinking I'll just *take you* out instead." His nostrils flare, breathing back to ragged.

It's a risky move, but I'm left with no choice. I can see the way he's spiraling. I step closer, and he does the same. I'm for sure within punching distance, and it wouldn't shock me if he did just that. But like I said to Darcy, I'll take whatever he hands out without retaliation.

"We just got back from Miami." I force the words out, working to keep my voice calm and steady when I'm anything but that underneath.

Jack looks off to the side, blowing out a cynical breath. "You didn't think you could get away with it in New York, so you took her away, where you wouldn't get caught. I fucking knew it. I knew you were a piece of shit, but I gave you the benefit of the doubt because even *I* didn't think you could be this fucking stupid."

If it wasn't for the bills on our caps, our foreheads would be touching as he gets right in my face. "Abbie never existed, did she?"

I swallow hard, bile rising into my throat. "No."

He puffs out another breath, eyes dropping to the ground before rising back to mine. "You're a fucking coward—you know that? Making up some bullshit about a chick so you could have your way in secret."

"It's not what you think it is," I say, wincing because while this absolutely isn't, it's a classic line everyone says when they've been caught red-handed.

"I'll tell you what it is," Jack bites out, jaw ticcing, molars grinding. "It's Archer Moore sticking his dick in whoever he wants and to hell with the consequences. You just couldn't leave her alone, could you? She was off-limits and a conquest you had to have, even if you knew it would set fire to our friendship and the team."

I see red. Despite understanding exactly why Jack would conclude what he has, he couldn't be further from the truth. I'm so fucking sick of being judged for my past and the choices I made before I fell in love with Darcy.

Smoothing a palm over my mouth, I can't suppress the sneer that pulls at my lips. "Be very, *very* fucking careful what you say next, Jack. My best advice would be not to judge what you don't understand."

His brows pull together, face still awash with rage. "If I don't understand and it's not what it looks like, then why didn't you come to me sooner? Why all the sneaking around?"

I open my mouth to tell him exactly why—that I was respecting my girl's privacy and wishes, but also because it was really none of his goddamn business until we decided to make it.

"Because I'm pregnant, okay? I just turned twelve weeks pregnant," Darcy bursts out, frustration lacing her voice.

Jack's head darts to his sister, and he takes a step back from me, his eyes falling to her stomach. Beneath the oversize sweatshirt she's wearing, you can't see her cute bump. Tears pool in the corners of her eyes, and all I want is to gather my wife in my arms and promise everything will be okay.

"Fuck it," I announce.

I do exactly that when I loop my arm around her shoulders, pulling her into my side. She buries her face into my hoodie, and my heart swells in response.

Her brother watches on, the blood draining from his face. "Y-you're pregnant? With Archer's child?" he finally pushes out.

"Yes," she whispers back, one hand falling to her stomach. "So, when you ask why we haven't said anything sooner, it's because we wanted to find the right time, and I only just finished my first trimester."

He points to her hand resting on her stomach, eyes growing even wider than before. "Wait, you got fucking married too?!"

I drop my head down to the floor.

What a fucking disaster.

"Yes," I reply, looking Jack straight in the eyes. "We did. But I'll repeat myself again: let's not do this here."

With a bright face and looking super excited, Kendra approaches from behind her husband. The second she registers he's talking to us, her face drops, turning as pale as my wife's.

"What's going on?" Kendra asks as she sidles up next to Jack.

The atmosphere is explosive. One false move or word, and Jack is going off at the deep end.

I'm not sure if it's the presence of his wife or he's finally processing our surroundings, but when he swallows thickly, I can tell he's holding back what he really wants to say. And right now, I'm grateful because I know he needs to calm down.

"Why don't we go back to our place and talk?" I suggest again, hoping this time, he'll accept our invitation.

I watch the way Darcy and Kendra exchange glances, wondering what Jack is going to say.

"That sounds like a good idea," Kendra agrees.

Holding up a hand, Jack shakes his head, and my hope dissolves. "No. Kendra just got off a long-haul flight, and I need some time to process what the fuck has happened so I don't go and say something I'll regret."

He looks at Darcy then, a gentler meaning in his eyes. "I'm

sorry, Darce, but I need a minute. I get why you didn't tell me about the pregnancy, but ... I don't know. I just feel like you're not thinking this whole thing through. It's like you're having a knee-jerk reaction to splitting with Liam and ..." He trails off, not knowing what to say next.

"I've thought everything through," Darcy quickly counters, her voice a touch sharper.

Tipping his head toward the ceiling, Jack then refocuses his attention back on me. "I've literally got nothing to say to you right now. The betrayal is too much for me to comprehend."

"We need a time to talk, away from heightened emotions and crowds, and I'll happily lay everything down for you," I reply, trying once more for him to see reason.

He smirks, and it isn't a warm, amused, or friendly one. "Yeah, I'm sure you will. But what I'm saying is, Archer, I'm not sure I'll ever be ready to talk to you. *Ever* again."

CHAPTER FORTY

ARCHER

Me: I'm guessing you've heard already.

Sawyer: Yeah. Collins told me, and I was planning to talk to you about it when I got to the rink. Figured face-to-face was better.

Me: It was bad.

Sawyer: Collins said Kendra thought he was going to hit you.

Me: Kendra isn't alone with those thoughts.

Sawyer: I'm not going to tell you I warned you because it's not helpful, and honestly, I get it. Sophie lost a baby at ten weeks, and she'd already told her parents and friends. It was hard as hell.

Me: Shit, I'm sorry.

Sawyer: Are you okay? Is Darcy okay?

> Me: Currently standing in the hallway outside the locker room, I can't bring myself to walk inside. Darcy is seeing her mom this morning. She's doing okay.

> Sawyer: I'm sitting in the parking lot, and I'll be inside in a couple of minutes. We can talk afterward. I'm not going to lie; this whole thing is going to be an uphill battle for the team. What I haven't said to you yet though is congrats. Married and about to become a family man. How does it feel?

Leaning against the locker room doorjamb and despite the shit show that was yesterday in the airport, I still feel incredible.

> Me: Amazing. It makes me wonder why the hell I fucked around all those years, you know? I know I've got some work to do in the locker room …

> Sawyer: For a lot of guys, until they become a family man, they don't understand how special it actually is. Welcome to the club, buddy. As for the locker room, I think you need to give it time.

> Me: He was pissed. You should've seen him.

> Sawyer: Oh, I can imagine. You knew it would go down like this though.

> Me: I love her so fucking much.

> Sawyer: I know you do.

"Moore."

Coach's stern voice interrupts my thoughts as I uncross my legs, pocket my cell, and look up into two cold steely-gray eyes.

Shit.

"Yes, Coach?"

He swipes a palm across his forehead before slapping it against his thigh. "I need to speak with you before practice." He thumbs to a side room.

I could ask him if everything is okay, but we both know it isn't.

Swallowing hard, I push off the jamb and follow behind him.

With his hand on the door handle, Coach pauses before opening. He doesn't turn to look at me, but speaks quietly, a serious undertone to his voice. "The discussion we're about to have needs to remain calm. I've got the GM wanting to know what the fuck is going on since a photo was leaked to the press this morning of you and Jack squaring up in the airport. The PR team had it taken down within minutes, so I doubt much narrative will come of it. That said, it didn't look good."

Nausea rolls through me. "Was Darcy in the picture?"

He looks at me then, surprised that was my first question.

It's the only question I have.

"No. Thankfully, she wasn't dragged into it."

"Okay, that's good," I say on a long breath that frees my lungs a little more.

Coach's hand tightens around the handle. "No, Archer, it isn't good." I can tell he's speaking to me as Jon, Darcy's stepdad. "You just set fire to team dynamics and have me questioning the direction of your moral compass."

When he opens the door to a small office, Jack is sitting in a black leather chair, resting his forearms on the desk in front of him.

For the briefest moment, his eyes flick to mine, but if I'd blinked, I would've missed the contact or the anger behind them.

A night's sleep doesn't appear to have done anything to calm him down.

"Take a seat." Coach rounds the desk and sits in his own chair on the other side. He pushes a keyboard away from him and mirrors Jack's position while I drop down onto the seat next to my center.

"How long is this going to take?" Jack bites.

Pulling off his cap, Coach sets it down on the desk. "It'll take as long as it takes. Practice is being run by Jensen right now."

"Not a great first impression for Schneider," Jack counters, and Coach lifts a brow.

"It's not our new defenseman I'm worried about. Because if we don't get this situation resolved, and fast, the GM is going to start dropping problematic players to the bench—or worse."

"I'm happy to sit here and talk for as long as it takes," I say, looking at Coach and then at Jack, who still won't offer me proper eye contact.

"Look at me, Jack," I tell him.

He scratches at his chin, eyes fixed on Coach. "I called Darcy a half hour ago because I needed to know the truth and I can't trust a word that comes out of your mouth. She told me you guys were playing around for a while before she fell pregnant." Finally, he gives me his attention. "Did you just marry her because you had gotten her pregnant? Because you knew the shit storm that would ensue and you wanted to get ahead of it with a shotgun wedding?"

He might as well have shot me instead, since his words blow me apart at the seams.

"That really and truly is what you think of me, isn't it?"

He swipes his tongue across his bottom lip. "Well, this time, you couldn't 'fuck and flee,' could you?"

I know what he's referencing. Back in his rookie season, we got to talking one night on an away series. I told him that was what I did with women to avoid any kind of commitment.

I close my eyes to temper the gnawing cringe. "I'm a very different man now. Darcy has changed me."

"A good man doesn't lie to his friends and teammates," he snips back.

I pull at the back of my neck, frustration coursing through

me. The second Abbie's name left my lips, I regretted it. Lying isn't something I do, but I felt like I had no choice but to play along. "It's not that black and white, Jack," I reply.

"I swear to fucking God if you hurt my baby sister and leave her stranded with a baby, I will tear you limb from limb," he growls so deep that I can hardly make out the words.

"Not going to happen," I volley back. "I'm in love with her."

Sitting back in his chair, Jack pokes his tongue into his cheek. "But you didn't respect me enough to be straight from the outset? Apparently, everyone else knew, apart from a few guys on the team and me and Jon."

I grip the metal handles on my chair so tightly that my knuckles turn white. "I respect you, Jack. I just don't think everything has to be all of your business all the time. And do you blame me when you react like this? You're like a fucking book; I can read you so easily."

Coach shifts in his chair, anticipating that this conversation is heading nowhere other than south.

"We're all personally involved in this, but the time for hashing out emotions isn't now." He leans forward, resting his elbows on the table. "What's important right now is your professionalism. You are two of my most valuable players, and we have had the best start to a season in a long fucking time. The GM and I do not want that fucking up."

I clear my throat, arms folded across my chest. "My ability to be professional and friendly isn't the issue here."

"You're precisely the issue!" Jack's temper frays as he points to the center of his chest. "Do you know how humiliated I am? I thought we were friends. I thought we had each other's backs."

"We do," I say quietly, emotion clogging my throat as I remember our exchange in the bathroom. "But I'll always put the woman I love first. And that woman is Darcy."

I watch his shoulders deflate, and I fucking hate it. I hate this for us.

"I'll always be there for my sister, and I'll always show up for my team." He pushes back his chair, clearly done with the conversation.

Coach doesn't stop his center as he makes for the door, pulling it open quickly.

Jack pauses, looking straight into the hallway. "But when it comes to you, Archer, I really think I'm done."

My head finds my hands as I drop my face down into them, voice muffled as I speak. "It wasn't supposed to work out this way. When we flew in from Miami, we planned to go and see him the next day, after this practice. He can't hear what I'm trying to tell him because he's so blinded by betrayal, and I don't know how to fix this."

For a few seconds, I wonder if Coach left the room with Jack. You could hear a pin drop; it's that quiet.

Finally, I hear him sit back in his seat.

"I have to admit, Archer, when Felicity told me last night, I spent the first hour with my jaw firmly glued to the floor. The next hour was spent trying to temper my rage. Now, in the cold light of day, I can see more clearly why you held off from saying anything. But that doesn't mean your reputation for fucking women around suddenly disappeared overnight. Darcy might be a grown-ass woman, but she also just got out of a toxic relationship, and I'm concerned to think she's potentially in another. You married her for visa purposes and because she was pregnant, and she had gotten pregnant because you were messing around in secret. And why were you messing around in secret?" His question is a rhetorical one as I lift my head to catch his raised brow. "Because you didn't want to get caught."

"That's not true." I shake my head at him. "I married your stepdaughter because I love her."

"Liam told Darcy he loved her too. Felicity's ex-husband, Elliott, told her he loved her. Both were absolute fuckers."

I'm back to squeezing the bars on my chair. "I'm not in their category. I pursued Darcy because I wanted her for more than just sex. She wanted fun. I was desperate for more."

He nods like he already knows this. Maybe Darcy told Felicity how it all went down. "I get your frustration, and that's why I'm not going off at the deep end on you. All I'm doing is setting out how others will see this. I was a guy with a reputation when I met my wife. I spent a lot of time convincing her I was the one, but what I didn't do was lie. Your biggest error here wasn't going after Darcy because you're right—you can choose to tell who you want and when; it was trying to cover up your actions with lies. That's what's eating at Jack and, to be really fucking honest, me too. You're my player, and I need to know I can trust every single guy on my team. I've told the GM he has nothing to worry about, both from the image leaked online and with the strained relationship between you and Jack. Do *not* prove me wrong, Moore."

I think he's finished when he leans forward again, his eyes locked straight on me.

"But more important than that, do *not* break my beautiful stepdaughter's heart. You fuck with her or your baby girl, and I swear to God, no trade or appearance on the farm team will compare to the way I will come down on you. You hurt them, you hurt my family."

I roll my lips together and lean forward, matching his determined stance inch for inch. "I'm happy you got that off your chest because you clearly needed to, Jon. However, allow me to participate in your cathartic exercise for just a second."

I offer him a warm smile that doubles as a warning of my own. "You don't need to concern yourself with thoughts of my two girls getting hurt because let me tell you this: if anyone—and I mean, anyone—lays a finger, passes a questionable glance, or fucks them over in any way while my feet are still on this earth, they'll wish they never took their first breath."

I push back my chair and stand, knocking my knuckles on the table twice. "And if you're looking for evidence of my promise, I'd suggest you give Liam a call."

CHAPTER FORTY-ONE

ARCHER

Four days, multiple unread texts, and one unanswered phone call later, and I'm still public enemy number one.

This morning, when I pulled Darcy into my arms, she asked me how I was feeling. She could tell this whole thing with Jack was getting to me.

She's right.

All I want to do is talk, but he won't let me in. The game against the Pittsburgh Flames was angsty. Not because of the score—we rolled them over four to one, narrowly missing out on another shutout. It was the tension that flowed from my center. When I asked if he had any of the stick tape we both used, the cold shoulder he gave me was palpable. I didn't need any, and I knew the kit guy would fix me up; I was just thinking of an excuse to engage him in a conversation.

Any kind of conversation.

It didn't work. All he did was shrug and turn toward his bench.

"Can you spot me?" Sawyer approaches from behind as I wipe the perspiration from above my brow.

Throwing my towel down, I try not to think about how I'd rather be anywhere else but here. If Darcy wasn't at work, finalizing the details of her maternity leave with Janine, I would for sure be thinking up reasons to split early and avoid another second of Jack's wrath.

"Sure thing," I blow out.

He drops a hand onto my shoulder, scanning the room for eavesdroppers. Tommy Schneider sits a few machines down, using the leg press. Wearing earbuds during any group session is Coach's pet peeve, so he went to town with full-on headphones.

"I know I said I wasn't getting involved, but ... do you want me to talk to him? I can try and smooth the land a little."

I shake my head on the way over to the Olympic bar and get into position, taking the weight before Sawyer lies down on the bench.

"No. It's fine. When he's ready to talk, he will."

From below me, Sawyer twists his lips. "You sure about that?"

He pushes out a few reps, and I take the weight back from him. "No, I'm not, but what other choice do I have? He's not giving me a fair chance to explain, and I'm tired of shots being fired at me unfairly."

"Unfairly?" a growl echoes from behind.

Fuck.

Replacing the weight back on the rack, I face Jack. He takes a pull from his water bottle, and I wait for him to elaborate because that's the first fucking word he's said to me by choice in the last ninety-six hours.

"This shit's hilarious! It's like some kind of standoff or something." Tommy thumbs over his shoulder toward the locker rooms. "I've got a couple of pistols if you want to duel. Could be fun, I guess."

"Not now, Tommy," Sawyer warns, rising from the bench and coming to stand in a place between me and Jack.

Tommy just grins, enjoying every second of the charged atmosphere.

"Why am I being unfair?" Jack speaks. "You expected to snap your fingers, and I'd be cool with everything?"

I drag a palm down my face, frustrated because I know whatever I say won't make any difference. "If you can't set your feelings aside for me, then maybe do it for Darcy. She's upset and panicking that I'm going to get traded by the GM if shit doesn't calm down."

He snorts. "Why would you get traded? We all played well against the Flames, and I supported you in the slot, like always."

"Come on!" I throw my hands up, voice several octaves higher. Thankfully, Jon isn't around to witness this. "You could feel the hostility from the moon, never mind the fucking family box."

"My kind of game."

"Shut up!" Jack and I shout at Tommy in unison.

Like he's chewing on some gum, he simply shrugs and leans back on the press, getting back to work and doing us all a favor.

Jack pushes a hand through his sweat-soaked hair. Like every other time his sister's been brought into the conversation, he mellows.

"Darcy knows this has nothing to do with her."

"Good fucking thing," I retort, really wishing I had more control over my mouth today.

Jack goes to spin on his heel, pointing to the treadmills on the other side of the room. A pang of sadness shoots through me. Only last season, we were laughing and joking around by them, winding Sawyer up over his date with Collins.

And now all he wants to do is retreat to them.

"Are we done?"

I step forward, determination pushing me on. "No, we're not done. Not by a long shot."

He crosses his arms over his chest, a classic defensive stance if ever I saw one.

"Okay, have your little speech in front of everyone. Don't forget to leave out the part where you lied—multiple times."

"I lied because this is how I thought you'd react!" I yell. "And all you're doing is proving me right."

He presses his lips into a thin line, biting back anger. "The first rule of a friendship is not to go behind each other's backs. Why couldn't you just be up front with me? I'm starting to wonder if I hadn't caught you in the airport, when would you have actually admitted to everything?" He throws his arms out, releasing a defeated breath. "It just fucking blows, and if the shoe were on the other foot, I would've never done that to you with Emma."

The conversation ends when Jack spins on his heel, shaking his head on the way over to the treadmills.

Sawyer watches him leave. "Time. He just needs time."

I nod in my center's direction. "And you think he's ready for the captaincy next year?"

He shrugs. "Yeah, I do. He hasn't taken any of this out onto the ice. The guy's hurt for personal reasons, and the next time you talk to him, it has to be in private."

"Oh, for fuck's sake, this is all I need," I say as Tommy grabs his training shirt, throws it over his shoulder, and waltzes toward us.

I'll give him something—the guy does not give a shit about anything.

"When I got traded, I was under the impression that this team was tight." Tommy looks around the room, tipping his head from side to side. "Apparently, it was a far cry from the shit show my dad played for."

"There's nothing wrong with the team," Sawyer grits out. "It's a disagreement between friends that will pass."

Tommy scratches at his chest. A motherfucking smirk I'd love to wipe clean from his face is still there. "You fucked his sister and got her pregnant, right? Then you married her, all before he found out." He puffs out a laugh. "Fuck me, I don't have a sister, but if my best friend did that behind my back, he'd never see the light of day." He keeps grinning, only wider this time.

"Drop it, Schneider," Sawyer demands.

His eyes rove around the gym. "Speaking of girls. That one with dark hair. She plays soccer and is a real fucking firecracker." He rubs his temple. "I swear I heard someone mention her name in the postgame bar."

"Jenna?" I say.

He snaps his fingers. "Yes, that's the chick. Hot as fuck," he purrs. "She have a boyfriend, or is she fair game?"

"Neither," I reply. "She's way out of your league."

He laughs, loving the heated exchange. This guy feeds off tension and controversy. "Says the guy who could only bag his girl by sneaking around behind her brother's back, getting her knocked up and then eloping. I mean, do you even plan on announcing to the world that you're together? You don't need to sneak around anymore now that you've been caught."

My anger, which has been simmering beneath the surface since Jack stalked off, spills over.

Big time.

Sawyer steps forward, ready to intercept any punches as I square up to Tommy. The guy is huge. With tattoos covering his entire upper half and hands, some even on his neck, he's an intimidating figure.

Not that he intimidates me.

"If you spent more time concentrating on your game and less on getting into other people's business and fights on the ice, it's possible people around here might actually like you."

He sneers, and I smile sweetly.

"Touched a nerve?" I continue. "You don't know shit about me, my wife, or my marriage, and that's how I intend to keep it. You walked into this team a few days ago, and all you've done is exactly what we predicted—stir shit. That kind of behavior isn't welcome here."

He motions behind him to where Jack's working out. "Your

assistant captain doesn't seem to agree. He's next-level pissed with you, and it shows. Maybe he can see something in you the others can't?"

Hands curling into fists by my sides, I glance at Sawyer for a modicum of control.

I can't punch this guy.

"However Jack feels about me right now is inconsequential. He's a good man, and in the foreseeable future, he will likely be your captain. He's pissed at me right now, but I know our friendship runs way deeper than the bullshit you're spewing." I drop my eyes down his body. "So, why don't you head back over to the leg press and start working on your quads?"

I'm surprised when he does just that, but not before he turns over his shoulder, throwing me the usual shit-eating grin.

I ignore it and focus my attention back on Jack, who's still pounding the treadmill.

"He's just like his dad," Sawyer says about Tommy on a headshake. "The GM made a mistake, bringing him into the team."

Reaching across to the Olympic bar, I grab my towel and water bottle, ready to get out of here and back to my girl when she's finished work.

"What's done is done. He's here now, and we need to try and make the best of it."

Sawyer nods, his captaincy mask slipping back into place. "Excluding him from Collins's birthday party in January isn't an option then?"

"No," I breathe. "Unfortunately not. Although I was surprised she's even having one when Darcy told me."

His smile grows wide. Anything about his fiancée, and this guy turns to a fucking puddle. "She's softening in her old age. It might have something to do with my son too."

I clap a hand on his shoulder, genuinely happy he and Ezra have found their person. "You're a good friend, buddy. Maybe I don't say it enough, but you are. You've got me out of a lot of binds in the past, but I want you to let go of this situation between me and Jack. You don't need to worry about it because I've got it handled. I know I've said that before, and it's blown up in my face, but this time, I promise you I'll make it right. Just concentrate on enjoying your final season in the NHL, okay?"

Although Sawyer hasn't officially announced when he's retiring, I don't need him to. I know my best friend well enough to sense when he's ready to hang his skates up.

"Despite everything going on right now, I know this season is ours. I'm determined to put the Cup in your hands because you deserve that, Man. You deserve it."

His eyes glaze as he clears his throat. "Where did that sentimental speech come from?"

I shrug, thinking about my girls and my new brother-in-law I'm desperate to fix things with. "I guess life perspective changes when you realize what's important. And you're really fucking important to me."

CHAPTER FORTY-TWO

DARCY

My favorite Brooklyn bakery, Rise Up, brings all the sensory goodness and comfort I've come to love about living in this city. The smell of freshly brewed coffee alongside baking, sparks a feeling of England, but with the added vibe of living in Brooklyn. It's also a favorite meetup spot for me and my girls. Whenever shit goes down or someone needs advice, the first place we gather is around a table at the back, armed with baked goods and ready to put everything right.

However, as I push through the entrance and the soft jingle of the bell above the door fills my ears, I'm struggling to find anything comfortable about today's visit or the reasons for it.

It's been twelve days since Jack caught us at the airport, and things show no sign of improvement. I know he hasn't fallen out with me; he messages me daily to check on how I'm doing or if I need anything. He was choked up when I told him the name we planned to give our daughter. But in spite of our open communication, things don't feel right. Vibes don't lie, as they say, and that phrase couldn't be more relevant to our relationship.

Truth be told, I'm pissed at my brother. I expected him to be disappointed in Archer for the ruse about Abbie and the initial sneaking around we had done. We had known back then that we were playing with fire. What I didn't anticipate was for him to shut my husband out entirely and for this length of time.

I didn't even tell him that Emily was Archer's idea, for fear of ruining the name-reveal moment. Maybe he already guessed it was his suggestion since it was the name Archer originally used for me in the boys' group chat, but that doesn't really matter. We should be able to work past this, or at least talk through feelings.

Instead, Jack's done the complete opposite.

Last night on the phone, Mum told me the GM is getting angsty, concerned that the team is fractured, even though Archer's game is on point and so are their results. Getting married was what Archer and I both wanted, but it was also to ensure we weren't separated. If Archer is forced out of the team, then I'll lose everyone around me as I follow my husband to another state in a huge country. The fact that Jack can't see that leaves me angry and frustrated.

So, last night, I called an emergency meeting between my girls and Mum. Clearly, the men can't and aren't going to sort their shit out. Might as well leave it to the girls.

"I got you the strongest decaf I could find." Kendra slides a steaming mug of coffee across to me as I pull off my coat and hang it on the back of my chair.

I take a seat as Collins, Kendra, Jenna, and Mum all drop their eyes to my stomach.

"Figured there was little point in hiding it now," I muse, pointing to my tight jumper dress. "And what do you mean *strongest decaf*? Isn't that a bit of a contradiction?" I say to Kendra, forcing a smile.

She tucks a piece of wavy blonde hair behind her ear. "I asked Ed to add an extra shot of vanilla."

I snort and bring the latte to my lips, enjoying the first sip before setting the mug back down and clearing my throat. "Thank you for meeting so last minute. It's just ... I need my girls right now."

From beside me, Mum takes my hand in hers. "My nine o'clock meeting with my client, the Barnetts, can wait."

"Anything for you." Jenna takes my other hand, and from opposite, Kendra and Collins smile at me reassuringly.

My senses sting as I work up the courage to speak what I know everyone else is thinking. "I'm worried my relationship with Archer has destroyed his friendship with Jack. Archer has been ... not himself at all. Yesterday, after dinner, he took my plate, planted a kiss on top of my head, and retreated into the home gym for hours. I took myself to bed because I'm constantly exhausted, and when I woke up at midnight, I found him sitting on the couch, scrolling through photos from last season. His heart is breaking, and I can't stand to watch it."

Kendra nods her head, fingernails tapping against the side of her mug. "Honestly, Jack is the same. I told him to go and talk with Archer, even if it's just to clear the air. But you know when an issue is left too long, it then creates a void between people that's arguably bigger than the initial problem? That's how I feel about this. He's hurting, and I get that." She looks at me, nothing but honesty in her eyes as she pauses. "I get why he's upset because so much has happened behind his back and without his friend being honest. He wasn't happy with me because I didn't tell him what was going on. Now, he understands my reasons for keeping your confidence and I only hope he can take a step back and see all this from Archer's perspective too. It's time to let bygones be bygones."

She pushes her coffee mug away like she's done saying her piece.

"When I told Jon about everything, he actually took it better than I'd thought he would." Mum rolls her eyes. "Naturally, he was disappointed he didn't know about your wedding, let alone get a chance to arrange the shit out of it." She chuckles and returns to a serious expression. "All things considered, he was relatively calm after an initial outburst." She clicks her tongue. "Obviously, he'll dismember Archer if he hurts you, but he is willing to give him a chance. I think that comes from experience more than anything—he knows what it's like to fight against a reputation as an unreliable playboy."

I turn to Collins. "You're quiet."

Taking a sachet of sweetener, she empties it into her coffee, rolling her lips together as she does. She's always been unreadable, but never more so than in this moment.

"I've lost a lot of people in my life. Some through premature death and others because I struggled to maintain a friendship through fear of getting hurt. The only true bonds I've made in my adult years are with the people sitting around this table and the two boys I have waiting for me back home. Before we know it, a beautiful baby girl is going to enter our lives, and I, for one, want to snuggle the shit out of her without awkward-as-ass silences. Unfortunately, I don't see that there's much we can do other than remind our men that friendships come before egos. That, and we'll kick their butts into next week if they don't sort their shit out."

Mum hums from beside me, Jenna nodding along with Kendra.

"Well, ladies, I have nothing more to add. You all speak sense and a lot of it," Jenna says. "I personally enjoy nights out at Lloyd's, and the last one was awkward as shit."

Everyone makes their agreement known, including me.

I release Mum's hand and drop a palm to my stomach, circling it slowly. "I'm praying when I reach my twenty-week scan and I can share more photos of Emily, that this will all be forgotten. Archer deserves to enjoy this pregnancy as much as I do, and all I can see is the sadness in him. I know he's not perfect, but who is? He loves me and ..." I trail off as my friends and family all look at me. I know I'm ready to say the words, but the first time will be to my husband. I clear my throat and continue, "Jack has nothing to worry about." I retake my mum's hand, squeezing it softly. "And neither does Jon. I don't think there's anything Archer wouldn't do for me or our baby."

When the elevator doors to our apartment open, I can tell Archer's home from the faint sound of music as it filters down the hallway.

He's working out. Again.

Dropping the tan tote I take everywhere these days, I head towards the sound of Tate McRae.

"Archer?" I call, pushing the soundproof gym door open, but finding no one inside.

I try our bedroom, but still nothing.

"Archer?" I call out again, a little louder this time.

As I step up to the spare bedroom door, the music grows louder, and paint fills my nostrils when I crack it open and peer inside. Archer has his back to me, halfway up a stepladder as he paints the back wall a bright yellow—a similar shade to the bows on my wedding shoes.

He's not wearing anything but a pair of light-gray athletic shorts and old white sneakers.

I pin my lip between my teeth as I observe the way the muscles in his back flex and roll with each stroke of the brush.

Jesus freaking Christ. That's my husband.

I stand, watching him for maybe thirty seconds more before the music ends and he climbs down from the ladder, immediately stopping when he turns and sees me.

"Hey." He drops the brush down into the paint tray and begins walking over to me, wiping his hands down his thighs to clean them. "I thought you'd be a while longer at Rise Up."

I'm too busy staring at his sculpted chest—which is dotted with paint—to answer, and he tips my chin to look at him.

"My face is here." He smirks, smoothing his lips over mine.

When he pulls back, his eyes fall to my stomach. The fitted jumper dress I'm wearing does nothing to hide my bump, just like the girls noticed earlier.

"Are you decorating the nursery?" I ask on a whisper, the way he's studying my body leaving me breathless.

Archer drops to his knees in front of me, rolling my dress up past my stomach to expose bare skin.

"Yes." He presses a single kiss to my bump. "I promised you we'd go shopping, and given another two weeks have passed since I originally planned, I want to get all the things—clothes, furniture, equipment for Emily. Anything and everything my wife wants. You know, the usual. I figured if the room's painted already, then we don't need to worry about messing up anything we buy."

I cup his face in my palms as he looks up at me. His eyes are one of my favorite features. "But we didn't discuss color themes."

His lips find my skin, and as he speaks, goose bumps break out. "I'm sorry, Darcy Doll. But Pip here told me that she wanted the same color as the bows on her mommy's wedding shoes."

"Is that so?" I say, although it's more of a gasp as he moves his mouth toward my apex.

With both hands, he tears my thong away from my body, tossing it across the room. Next, he kisses just above my pussy, adding a swipe of his tongue for good measure.

"Did I guess the color correctly?" he asks, hooking one of my legs over his shoulder. "Because your pussy tells me I did."

He swipes a finger through my wetness.

"Yes," I moan.

In one easy motion, Archer picks me up in his arms, carrying me over to the stepladder.

"I wanna fuck my wife," he rasps into the crook of my neck.

Who am I to say no?

"Yes," I reply, already desperate for his cock.

When he sits me on a wooden rung, Archer pushes his shorts to the floor and steps out of them. Eyes dark and totally naked, thigh tattoo visible for me to salivate over.

I reach out and grab his hip, pulling him toward me. He's hard and leaking already.

"Are you okay?" I ask softly.

I don't need to elaborate; he knows I'm referring to everything going on with Jack and the team.

Archer blows out a long, steadying breath, his broad shoulders dropping. He wraps a large palm around his cock and inches forward, holding the stepladder steady with one hand and pushing my thighs apart with his knee.

"I'm fucking great whenever I'm with you."

I place my hand in the center of his chest, asking him to stop for a second.

He does, and I study his expression.

"You've spent a lot of time telling me everything will work out fine. Now it's my turn to offer you that same reassurance."

"We've been through so much to get here, Darcy." He presses his forehead against mine, looking down between us. "It feels like I've had to fight everything and everyone to be with you, and I'll fight even harder if that's what it takes."

I tip his chin up to look at me. "I'm telling you Jack will come around. I'll make it happen. This wise guy once told me that when a person loves someone enough, it isn't possible for bad shit to happen because that person simply won't let it."

The purest blue eyes find my own. "Do you ..."

I nod my head without hesitation. "Yes. I do. I love you, Archer. I love everything about you. I love your kind heart and the passionate way you care for me and our baby. I love your mind and the way it wants to learn sudoku and all the things that make me happy."

A single tear falls from his left eye, marking a track down his cheek.

My small palm is dwarfed by my husband's broad chest, his heart beating a fast rhythm against it. "I love your past and everything you were before you met me. I embrace all of it because that's what makes you special. No part of you has ever been or will ever be too much for me. You were and are exactly who I love. I see you, Archer Moore."

Sometimes, no more words need to be spoken, only actions.

With a wetness that still shines in his eyes, Archer pushes himself inside me.

I immediately grip the sides of the ladder as we take each other in, bound in a lock of blissful emotion.

After a few seconds, he begins gliding in and out of my pussy, leaning down and sealing his mouth over mine.

When he whispers that he loves me, I swallow down his declaration. I want our baby girl to learn that this is how a woman should be loved. This is the only kind of love I want her to experience.

Shivers trickle down my spine when he wraps my leg around his waist, and I whimper in response to the way he drives deeper.

As I cling on to the ladder, Archer fucks me with abandon. I never thought it was possible to be fucked in a way that filled my heart with so much love. My husband proves that theory wrong.

He draws out my orgasm when it hits, pulling out and sliding in slower so I can feel the full benefit of his dick, along with its accessories.

"Does this cock make my wife feel good?" he croons, sliding all the way back inside me again.

"Don't stop," I plead. "Don't you dare fucking stop, Archer."

"I'm never going to stop loving you, Darcy."

"But you just did," I groan, tipping my head up toward the ceiling when Archer's body stills.

He looks over his shoulder toward the door and then back at me, eyes wide and cheeks flushed.

"Shit. Someone's at the door."

CHAPTER FORTY-THREE

ARCHER

I have never grabbed my clothes and gotten dressed so fast in my fucking life. And trust me when I tell you that for me, that's really saying something.

I know who's standing on the other side of the door. I don't need to check my smart doorbell to confirm it. Only Jack could time his visit to absolute fucking perfection, and for some reason, he's always had a specific knock.

With my hand on the door handle and while thanking myself on repeat for updating the security code to the elevator recently, I check over my shoulder to make sure Darcy's in the bathroom, taking a bath and not racing through the apartment, naked, because that's the last fucking thing I need when I open this door.

"She fucking loves me," I whisper to myself, a shot of adrenaline kicking up my heart rate.

Drawing in a deep breath, I drop my eyes to be sure my dick has definitely deflated and pull the door open.

My gut was right.

"Hey," Jack greets me beneath a Blades baseball cap. He casts his attention down the hallway, closing his eyes like he doesn't particularly want to be here.

"Did Kendra make you come over?" I ask, stepping to one side so he can enter.

For a brief second, he hesitates, but then moves forward, and I close the door behind him, determined not to be the next one to speak. He's barely said two words to me outside of the rink, and if there's any hope for our relationship, it's time he started talking.

"Is Darcy here?" he asks.

Heading over to the kitchen, I do what I always do when Jack stops by my place to watch game footage or generally hang. With my arm outstretched, I offer him a beer.

"She's taking a bath, and she'll probably be a while," I reply, feeling the tension grow thicker with each second.

He stands next to the island with both hands in the pockets of his jeans, staring at the bottle I'm offering, like if he accepts it, then he's somehow yielding.

Don't leave me hanging, please.

Finally, he steps forward and takes the bottle. He doesn't immediately twist the cap and take a pull, like he usually does, instead setting it down on the counter in front of him.

"Why are you here?" I try a different tactic since he ignored my question about Kendra.

He shrugs, turning on his heel as he heads over to the floor-to-ceiling window.

"You're right; Kendra did tell me to come since the girls are freaking out over how things are between us. I was in this part of town, picking something up for Emily, and the next thing I know, I'm standing outside your door, having listened to my wife," he explains, his back still to me.

"Something for Emily?" I repeat, a dose of love spreading inside my chest.

He nods. "Yeah. I have it in my truck, but I'll save it for after she's born."

My throat tightens, and I take a sip of beer in an attempt to temper my emotions.

"What did you get her?"

Turning to look at me, he can't hide the subtle smile as it plays on his lips. "You'll see come the birth."

Something about that statement gives me hope, like he isn't going to cut me out completely.

Feeling like now is the best opportunity I'll get, I decide to approach with caution. "Are you ready to talk?"

Jack walks over to the couch and takes a seat, and I sit on the coffee table opposite him, forearms resting on my knees as I wait, yet again, for him to speak.

"I guess that's why I'm here, although I still don't know what to say. I'm just sick of this awkward atmosphere."

"That you created," I counter, immediately regretting that I did.

Jack goes to stand, but I hold up a hand.

"I'm sorry. Don't go. I'm frustrated, is all. I've been waiting to clear the air, and you haven't given me the chance."

Thankfully, he sits back down, twisting his hands around.

"I hate seeing you like this."

Jack's brows pull together. "Like what?"

I circle my own face. "I'm used to the golden retriever Jack. The one who can't stop talking and ripping the shit out of me. I can't remember the last time I saw you smile."

"When did you start sleeping with my sister?" He glosses over my previous comment, no sign of the old Jack reemerging.

But at least he's talking, and at this point, I'll take whatever he'll give me to start an open dialogue. This isn't just about me or him or the team. This is about my wife and the way I can see how this whole thing is cutting her up.

"The night of her birthday party."

I watch the way his jaw tics.

"That was over three months ago. You've been keeping all this a secret for that long?!" He huffs out a disbelieving breath.

"No, wait. Of course you have. She's over fourteen weeks pregnant."

"Fourteen weeks and two days, and starting to show." I'm so fucking proud, and I wear the smile to match. "She's doing so well, taking everything in her stride with the vitamins and shots she needs. We had a blood test at eight weeks, and she got through it like a pro. I distracted her with a story about me being an idiot when I was younger, and the test was over before she knew it."

Jack scrubs a hand over his mouth, his face softening. "I never even thought about her fear of needles."

I nod once and recall the look of absolute dread when the phlebotomist visited that day. "I remembered you talking about Darcy's fear of needles and figured she'd need some extra support through the pregnancy."

Something like understanding creeps into his stoic expression, and my hope blooms a little brighter. I decide to keep talking since I can sense he's way more receptive.

"Darcy getting pregnant when she did was never in our plan. That said ..." I eye him cautiously. "I won't lie to you again and tell you that I hadn't thought about what it would be like to spend a life with her. The number of times I wanted to sit you down and unload my feelings—"

"Then why didn't you?" he asks. "I'd have had way more respect if you'd come to me at the start."

Twisting my hands around anxiously, I know how important these next few minutes are to the future of our friendship and family.

"For the exact same reasons you waited four years to tell Kendra how you felt—fear of rejection. I've spent my entire adulthood jumping from one woman's bed to the next with zero chance of catching feelings. It wasn't because I was scared of the concept of a relationship, more that I didn't want one. That was, until I did and with the one person who was off-limits, and that thought *did* scare me shitless. With Darcy, all it took was a few minutes in her company, and I was enraptured—fucking ruined, to be honest. I got the opportunity to get to know her on a platonic level, and I'd never done that with a woman. Again, it was something I'd never *wanted* with any other woman."

I pause and let him absorb my words. Jack remains still as he studies me carefully.

"Darcy made it pretty fucking clear she wanted to have fun with guys after Liam, and honestly, I got it—why she'd want to keep her heart at a safe distance from other pricks who could tear it apart again. But when she moved to New York and started going out and garnering male attention right in front of me, my remaining willpower dissolved entirely."

Jack goes to speak, but my emotions are so high that I hold up another hand, needing to get everything out into the open after two years of hiding.

"No matter how many times I considered coming to you and explaining how I felt and what my intentions were with your sister, I couldn't envision an outcome where you'd understand or take me seriously. And then when you found out Liam had cheated, it was like big-brother mode hit a whole new level."

I puff out a defeated breath.

"I had you on one side, warning me to keep my distance when, in fact, I was the only guy who had honest intentions with Darcy. Then, on the other side, I had the girl of my dreams telling me all she wanted was fun." My voice shakes slightly on the final word. "Because that's all I could possibly be good for, right? That was a reputation I'd built for myself, and it was one that nearly cost me everything."

"Archer ... I ..." Jack starts, but stops himself as he struggles to find the right reply.

I keep going, feelings finally spilling from me in one cathartic declaration after the next.

"After a while of having safe and exclusive fun together, I was starting to feel like the only person who was going to get hurt was me, although that was a risk I accepted just to be near her and spend time with her. That's when she got pregnant. Darcy was convinced I'd run a million miles away from her and any responsibility." I look him dead in the eyes. "I didn't. Hearing her say she was carrying my baby was the single best news I'd ever heard, and the only place I wanted to be was by her side."

An involuntary, cheek-aching grin overtakes my face as I recall the start of my wife falling in love with me.

"Witnessing the way each hug became tighter and each kiss grew deeper was incredible. It was like we were part of this bubble we never wanted to burst. Outside of its walls, we knew a shitstorm was ready to rain down, but while we had our bubble's protection, nothing could stop us. Nothing can stop the way I worship your sister."

When I next lift my eyes to my friend, his shine with pools of emotion.

"You accused me of marrying your sister because I got her pregnant." I shake my head as the devastation I felt when he said it trickles through my veins once again. "It's true that we married in secret because we knew her employment visa was time-sensitive. Also, there was no way you wouldn't do everything in your power to either stop us out of anger or at least make it really fucking difficult."

Jack doesn't argue as he continues to listen.

"The bottom line is, Darcy can do what she wants. She can be with who she wants. She chose me, and there's no way I wouldn't have put a ring on her finger or had yellow bows stitched onto her wedding shoes whenever she gave me the honor of being her husband. Circumstance brought our timeline forward, but my love for her has always been real."

Against the backdrop of nothing other than the faint noise of the world outside, I swear I hear Jack swallow as he scuffs his sneaker against the floor.

"And the Abbie thing?" he asks quietly.

I push a hand through my hair. "If there's one part of this story I regret, it's allowing you to conclude I was seeing someone else. I want you to know I don't lie, but I am a human being, and I made a mistake. I was so desperate to keep seeing Darcy that Abbie gave me a good cover story as I soaked up whatever time I could get with the real woman I was dating, even if only in my head." I chuckle darkly. "Jesus, if you knew some of the stuff I did to keep her safe or in my life, then—"

Smiling, Jack interrupts my rambling. "I honestly don't want to know, Archer. You're your own brand of unhinged, and so long as Darcy is good with the possessive vibes you give off, then I guess I'm okay with it too."

"Does this mean we're good?" I ask carefully.

When Jack stands up for a second time, I don't stop him. Instead, I do the same.

Pulling off his cap, Jack holds it down by his side. He releases a tension-easing breath, and I find myself mimicking his exhale as we stand a few feet apart.

"I misjudged you, Archer. I don't know if it was blind rage or my ego getting the better of me, but I did. Honestly, it's probably why I showed up here today because despite my anger and hurt, I knew you weren't the kind of person who would easily betray a friend or the sister he protects with his life." He shakes his head slowly. "The Liam scenario fucked with my head because I'd seen how badly my blood dad treated my mum. Liam reminded me of him, and all I wanted for Darcy was happiness and good people around her as she moved to New York. Truth is, I should have more faith in my sister's judgment of people, along with my own. I should also probably listen to my wife when she tells me I'm being a prick."

He holds out a hand, and I close the whole distance, wrapping my arm around his back. A feeling of relief floods through me as wetness settles onto my eyelashes for the second time today.

"It's going to take time to fully heal from all this, but ... yeah, we're good, Archer," he whispers. "Welcome to the family, buddy."

CHAPTER FORTY-FOUR

DARCY

My brother might be one of the most recognized NHL players right now, but that's nothing compared to Archer Moore's fame. Wherever he goes, the press follows. I think there comes a point where a player can be bigger than the sport they actually play, and in my husband's case, I'm pretty certain that's true.

How our relationship hasn't been fully leaked to the media, I'll never know. We haven't been completely discreet since Jack and Jon found out, but we have kept a relatively low profile, I guess.

Until tonight.

"Are you nervous?" Kendra taps me on the shoulder.

"Yes—no—maybe," I say on a shrug. "Okay, I'm definitely shitting it a little bit."

Kendra throws her head back and laughs. I know on the other side of the exit doors to the players' parking lot, there are cameras and reporters waiting to catch a glimpse of us. When Archer pulled off his helmet and blew a kiss to the family box, it ignited what were already low-grade rumors that he was seeing someone. And since things are starting to improve with my brother—thank Christ—we figured it was time to address those rumors."

Kendra reaches out, wrapping her arm around my shoulders. "It will go a bit wild initially, especially since you're Jack's sister, but then it'll die down." She kisses the side of my head. "Jesus, you smell good."

I flick my hair back and smile. "The latest Chanel. I'm not sure if I like it as much as last season's fragrance, but it's got that citrus undertone, you know?"

"Hey, Darcy Doll." Archer's breath hits the side of my cheek as he takes my chin between his thumb and forefinger and turns my face toward him.

He looks delicious in a dark blue suit and a white shirt, open at the collar, his platinum chain shining against his freshly showered skin.

His eyes drop to the baby-blue jumper dress I'm wearing. "Are you showing off our baby, Darcy?"

"I am," I reply, feeling my cheeks flush hot.

He brushes his lips over mine, smiling into me. "Lesson four in Archer Moore: I've been desperate to do this since I first laid eyes on you."

"What?"

"This. No more hiding in parks, movie theaters, or at home." Interlacing our fingers, he holds his wash bag in the other hand and guides me down the hallway toward the exit.

When he reaches the doors, he pauses for a second, offering me a cheeky wink before he pushes out into the evening, and immediately, a few cameras begin flashing, multiple reporters asking questions. There aren't many since security only allows a certain number outside, and they can't reach us behind the fences, but still, they're rowdy and desperate for information.

I know they're here because it's Archer, but when a reporter asks about my baby bump, I stop and turn toward him.

"Archer, is this your new girlfriend? There have been whispers circulating for some time now that you're dating ..." another reporter asks as his eyes drop to my stomach.

I smooth a palm over my bump, and Archer steps toward the reporter, my hand still in his as he squeezes it tightly.

"The whispers are true," Archer confirms, picking our joined hands up and kissing across my knuckles. "As some of you may already know, this is Darcy—sister of Jack Morgan, stepdaughter of my coach, and as of very recently, my wife and the mother of my unborn child."

A flurry of conversation breaks out among the reporters as more cameras flash. Archer doesn't flinch at the attention, and I can't say it makes me feel uncomfortable. I've seen enough attention paid to Jack to know what I'm walking into.

"How many weeks are you, Darcy?" another male reporter shouts up.

Archer goes to respond, but then stops himself, allowing me to answer.

"A little over fifteen weeks." I smile when Archer cups the side of my face, bringing his lips down to mine.

"You two look very in love," a female fan croons as Archer steps forward to sign autographs.

"Darcy is the best thing that's ever happened to me. Sometimes, I have to pinch myself to know she's really mine," he replies. The sincerity and awe in his voice as he turns to look at me sends my head spinning out.

"Thanks for showing up tonight. I'm happy we got the win and another shutout against Philly." Finishing up on a Blades cap, he hands it back to the female fan, along with a pen, and then retakes my hand as we walk toward his car and head for our usual postgame meetup at Lloyd's Bar.

"Where's Emma?" I ask with excitement as we step into the private area, still hand in hand.

We're way later than expected since Archer wouldn't let me leave his car, my sore lips evidence of his reluctance. I'm desperate to meet his sister, even if it's only briefly as she passes through town.

He points in front of him toward a dark-haired beauty talking with Jenna, Collins, and Kendra. "That's Emma."

"Oh Jesus." I stop dead in my tracks. "She's stunning. Like, mega stunning."

Archer low chuckles. "She has her brother's genes. What did you expect?"

I roll my eyes at him. "I don't know. Maybe a little more humility."

He full-on cackles as he wraps an arm around my shoulders and leads me over to Emma. We didn't meet at the game since she was seated rink side with a couple of friends, but now that I've got my chance, my inner social butterfly is ready to take full advantage.

Archer ruffles a hand through his baby sister's hair, pulling her attention toward us. "Ems, how's it going?"

She spins around. Piercing blue eyes, just like Archer's, capture my attention, along with high cheekbones and a huge smile that reminds me of Julia.

"Hey!" she squeaks, throwing her arms around Archer's neck.

"I thought you weren't coming; you took so long to get here. Either that or you were both mauled by the media." She winces. "I saw the photos and footage; they were like savages."

I look up at my husband as he flushes at the memories of the dirty things he just did to me in his car. We both know the media isn't the real reason we're late.

"We got a little sidetracked." He motions to me. "This is Darcy, but I guess you already worked that one out."

It's like she's met me a hundred times before when Emma pulls me into her arms. "Now that I've forgiven Archer for not inviting me to your wedding, I'm delighted to meet you, Darcy."

Her eyes drop to my stomach, and she gasps. She's already aware I'm pregnant, but I guess seeing it in the flesh hits differently.

"Can I?" she requests, her palm hovering over my bump.

"Sure." I giggle as she wastes no time at all.

"Oh my God, have you felt her kick yet?" Emma asks as Archer steps away from us to order drinks.

Collins, Kendra, and Jenna all gather around me, each taking a turn to caress my bump.

"Not yet," I reply. "But we're hoping to soon. They say it can happen anytime after sixteen weeks."

Emma nods softly. "I'm sorry I haven't been in touch sooner. I don't really have an excuse other than I'm one of those crazy people who travels the world, and, yeah ... I kind of needed to decompress from family stuff after my mom and dad divorced."

"Ugh, parental divorce," Jenna drawls. "I hear you, girl. No matter how old you are, that shit gets to you."

I nod immediately, shrugging my jacket off and hooking it over my bag. "My parents divorced when I was a teenager. Then our family got separated across different continents."

Emma tips her head to the side, studying me. "Other than your sexy British accent, I can see why my brother and mom love you so much. You've got that ..." she clicks her fingers, reminding me so much of Archer with her confident actions.

"*Je ne sais quoi?*" Collins adds, making us all laugh.

"I think it's your big eyes," Emma muses. "You remind me of a—"

"Doll?" Archer finishes for her, passing me the mocktail version of a cosmo.

I take a sip and close my eyes.

"Pretending it's alcoholic?" Jenna asks.

I nod once, eyes still closed. "If I try hard enough, I swear I can taste the Cointreau."

"Only six and a half months to go, and you'll be able to taste it for real." Kendra picks up her soda and takes a sip. "Maybe we can mourn the loss together until then."

Every single head whips her way.

"Wait," Jenna announces. "Are you ..."

To my disappointment, Kendra shakes her head. "No. Although we've removed the goalie, if you catch my drift." She winks, and Archer kisses me on top of the head, moving across the room to join the boys. "We figured now was as good of a time as any to start trying. If we have a baby, then I'll still be young enough to get back into shape and pick up my career from there."

I nod along with Collins but see the discomfort as it flashes, very briefly, in Jenna's eyes. I can sense she feels like she's being left behind, and that breaks my heart for her. I've always known she's kind and caring and deserving of love, but that night she stayed in my apartment meant the world to me. She's the type of girl who loves her friends fiercely but quietly, not looking for recognition.

"When do you head back home to Philadelphia?" I ask Emma.

She shrugs a shoulder. "I'm not sure, probably in the next couple of days. Right now, I'm between jobs and crashing at a friend's place while in New York. I went to college with her, and she's a big Blades fan."

"All right, ladies."

I force back an eye roll as Tommy Schneider approaches our group, setting his empty pint glass down on a table next to him before turning to us.

The last time I saw him was after a game in the players' private bar, and I avoided talking to him. This is the first time I've met him face-to-face, and already, he's every bit the asshole Archer and Jack described him as.

With his messy brown hair and even darker brown eyes, I can't deny he's hot. The smattering of freckles across the bridge of his nose are a complete contrast to the tattoos that cover both arms and hands, all the way to the tips of his fingers.

I look around our silent group and catch sight of Jenna as she averts her eyes from him, taking a sip of her beer.

Tommy must notice her reaction as he smirks and studies her, running his tongue along his bottom lip.

"Hello there, Jenna." Tommy cuts through the awkward tension, scratching at the side of his jaw.

She lifts her head to look at him, complete disdain all over her face. "Hi."

Clearly unaffected by her clipped response—if anything, only encouraged—Tommy reaches forward and takes the glass from her hand, sniffing the contents.

Jenna freezes in place, jaw agape at his audacity. We're all in shock as he brings the glass to his lips and takes a large pull.

"What kind of woman drinks beer—and an IPA at that?" he teases, laughing to himself as he does it.

Jenna just shrugs, snatching the glass back and downing the rest before setting it on the bar beside her.

It's like none of us are here as they both pin each other with glares.

"I'm sorry?" She raises a single brow. "Did I pass out and miss the part where I was supposed to give a fuck about what you thought?"

Collins snorts at the kind of comeback she'd make.

Tommy doesn't react at all, continuing to smile at Jenna. "I bet you impress all the guys with an attitude like that."

"Was this your attempt to woo me, or can I save my applause for later?" Jenna volleys back.

I cast a quick glance at Emma to check she's okay, but she only looks amused at the back-and-forth between them.

"Ooookay ..." Kendra cuts through the tension, flicking her hair over her shoulder. "Now that we've established long-lasting friendships, I'm going to take a seat in the booth."

Collins and Jenna nod in agreement as all three step out of the circle, and Tommy steps up to the bar, leaving me and Emma alone. I exhale a slow breath.

"He's a bit of a dick, isn't he?" she whispers, thumbing over her shoulder toward Tommy.

"Yep. I give him a season, maybe two at best," I reply, taking another sip of my mocktail.

She twizzles a piece of long, dark hair around her finger, observing the boys as they laugh and joke about their league domination.

"He's happy, really happy. I can't remember the last time my brother was this genuinely light. For most of his life, it's felt like an act—fun-loving Archer, always the guy to crack jokes and never takes life too seriously."

"He's not always been happy?" I ask, that thought settling heavily in my stomach.

She shakes her head. "No, Archer's always been happy. I just got the feeling that he wanted more beyond hockey and playing around with other women, even if he never admitted that himself. I can sort of relate to that because I haven't found my person either. Sometimes, I thought it might be the arguments and unhappy marriage between my mom and dad that bled into our adulthood, holding us back from believing in a happy ending."

"But you don't believe that now?"

Emma's eyes move back to mine. "No." She smiles. "I simply

think he hadn't found the one woman who could bring him to his knees and make him want to settle down. And that gives me hope, you know? Hope that I can find my person one day too. I've always looked up to my brother; with his career and success, he set the bar for me to want more out of life."

She steps forward and wraps me in a hug. "Now, I'm thinking all I want is the kind of love you both share."

CHAPTER FORTY-FIVE

DARCY

"You cannot tell me that this wouldn't look so fucking cute on our daughter."

One fist propped on my hip, I eye my husband carefully as he holds up a gawdy-looking patterned dress.

"It looks like wearable carpet."

Archer's brows knit together as he twists the dress around by the hanger, studying it carefully. "I was thinking about it for next Christmas."

I drop my head down and laugh. "We need to focus on the right now."

He hooks the dress back on the rack and stalks toward me, tipping my chin up with his finger. "Well, right now, all I can think about is how fucking stunning you are." His free hand splays across my stomach. "And all I want to do is see you in that lingerie set I just bought."

My cheeks heat when he presses his mouth to mine, festive music playing in the background. For the day before Christmas, the shops are pretty quiet, and I've had the best time baby and clothes shopping.

"You realize I'm right here, don't you?" Jack groans from beside us. "And there is zero reason why you need to pet in public."

I twist my head and look at my brother. Being able to spend time with him without feeling like I'm hiding my whole life is everything, but having him accept Archer as the man I want and will make me happy? That makes me a whole new level of content.

"Pet?" I reply. "Who even says that word anymore? Do you mean make out or get it on?"

Jack closes his eyes and groans again. "It's seeing you all over each other. I don't want to think about my sister and best friend … you know … getting it on." He finishes the last part of the sentence in a pained way.

"Oh my God, check out these cute maternity dresses!" Kendra comes barreling toward me with two versions of the same maxi dress. One yellow, one blue.

I step away from Archer, and she holds them up against me, twisting her lips to the side in thought.

"I mean, they're definitely cute. I'm not sold on how horizontal stripes will look." Her face lights up. "I genuinely think you're going to be huge in your third trimester."

"Thanks," I reply dryly, taking a dress from her and inspecting how stretchy the material is.

"You're going to be fucking stunning in your third trimester." Archer leans into my ear, his voice low and gravelly. "Although we might need to fuck doggy style more often because of, you know, logistics."

"Still here," Jack sings.

"You don't need to be," Archer chimes back.

Jack pushes his jacket sleeve up his arm, checking the time. "Regardless of where I am right now, we need to be at the steak house in thirty minutes for the table I booked."

I scrunch my nose up at the thought of a slab of red meat. Well cooked or not, it grosses me out. I remember Kate turned vegetarian when she was pregnant with the twins, and now I'm beginning to see why. How in the hell I'm going to get through a full Christmas dinner tomorrow, I have no idea.

"You want Taco Bell, don't you?"

"Yes," I whisper back at my husband. "With extra cheese sauce, rice, and beans."

When I turn to locate my brother and Kendra, they're across the other side of the store, Kendra showing him more maternity clothes as he nods along agreeably.

My shoulders deflate as I stare up at Archer. "The exhaustion is really starting to set in now. Between work and the holiday season, I'm ... I'm struggling. All I want is Taco Bell, a soft blanket, and my favorite movies on repeat."

Archer looks down at the bags he's holding from previous stores we visited. Anything I remotely liked, he took it straight to the counter, whether it was a cute romper set for Emily or sexy underwear for me.

He really is that freaking perfect.

"Then why don't we do that? I noticed they have this really cool documentary about Alan Turing on Netflix. He's the guy from *The Imitation Game*." He winks proudly, and I can't help the giggle as it escapes my chest.

Archer presses a kiss across the bridge of my nose. "All I want is for you to be happy and comfortable. If I were any good at editing, I'd do your job for you too. Somehow, I think Janine might notice a decline in quality though."

I giggle again, losing count of how often my husband makes me laugh. "I've never been happier, truly. I think I just need to sleep for a thousand years once tomorrow is over. Jon has gone to a lot of trouble with the dinner, and I'm looking forward to seeing your mum again. I don't want to let anyone down."

He takes the maxi dresses from me and hangs them over his shoulder. "I don't think you could ever let anyone down, Darcy. My sister genuinely thought you were one of the best people she'd ever met. My mom can't stop talking about you every time

I call her. And I know when my dad finally meets you, he'll love you too."

If there's one thing about pregnancy I've learned so far, it's that one second you can be ready to cry your eyes out, craving the comfort of your partner. Whereas, in the next, all you can think about is his cock and how you're desperate to ride it. This is especially accurate when your husband is Archer Moore.

My eyes rove the empty store, Jack and Kendra still busy shopping and the assistant distracted with her phone, fully in holiday mode.

I lace my fingers through his. "Follow me."

Guiding him toward the changing rooms, I find a large corner cubicle and pull back the curtain.

"Take a seat," I instruct, pointing at a plush couch in the corner.

Without hesitation, Archer does as I ask, and I pick up one of the luxury shopping bags he's been carrying around for the past hour.

I know he's desperate to see me in the lingerie set he bought at the first store, and all I want to do is show him.

When I shrug off my jacket and go to pull my dress overhead, Archer shifts in his seat, swallowing thickly.

The lacy white thong isn't something I'd usually go for since I prefer dark underwear. But when I saw the way my husband's eyes darkened in response, I knew this would be a gift for him as much as it was for me. It was the fastest purchase in human history as he took it to the counter and had it bagged, all before Jack could notice what we were doing.

The bra is a balconette style, making the most of my modest chest, which is slowly getting fuller by the week. Something else Archer loves about pregnancy.

He leans back, spreading his thighs wide as he watches me get undressed silently. The atmosphere between us is charged to fuck, only made hotter with the risk of being caught.

A few more seconds, and I'm standing in front of him, completely naked, my body burning from head to toe.

"What do you want me to try on first? The thong or the bra?"

He reaches forward and pulls out the thong, dangling it on the end of his finger. He's so turned on; I can see by the way his jeans tent at the front.

"I want to see you in this, Darcy," he replies darkly, biting off the tag with his teeth.

Pulsing at the way he says my name, I take the thong from him and slowly step into it, pulling the thin strap up my thighs.

"What now?" I ask, my voice barely audible over the soft background music.

Archer rises from the sofa. Standing in front of me, he hasn't laid a single finger on my skin, yet the anticipation of his touch alone burns white-hot pleasure throughout my body.

"Why did you bring me in here, Doll? What do you want me to do to you?"

I grow damp at the question I'm confident we both know the answer to.

"Is it because you want me to fuck you?" he continues, dipping a single finger beneath my thong's waistband. "You know what I think?"

I roll my lips together, yearning for him to move his hand lower and slide his fingers through me.

"What's that?"

Like he can read my mind, he dips a hand into his pocket and pulls out his phone.

"I think you want me to rail you hard and take photos as evidence."

My entire body flushes as I respond in a breathy voice, "Yes."

Archer wastes no time as he takes a step back and snaps a picture of me wearing only the thong, smirking when he throws his phone onto the seat.

When he finds my opening, he pushes a thick finger inside. I sag against the pleasure, looping an arm around his neck.

"I also think while you love having your brother here, helping us shop and prepare for the arrival of our baby, you miss the way we used to fuck in secret. Do you like it when I fuck you in secret, Darcy?"

I lift onto my tiptoes, our lips ghosting over each other. "Yes. I like to have lots of fun."

In a split second, my back is against the cubicle wall, one hand under my ass, Archer pinning me in place as he undoes his jeans and pushes them down, along with his boxers.

I'm suspended and ready to be filled when I feel something foreign, and I immediately look down at my stomach.

"What is it?" Archer asks, looking and sounding concerned.

I've never been pregnant before, but I know from the baby books we've read together and the conversations with our doctors that it's possible to feel them as early as sixteen weeks.

Bringing a palm to my bump, I rub small circles over it. "I-I think Emily just kicked for the first time."

Archer's brows knit together as he tries to process my words. "She did?"

His hand immediately covers mine, and just as I pull it out from underneath—hoping that she'll kick again and Archer will be able to feel it fully—she does. His breath catches in his throat, eyes growing wide with amazement.

"Holy shit. Our baby girl is saying hello."

Love overtakes me, a flurry of warm fuzziness filling my chest. "She is," I whisper.

He waits for a few more seconds, but no more kicks materialize.

"I think she went back to sleep," Archer says, brushing his thumb over the small beginnings of a stretch mark.

I nod once, imagining her getting comfortable in there. "Probably just changing position in her little womb."

"Little womb," he repeats back, lips pulling into a warm smile.

I didn't think it was possible, but when Archer kisses me, I'm certain he just fell harder for me and our daughter.

Archer sucks and nips at my neck, taking all of my weight as he holds me by the thighs, spreading them as wide as I can go before entering me quickly.

Pieces of dark hair fall over his slick forehead, partially covering his feral eyes. I know he loves the thought of getting caught as much as I do; I can tell by the feel of his cock—how hard he is, how big it grows inside me.

"How's that?" he murmurs into the side of my neck, licking his tongue over my collarbone. "Does my wife like getting dicked down by her husband like this?"

"Yes." All I can manage is a whimper, and it's probably just as well since if I could find my voice, I'd be screaming my response.

Archer slows his pace, dropping his head to observe the way I take him.

"Look," he croons, drawing his bottom lip between his teeth. "Look how beautiful our bump is, along with the dick that created it. You let me fuck you so well."

I feel my release as it trickles down my thighs. I'm so wet and spread impossibly wide for him.

"You're all over me, coating your husband in secret while your brother is just in the next room."

More release covers his dick as I tighten around him, right on the edge of losing it completely.

"Come for me, Darcy."

I shake my head, scared if I do, then I'll be unable to temper my cries.

Archer clamps his mouth over mine, driving deeper and harder with thrusts that push me into a pleasure-induced trance. My orgasm ripples through my veins, seizing every muscle, igniting every nerve I possess.

As he licks into me, my pussy locks on to his dick, and I feel the way he throbs, liquid heat spreading throughout my lower half. I'm not sure Archer has ever come this hard, and by the way he shudders and shakes in response, he's fighting to stay quiet too. He drops his face back into my neck, growling out the remains of his high.

I'm a strange kind of satiated—caught in the bliss of the orgasm he just gave me, yet still desperate to have his dick all over again.

Pregnancy can be a wonderful thing.

A throat clears from the other side of the curtain, and Archer's growl turns humorous.

"We're going to be late for the steak house," Jack grinds out, the pained lilt in his voice earlier sounding even more intense.

"Yep," Archer acknowledges, shoulders shaking with silent laughter as he presses his still-hard cock further inside me. "We're just making sure these dresses are right for Darcy."

"Of course you are," Jack groans. "I have no doubt you're making sure every inch fits perfectly."

CHAPTER FORTY-SIX

ARCHER

Jack has added you to a new group chat.

Jack has renamed the group chat: Stop Banging My Sister.

Jack: Just leaving this here …

Sawyer: For the record, I have never banged your sister.

Jack: I know. You're here for moral support.

Me: You can't complain now that I'm your brother-in-law.

Jack: You know what you did …

Sawyer: *sighs into my beer* What did he do this time?

Jack: Yesterday, we went shopping together. I thought, why not? It'll be nice to buy baby clothes and spend time as a family.

> Jack: The first store—FIRST STORE—we walk into, and Archer's sneaking off to pay for sexy lingerie.
>
> Sawyer: For himself?
>
> Me: I would look good in a thong. For sure.

From the couch on the other side of Jon and Felicity's living room, Jack narrows his eyes at me before he gets back to typing.

> Jack: I just ate.
>
> Jack: No, Sawyer, for my sister. He snuck off to pay for sexy lingerie FOR MY SISTER while he thought I wasn't looking.
>
> Sawyer: Which begs the question, why were you looking?
>
> Jack: It was an unfortunate moment. Anyway, that isn't the worst part or the point.

"Does anyone plan on sitting back around the table for the dessert I made, or should I throw it all at you instead?" Coach—or Jon, as I now call him out of rink time—props his hands on his hips as he scans the room with narrowed eyes.

Looking at Jon, dressed in a blue striped apron with *Morgan's Marvelous Meals* stamped across the front, I'm slowly figuring out why Jack has consistently refuted that he's turning into his stepdad.

He absolutely is.

Throwing my brother-in-law a grin, I type out my next message without looking, my eyes on him the whole time.

> Me: What was the worst part of the shopping trip, Jack?
>
> Sawyer: I don't want to know. I also just ate.

> Jack: I don't have any hard evidence—thank Christ—but in another store, I'm fairly certain he took Darcy into a dressing room, claiming he was helping her try on dresses, and then ... you know ... while she was wearing said lingerie.

Sort of correct.

> Sawyer: All I want to do is make a joke about hard evidence. But I have a teenage boy and I'm in my mid-thirties. I shouldn't be this way.

> Me: Very perceptive, Morgan. Although it wasn't my idea. Your baby sister likes me to fuck her brains out in risky places. What can I say? I don't make the rules. I simply follow them like a good boy.

> Jack: ...

> Sawyer: You're regretting starting this conversation, aren't you?

> Jack: I'm regretting a lot of things right now.

I laugh at the way he holds his cell out in front of him, head sagging between his shoulders.

"Are you tormenting my brother again?" Darcy comes to sit across my lap.

I look up into her pretty eyes. She's curled her hair into waves today, and I loop one around my finger as they cascade down her glittery pink bodycon dress. The yellow diamond earrings I bought her for Christmas match her engagement ring perfectly. She looks fucking breathtaking.

"Making up for lost time," I reply, setting a tender kiss to her shoulder.

"Listen, while I get that all of us were young and in love at some point, I'll have none of that petting in my place, thank you very much," Jon announces, pointing at us with a spatula. "You're still on probation with me, remember?"

Mom snickers from across the table. She's been talking to Felicity, Darcy, and Kendra all day, and honestly, witnessing her beaming smile as she girl-talks with my new family is definitely the greatest gift I could've wished for this holiday period.

"Can I offer my coach a little advice?" I lean back in my chair to look at Jon, one palm resting on Emily as Darcy starts up talking with the girls again.

Jon spins on his heel as Jack plops down next to me, stealing a honey-roasted parsnip from my plate. As if he didn't already eat a whole-ass turkey.

"Don't push it, Archer," Jon warns, showing me his back before he sets a pan on the stove in front of him.

I decide to push it because ... it's me.

"The turkey was delicious and everything," I say, smirking around my beer glass as I lift it to my lips. "Although I'd have added champagne to the broth and cooked away the alcohol in the final stretch. I find it helps to keep the meat moist."

Darcy makes a retching sound from above me. Any mention of meat, and she's heaving. Just like me when I saw the nut roast she planned to eat.

Jon pauses his movements around the kitchen, narrowing his eyes at me.

You cannot tell me Jack and Jon aren't the same person.

He quirks a brow, wiping his spare hand over his apron. "Are you telling me you can actually cook, Archer?"

I shrug and set another kiss on my wife's shoulder. "I'll tell you what I told Jensen one time in practice: if you, me, and him had a cook-off, I'm confident I'd blow you both out of the water."

Darcy joins the conversation, tipping her head at me. "I can confirm the boy can cook. I've had some of the best meals ever from the comfort of his bed. Like the other morning," she starts, and I loop my arm around her waist, so fucking proud that she's mine, "I was feeling nauseous again. Next thing, he's bringing me a homemade dal curry, along with brown rice and a coriander naan bread." She imitates a chef's kiss. "Perfection. My craving for beans and pulses was immediately satiated, and the nausea suppressed."

Jon motions behind him to the stove. "Well, why aren't you up here, proving your worth?"

Wrapping Darcy tighter in my arms, I bury my face into her hair. "Too busy loving my girl."

"Ugh, I just love him," Felicity coos from across the table, heart eyes when she looks at me and her daughter. "I'd say my son-in-law has already proven his worth."

"Hmm," Mom replies, twisting her wineglass around on the table. "I have a few stories I can tell that might change your mind."

I pull my thumb and forefinger across my mouth, begging for her silence. There are plenty of secrets my mom can unearth about me—mostly when it comes to my past with women—but I know she won't go there.

She just laughs, and my heart swells even bigger. The temptation to drop that I just bought her a place a few blocks from my and Darcy's penthouse is overwhelming, but I decide to wait until tomorrow, as I originally planned since it's when we can get access to show her around. Emma's already called dibs on the room she wants when she comes to visit.

"Oh!" Darcy announces, excitement lighting up her face when she looks at me. She rests her palm over my hand. "Did you feel that?"

Don't cry around the dinner table, Archer.

When Emily kicks again, Jon throws his spatula down and races toward us. "Can I feel?" he asks Darcy, an emotion I've rarely seen before in his eyes.

Felicity and Mom rise from their seats, too, and a circle forms around my wife.

Jon holds up a hand to everyone. "I think you'll find I called first go. Granddad Jon wants to meet Emily."

As if following his instruction or maybe just to humor my demanding coach, Emily kicks again, and his face lights up. I know Jon met Felicity when she was thirty-nine and Darcy and Jack were almost college age. A stranger could argue he might've wanted children of his own, but from the way he protects, loves, and defends his stepchildren, along with the proud look in his eyes right now, I'd say he feels rich enough.

"I'm so proud of you, Darcy," Jon says, a shine to his eyes that I know isn't from when he was cutting onions earlier.

He steps aside, and Felicity rests her palm across her daughter's stomach.

"Typical," she moans. "Everyone performs for my husband, but the second I get a look in, it goes—" She cuts herself off, eyes darting to Darcy's bump. "Wow. She really is incredibly active, isn't she? Just like her mumma."

She turns over her shoulder to look at Kendra. "Fair warning though: this one here"—she points at Jack—"slept through the majority of my pregnancy, including all of the scans. It was even a struggle to work out if we were having a boy or a girl—he wouldn't move to show us."

Don't say it, Archer. Don't say it.

"I mean, I guess body parts have to be large enough to show up on the monitor in the first place."

Jack turns to look at me, one brow raised aggressively. "Divorce this asshole, Darcy. We don't need that kind of negativity in the family."

"I can vouch that—"

"Yes, yes. I don't want a full-blown discussion about my center's dick size," Jon quickly interrupts Kendra, shuddering at the thought.

Laughter fills the room as Kendra, Jack, and Felicity all help clear the table and serve dessert when my eyes briefly connect with Mum's.

She leans forward, both elbows braced on the table in front of her, chin resting in one palm. And when she flicks me a single wink, I know exactly what she's saying—she's proud of me, proud that I went after the girl I wanted and made her mine.

CHAPTER FORTY-SEVEN

DARCY

Years ago, Mum once said to me that life can deal us a set of cards we least expect. It's what we do with them that really matters. We can either fold or make the best of what we have.

I feel like the past few months have taught me the true meaning behind that statement. Sitting next to Archer Moore, my husband and father of our eighteen-week unborn baby, was not how I anticipated life in New York to play out for me.

It was in the stars though.

When I moved to Brooklyn, I was hurting, even if I didn't let it show. I was scared to embark on a new career after graduating and pursue my dreams in editing. Even if I pretended like I'd gotten my shit together, I felt like I had anything but.

I kept reminding myself that several years ago, when I was much younger, Mum had done something similar when she stayed in Seattle and made difficult decisions to go after the life she wanted to live. In the end, she made some of her greatest friends and met a husband most women could only dream of having by their side.

To some extent, it feels like I've followed in my mum's footsteps. I always saw her time in Seattle as a second act in her life, and while I'm younger than she was when she met Jon, I can't help but feel a similar kind of way.

It's easier to try and control every element of your life because that way, the days seem safer, more predictable, and fear of the unknown doesn't creep in. But when you play it safe, you risk missing out on undiscovered chapters or dismissing people who couldn't be more perfect for you and the life you truly want to live.

Sure, I have dreams of opening my own editing business one day. The friends I have around me in Collins, Kendra, and Jenna are real-life inspirations to me as they kill their respective careers daily.

But right now, in this moment, driving to my friend's birthday party with my husband's palm resting on my rounding stomach, is exactly where I want to be. I wouldn't change the cards I'm holding because this hand is perfect.

"You make me nervous when you're quiet, Doll." Archer glances across at me as we head toward the private bar Sawyer has booked out. "I don't think your mind ever stops, does it?"

"Not really," I reply as he pulls into a designated parking spot for the valet.

Placing the car in park, he reaches across, cupping my cheek in his warm, rough palm. "You know you can let those brain cells rest a little now that you have me. We're a team, and we will work everything out together."

I place my hand over his, feeling my shoulders relax a fraction. "The DARCher bubble never really burst, did it?"

Archer studies me with intrigue. "DARCher bubble? I've never heard that before." He leans across and sets a kiss against my lips. "But I love it. Our bubble never burst when we allowed others into our secrets, Darcy. It only made us stronger. I promise there will always be parts of us and our life that only we know."

"Like what?" I ask, my heart rate picking up as he kisses my jaw.

"Like the way you chew the tip of your pencil when you're thinking through a puzzle. Or the way you fold your foot behind the other when you're standing at the sink."

Another kiss, and I can feel my pulse as it throbs.

"How I knew you wanted me to be a pussy preventer that day with Harry at the bar. And how I punched a guy last August when he was all over you one second and chatting shit about you the next."

I pull back, jaw agape. "You did *what?*"

He winces, that rare flush of color spreading across his high cheekbones. "The night Sawyer and Collins got engaged ... there was this dude you were flirting with in the bar we went to afterward."

I shake my head, remembering clearly who he was and that I kissed him. Truthfully, I had every intention of heading back to his place, like he'd suggested. But when he went to the restroom, he never came back, and I assumed he'd changed his mind and tried not to take it personally. I think at that point, I concluded being a playgirl probably wasn't suited for me.

"Wait ..." I pause, slowly putting the pieces together. "You punched him in the restroom, didn't you?"

Archer scratches at the back of his neck, a playful but pleading puppy-dog look in his eyes. Almost like he's been caught chewing on something he shouldn't.

"He was talking shit about you. I saw red and fucked up his jaw." He winces again, gripping his steering wheel tightly. I can sense his anger even now, months after he hit him. "*No one* gets to look at my girl in the wrong way, never mind disrespect her. I was convinced I'd fucked up with you and the guy would leak it to the press. He didn't, and I got away with it."

Is it wrong that my thong just grew damp?

"You told Liam to take a hike too, didn't you?" I ask, unsure if he did, but starting to suspect Liam's disappearance might have to do with my spouse.

Archer's eyes grow wide, a flash of panic shooting through them. "How do you know about that?"

I shrug a shoulder. "I didn't, until you just admitted it. He dropped off the face of the earth, and that's not like him. Normally, he likes to fuck with my head as much as possible."

"He's a fucking prick I want to pummel into the ground, but also kiss and thank him for letting you go, all at the same time. There was no way I was allowing him back into your—our lives."

Like I do so frequently, I tip my head to one side, teasing him with a grin. "You're really freaking intense, Thigh Boy. You know that, right?"

He returns the expression. Playboy Archer might be long gone, but something tells me his trademark cockiness will always remain.

I hope it does.

"I'm willing to bet that there is no one in this world—universe, in fact—that's as down bad for their girls"—he rubs a thumb over my stomach—"as I am for mine."

"If I drink another mimosa, I'm one hundred percent going to puke," my friend announces.

I push the glass along the bar toward Collins. "I believe in you, babe. You've had two drinks all night. Plus, I'm intrigued what drunk Collins is like."

"Same." Sawyer approaches his fiancée from behind, setting a kiss on top of her head. "I want to know how much crazier you get when you let all your inhibitions drop."

She rolls her eyes and picks up the glass, taking a tentative sip. I do the same with my soda, watching as Archer talks with a few of his teammates.

"Last birthday as a Mackenzie," I breathe out around the rim of my glass.

She smiles, creases forming around the corners of her eyes. "Ezra picked out his suit last weekend; it matches his dad's, apparently."

"It does." Sawyer kisses the top of her head, as infatuated with her as he was the first night he clapped eyes on his future wife. "I'm desperate for clues about the dress, but this one here isn't giving anything up. I don't know how I'm supposed to hold out until July."

Collins shifts out from underneath Sawyer, twisting her neck to look up at him. "I'm not wearing a dress—well, not a white one anyway." She shivers and turns to look at me. "Can you see me in white? Seriously?"

Right now, all I can see is Archer's face when the doors opened to the private room where we married and how incredible I felt, wearing something the total opposite of what I'd have gone for.

"I think you should—go white, that is. Play it a little dangerously."

The second my hand smooths across her hip, shouting penetrates the loud music.

"What the fuck?!" Sawyer announces, already halfway across the room to join Archer as they both make a beeline for Tommy.

I slide my drink back onto the bar, Collins doing the same as we both scurry over to Jenna, who's now all up in Tommy's face.

"I'm sorry, but if you're going to talk bullshit, then own it," she bites out.

Tommy scoffs at her, his menacing brown eyes laser-focused on my friend.

I'm ready to step in like my five-foot-three ass could do something when a huge—and I mean, freaking huge—guy stands up next to her. With similar dark hair and brown eyes to Jenna, he wraps an arm around her shoulders.

"That's Holt," Kendra whispers from beside me.

I don't know when she joined me and Collins. Clearly, I was too locked in on what's going down.

"As in her brother?" I reply.

Collins nods slowly from the other side of me. "Yeah. He arrived a few minutes ago. He just got off a flight from Paris. He's here to visit his family for a few days since there's a short break in the rugby season."

Kendra clicks her tongue as Tommy squares up to Holt. "I wouldn't fucking do that if I were you, Tommy," she whispers beneath her breath. "Rugby guys are born to take people out. They do it for a living."

"You're a fucking piece of shit," Holt spits at Tommy, although I didn't catch whatever bullshit Tommy just spewed at him.

It doesn't surprise me since his dad was underhanded with everything he said and did too. Like father, like son, I guess.

At first, I think Tommy's either thought better of his chances or overheard Kendra's whispered warning when he shoves both hands into the pockets of his pants, turning to walk away.

I was wrong. He just wanted Holt to drop his guard.

Jenna's screams cut through the room as the music grinds to a standstill seconds after Tommy's knuckles connect with the underside of Holt's jaw, pushing him back into the table behind him and causing drinks to spill everywhere.

"Oh fuck, no!" Archer and Sawyer immediately pin Tommy's

arms behind his back as Jack takes a stance right in front of him, blocking his path to Holt.

How Jenna's brother doesn't retaliate, I have no idea. What I do know from my time in college is, rugby players aren't just taught the skills of their game, but discipline and control are drilled into them from a very young age.

"I can't believe he just hit him," Kendra gasps. "H-he just fully punched the shit out of Jenna's brother."

"Me neither," Collins agrees.

"I can," I add with a headshake, and they both turn to look at me. "His last name's Schneider."

CHAPTER FORTY-EIGHT

ARCHER

Last year, I spent Valentine's Day scrolling aimlessly through Darcy's social media profiles, tormenting myself as I imagined her waking up in someone else's bed.

This year, she's my wife and in our bed. Where she belongs, where she's always belonged.

As I reach across and pull the duvet over her twenty-three-week pregnant belly, I carefully set a kiss above her navel. Emily is just as active as she was when we first started to feel her kick, and I'm addicted to the tiny movements beneath my palm.

I can tell she's going to have sass, just like her mommy. Personally, I think she's going to be just like Darcy in every way. Her eyes, her hair, lips, nose, cheeks, chin ... all of it. I also hope she sleeps like her mommy does because that shit will make our lives way easier. Darcy told me that before we started sharing a bed, she'd have disturbed nights where her brain didn't stop. I've never witnessed any of that, only the peaceful snorts she puffs out into our bedroom while I lie awake, staring at her like the crazy person I am.

Although that's not strictly true. I was awake most of last

night for another reason. It's been a while since I got my thigh tattoo, and I forgot how fucking painful—and sore—they are immediately afterward.

Technically, I shouldn't be getting any while in the middle of the regular season, but when Coach found out what I planned, he turned a blind eye. Call it special family privileges or that he's too caught up in the constant fights and issues Tommy keeps creating for the team. I knew he was a bad trade, and he's proving us right. After the fight at Collins's party, Jenna has stopped coming to games, refusing to be anywhere near him. Even Sawyer has decided to extend his career for a further season. He plans to step down as captain in the offseason, but will stick around with Jensen Jones to help steady the ship.

When it comes to my new tattoo, I guess I could've waited until the offseason, but if you haven't worked out by now that I'm the most impatient person on the planet, then I guess you don't know me that well at all.

What I want, I get, and what I wanted was my daughter's twenty-week scan tattooed across my left pec.

It's barely light outside as I throw back the rest of the duvet, and Darcy squirms in response to the cool morning air as it meets her skin.

Keeping my mouth moving, I descend my lips and tongue from her navel to her bare pussy, and she spreads her legs instinctively, inviting me to help myself.

"You love to use me, don't you, Doll?" I croon, moving further down the bed until my head's perfectly positioned between her thighs. I part her wider and push two fingers inside her damp pussy, circling her tight ass with my thumb.

Her hips lift from the bed, but I hold her down with an arm, taking my first taste of her.

"I plan to play with this pussy all day. Is that okay with you, wife?"

Her hands dive into my hair, tugging at the roots when I nip at her clit. My fingers continue to slowly pump her, searching for Darcy's first high before she's barely opened her eyes.

"I'm feeling like a bad boy today," I rasp against her entrance, pulling my head back and slapping her clit with my palm, making her jolt and writhe. "I don't want to move from our bed. You're not at work, I don't have practice, and it's the most romantic date of the year."

She whimpers when I pull out my fingers and spit onto my thumb, reentering her pussy and pushing the tip of my thumb inside her tight hole, teasing and coaxing her gently.

After a few seconds, I pull out of her ass, crooking my fingers to massage her front wall. Her cunt weeps for me, pools of release trickling down my hand.

"God, Jesus, Darcy. You're such a wet fucking girl—you know that?" I rarely talk or think about my past with other women because my future only involves one. But I have never known a girl to get so wet during sex.

I like to think she saved it all up for me, and that thought sends blood shooting straight to my cock.

Like some sort of caveman, I growl against her, swiping my tongue from one hole to the next, considering all the ways I plan to take them throughout the day.

"How do you want me first?" I ask, my voice laced with lust and body trembling with need.

"I want you naked," she replies, tugging at the hem of the T-shirt I've worn all night, trying to hide the tattoo I got yesterday but wanted to reveal this morning.

"But I'm hiding something under there," I tease, my mouth hovering over her pussy.

She yanks on my shirt again. "Archer, you can't say shit like that and then continue going down on me like it was nothing."

Slowly and with a grin wider than the Brooklyn Bridge, I kiss my way up her body, only stopping when our lips are millimeters apart.

"Lesson number five in Archer Moore: I can lick your pussy

whenever and under whatever circumstances I want." I reach down between us, guiding my cock inside her. "Because my wife's cunt is mine, to stretch out and fill as I please."

She whimpers when my piercings slide into her opening, both legs clamping around my ass. She needs me deeper.

"Have you ever wanted and loved someone so much that you wish your bodies could just merge?" Darcy whispers against my parted lips. "At the risk of sounding like an ungrateful bitch, just you being inside me doesn't feel like enough anymore."

I know exactly what she means. "I'm happy you're finally catching up to my feelings." Still inside her, I pull up to a kneeling position, and she unwraps her legs from around me. "But what if I told you I did something yesterday that merges us and our family forever?"

Her eyes fall to the hem of my shirt when I cross my arms over my chest and pull it over in one motion. Although my tattoo is still fresh and wrapped, I replaced the initial bandage with a clear film so Darcy can see it.

Already big blue eyes grow even wider when they fall to my pec, a tiny gasp leaving her throat.

"Y-you ..." She's lost for words, pointing at my chest as she tries to form a coherent sentence. "When did you get this done?"

I drop down and brace my elbows on either side of her head as my dick makes slow strokes inside her tightening pussy. "Yesterday, after morning skate. The second we got the scan images, I booked in with the same artist who had done my thigh tattoo. Do you like it?"

She trails her dainty fingers over the image. "Archer, I ... you got Emily tattooed on your body. It's the most incredible thing I have ever seen."

My heart swells, and I sit back again, this time bringing my girl with me until we're fucking in the lotus position. I know this one's good for her, she likes me deep, and I like to feel her swollen belly as she grinds against me, taking all that she wants from my body.

"When Emily's born, I want to get yours and her fingerprints just underneath it."

Darcy lifts up and sinks back down onto me, tipping my chin up with her forefinger as she kisses me with a passion so deep that I swear to God, my soul leaves my body.

"I love you, Archer. With everything I have, I love you so much."

When her first orgasm hits, she spreads her legs wider, a crimson flush overtaking her flawless complexion. Her blue eyes are glazed, pouty pink lips parted as a climax so strong suspends her in a euphoric trance.

Throughout the years I've known this girl, I've thought on multiple occasions that she couldn't get any more beautiful. This moment, right here, blows everything out of the water.

Her skin glows from my growing baby, a sheen of perspiration covering her skin as she rides my cock with abandon. I know our bedsheets are fucked, and I know I won't be able to hang on much longer as my balls tighten. I'm ready to let go and imprint this image of my wife in my memory, just like I have our daughter on my skin.

"You've changed my life, Darcy." At first, I can't be sure if I said the words out loud, but when Darcy's eyes grow glassier, I realize I did. "You made me believe in love," I continue, emotions spilling out of me in the way I know I'll empty inside her any minute. "My life was happy, but you gave it meaning. I've got everything to live for beyond my years as a hockey player."

Minutes—albeit I don't know how many—pass where all we do is make out and fuck each other slowly. The flush painting Darcy's skin only grows deeper with every orgasm I give her until I really am at the point of zero return.

"I'm going to come." My words are weak as I buckle under the intensity of her love, shooting deep inside my wife.

Darcy flops into my chest as we both come down from our joint high. She reaches a hand up, tugging on my chain and asking for my mouth. "I've got something I want to give you. I was going to wait until tonight, but I don't think I can," she confesses between kisses.

I push a few strands of damp hair away from her face. "I'm supposed to be the one who spoils you."

As she pulls back to reach for the nightstand, my cock slips out of her, and immediately, I want back inside.

Fuck me, today is going to be epic.

"Yeah, well, suck it up, Thigh Boy." She giggles, pulling a long black box from the drawer.

Darcy kneels in front of me, eyes sparkling with excitement just before she cracks the lid.

"I know you bought the last one for yourself, and I don't want you to think this is in any way replacing it. But ..." She trails off as I try and take in the yellow gold chain. "I figured it was time to buy you another. As a reminder of how far you've come."

Taking the small golden dog tag between my fingers, I turn it around to see those exact words—*How far you've come*—along with, *All my love, Darcy Doll*, written underneath.

Without any more words exchanged, she sets the box down and plucks the chain from its black velvet cushion, dangling it between us.

"I've met three types of dads in this world." She begins talking as she unclasps the chain and hangs it around my neck. "One I share DNA with, but rarely speak to since he can't be bothered to get in touch." She secures the clasp and takes my face between her hands. "Another who loves me like his own daughter and who, oftentimes, I wish were my blood father."

I swallow down my emotions. "And the third type?"

She just smiles, eyes searching my face. "The third is his own unique brand—the kind who inks his daughter onto his body and treats his wife like an absolute queen. The kind of dad who has so much talent, but never really discovered his true gift until he fell in love with a girl and found out she was having his baby." She takes my hand in hers. "He's courageous and loves without question. He's funny and smart—he can even solve master sudoku puzzles." A single bubble of laughter leaves her as she strokes her thumb under my eye, wiping away a single tear as it hits my cheek.

"To the onlooker," she continues, "he might be the most unlikely dad—all about fun and messing around with women. But lesson by lesson, he taught his baby mama that the world was wrong to conclude that he was anything other than perfect."

EPILOGUE

June

DARCY

"I can't do this. I take it back. We can't have a baby—because I *can't do* this."

Panic snakes up my spine, slithering into and overtaking every part of my mind.

All the positive vibes I had earlier?

Gone.

All the excitement I felt when we walked into the hospital?

Vanished.

The baby birthing mixed tape with all my favorite songs—which was essentially a One Direction album—that Archer created for me?

Fuck. That. Shit.

There is no way a baby is being birthed from my vagina. I don't care that there's history spanning hundreds of thousands of years ready to prove me wrong. I will not push a full-sized baby from this body.

As I pace—or more like waddle—around the delivery suite, Archer tests the water temperature in the birthing pool I was determined to book.

"Just so we're clear ..." I pant and wince as another contraction hits me. "We aren't having any more babies."

Shaking drops of water from his hand, Archer stands and walks toward me as I continue circling the room.

"And why did you have to wear gray sweatpants today?" I snap, clutching my back because the heat pads that are supposed to relieve pain are doing nothing but pissing me off. "You know I struggle to be mad at you when you wear gray sweats."

His cocky smile emerges, and all I want to do is wipe it from his face. "Why do you think I wore them? I like to think of them as my mid-labor body armor."

He tips his head to the birthing pool as I drop mine to his chest.

Archer wraps his arms around my lower back and rubs it gently. "The doctors said you could use the water whenever you're ready."

I sob into his shirt. "Mum never warned me that labor was this bad. Why did she lie to me?"

The soft beating of his heart causes me to breathe a little slower as Archer continues to hold me against him.

"It's not too late if you want me to call her. I know she's only downstairs, waiting anxiously for news."

I peer up at my husband. He looks and smells incredible, unlike me, who has been laboring for the past ten hours with very little to show for it. Only the puke stains on the oversize Blades top I'm wearing serve as evidence of my struggle.

Shaking my head, I grind my teeth and pull at his shirt when another contraction hits me. "No. We stick to the original plan. Unless anything goes wrong—"

He tips my chin back up to look at him, confidence the only emotion on his face. "I don't want you to even start thinking about going down that route. Nothing is going to go wrong."

"How do you know?" I rush out, another wave of panic slamming into me when I remember the doctor said I was only four centimeters dilated. I have another six to go. There's no way I can sustain this; the pain is only going to get worse.

Of their own volition, my arms flop down to my sides, any energy I had remaining almost completely depleted.

Archer drops one hand into mine and slowly walks us across to the corner, where the birthing balls are kept.

He lowers me gently onto a green one and then takes a seat on a blue one opposite, this time holding both my hands in his.

We bounce on them slowly, just as we've done time and again in our apartment. He even brought one to the last game of the playoffs—which they lost, thanks to Tommy fucking Schneider—just to make sure I was comfortable.

"Look at me, Darcy." His voice is gentle but demanding.

Lifting my eyes to his, I can feel the tears of overwhelm as they begin to surface, but none spill onto my cheeks.

Jesus, I'm too exhausted to cry.

"Nothing bad is going to happen because I'm here. I know I've said a thousand times that I'll never let anything hurt you or Emily, and that's because I *mean it.*" He bites out the final two words of his statement, trying to hammer home his point. "My life is nothing without you in it."

There's a quick tap on the door before a female doctor and nurse enter, and I spin back around to face Archer.

He nods at me reassuringly, squeezing my hands in his.

"Okay, Darcy." The doctor begins speaking, tapping the bed with her hand before pulling on surgical gloves.

"They're latex-free, right? My wife has an allergy," Archer quickly asks.

She smiles over at him. "Yes, Mr. Moore. We have it in our notes, and the previous doctor informed me too. Please don't worry."

Archer's shoulders drop an inch as he stands and helps me off the ball.

"If I can ask you to come and lie down on the bed for me in the usual position, we can check how far along you are."

I buckle over the bed just as I reach it, groaning into the mattress while Archer stands behind me, practically holding me upright.

"The contractions are definitely getting stronger and closer together." Archer speaks for me. "She's exhausted."

When I try to swing a pathetic leg onto the bed, Archer takes my entire weight, and he carefully lifts me onto it. I don't miss the swoonworthy look the nurse gives him.

I internally roll my eyes. *First it's the phlebotomist, now my nurse.*

"Well, I'm pleased I can bring you good news." The doctor pulls a white sheet back over my lower half and snaps off her gloves, tossing them into the medical rubbish bin. "You're now seven centimeters dilated and making great progress."

I could cry. Both from the pain and the fact that, *finally*, my labor is starting to move forward. I'm aware that some poor women labor for days without much progress, but I couldn't be of those women. I was ready to wilt at the first contraction.

The doctor points toward the birthing pool. "Do you want to try now, Darcy? I suspect the baby won't be all that much longer."

Another contraction rips from me, this one much stronger. "I don't know if I've got it in me to get off this bed and in there," I wail, throwing my head back into the pillow as I grit my teeth through it.

"I've got you," Archer says, curling his arms under my body.

"Sir, I'm not comfortable with you carrying your wife anywhere."

We're already halfway over to the birthing pool when Archer turns with me in his arms.

"My wife made it clear that it was her dream to birth our daughter in the pool with yellow sensory lighting. And that's what she's going to get."

He leans down, placing a kiss on my forehead. "I'm going to lower you into the water now, okay? Then I'll take off your shirt so you don't overheat. I'll reduce the lighting to get it all cozy for you, and we'll work through this together."

Partly because I don't have the energy for words, but also because I've now joined the nurse's involuntary swoon session, I nod and let Archer do as he described.

When the nurse and doctor leave the room, Archer walks over to the lighting panel and sets it up just as I originally planned.

A couple of seconds later, another contraction hits me, but the weightlessness of the water takes the slightest edge off it. Don't get me wrong; I still want to scream blue murder, but somehow, the warmth against my skin helps to alleviate the unbearable, gripping pain.

"Are you sure you don't want pain relief? It's not too late, and you don't need to be a hero about it," Archer asks, swishing a little water against my baby bump.

"No. I've come this far," I say, shaking my head and closing my eyes. "This is a battle I'm having with myself."

"Okay, we're starting to crown. We only need a couple more really big pushes from you, Darcy."

Nope. It's a hard nope from me.

I shake my head profusely as Archer takes me into his arms. Around ten minutes ago, he stripped down to his boxer briefs and climbed into the pool with me.

"You can, Darcy Doll. I know you can. What do you need?"

"I j-just n-need this baby out." My cries are now full-blown wails. "Can you push her out for me?"

Another contraction builds, and I wrap my arms around Archer's neck, digging my fingernails into his shoulders.

"That's it. Take it out on me. Just keep pushing." He kisses my sweat-soaked forehead, murmuring against my skin, "I've never loved you more than I do in this moment."

The midwife leans down into the pool. "One more, Darcy, and we'll have her."

I have no idea where the strength comes from when I lift my head to look at Archer. The burning and pain are unbearable, but I know we're so close to starting a family.

"One more," he whispers. "One more, and she's ours."

On a cry I know will summon my entire family upstairs, I deliver Emily into the pool, and the midwife quickly reaches down and gathers her up, immediately placing her on my chest.

"She's got your features; I can tell she's just like her mama." Archer's shaking voice is the only sound I hear between my own sobs and the tiny cries leaving my daughter.

Emily's eyes are still closed, but as the nurse quickly takes her from me to clean, weigh, and wrap her, I can already see the resemblance.

"I'm so fucking proud of you, Darcy." Archer wraps his arms around me, pressing his forehead against mine. The weight of my exhaustion has fully lifted, replaced with a pure exhilaration I've never felt before. "Do you want me to ask everyone downstairs to leave visiting for a while? We can have people around when we get back home."

I shake my head, ready to get out of the pool and hold Emily again as she begins to cry. "No. Invite them up. They've all waited, and I want them to see how beautiful she is."

A half hour later, I'm tucked up in bed with a fresh set of nightwear and my messy hair somewhat controlled in a bun Archer attempted for me.

My husband shakes his head in awe as he slowly walks around the room, holding our daughter in his arms. "I can't believe she has emerald eyes. I was sure they would be blue."

He's a complete natural, and it's already obvious who Emily favors.

A girl after her mommy's heart.

"Oh, I can," Mum adds, readjusting my bedsheets in the usual fussing way she does. "She has her grandma Morgan's eyes."

"I don't know about that," Julia chimes in, tucking the sheets on the other side. "I'd say mine are more of a bluey-green and I can see that color in Emily's."

Archer takes a seat in the corner of the room, smiling at me as he cradles Emily to his bare chest, her tiny hand curled around his little finger. "That's you right there, Pip. Etched onto Daddy forever." He drops his eyes to the tattoo on his left pec, and my heart squeezes.

"Do you have enough baby clothes in this bag?" Mum asks sarcastically, taking a few sets out and laying them down on the dresser in front of her. "I was just wondering if you'd packed for a vacation or a stay in the hospital."

I snicker when Archer rises from the chair and walks over to me, lowering a sleeping Emily down on my chest.

"Are we okay to come in?" Kendra knocks lightly on the door, peeking her face around the side.

With a finger to his lips, my husband silently nods at Kendra.

She enters, Jack and Jon following closely behind. All three head straight over to me, and Archer lies down on the bed beside us, wrapping an arm around my shoulders.

Kendra's hands come straight to her mouth, hearts bouncing in her eyes when she takes Emily in. "I don't even know what to say. She's absolutely beautiful."

"Eight pounds of pure perfection," Archer coos.

"Can I hold her?" Jack's voice is broken when he speaks. "Or will I wake her?"

"Yes, of course," I whisper as Jack steps forward and carefully lifts her from me.

"Make sure you support her neck," Archer instructs, rising from the bed and showing Jack what to do.

"Actually, can you do me a favor?" Jack asks Archer. "I have something in my hoodie pocket that I need you to show Emily."

Everyone in the room is intrigued when Archer dips his hand into the front pocket of my brother's hoodie, pulling out a red top.

Holding it by the collar, he lets it unravel. "This is what you picked up for her in town that time, isn't it?"

Jack snickers, loving arms wrapping tighter around his niece. He looks so proud of her. "She's a Morgan and no one can tell me otherwise."

Despite his disapproving headshake, I see the emotion in my husband's eyes as he places the tiny jersey over the end of my bed, my brother's last name and number stamped across the back.

Jon stands there, a palm over his mouth as he takes it all in.

"Are you okay?" I ask, offering my hand out for him to take.

He wraps his big palm around mine, still no words materializing as he motions toward Emily.

"Wait, what's this?" Mum speaks up, pulling something round and brown from my bag. I don't immediately register what it is until she drops a piece of string between her fingers. "Darcy"—she chuckles softly—"why on earth did you pack a conker?"

"I didn't," I quickly reply, gaze resting on my husband as he takes it from Mum and turns it around in his hands.

"I did," Archer confirms, and it's then I see the *E* neatly carved into the side of the conker. "Someone once told me that conker fights make a great family game." He shrugs a shoulder and walks over to Emily and Jack, handing my brother the conker. "I figured that we could revive that tradition and you could teach my daughter how to kick some butt."

My eyes might be blurry, but I don't miss the moment as it passes between both men.

"Oh my." Mum is the only one to speak as Archer makes his way over to me, leaning down so only I can hear what he says next.

"Here's your sixth and final lesson, Darcy Doll: your brain might be able to recall everything I've ever said, but my heart hangs on your every word. Forever living in our DARCher bubble."

THE END

Tommy's story is coming in September 2025. Pre-order his book now!
https://geni.us/FullTiltBlades

ACKNOWLEDGMENTS

My Husband: You know this one has been a while in the making, and the level of pressure I put myself under to do Darcy and Archer's story justice was, at times, crazy. Thank you for always being the voice of reason and helping me take downtime to switch off when I needed it. We are living in our own bubble, and I'm forever thankful to have you in my life.

My Dad: This one feels like a milestone for us both. My seventh book and the couple I've been talking to you about for so long now. At times, I wasn't sure I could reach the end goal and publish this one, but you knew all along I could do it. I hope one day to share the same faith in myself that you always have in me.

My little boy: I hope one day you find a love like Archer and Darcy's. You deserve all the good things that are coming your way. This fall, we'll have our very own conker championships!

My Beta Team: I don't think I've ever needed a group of girls as much as I needed you for this one. The way you screamed—and cried—over Archer and Darcy was everything. You know how much I appreciate each and every one of you.

Nay: I'm running out of ways to say thank you. Thank you for the advice you give me, for the 'cleansing' voice notes we send back and forth. For the lunch dates and the planned dates and the random phone calls at whatever time at night. You are a true friend beyond books, but equally, the kind of bestie I would write about. Thank you for being you.

Lauren: I know your love for JJ runs deep, so naturally, I had to write you another obsessed hockey goalie. Thank you for all your love, help and advice.

To Autumn and all at Wordsmith Publicity: Another book together on this incredible ride I know I wouldn't be on without your ongoing care and guidance. Autumn, this is the book—the one you planted in my head over tacos back in May last year and the one we have both been so excited to work on. Darcy and Archer are everything I dreamed they would be. Our girl *finally* has her book!

To the Bookstagram community: The one we've been waiting on is here! We've been screaming about these characters since I don't even know when and now they're sitting in our kindles and on our bookshelves. This book feels like coming full circle on a story that started with my debut, and I couldn't be more grateful for all of your love and support throughout this past year. I love you all!

To all my readers: I truly hope that Darcy and Archer are everything you want them to be. This book was an absolute joy to write. That said, it certainly wasn't the easiest but, to me, that makes their story all the more beautiful. With every page, I wanted this to be the magical story we knew Darcy deserved from the early chapters of Boarded Hearts. I'm pretty sure she got the ultimate upgrade in Archer Moore! Thank you for picking up my books and showing them so much love. I appreciate each and every one of you! Ruth x

ABOUT THE AUTHOR

Ruth Stilling is an avid romance reader turned writer. Having spent many years reading about and dreaming of her ideal book boyfriend, she finally decided to create her own and to share them with the rest of the world.

Living in a small town in Derbyshire, England, Ruth is an introvert by nature and spends much of her time talking with her equally book-crazy friends from across the globe.

When she isn't writing your next book boyfriend, Ruth enjoys watching all kinds of sports and is an Aston Villa and Derby County fan. The outdoors is a real favorite, and if the British weather were kinder, she would spend all her time writing outside.

Ruth is a wife to her best friend and number one cheerleader, whom she married in 2015, and a mom to her beautiful son, who has shown her a new perspective on life—enjoy and celebrate who you are as a person and cherish those who are there for you through rain and shine.

Ruth is incredibly excited to share Shots Fired, the third installment in her second generation series, The Blade Kings!

You can follow Ruth and keep up to date with what's coming next via Instagram and TikTok by searching @authorruthstilling

Printed in Dunstable, United Kingdom

65204731R00241